the gentlemen's hour

Don Winslow has worked as a movie theatre manager, a production assistant, and as a private investigator. In addition to being a novelist he now works as an independent consultant in issues involving litigation arising from criminal behaviour. His novels include *The Death and Life of Bobby Z, California Fire and Life, The Power of the Dog, The Winter of Frankie Machine* and *The Dawn Patrol.*

ALSO BY DON WINSLOW

The Dawn Patrol

The Winter of Frankie Machine

The Power of the Dog

California Fire and Life

The Death and Life of Bobby Z

While Drowning in the Desert

Isle of Joy

A Long Walk up the Water Slide

Way Down on the High Lonely

The Trail to Buddha's Mirror

A Cool Breeze on the Underground

DON WINSLOW

the gentlemen's hour

Published by William Heinemann 2009

2 4 6 8 10 9 7 5 3 1

First published in Great Britain in 2009 by
William Heinemann
Random House, 20 Vauxhall Bridge Road,
London SW1V 2SA

www.rbooks.co.uk

Addresses for companies within The Random House Group Limited can be found at: www.randomhouse.co.uk/offices.htm

The Random House Group Limited Reg. No. 954009

A CIP catalogue record for this book is available from the British Library

ISBN 9780434019250

The Random House Group Limited supports The Forest Stewardship Council (FSC), the leading international forest certification organisation. All our titles that are printed on Greenpeace approved FSC certified paper carry the FSC logo. Our paper procurement policy can be found at: www.rbooks.co.uk/environment

Typeset by SX Composing DTP, Rayleigh, Essex
Printed and bound in Great Britain by
Clays Ltd, St Ives Plc

"But I don't need that much
Sugar in my cup,
No, I don't need that much . . ."

– Nick Hernandez,
Common Sense,
'Sugar In My Cup'

the gentlemen's hour

1

Kansas.

See 'flatter than.'

Like the ocean this August morning in Pacific Beach, San Diego, California.

Aka Kansas.

As the Dawn Patrol gives way to the Gentlemen's Hour.

2

Earth, air, fire and water.

The four elements, right?

Let's let air go for a minute – except in LA, it's pretty much a given. Fire's not the topic either – for now, anyway.

Leaving earth and water.

They have more in common than you'd think.

For example, they can both look static on the surface, but there's always something going on underneath. Like water, earth is always moving. You can't necessarily see it, you might not feel it, but it's happening anyway. Beneath our feet, tectonic plates are shifting, faults are widening, quakes are tuning up to rock and roll.

So that dirt we're standing on, so-called 'solid ground?'

It's moving beneath us.

Taking us for a ride

Face it – whether we know it or not, we're all always surfing.

3

Boone Daniels lies face up on his board like it's an inflatable mattress in a swimming pool.

He's half-asleep. The sun that warms his closed eyes is already burning off the marine layer relatively early in the morning. He's out there as usual with the Dawn Patrol – Dave the Love God, High Tide, Johnny Banzai, Hang Twelve – even though there's no surf to speak of and nothing to do except talk story. The only regular not present for duty is Sunny Day who's in Oz on the Women's Professional Surfing Tour and also making a video for Quicksilver.

It's boring – the torpid dog days of late-summer, when Pacific Beach is overrun with tourists, when most of the locies have basically sung 'See you in September,' and the ocean itself can't work up the energy to produce a wave.

"Kansas," Hang Twelve complains.

Hang Twelve, thusly glossed because he has a dozen toes – fortunately six on each foot – is the junior member of the Dawn Patrol, a lost pup that Boone took under his arm when the kid was about thirteen. White as a Republican National Committee meeting, he sports Rastafarian dreadlocks and a red retro-beatnik goatee, and despite or perhaps because of his parents' many acid trips, he's an *idiot-savant* with a computer.

"Have you ever been to Kansas?" Johnny Banzai asks, sounding a little aggro. He doubts that Hang has ever been east of Interstate 5.

"No," Hang answers. He's never been east of Interstate 5.

"Then how do you know?" Johnny presses, in full-on interrogator mode now. "For all you know, Kansas could be covered with mountain ranges. Like the Alps."

"I know there's no surf in Kansas," Hang Twelve says stubbornly, because he's almost certain there's no ocean in Kansas, unless maybe it's the Atlantic, in which case there's probably no surf either.

"There's no surf in San Dog," Boone offers. "Not today, anyway."

Dave, lying on his stomach, lifts his head off the board and pukes into the water. Again. Boone and Dave have been boys since elementary school, so Boone has seen Dave hung over many, many times, but not quite like this.

Last night was 'Mai Tai Tuesday' at The Sundowner.

"You gonna live?" Boone asks him.

"Not enthusiastically," Dave answers.

"I'll kill you if you want," High Tide offers, propping up his big head on one big fist. The origin of the 375-pound Samoan's nickname is obvious – he gets into the ocean, the water level rises; he gets out, it falls. Simple displacement physics. "Something to do, anyway."

Johnny Banzai is all over it. "How? How should we kill Dave?"

As a homicide detective for the San Diego Police Department, killing Dave is right in Johnny's wheelhouse. It's refreshing to put his mind to a murder that *isn't* going to happen, as opposed to the three all-too-real killings he has on his desk right now, including one he doesn't even want to think about. It's been a hot, tetchy summer in San Diego – tempers have flared and lives have been extinguished. A vicious drug war for control of the Baja Cartel has spilled across the border into San Diego, and bodies are turning up all over the place.

"Drowning him would be easiest," Boone suggests.

"Hello?" Tide says. "He's a *lifeguard*?"

Dave the Love God *is* a lifeguard, only slightly more famous for the lives he's saved than the women he's slept with on his one-man crusade to boost San Diego's tourist industry. Right now, though, he's belly down on his board, moaning.

"Are you kidding?" Boone asks. "*Look* at him."

"Drowning is too blatantly ironic," Johnny says. "I mean, the headline *Legendary Lifeguard Drowns In Flat Sea*? It doesn't work for me."

"Do you have your gun?" Tide asks.

"In the *water*?"

"If you were my friend," Dave groans, "you'd paddle in, get your pistol from your car, and shoot me."

"Do you know the paperwork involved in discharging your firearm?" Johnny asks.

"What's in a Mai Tai anyway?' Boone wonders out loud. He was also at Mai Tai Tuesday, his office being next-door to The Sundowner and he being sort of an unofficial bouncer for the joint. But he left after having only a couple and went back to his office, upstairs from the Pacific Surf Shop, to see if there were any e-mails from Sunny or any offers for work. Zippo on both, Sunny being really busy and the private investigation field being really not.

Boone's not so bummed about the work, but he does miss Sunny. Even though they have long been 'exes,' they're still good friends, and he misses her presence.

They all shut up for a second as they feel a wave building up behind them. They wait, feel the slight surge, but then the wave gives up like a guy who's late for work, just can't get out of bed, and decides to call in sick.

Later.

"Could we get back to killing Dave?" Tide asks.

"Yes, please," Dave says.

Boone drops out of the conversation.

Literally.

Tired of making talk, he rolls off his board into the water and lets himself sink. It feels good, but then again, Boone is probably more comfortable in the water than on land. A prenatal surfer in his mother's womb, the ocean is his church, and he's a daily communicant. Working just enough to (barely) support his surfing jones, his office is a block from the beach. His home is even closer

– he lives in a cottage on a pier over the water, so the smell, sound and rhythm of the ocean are constants in his life.

Now he holds his breath and looks up through the water at the relentlessly blue summer sky and pale yellow sun, distorted by refraction. He feels the ocean gently pulse around him, listens to the muted sound of the water running over the bottom, a scant ten feet or so below, and contemplates the state of his existence.

No serious career, no serious money (okay, no money at all), no serious relationship.

He and Sunny had split up even before she got her big break and went off on the pro tour, and although there is that thing with Petra, who knows where that's going? If anywhere. They've been 'seeing' each other casually since last spring but haven't closed the deal and he's not sure he even wants to because he has a feeling that Petra Hall would not be into the friends-with-privileges thing, and that if they did sleep together, he *would* instantly have a serious relationship.

Which he's not sure he wants.

A relationship with Petra 'Pete' Hall is heavy-duty reef break, nothing to be trifled with. Pete is gorgeous, smart, funny and has the heart of a lion, but she's also a career-driven lawyer who loves to argue, ferociously ambitious, and she doesn't surf.

And maybe it's too much, on the end of what's been a heavy year.

There was the whole Tammy Roddick case that brought Petra into Boone's life, and blew up into a massive child prostitution ring that almost *cost* Boone his life; there was Dave blowing the whistle on local gangster Red Eddie's smuggling op; the big swell that rolled in and changed all their lives; and Sunny riding her big wave, making the cover of all the surf mags, and leaving.

Now Sunny was off riding her comet, and Dave was in limbo waiting to see if he'd ever have to testify in Eddie's constantly delayed trial, and Boone was treading water on the edge of a relationship with Pete.

"Is he coming up?" Hang asks the others, starting to get concerned. Boone's been down there a long time.

"I don't care," Dave mumbles. I'm the one who's supposed to

die, he thinks, not Boone. Boone's not hung over, Boone didn't down double-digit Mai Tais – whatever the hell they're made from – last night. Boone doesn't deserve the dignified relief of death. But Dave's lifeguard instincts take over and he looks over the edge of his board to see Boone's face underwater. "He's fine."

"Yeah," Hang says, "but how long can he hold his breath?"

"A long time," Johnny says.

They've actually had breath-holding contests, which Boone invariably won. Johnny has a dark suspicion that Boone is actually some kind of mutant, like his parents were really space aliens from an amphibian planet. Holding your breath is important to a serious surfer, because you might get held under a big wave and then you'd better be able to go without air for a couple of minutes because you're not going to have a choice. So surfers train for that eventuality, which, in reality, is an inevitability. It's going to happen.

Johnny looks down into the water and waves.

Boone waves back.

"He's good," Johnny says.

Which leads to a not very animated discussion of whether it's possible for a person to intentionally drown himself, or whether the body would just take over and force you to breathe. On a cooler day, with more active surf, this is the sort of topic that would have engendered ferocious debate, but with the sun stinking hot and the surf a no-show, the argument falls as flat as the sea.

August blows.

When Boone finally pops back up, Johnny asks, "Did you figure out the meaning of life?"

"Sort of," Boone says, climbing back on his board.

"We're dying to hear," Dave mutters.

"The meaning of life," Boone says, "is to stay underwater for as long as possible."

"That wouldn't be the *meaning* of life," Johnny observes, "that would be the *secret* of life."

"Okay," Boone says.

Secret, meaning, secret meaning, whatever.

The secret meaning of life might be just as simple as the Dawn Patrol itself. Spending time with good, old friends. Doing something you love with people you love in a place you love, even when there's no surf.

A few minutes later they give up and paddle in. The Dawn Patrol – that early-morning, pre-work surf session – is over. They have places to go to: Johnny's coming off the night shift but needs to get home because his doctor wife is on days, Hang has to open Pacific Surf, Tide is due at his gig as a supervisor in the Public Works Department, responsible for storm drains even when there are no storms to drain. Dave needs to man the lifeguard tower to protect swimmers from surf that doesn't exist.

The Dawn Patrol – Boone's best friends in the world.

He doesn't go in with them, though.

Having no work at the moment, there's no point in going into the office to see if the red ink has gotten any redder.

So he stays out there for the Gentlemen's Hour.

4

The Gentlemen's Hour is an old surfing institution.

The second shift on the daily surfing clock, the Gentlemen's Hour follows the Dawn Patrol in the rotation, as the hard-charging younger guys from the early-morning session go to their j-o-b-s, leaving the beach to the older *veteranos* – the retirees, doctors, lawyers and successful entrepreneurs who have the 9-to-5 in the rear-view mirror.

Now, young guys can stay for the Gentlemen's Hour, but they'd better know and observe the unwritten rules:

1. Never jump in on an old guy's ride.

2. Never hot-dog by doing stuff your younger body can do that their older ones can't.
3. Never offer your opinion about anything.
4. Never, *ever* say anything like, 'You already told us that story.'

Because the gentlemen of the Gentlemen's Hour like to talk. Hell, half the time they don't get into the water at all, just stand around their classic woodies and talk story. Share memories of waves out of the past, waves that get bigger, thicker, meaner, sweeter, longer with time. It's only natural, it's to be expected, and Boone, even when he was an obnoxious gremmie – and there were few more obnoxious – found out that if you hung around and kept your stupid mouth shut, you could learn something from these guys, that there really was a pony under all the horseshit.

Everything you think you're seeing for the first time, these guys have already seen. There are still old boys out on the Gentlemen's Hour who invented the sport, who can tell you about paddling out into breaks that had never been ridden before, who can still give you a little vicarious glow from the Golden Age.

But some of the guys on the Gentlemen's Hour aren't old, they're just successful. They're professionals, or they own their businesses, and everything is going so well they don't have to show up anywhere except the beach.

One of these fortunates is Dan Nichols.

If you were going to make a television commercial featuring a forty-four-year-old California surfer, you'd cast Dan. Tall, rugged, with blond hair brushed straight back, tanned, brilliant white smile, green-eyed and handsome, Dan is the male version of the California Dream. Given all that, you'd also think you'd hate the dude, but you don't.

Dan's a cool guy.

Now, Dan didn't grow up anything like poor – his grandfather was in real estate and left him a tidy trust fund – but Dan took that nest egg and hatched a whole lot of chickens. What Dan did was marry his vocation and avocation, building a surf clothing line that just exploded. Started with a little warehouse in PB, and now has his own shiny big building in La Jolla. And you don't have to be in San Diego to see Nichols' 'N' logo, you can see kids wearing Dan's gear in Paris, London and probably Ouagadougou.

So Dan Nichols has many, many bucks.

And he can really surf, so he's a member-in-good-standing of the PB Gentlemen's Hour. Now he paddles out behind the barely discernible break and finds Boone sunbathing on his longboard.

"Boone, what's up?"

"Not the surf," Boone says. "Hey, Dan."

"Hey, yourself. What keeps you out past the Dawn Patrol?"

"Sloth," Boone admits. "Sloth and underemployment."

If Boone weren't *self*-employed he'd be *un*employed, and very often it amounts to the same thing anyway.

"Actually, that's what I wanted to talk to you about," Dan says.

Boone opens his eyes. Dan looks serious, which is unusual. He's normally jovial and ultra-laid-back, and why not? You would be too if you had double-digit millions in the bank. "What's up, Dan?"

"Could we paddle out a little farther?" Dan asks. "It's kind of personal."

"Yeah, sure."

He lets Dan take the lead and paddles behind him another fifty yards out, where the only eavesdroppers might be a flock of brown pelicans flying past. Brown pelicans are sort of the avian mascots of Pacific Beach. There's a statue of one by the new lifeguard building which, even now, Dave is climbing to begin another day scoping *turistas*.

Dan smiles ruefully. "This is hard . . ."

"Take your time," Boone says.

Probably Dan suspects that an employee is embezzling, or selling secrets to a competitor or something, which would seriously bum him out, because he prides himself on running a happy, loyal ship. People who go to work at Nichols tend to stay, want to spend their whole careers there. Dan has offered Boone a job any time he wants it, and there have been times when Boone's been almost tempted. If you're going to have a (shudder) 9-to-5, Nichols would be a cool place to work.

"I think Donna's cheating on me," Dan says.

"No way."

Dan shrugs. "I dunno, Boone."

He lays out the usual scenario: She's out at odd hours with murky explanations, she's spending a lot of time with girlfriends who don't seem to know anything about it; she's distant, distracted, less affectionate than she used to be.

Donna Nichols is a looker. Tall, blonde, stacked, leggy – an eleven on a California scale of ten. A definite MILF if she and Dan had children, which they don't. The two of them are like the poster couple for the SoCal Division of the Beautiful People, San Diego Chapter.

Except they're nice, Boone thinks. He doesn't know Donna, but the Nichols have always struck him as genuinely nice people – down-to-earth, amazingly unpretentious, low-key, generous, good community people. So it's a real shame that this is happening – *if* it's happening.

Which is what Dan wants Boone to find out. "Could you look into this for me, Boone?"

"I don't know," Boone says.

Matrimonial cases suck.

Mega-sleazy, sheet-sniffing, low-rent depressing work that usually ends badly. And you're always left feeling like some leering, peeping-tom pervert who then gets to present the client with proof of his or her betrayal, or, on the other hand, confirmation of the paranoia and mistrust that will destroy the marriage anyway.

It's a bad deal all around.

Only creeps enjoy doing it.

Boone hates matrimonial cases, and rarely if ever takes them.

"I'd consider it a personal favor," Dan says. "I don't know where else to turn. I'm going crazy. I love her, Boone. I really love her."

Which makes it worse, of course. There are a few thousand deeply cynical relationships on the Southern Californian marital merry-go-round – men acquire trophy wives until the sell-by date does them part; women marry rich men to achieve financial independence via the alimony route; young guys wed older women for room, board and credit-card rights while they bang waitresses and models. If you absolutely, positively *have* to do 'matrimonial,' these are the cases you want, because there's very little genuine emotion involved.

But 'love?'

Ouch.

As has been overly documented, love hurts.

It's sure laying a beat-down on Dan Nichols. He looks like he might actually cry, which would violate an important addendum to the rules of the Gentlemen's Hour: There's no crying, ever. These guys are old school – they think Oprah's a mispronunciation of music they'd never listen to. It's okay to *have* feelings – like if you're looking at photos of your grandchildren – but you can never acknowledge them, and showing them is *way* over the line.

Boone says, "I'll look into it."

"Money is no object," Dan says, then adds. "Jesus, did I really say that?"

"Stress," Boone says. "Listen, this is awkward, but do you have . . . I mean, is there anyone . . . a guy . . . you suspect?"

"Nobody," Dan says. "I thought you might tail her. You know, put her under surveillance. Is that the way to go?"

"That's one way to go," Boone says. "Let's go an easier way first. I assume she has a cell phone."

"I-phone."

"I-phone, sure," Boone says. "Can you access the records without her knowing it?"

"Yeah."

"Do that," Boone says. "We'll see if any unexplained number keeps coming up."

It's kooky, but cheaters are amazingly careless about calling their lovers on the cellies, like they can't stay off them. They call them, text them, and then there's e-mail. Modern techno has made adulterers stupid. "Check her computer, too."

"Got it, that's good."

No, it's not good, Boone thinks, it reeks. But it's better than putting her under surveillance. And with any luck, the phone records and e-mails will come up clean and he can pull Dan off this nasty wave.

"I'm going out of town on business in a couple of days," Dan says. "I think that's when she . . ."

He lets it trail off.

They paddle in.

The Gentlemen's Hour is about over anyway.

5

In the middle of August, on a ferociously hot day, the man wears a seersucker suit, white shirt and tie. His one concession to the potentially harmful effects of the strong sun on his pale skin is a straw hat.

Jones just believes that is how a gentleman dresses.

He strolls the boardwalk along Pacific Beach and watches as two surfers walk in, their boards tucked under their arms alongside their hips.

But Jones' mind is not on them, it is on pleasure.

He's reveling in a memory from the previous day, of gently, slowly, and repeatedly swinging a bamboo stick into a man's shins. The man was suspended by the wrists from a ceiling pipe, and he swayed slightly with each blow.

A less subtle interrogator might have swung the stick harder, shattering bone, but Jones prides himself on his subtlety, patience and creativity. A broken shin is agonizing but hurts only once, albeit for quite some time. The repetitive taps grew increasingly painful and the anticipation of the ensuing tap was mentally excruciating.

The man, an accountant, told Jones everything that he knew after a mere twenty strokes.

The next three hundred blows were for pleasure – Jones', not the accountant's – and to express their common employer's displeasure at the state of business. Don Iglesias, patron of the Baja Cartel, does not like to lose money, especially on foolishness, and he hired Jones to find out the real cause of said loss and to punish those responsible.

It will be many months before the accountant walks without a wince. And Don Iglesias now knows that the origin of his losses is not in Tijuana, where the beating took place, but here in sunny San Diego.

Jones goes in search of an ice cream, which sounds very pleasant.

6

AK-47 rounds shatter the window.

Cruz Iglesias dives for the floor. Shards of glass and hunks of plaster cover him as he reaches back for his 9mm and starts to fire onto the street. He might as well not bother, the machine-gun fire from his own gunmen dwarfs his efforts.

One of his men throws himself on top of his boss.

"Get off me, *pendejo*," Iglesias snaps. "You're too late anyway. *Dios mio*, if my life depended on you . . ."

He rolls out from under the sweaty *sicario* and makes a mental note to require the use of deodorant for all his employees. It's disgusting.

Within the hour he's come to the conclusion that Tijuana is just too dangerous during his turf war with the Ortegas over the lucrative drug market. Times are hard – the pie is shrinking and there's no room for compromise – especially with his recent losses. Three hours later he's in a car crossing into the USA at San Ysidro. It's not a problem – Iglesias has dual citizenship.

The car takes him to one of his safe houses.

Actually, it's not too bad a thing to be in San Diego – if you can tolerate the inferior cuisine. He has business there that needs his attention.

7

Boone walks to the office, upstairs from the Pacific Surf Shop where Hang Twelve is pretty busy renting boogie boards and fins to tourists. Hang has a family of five on his hands, the kids arguing about which color board they're going to get. Hang looks real happy, not. Speaking of unhappiness, he warns, "Cheerful's up there."

Ben Carruthers, aka 'Cheerful,' is Boone's friend, a miserable, saturnine millionaire who would qualify for the Gentlemen's Hour if he didn't actually loathe the water. He's lived in Pacific Beach for thirty years and has never actually been to the beach or the Pacific.

"What do you have against the beach?" Boone asked him once.

"It's sandy."

"The beach *is* sand."

"Exactly," Cheerful answered. "And I don't like water either."

Which pretty much does it, beach-wise.

Cheerful is, to say the least, eccentric, and one of his weirder things is a quixotic crusade to stabilize Boone's finances. The utter futility of this exercise makes him blissfully unhappy, hence the sobriquet. Right now he has his tall frame slouched over an old-style adding machine. His slate-gray hair, styled in a high-crew cut, looks like brushed steel.

"Nice of you to make an appearance," he says, pointedly looking at his watch as Boone comes upstairs.

"Things are slow," Boone says. He steps out of his boardshorts, kicks off his sandals and goes into the little bathroom that adjoins the office.

"You think you're going to speed them up by not coming in 'til eleven?" Cheerful asks. "You think work just floats around on the water?"

"As a matter of fact . . ." Boone says, turning on the shower. He tells Cheerful about his conversation with Dan, adding with a certain sadistic satisfaction that Nichols is FedExing a substantial retainer.

"You demanded a retainer?" Cheerful asks.

"It was his idea."

"For a moment," Cheerful says, "I thought you had learned some fiscal responsibility."

"Nah."

Boone steps into the shower just long enough to rinse the salt water off his skin, then gets out and dries off. He doesn't bother to wrap the towel around himself as he steps back into the office to look for a clean shirt – okay, a reasonably un-dirty shirt – and a pair of jeans.

Petra Hall is standing there.

Of course she is, Boone thinks.

"Hello, Boone," she says. "Nice to see you."

She looks gorgeous, in a cool linen suit, her black hair cut in a retro-pageboy, her violet eyes shining.

"Hi, Pete," Boone says. "Nice to be seen."

Smooth, he thinks as he retreats back into the bathroom.

Idiot.

8

"Business or pleasure?" he asks when he comes back in, Petra having handed him a shirt and jeans.

She gave him his clothes a tad reluctantly because (a) it's fun to see him embarrassed; and (b) it's not exactly painful to see him in the buff, Boone Daniels being, well, *buff*. He's tall and broad-shouldered, with the lean, long muscles that come from a lifetime of paddling a surfboard and swimming.

"And why can't business *be* a pleasure?" she asks in that upper-class British accent that Boone finds alternately aggravating and attractive. Petra Hall is a junior partner at the law firm of Burke, Spitz and Culver, one of Boone's steadier clients. She got her good looks and petite frame from her American mother, her accent and attitude from her British dad.

"Because it usually isn't," Boone answers, feeling for some reason that he wants to argue with her.

"Then you really should find a new line of work," she says, "one that you can enjoy. In the meantime . . ."

She hands him the slim file that was tucked under her arm. Boone nudges a copy of *Surfer* magazine off the cluttered desk to make a little room, sets the file down and opens it. A deep red flush comes over his cheeks as he shuts the file, glares at her and says, "No."

"What does that mean?" Petra asks.

"It means no," Boone says. He's quiet for a second and then says, "I can't believe Alan is taking this case."

Petra says, "Everyone has the right to a defense."

Boone points down at the file. "Not him."

"*Every*one."

"Not *him*."

Boone glares at her again, then slides his feet into a well-worn pair of Reef sandals and walks out.

Petra and Cheerful listen to him pound down the stairs.

"Actually," she says, "that didn't go as badly as I anticipated."

Petra had known before she asked that the Corey Blasingame case was deeply hurtful to Boone, that it put into doubt everything he believed in, everything that he'd built his life upon.

9

Kelly Kuhio was a freaking legend.

No – K2 was a freaking *legend.*

Build a surfing pantheon? KK's in it. Carve a Mount Surfers' Rushmore? You're going to be blasting Kelly's face into that rock. Just make a list of the all-time good guys who've ever ridden a board? Kelly Kuhio is in your Top Ten.

Nobody who ever met Kelly Kuhio did anything but like and respect him, he was that kind of dude. Soft-spoken, understated, ultimate cool, Kelly had a way of making people want to be better than they were, and a lot of guys on the Gentlemen's Hour could tell stories about how they went out and did just that.

Kelly was the epitome of a bygone era.

The time of the Gentleman Surfer.

As a kid, Boone literally sat at his feet, because K2 was a good friend of Boone's mom and dad, both of them well-known surfers both in San Diego and K2's native Kauai. So K2 – 'Uncle K' to Boone – would come to the house and talk story, and Boone just kept his pie-hole shut and his ears open.

Stories? Are you kidding me? Out of the mouth of Kelly Kuhio? Just look at the man's life. Born in Honolulu, K2 was the Hawaiian state surfing champion at the age of thirteen. That's *thirteen*, Jack, an age when most gremmies are only champs at . . . well, it ain't surfing.

And Kelly wasn't some dumb, mutant muscle freak, either. Actually he was slight of build and smart, went to Punahou School on a scholarship and was 4.0. After school he went up to the North Shore, because that's where the waves were, and it was K2 who figured out how to shape a board that could survive the wicked hollow tubes up there. K2 became known as 'Mister Pipeline,' winning the Masters' so often they practically put his name on it.

Then he got bored with that and started traveling.

Dig, it was K2 who first explored Indonesia, K2 who found that great left-hand point break that eventually became G-Land. Should have been K-Land, except Kelly was too modest to hang his tag on it. But now all the boys who make the pilgrimage to Indo on the Unreconstructed Hippie Surf Safari are following in the footsteps of K2, whether they know it or not.

When Laird and Kalama and the rest of the Strapped Crew started to figure out the big wave, tow-in thing, they went to K2 to advise them how to shape their boards. Kelly enthusiastically helped them but didn't go out in the 60-footers himself. In his forties then, he knew that was a young man's game and K2 was too cool to try to desperately hang on to his youth. He had nothing to prove.

When Kelly freaking Kuhio decided to move to California it was a *big deal*. He came at the behest of the surf clothing companies, to promote their products, and then he stayed. Did a few small parts in films, made public appearances, was basically just being K2. He liked SoCal, he dug the San Diego vibe, he just hung out.

The boys couldn't believe it. They'd be on the beach and there was K2 out there, cutting his elegant lines, making it look so easy, so casual. And he'd invite you out there to surf *with* him –'Come on out, brother, the water is fine, plenty of room for everyone' – and give you little tips if you were open to them. (He shifted Sunny's stance by *three inches*, and it made all the difference.) K2 was all about the aloha, the community, the peace.

K2 was a Buddhist since his early days hanging out with the Japanese community in Honolulu. A serious, two-meditation-sessions-a-day, lotus-position Buddhist, but he never shoved it at you. K2 never shoved anything at anybody, you just looked at him and learned, and it was K2 that pointed Sunny toward Buddhism and probably never knew it. She just admired his energy, his presence, and wanted it for herself.

Other things K2 did?

Coached surfing at a local high school.

Sit back and ponder that a little bit. You're a high-school baseball player, and Hank Aaron shows up one day and is going to stay and teach you how to swing the stick? You play a little b-ball and Michael Jordan volunteers to spend his afternoons and weekends perfecting your jumper? Are you kidding me?!

K2, Mister Pipeline, the Zen Master himself, out there showing kids how to surf and how to do it right, how to carry themselves, how to behave, how to treat other people. K2, Mister Pipeline, the Zen Master, telling them to stay in school, spurn drugs and gangs. If you're a kid and you're hanging with K2, it's cool to stay clean and straight, cool to stay off the corner, maximum cool to hang with that man, eat PB&J and learn ukulele chords.

Get it – K2 had Samoan gang bangers out there on Saturday mornings with trash bags, cleaning up the beaches around O'side and laughing the whole time. K2, more silver than black in his full head of hair by then, had black kids from Golden Hill in the water on body boards, talking about saving their money to get the real thing. There was a downturn in gang violence, most of it having to do with sheer demographics, but the local police laid a piece of it right on K2's doorstep.

K2 showed up at the charity events and the walk-a-thons, always found some piece of memorabilia to donate to school auctions, never said no if he could find a way to say yes.

He became a fixture at the PB Gentlemen's Hour, standing around the beach talking story, more often out in the water catching rides, his style still elegant if less hard-charging. Boone would see him around from time to time, at Jeff's or The Sundowner, or just on the beach or some surf event. K2 would always ask for his parents, they'd exchange a few words. Every now and again they surfed together.

Boone admired him, looked up to him, learned from him.

He wasn't alone in that – for good reason, San Diego loved that man.

He was a hero.

Maybe a saint.

Then Corey Blasingame killed him.

10

It happened outside The Sundowner.

Which makes what happened all the worse, because the restaurant-bar-hangout is an icon of the San Diego surf scene. Faded photos of great local surfers riding their waves decorate its walls; famous surfboards that have provided some of those rides hang from its ceilings.

It goes beyond memorabilia, though. The Sundowner stands for the brotherhood – and, increasingly, the sisterhood – of surfing. A hangout like The Sundowner stands for the surf ethic – peace, friendship, tolerance, individuality – an overall philosophy that people sharing a common passion are, indeed, a community. In short, everything that Kelly Kuhio taught by example.

In Pacific Beach, that community gathers in The Sundowner. To share a meal, a drink, some stories, some laughs. From time to time, a few tourists might come in and get over-refreshed, or some chucklehead from east of the 5 might walk in looking for trouble – which is where unofficial bouncers like Boone, Dave or Tide might be asked to intervene – but surfers never cause problems in The Sundowner. Sure, a surfer might have a few too many beers and get silly-stupid and have to be carried out by his buddies, a guy might yank on the floor (see Mai Tai Tuesdays), a boy might try to surf a table and end up in the E-Room for a few stitches, but *violence* just doesn't happen.

Well, didn't used to.

23

The ugly, painful truth is that violence has been seeping into the surf community for some time, really since the mid-eighties, when the drug-blissed hippie surfer era gave way to something a little edgier. Over the years, grass gave way to coke, and coke gave way to crack, crack to speed, speed to meth. And meth is a violent fucking drug.

The other thing was overpopulation – too many people wanting a place in the wave and not enough wave to accommodate them; too many cars looking for a place to park and not enough spaces.

A new word crept into surf jargon.

Localism.

Easy to understand – surfers who lived near a certain break and surfed it their whole lives wanted to defend their turf against newcomers who threatened to crowd them out of a piece of water they considered their *home* – but it was an ugly thing.

Locies started to put up warning signs: 'If you don't live here, don't surf here.' Then they began to vandalize strangers' cars – soap the bodies, slash the tires, shatter the windshields. Then it got directly physical, with the locies actually beating up the newcomers – in the parking places, on the beach, even in the water.

Which, to surfers like Boone, was sacrilege.

You didn't fight in the water. You didn't threaten, throw punches, *beat people up*. You *surfed*. If a guy jumped your wave, you set him straight, but you didn't foul a sacred place with violence.

"Fighting in the line-up," Dave opined one Dawn Patrol, "would be like stealing in church."

"You go to *church*?" Hang Twelve asked.

"No," Dave answered.

"Have you ever *been* to church?" High Tide asked. He actually has – since he left his gang-banging days behind, Tide goes to church every Sunday.

"No," Dave answered. "But I knew this nun once—"

"I don't think I want to hear this," Tide said.

"Well, she wasn't still a nun when I knew her—"

"That I believe," Boone said. "So what about her?"

"She used to talk about it."

"She used to talk about stealing in church?" Johnny Banzai asked. "Christ, no wonder she was an ex-nun."

"I'm just saying," Dave persisted, "that fighting while surfing is . . . is . . ."

" 'Sacrilegious' is the word you're searching for," Johnny said.

"You know," Dave answered, "you really play into a lot of Asian stereotypes. Better vocabulary, better in school, higher SAT scores . . ."

"I *do* have a better vocabulary," Johnny said, "I *was* better in school, and I *did* have higher SAT scores."

"Than *Dave*?" Tide asked. "You didn't have to be Asian, you just had to show up."

"I had other priorities," Dave said.

Codified in the List Of Things That Are Good, an inventory constantly under discussion and revision during the Dawn Patrol, and which conversely necessitated the List Of Things That Are Bad, which, as currently constituted, went:

1. No surf
2. Small surf
3. Crowded surf
4. Living east of the 5
5. Going east of the 5
6. Wet-suit rash
7. Sewage spills
8. Board racks on BMWs
9. Tourists on rented boards
10. Localism

Items 9 and 10 were controversial.

Everyone admitted to having mixed feelings about tourists on rented boards, especially the Styrofoam longboards. On the one hand, they were truly a pain-in-the-ass, messing up the water with their inept wipeouts, ignorance and lack of surf courtesy. On the other hand, they were an endless source of amusement, entertainment and employment, seeing as how it was Hang's job to rent them said boards, and Dave's to jerk them out of the water when they attempted to drown themselves.

But it was Item 10, localism, that sparked serious debate and discussion.

"I get localism," Tide said. "I mean, we don't like it when strangers intrude on the Dawn Patrol."

"We don't like it," Johnny agreed, "but we don't beat them up. We're broley."

"You can't own the ocean," Boone insisted, "or any part of it."

But he had to admit that even in his lifetime he had witnessed the gradual crowding out of his beloved surf breaks, as the sport gained in popularity and became cultural currency. It seemed like everyone was a surfer these days, and the water *was* crowded. The weekends were freaking ridiculous, and Boone was tempted sometimes to take Saturdays and Sundays off, there were so many (mostly bad) surfers hitting the waves.

It didn't matter, though; it was just something you had to tolerate. You couldn't stake out a piece of water like it was land you'd bought. The great thing about the ocean was that it wasn't for sale, you couldn't buy it, own it, fence it off – hard as the new luxury hotels that were appearing on the waterside like skin lesions tried to block off paths to the beaches and keep them 'private.' The ocean, in Boone's opinion, was the last stand of pure democracy. Anyone – regardless of race, color, creed, economic status or the lack thereof – could partake of it.

So he found localism understandable but ultimately wrong.

A bad thing.

A malignantly bad thing, because more and more often, over the last few years, Boone, Dave, Tide and Johnny all found themselves playing peacemaker, intervening in disputes out on the water that threatened to break into fights. What had been a rare event became commonplace: preventing some locies from hammering an interloper.

There was that time right at PB. It wasn't the Dawn Patrol, it was a Saturday afternoon so the water was crowded with locals and newcomers. It was tense out on the line, too many surfers trying to get in the same waves, and then one of the locals just went off. This newbie had cut him off on his line, forcing him to bail, and he sloshed through the whitewater and went after the guy. Worse, his buddies came in behind him.

It would have been serious, a bad beat-down, except Dave was on the tower and Johnny was in the shallows playing with his kids. Johnny got there first and got between the aggro locies and the dumb newbie and tried to talk some sense. But the locies weren't having it, and it looked like it was on when Dave came up, and then Boone and Tide, and the Dawn Patrol combo plate got things settled down.

But Boone and the other sheriffs from the Dawn Patrol weren't at every break, and the ugly face of localism started to scowl at a lot of places. You started to see bumper stickers proclaiming 'This is protected territory,' and the owners of those cars – too often fueled by meth and beer – felt entitled to enforce the edict. Certain breaks up and down the California coast became virtual 'no-go' zones – even the surf reports warned 'foreigners' to stay clear of those breaks.

What evolved were virtual 'gangs' claiming ocean turf.

It was ridiculous, Boone thought. Stupid. Everything that surfing isn't. Yeah, but it *was*. A scar on the body oceanic, even if Boone didn't want to look at it.

But he *never* expected to see it in The Sundowner.

The Sundowner is old school. Go in there, you'll find guys from the Dawn Patrol, from the Gentlemen's Hour, surfers from the pro tour, out-of-towners on a pilgrimage to a surf mecca. Everyone is welcome at The Sundowner.

Maybe Boone should have seen it coming. The signs were all there, literally, because he started to see them in the windows of other joints in Pacific Beach, reading 'No caps. No gang colors.'

Gang colors?!

Freaking *gang colors* on Garnet Avenue?

Yeah, and it was a problem. The past few years, gangs started to come to PB. Gangs from Barrio Logan and City Heights, but also local gangs, surf gangs – *surf freaking gangs* – claimed clubs and whole blocks as their partying turf and defended them against other gangs. More and more bars began to hire full-time professional bouncers and security, and the streets of laid-back, surf-happy PB got sketchy at night.

But that couldn't happen at The Sundowner.

Yeah, except it did.

11

Petra slides into the booth across from Boone.

He pretends to study the menu, which is ridiculous because Boone has had breakfast here almost every morning for the past ten years. Not only does he already know what he wants, the waitress already knows what he wants because he always orders the same thing.

The waitress, Not Sunny, is a tall blonde, leggy and pretty, and Petra wonders if there's some sort of secret breeding facility in California where they just crank out these creatures, because there seems to be an inexhaustible supply. When the original Sunny left her job at The Sundowner to go off on the professional surfers' tour, the new tall, blonde and leggy replacement appeared immediately in a seamless progression of California Girls.

Nobody seems to know her real name, nor does she seem bothered that she has been tabbed Not Sunny, doomed to exist in Sunny's shadow, as it were. Indeed, Not Sunny is a pale version of her namesake; on the surface as pretty, but lacking Sunny's depth, intelligence and genuine warmth.

Now Not Sunny stares at Boone and says, "Eggs *machaca* with jack cheese, corn *and* flour tortillas, split the black beans and home fries, coffee with two sugars."

Boone pretends to study the menu for an alternative, then says, "Just flour."

"Huh?"

"Just flour tortillas, not corn."

Not Sunny takes a moment to digest this change in her world, then turns to Petra and asks, "And for you?"

"Do you have iced tea?"

"Uh, yeah."

"I'll have an iced tea, please," Petra says. "Lemon, no sugar."

"Lemonnnnn . . . no sugar," Not Sunny says to herself as she walks away to place the order, which, in fact, the cook had thrown on the grill the second he saw Boone come through the door.

"Oh, put the menu down," Petra says to Boone.

Boone puts the menu down and looks at her. It isn't a nice look.

"Why are you so angry?" she asks.

"Kelly Kuhio was one of the finest people I ever knew," Boone answers. "And your piece-of-shit client killed him."

"He did," Petra says. "I'm by no means convinced, however, that he's guilty of first-degree murder."

Boone shrugs. It's a slam dunk – if the DA can put Corey on death row, good for her. Mary Lou Baker is a tougher-than-nails veteran prosecutor who doesn't lose a lot of cases, and she is coming *hard* on this one.

Hell, yes, she is, because the community is *outraged*. The killing made the headlines every day for two weeks. Every development in the case makes the paper. And the radio talk show jocks are all *over* it, demanding the max.

San Diego wants Blasingame in the hole.

"I'll tell you what I *am* convinced of, though," Petra says. "I'm convinced that this city has formed a collective lynch mob for Corey Blasingame because he's bad for the tourist industry upon which the economy depends. San Diego wants families to come to Pacific Beach and spend money, which they're not likely to do if the area gets a reputation for violence. So the city is going to make an example of him."

29

"Yeah?" Boone asks. " You have any other kook theories?"

"Since you asked," Petra says, "I think you're so angry because this stupid tragedy has shattered your image of surfing as some sort of pristine moral universe of its own, removed from the rest of this imperfect world where people do horrible things to one another for no apparent reason. Poor, stupid Corey Blasingame has spray-painted his violent graffiti all over your cozy Utopia and you can't deal with it."

"You mind if I sit up, Doc?" Boone asks. "Or should I just lie down on the floor, seeing as how there's no couch?"

"Suit yourself."

"I will," Boone says. He cranks his neck to see Not Sunny leaning against the bar and says, "Make that to go, please?"

Petra says, "Coward."

Boone stands up, digs in his jeans' pocket and comes out with a couple of crumpled dollar bills that he tosses on the table as a tip. Chuck Halloran, the owner, won't allow Boone to pay an actual tab.

"No, I mean it," Petra says. "Not only are you afraid of taking a hard look at yourself, you're also afraid that if you take this case, all your surfing buddies will think less of you and throw you out of the fraternity. I wouldn't have thought it of you, but you leave me with no other choice."

"On second thought," Boone says to Not Sunny, "just cancel the order."

He walks out the door. Not Sunny comes over to the table. "Do you still want the iced tea?"

Petra sighs. "Oh, why not?"

Not Sunny sets the glass on the table.

We have something in common, Petra thinks.

We're both not Sunny.

12

The night that Kelly Kuhio was killed, PB was rolling with tourists and locals out for a good time. The bars were full and spilling out onto the sidewalks, the beer and wine were flowing, music was pulsing from the clubs and cruising cars with the bass turned up.

Dave and Tide were in The Sundowner, hogueing a platter full of fish tacos, just cooling it out after a day-long session. Dave was burned out from a double-shift, Tide was bored from a week of supervising bone-dry storm drains. They were sitting at their table, speculating on where Sunny might be at that moment, somewhere in the world, when the aggro started.

Yelling coming from the bar.

Corey Blasingame was a local kid, nineteen or so, who usually surfed out at Rockpile. Corey could ride a wave, but that was about it – he had no flair, no skill that would distinguish him. Now he was sporting a shaved head and a hoodie in the middle of freaking summer, although the sleeves were cut off to reveal his tattoos.

He had three boys with him – domes also shaved, ripped T-shirts and hoodies, baggy cammie trunks over ankle-high Uggs – and there was some ridiculous crap going around about these guys glossing themselves the Rockpile Crew, how they charged themselves with keeping 'law and order' at that La Jolla break, just up the road from Pacific Beach, how they kept the 'foreigners' out of their water.

A surf gang in La Jolla. Totally goobed. You know, La Jolla? The richest place in America? Where grown men with silver hair shamelessly wear pink polo shirts? A *gang*? It was so funny you almost couldn't laugh at it.

Tide did. When Boone brought up the ludicrous nature of a La Jolla gang during the Dawn Patrol, Tide said, "They got gangs in La Jolla. Doctor gangs, lawyer gangs, banker gangs. Those mean fuckers will rip you up, man, you don't replace a divot."

"Art gallery gangs," Dave added. "You don't mess with them janes, you value your junk."

Anyway, the Rockpile Crew was up front, demanding service which the bartender had refused because they were under-age. They started yapping about it, arguing, chanting 'Rockpile Crew' and just generally being pains-in-the ass, disrupting the nice vibe of the evening. Chuck Halloran, the owner, looked out from behind the bar at Dave, like, can you give me a hand with this?

Kelly Kuhio was in a booth with some friends, and he started to get up. Dave saw this and waved him off, like, I got this. That was the thing, Boone thought later, after it all went south – Kelly wasn't even involved in the hassle. He just sat in his booth drinking grapefruit juice and hitting some nachos. He had nothing to do with it.

For that matter, Boone had nothing to do with it, either. He was MIA from The Sundowner that night, on a date with Petra.

So it was Dave who got up from his chair and edged his way through the crowd to the bar and asked Corey, "What's up?"

"What's it to you?"

Dave looked at Corey's eyes and he could see the kid was jacked up. Certainly on beers, but probably something more – meth or speed or something. The boy was hopping up and down on the balls of his feet, his fingers flexing. Still, Dave could also tell from the look in his eye that Corey didn't really want a fight, that he was looking for a face-saving way to back down.

No problem, Dave thought. I'm all about the peace. Yeah, not really. Dave actually likes to go, but that's not what Chuck needed at the moment, and anyway, K2 was in the house, and The Man deplored violence. So Dave said, "Dude, you're too cool to want to cost Chuck his license, right? And I don't want to throw with you, you look tough, man."

Corey smiled and it should have been over right there.

Except that one of Corey's crew didn't want it to be over.

Trevor Bodin was a punk. Unlike Corey, Trevor had the build to back it up. Trevor did his time in the gym, and in the dojo, and he fancied himself some kind of mixed martial artist, always yapping about breaking into the Ultimate Fighting Championship.

Now Trevor opened his pie-hole to say, "You don't want to mess with us, man."

It was all too predictable that Bodin would want to keep this flame burning. Unlike a UFC octagon, he was surrounded by his boys who could pull his nutsack out of the fire if he got in trouble, so Trevor was real brave and mouthy.

"What's this have to do with you?" Dave asked him.

"What's it have to do with *you*?" Trevor answered.

Which was, like, a mistake.

Dave stepped forward and just kept walking, moving the guy toward the door. Tide did the same with Corey and the two other Rockpile Crew, and not one of them, not Corey or Trevor or Billy or Dean, did a damn thing about it. They didn't push back, they didn't throw, they just let themselves get ushered out onto the sidewalk.

Which was good thinking for morons. They were looking at two Pacific Beach *legends*, and the legends wanted them out of there, and they were just smart enough to go. But not smart enough to keep their mouths shut. It was almost comical, Corey hopping so he could yell over Tide's shoulder, "Rockpile Crew! Rockpile Crew!"

"Whatever," Dave said. "Move along."

"You don't own the sidewalk," Trevor said.

"You want to see what I own?" Dave asked.

Trevor didn't. Neither did the rest of the crew. They strutted up Garnet, chanting, "Rockpile Crew! Rockpile Crew!"

Dave and Tide went back to the bar and laughed about it.

Nobody was laughing about it the next day.

Because Kelly Kuhio was in a coma.

13

Boone walks straight to the beach.

Where he always goes when he's pissed off, sad, or confused. Looks to the ocean for an answer, or at least solace.

Pete's full of shit, he thinks as he looks at the torpid sea. Classic defense attorney bullshit. It's always somebody else's fault, not the poor criminal's. He's just a victim of society. 'Lynch mob' my aching ass. Four guys going to a man's house and beating him to death, that's a lynch mob.

Except Pete's not some knee-jerk, NPR-addicted, Volvo-driving, crunchy granola, left-wing type. She enthuses about the Laffer curve, thinks litterers should get jail time and owns a gun, for Chrissakes. Hell, if she wasn't getting paid to do the opposite, she'd be out to hang little Corey from the yard-arm.

The beach is crowded today, mostly with families. Lots of kids running around, and they don't seem to care that there's no surf. The mommies and daddies sure like it, they can relax and let the kiddies ride the boogie boards in the tiny whitewash. Other kids are tossing Frisbees, playing paddleball, making sandcastles. A few women are asleep in beach chairs, paperback books lying open on their laps.

Up on Crystal Pier people are strolling around, enjoying the view, the sunshine, the blue water. A few fishermen cluster at the end of the pier, their lines stretched down into the water, pretty much just an excuse to be out there on a day when the fish aren't biting. Below the pier a few lunchtime surfers are out, more from habit than hope that any decent wave is going to come along. Still, it's better than sitting in the office cubicle waiting for the bell to sound again and summon them back to whatever shit is waiting on their desks.

Pete's right about the lynching thing, Boone reluctantly concedes. The papers have been full of editorials and letters demanding strong reaction to the Kuhio murder, and the radio talk shows have been hammering the deterioration of Pacific Beach, the callers and hosts screaming for a 'crackdown.'

So dumbass Corey takes some of that weight. Is that so unfair? He killed someone.

Case closed.

Or is it? Was it the punch that killed Kelly, or the sidewalk? You've been in a few scuffles yourself, thrown a couple of punches. What if the addressee of one of those had fallen backward, hit his head on something unforgiving that cancelled his reservation? Would that have made you guilty of murder, justifiably put you in a box the rest of your life?

It depends.

On what?

On the very shit that Alan Burke wants you to look into. You know the game – a top-notch trial lawyer like Alan is too smart to try for an acquittal, he'll try to get the jury to go for a lesser charge, and he'll angle his case toward the sentencing hearing. That's if he takes it to trial at all – he'll probably try to find some facts that might persuade the DA to cut the kid a deal instead.

Boone looks back out at the ocean, where a flock of pelicans skim over the surface. A weak breeze wafts a scent of salt air and suntan lotion.

Is Pete right? Boone wonders. Is that what has you so jacked up? That this murder confirmed something you've known for a long time but didn't want to admit – that surfing isn't the Utopia you always wanted it to be? Needed it to be?

He decides to go see his priest.

14

Dave the Love God sits atop the lifeguard tower.

Boone walks to the base of the tower and asks, "Permission to come aboard?"

"Granted."

Boone climbs up the ladder and sits down next to Dave, who doesn't as much as turn his head to acknowledge his presence. Dave stares steadily out at the water, the shallows of which are packed with tourists, and doesn't take his eyes off it. Sure, the ocean is placid, but Dave knows from experience how quickly tedium can turn to terror. While the running joke among the Dawn Patrol is that Dave uses the tower as a vantage point to scope *turista* women – which he does – the actual truth is that when Dave is on duty and people are in the water, he is deadly serious about his job.

It's the rule that Boone's dad drilled into him, the rule that they all grew up with:

Never turn your back on a wave.

Never turn your back on the absence of a wave, either, because the second you do, a real thundercrusher will rise out of nowhere and smack you down. The ocean may look like one thing on the surface, but there's *always* something different happening underneath. That something could start a thousand miles away and then be headed toward you and you'll never know about it until it happens.

Dave's been on duty on a totally placid day when a freak rip comes in and takes a few swimmers out and then it's on, and the few seconds it might have taken him to get over his surprise would have cost those people their lives. As it was, he wasn't surprised, never surprised by the ocean, because, as much as we love her, she's a treacherous bitch. Moody, mercurial, seductive, powerful and deadly.

So Dave's head never turns toward Boone as they talk. Both men look straight out at the water.

"Your take on something?" Boone asks.

"You come seeking wisdom, Grasshopper?"

"Do you think," Boone says, "that we're a smug, self-anointed elite that can't see past our own zinc-oxide-covered noses?"

Dave touches the bridge of his nose to check that the zinc-oxide is still fresh. Then he says, "Sounds about right."

"What I thought." Boone says, getting up.

"That's it?"

"Yup."

"'Bye."

"Thanks."

"*Nada*."

Boone walks up the beach.

15

Boone only knows what happened that night from the newspaper accounts and the usual beach-bongo telegram system of rumors that went around PB.

But here's how it went.

Kelly Kuhio walked out of The Sundowner a little after midnight, stone-cold sober, on his way to his car in a parking lot on the corner.

He never made it.

Corey Blasingame – drunk, stoned, high on whatever – stepped out of the alley, backed by his crew, walked up to Kelly and punched him.

Kelly fell backward and hit his head on the curb.

He never regained consciousness.

They unplugged him from life support three days later.

16

Petra sits and sips her tea.

Very unlike her, to sit and do nothing, but she's sort of enjoying it, sitting and musing about Boone.

An odd man, she thinks. Simplistic on the surface, but extraordinarily complicated below. A maelstrom of contradictions beneath a placid-seeming sea. A Tarzan-like surfer boy who reads Russian novels at night. A devoted glutton of junk food without an ounce of body fat, who can grill fish to a turn over an open fire. A philistine who, when jollied into it, can talk quite intelligently about art. A disillusioned cynic with barely concealed idealism. A man who will desperately sprint away from anything that resembles emotion, but a deeply sensitive soul who might simply be the kindest and gentlest man you've ever met.

And attractive, damn it, she thinks. And frustrating. They've been sort of dating for some three months now and he's attempted nothing more than a quick, virtually chaste brush on the lips.

No, he's been terribly well-behaved, a real gentleman. Just two nights ago she had dragged him to a charity event at the La Jolla Museum of Contemporary Art and he showed up wearing a smart summer khaki suit, with a blue Perry Ellis shirt he certainly couldn't afford, and had actually had his hair cut. He'd been wonderfully tolerant of all the chit-chat, and even wandered around the gallery with her and made some sharp observations about some of the pieces, though none of them were depictions of breaking waves or wood-sided station wagons from the 1950s. And, in truth, he'd been absolutely charming to the other guests and the hosts, displaying a surprisingly detailed knowledge of the charity in question, and Petra had quite bristled at a colleague's ladies' room remark that her 'boy toy cleaned up nicely.'

But he stood at her doorway later that night as if his feet were planted in the concrete, gave her a polite hug and a perfunctory kiss, and that was it.

Do I want more? she asks herself. Certainly in this day and age, and as a modern, liberated woman, if I wanted more I could go after it. I'm perfectly capable of making the first move.

So why don't you? she asks.

Are you feeling the same ambivalence that he is? Because clearly he's attracted to you, else why would he ask you out repeatedly, but he seems hesitant to take it to the next level. As are you, to be honest. Why is that? Is it because we know that we're so different and it would therefore never work? Or is it because we both know in our heart of hearts that he's not yet over Sunny?

Is that a 'yet,' she wonders, or an 'ever?'

And do I want him or not?

This attitude about Corey Blasingame certainly argues against it. How an intelligent person could take such a knee-jerk, 'law-and-order,' vengeful, Dirty Harry, unenlightened stance . . .

17

There were paddle-outs for Kelly Kuhio all over the world, timed to go off at the same moment.

The one in San Diego was especially poignant.

They went out just before dawn to wait for the sun, as Kelly had for his morning meditations. Everyone brought a flower *lai* and tossed it into the water. Someone played a tune on the uke while someone else sang a song in Hawaiian, then a Buddhist monk said a prayer. Then anyone who wanted shared a memory or a thought about Kelly – his kindness, his superb skill, what he taught, how he was, his gentle humor, his strong compassion. There was some laughter and a lot of crying.

Boone didn't say anything, he just fought to hold back his tears.

What impressed him the most were the black and Mexican kids that paddled out even though most of them couldn't swim and looked scared shitless. Boone kept an eye on them to make sure they made it back okay, which they did.

They just wanted to pay their respects to the man.

Now Boone looks out at the same piece of water and remembers that day. He also remembers something that Kelly said to him one Saturday afternoon. Boone had been helping him keep a bunch of inner-city kids from drowning themselves while body-boarding down at La Jolla Shores, and a tired Boone asked Kelly why he went to all this trouble.

In his famously soft voice, Kelly answered, "You and I were lucky. At a very early age we found something that we loved, something that made our lives worth living. And I can't but believe that if you think your own life is worth living, you value other people's lives as well. Not everyone is as lucky as us, Boone."

Now Boone argues with Kelly Kuhio's memory. *Yeah, but, Kelly, the kids you worked with had nothing. The kid who killed you is a rich, spoiled little bastard who grew up with every advantage.*

Then he hears Kelly's dry, humorous voice. *Apparently not, Boone.*

So you're going to help Corey Blasingame, Boone tells himself. Stop flailing around like a barney, you know you're going to do it.

Because Kelly Kuhio would want you to.

18

Boone walks back into The Sundowner and sits down at the booth.

Not Sunny sighs and turns to the cook.

"Got it," the cook says.

"Why me?" Boone asks. "Why not some other PI?"

"Because you know the scene," Petra answers. "Another PI would take God knows how much time just to catch up on a learning curve that you already know."

"Why did Alan take this case?" Boone snaps.

"Corey's father is an old fraternity brother," Petra says.

"So I take it he can handle Alan's bill."

Petra nods.

"Doctor? Lawyer? Indian chief?"

"Real estate developer."

"I hate him already."

This is true. Generally speaking, Boone would have every real estate developer in Southern California put on a bus and driven over a cliff, if it wouldn't kill the bus driver. If he can find a bus-driving real estate developer, though, it's on.

Not Sunny sets Boone's plate down. He takes a big bite of the reheated *muchaca*, then says, "I won't help you go for an acquittal."

"We're not asking that," Petra says. "Just a sentence that reflects the facts, that a drunken teenager threw one punch with unfortunately tragic consequences, as opposed to the mob mentality that's driving an inflated first-degree murder charge. We don't want to go to trial,

Boone. Just try to get enough leverage that we can make a deal that resembles justice."

They want to knock it down to voluntary manslaughter. Boone knows that the State of California has mandatory sentencing guidelines – a vol man plea bargain could get Corey anywhere from 24 to 132 months in prison. Figure it somewhere in the middle range . . .

"Tell Alan I'll take the case."

"Actually, I already did."

Because with all your contradictions you're really a very simple man, she thinks.

You'll do the right thing.

She reaches over to his plate, tears off a piece of tortilla and says mildly, "There's a slight problem . . ."

Actually, six slight problems.

Five eyewitnesses.

And Corey's confession.

19

Since starting to date Pete, Boone has gained an appreciation of British understatement.

If she says she's 'a bit peckish,' it means she's starving; if she's 'a tad annoyed,' she's really approaching near homicidal rage; and little Corey's having 'a slight problem' means he's totally screwed.

Calling Corey's confession 'a slight problem' is like tagging a tsunami 'a little wave,' Boone thinks as he looks over the file. It could sweep Corey off the beach and carry him all the way to San Quentin, never to be seen again.

Here's what stupid Corey wrote:

'We were outside the bar waiting because we were pissed that

they threw us out of there earlier. So I saw the guy coming out of the bar and decided to mess him up. I walked up to him and hit him with a Superman Punch.'

A 'Superman Punch?' Boone asks himself. What the hell is a 'Superman Punch?'

'I saw his lights go out before he hit the ground. Other than that, I have nothing to say.'

'Other than that?' Boone wonders. Other than *that*, you moronic dweeb? Other than admitting to premeditation, then the premeditated act, then providing testimony that your random victim was killed by your punch and not the fall? Yeah. Other than that, good time to clam up, dim-bulb. Efficient writing style, though – Life Without Parole in five crisp sentences. Hemingway couldn't have done it better.

Three of the witness statements are from his little friends.

Corey's Rockpile crewmates threw him under the bus.

Typical of gangs, Boone thinks. It's all 'brothers forever' until they start doing the hard math of murder one *v.* accessory to manslaughter *v.* witness with immunity, then the brotherhood goes Cain and Abel.

Of course, the police were shaping the case that way from moment one. They had two other eyewitnesses who would testify to Corey throwing the fatal punch so the cops went to work on the potential co-defendants, making sure that they had Corey sewn up tight in the net.

Technically, they could book all four for murder – doubtless that was their opening gambit – but in practice they could never make anything but an accessory charge stick so they put a bright light over the 'Exit' door for three of them to find their way.

Trevor's statement is priceless.

'We were hanging in the alley when we saw this guy come down the street. Corey said, "Check it out – I'm going to mess with him. I'm going to fuck him up." I tried to restrane him . . .'

'Tried to restrane him,' Boone thinks. Three years on the SDPD, Boone recognizes 'copspeak' when he hears it.

Trevor was coached.

They just couldn't coach him to spell.

A nice touch of authenticity, though.

And the *'I'm going to fuck him up'* is really bad news.

'. . . but Corey shook me off, walked up and hit the guy with a Superman Punch.'

This Superman Punch, Boone thinks, seems to be like a *thing*, whatever it is.

'Then I heard this really bad "crack" sound when Mr. Kuhio's head hit. I knew it was real bad then. I said to Corey, "What did you do, dude? What did you do?"

'I know we should have called 911 and stayed, but we got freeked out and scared and so we got back in the car and drove away. I was crying. Corey was yelling, "I got him! I got the motherfucker. Did you see me get him?"'

Yup, Trevor has the shovel out and he's digging like mad. With a helping hand from the investigating officer.

Boone could practically hear the detective in the interview room with dumbass Trevor: *This might be your last chance to help yourself, guy. The train is pulling out of the station. There's a big difference between a witness and an accessory, kid. The former gets to go home, the latter gets to take showers with the Mexican Mafia.* Then he slides a pad of paper and pen across the table and tells Trevor to start writing.

Write for his life.

Then the cops buzz back and forth like bees, cross-pollinating Trevor Bodin with Billy and Dean Knowles. Have them toss as much shit as they can at each other, but especially on Corey. A little expository writing workshop, there in the precinct house. Pencils up, students, be sure to use vivid verbs and lively adjectives. Tell it in your own words, find your inner voice.

The one kid who didn't get a tutorial was Corey. They just handed him the suicide pen and told him to write. *"Just stick the point in your belly, son, and slash up and across. And try not to leak your bloody entrails on our furniture, kid."*

The investigating officers on the file were Steve Harrington and John Kodani.

Johnny Banzai.

A slight problem there.

Even with the jump-in rule.

Boone and Johnny established the jump-in rule shortly after Boone got his PI card and they realized that their lines were going to clash from time to time. So the rule is just an understanding that their business lives are sometimes going to conflict with their friendship – that sometimes one of them is going to have to jump in on the other guy's wave, and it's nothing personal.

Yeah, but . . .

This threatens to get real personal, because for Boone to do his job he's going to have to attack Johnny's work, his professional ethics. Which is not something you do to a friend and, no mistake, Boone and Johnny Banzai are friends.

They've been boys since they were freshmen law enforcement majors at San Diego State. In those days, Johnny used to surf down in Ocean Beach, and it was Boone who told him that he should check out PB Pier, Boone who made sure that he didn't catch any locie aggro as a newbie. Yeah, that didn't take long – when the PB boys saw Johnny shred that wave like he was born in it, when they caught how cool a guy he was, they took him right in.

Yeah, Boone and JB are friends, as in . . .

Boone was the best man at Johnny's wedding (and studied for weeks to learn enough Japanese to properly greet Johnny's grandparents). As in . . .

If Johnny and his wife both had to work a weekend day, they'd leave their boys with Boone and Dave at the beach and never give it a second thought because they knew that Boone and Dave would die before they'd let anything happen to those kids. As in . . .

One of those kids, the younger son, is named James Boone Kodani. As in . . .

The normally ultra-peaceful Boone clocked some clown who called Johnny a 'slant' right here in this same Sundowner. As in . . .

When Boone had his problems over the Rain Sweeny case, when he was a pariah on the force, it was J Banzai – and only J Banzai – who stood by him, who'd be seen talking to him, who'd sit down and have lunch with him. And although Boone never knew it, after he pulled the pin, it was Johnny B who whipped out his judo and put an epic ass-kicking on three – count them, *three* – cops who bad-mouthed Boone in the locker room. As in . . .

JB came to visit Boone in his crib almost every day during Boone's long months of lying around feeling sorry for himself. It was JB who kicked his ass to get off the sofa, JB who commiserated with him when Sunny couldn't stand it anymore and threw him out, Johnny Banzai who told him, 'Get back to the ocean, bro. Get back in the water.' As in . . .

They're friends.

So this ain't gonna be fun.

20

Boone ponders this as he gets into the Deuce to meet Pete over at the central jail downtown. That he's going to have to take a chunk out of one of his oldest friends in order to save garbage like Corey Blasingame.

And classic Johnny to catch the biggest case in San Dog and not mention it. Then again, JB usually keeps his cards pretty close to his chest where his cases are concerned, especially after Boone left the police force. They can talk shit out on the line-up, but there's a lot of shit they can't talk anymore.

The Deuce is a used Dodge van, the replacement for the legendary Boonemobile, which went out in a Viking funeral last April.

"This is your chance, you know," Petra had pointed out to him, "to own a real, grown-up sort of car."

Not really – the insurance payment on the Boonemobile had been exactly zero, Boone having been honest about the fact that he set the van on fire himself and also pushed it off the edge of a cliff. So there wasn't a lot of cash to go out and buy a 'real, grown-up car,' not that Boone wanted one. He wanted, and bought, another old van that he could fit his stuff in. A vehicle that cannot carry a surfboard is a sculpture.

"Then," Petra said, graciously yielding to the inevitable, "this is your chance to own a vehicle that does not have a sophomoric name."

"I didn't name the Boonemobile," Boone said, a little defensively. "Other people did."

The other people – Dave, Tide, Hang, Johnny and most of the greater San Diego surfing community – inevitably called the 'new' van Boonemobile II, after its iconic predecessor. The really annoying thing for Petra was that the replacement van acquired not one, but two monikers, because Boonemobile II was too long – so the nickname got a nickname of its own – 'Deuce.'

"You know," Johnny said, "guys who are 'the third' get tagged 'Trey.' Let's call Boone's second van 'Deuce.' "

So, Deuce it was.

She's waiting in the parking lot when he gets there.

"Your boy is driftwood," Boone says.

Washed up on the beach.

"I can't allow myself to think that way," Petra answers.

"How are you going to get around the confession?" Boone asks. Some waves you don't get around, over, or under. They just crush you. Out.

Petra shrugs. "Confusion? Coercion? A cop putting ideas into his head? That sort of thing does happen."

"Not with John Kodani," Boone says.

JB will definitely play hardball and he doesn't always throw straight down the middle. No, Johnny hurls some filthy junk – curveball, sliders, even the occasional knuckleball – but he's always going to catch the edge of the plate. Banzai wouldn't just rear back and throw a spitter at someone's head – convince some stupid kid that he did something he didn't.

"The first thing we have to do," she says, ignoring the 500-pound gorilla, "is to demonstrate that the Rockpile Crew isn't a 'gang.' The 'special circumstances' on the first-degree charge hinge on the allegation of gang activity."

"The Rockpile Crew *is* a gang," Boone says.

"Mere association and group self-identification do not meet the legal threshold required of a 'gang,' " she answers. "For instance, is the Dawn Patrol a gang?"

"Sort of."

"The 'gang' has to exist for the furtherance of criminal activity," she says. "I don't think that The Dawn Patrol engages in organized criminal activity."

Clearly, Boone thinks, she's never seen the Dawn Patrol hit a lunch buffet. Okay, the 'organized' thing is a stretch.

"Like murder?" he asks.

"Only," she insists, "if the murder is a direct consequence of, and/or in furtherance of, the stated criminal activity. It can't be merely coincidental."

Boone wonders how Kelly's loved ones might feel about his murder being 'merely coincidental,' but keeps the thought to himself. "So we need to find out if the Rockpile Crew was involved in anything other than the violent defense of its turf – say, drug-dealing or something like that."

"Precisely," she says. "Although I suppose it would be prudent to find out if any of these gangs of 'locies' – is that what you call them? –"

"Okay."

"– derive any financial profit from the defense of said turf," she says. "For instance, if they're practicing extortion, or charging 'taxes' for the use of the water, that would constitute a 'gang' under the legal interpretation."

So, Boone thinks, if the Rockpile Crew says "You can't surf here" and enforce it, they're not a gang. If they say, "You can't surf here unless you give us twenty bucks," and enforce that, they are. You gotta love the law.

What about the big five-star hotel chains that are buying up the coastline, and do everything they can to keep the public from getting access to 'their' beaches? Are they a gang under the law?

Oughta be.

Bet they're not.

He asks, "What does Corey say about it?"

"I don't know," she says. "Let's go ask him."

To meet Corey is to take an instant dislike to him.

In the interest of efficiency.

Clad in an orange jumpsuit, he slumps in a chair in the interview room and refuses to look at either Boone or Petra. He's thin and pale, but his shoulders and biceps are big, his head shaven, and he maintains a sullen, anti-social expression.

"Corey," Petra says, "this is Mr. Daniels. He's here to help on your case."

Corey shrugs. "I have nothing to say."

Boone shrugs. Sure, *now* you have nothing to say. Bad timing on your part going Marcel Marceau *now*.

"Since writing his statement, that's all he's ever said," Petra remarks to Boone. She turns back to Corey. "There's tremendous variation in what you could be convicted of, Corey. From involuntary manslaughter, in which case you'd be released for time served, all the way to murder with special circumstances, in which case you're looking at life without parole."

Corey sighs. Like he's bored out of his mind, like he could give a rat's ass, like he's so gang, so down, so tough, that killing someone is No Big Deal. "I have nothing to say."

"Please help us to help you," Petra says.

Corey shrugs again.

"Forget it," Boone says to her. "Let him slide."

A lot of people have drowned, he thinks, trying to save a drowning swimmer. And this one isn't even worthy of saving. Let him go.

Petra doesn't. "Your father retained us to—"

Which seems to spark a small flame, anyway. "Hey," Corey says, "you want to make my dad happy so he pays your bill, knock yourselves out. It has nothing to do with me."

"It has everything to do with—"

"No," Corey says. "Trust me – it doesn't."

He gets up.

"Sit down," Boone says.

"You gonna make me?"

"Maybe."

Corey sighs again but he sits down and stares at the floor.

"Tell me about the Rockpile Crew," Boone says.

"Nothing to say," Corey says. Except he goes ahead and says it. "We surf, we party, we brawl. S'bout it."

Kid sounds like a bad hip-hop lyric, Boone thinks. "You deal?"

"Nah."

"What about the juice?"

"Say again?"

"Don't jack me around, I'm not in the mood," Boone says. "The steroids – you sell, or you just use?"

"I just use," Corey says.

"Where do you get them?"

"I have nothing to say." Corey smiles. He looks up from the floor and smiles at Petra. " 'Life without parole?' Do I look like some taco to you? I'll get *probation*, the money my dad's paying."

He gets up and the guard leads him out.

21

"I have nothing to say," Boone says out in the parking lot.

"Funny," Petra says. "Very droll."

It's freaking hot out there. The sun is doing its hammer-on-anvil routine and just *pounding*. Even Petra is sweating – check that – *perspiring*.

"No, I can see why you're eaten up with sympathy for the kid," Boone says "It's his warmth, humility, intelligence, his sense of true remorse for what he did . . ."

"Come on, Boone," she says, "you can see through the bluster. He's a child, he doesn't know how to react. The vacillation between depressed fatalism and unreasonable optimism is quite telling. The arrogance is covering up fear, the seeming indifference is to mask shame."

"See," Boone says, "I think that underneath all that surface arrogance is a deep arrogance, and the sham indifference masks a genuine indifference."

She unlocks her car and slides into the driver's seat. "In any case, it's our job to defend him."

"He made that point, yeah."

Because he ain't some 'taco,' a Mexican that would have to pay bust-out retail for what he did. No, Corey's pretty sure that his white skin and his daddy's money are going to get him a good deal.

It's a reasonable assumption, but it's wrong. This time the community is outraged and demanding action; the very privilege that Corey's banking on is going to boomerang on him, and he just doesn't get it yet.

He's thinks it's business as usual, but it isn't.

There's another factor here, Boone thinks, feeling old. It's the video-game generation – they always think they can hit the re-set button and get a new game. If nothing is real, if it's all virtual, then there are no real consequences.

"How did you know about the steroids?" Petra asks.

"I looked at him," Boone says. "He's juiced – his muscles are too big for his bones, the shaved hair is thinning. I think he might have been juiced up that night."

"'Roid rage?"

"Maybe."

"I'm not sure it's a viable defense anyway," she says. "But it's worth looking into. Where else do you want to take it?"

Boone starts off with where he can't take it. He can't talk to Trevor Bodin or the Knowles brothers because their lawyers know that their interests conflict with Corey's and won't let the interviews happen. Those kids, smarter than Corey, started making their deals right in the police interview rooms. The best they can hope for is that Alan takes a chunk or two off the rest of the Crew's credibility during cross-exam, but that's about it. So that's no good. But he can run down more info on the Rockpile Crew and the 'gang' issue, find out what they were all about.

Boone sums all that up for Petra, and then says, "If Corey takes that attitude into a trial, Mary Lou will ride it to a max sentence."

"I'm sure," Petra says. "Find out about him, Boone. Open him up for us, get us something we can use."

"I'm not a shrink, Pete," Boone says. "Neither are you."

She just doesn't get that Corey Blasingame is exactly what he seems to be – a rich, spoiled, uncaring piece of crap who threw an unlucky punch and is going to ride that wave all the way to the bottom because he's too stupid and arrogant to even try to bail. No, Corey's in the impact zone and no one's coming in with a jet ski to pull him out.

Yeah, except Kelly Kuhio is pushing Boone onto the ski.

"Just get us the information," she says. "We'll figure out what to do with it."

"You got it."

Not a fun job, but then again, most of them aren't.

Why they call it 'work.'

And the work of this case will be not so much to find out *what* Corey did, but *why*.

"You, uhhh, doing anything tonight?" asks Boone.

Smooth, he thinks, very smooth.

Barney.

She frowns. "Getting together with some people from the office. A retirement celebration for one of the partners. Sort of optional mandatory. Sorry."

"No worries." Optional mandatory?

"Another time?"

"Sure."

She blows him a kiss, closes the door, and pulls out.

Boone gets back into the Deuce.

She probably does have an office thing tonight, he thinks. Or she's free, but doesn't want you to think that you can ask her out on short notice like that. He makes a mental note to consult on this with Dave (not-for-nothing-known-as) the Love God, then remembers that Dave has asked women out – or more accurately in – with less than thirty seconds' notice.

The lawyer world, he decides, is very different from the surfer world.

Different waves, different rules.

Speaking of which, he decides to use what's left of the afternoon by driving up to La Jolla to check out the break known as Rockpile.

22

Depending on who or whom you believe, the name 'La Jolla' (pronounced 'Luh Hoya') comes from the Spanish, and means 'The Jewel,' or from the Native Americans, and means . . .

'The Hole.'

Boone goes with the latter interpretation, just to piss people off, and because it's funny – one of the most beautiful, expensive, exclusive and snooty neighborhoods in America getting tagged a hole. Also because the NAs owned it and should know what they called it.

Not that they meant anything pejorative, the 'hole' in question probably referred to the caves in the coastline bluffs, and the area was almost certainly a paradise back then, when the original inhabitants lived by fishing, gathering shellfish and doing a little light hunting and farming, before the Spanish friars arrived and decided that the people were better off being Christian slaves than free 'savages.'

Actually, La Jolla stayed pretty quiet and bucolic for a long time as it didn't have much to offer besides those caves, pristine beaches and gorgeous scenery. There were no natural harbors, for instance, nowhere to dock a fishing fleet. It was just a long stretch of grassy coastline with some picturesque rock formations and red seaside cliffs with holes in them, until the real estate boom of the 1880s came along and the Sizer brothers surveyed and bought up some land for $1.25 an acre. Not a bad investment, Boone thinks as he drives up from Pacific Beach, because acre lots in that neighborhood now go for $2,000,000, if you can get them.

Then in 1890, the local newspaper heiress Ellen Browning Scripps decided that she was an artist, and that La Jolla was a good place for art, so she started an artists' colony. Art colonists started to build arty little beach cottages in the downtown neighborhood still known as 'The Colony.' You can find galleries there today along Prospect or Girard, together with five-star hotels, expensive boutiques, restaurants, nightclubs and office buildings, and the La Jolla Museum of Contemporary Art occupies a prominent place on the bluff, but the art most practiced in contemporary La Jolla is the art of the deal.

Boone also likes 'The Hole' etymology because his route takes him near the infamous La Jolla sinkhole.

A little less than a year ago, an area about the size of a football field simply sank into the earth, taking eighteen $2-million homes with it. City engineers warned the residents just the day before that they shouldn't sleep there that night, but most did. No one was seriously hurt, but a bunch of people had to be rescued.

The papers called it a landslide, the television reporters deemed it a 'sinkhole,' the geologists referred to it as a 'breakaway,' and the chief city engineer, in Boone's favorite comment, said, 'This is a geologically active area.' No shit, Boone thinks as he drives near the disaster site – an entire neighborhood just fell into a hole, which is just about as active as it gets.

Maybe, Boone thinks, the Native Americans knew something we didn't.

Like, don't build over a hole.

He takes a left and turns down toward 'Rockpile,' further proof of the area's geological hyper-activity.

The rock pile that gives the break its name is a stack of red boulders, now splattered white from seagull guano, that clearly broke off from the cliffs sometime in the undetermined past and landed in the water. Like any formation of solid matter in the ocean, it created something for waves to 'break' on, in this case a tasty outside left, very attractive to the spiritual descendants of Ellen Browning Scripps and to surfers.

So you have two very different types of people that frequent Rockpile: Artsy ladies in sensible shoes and big hats with their easels, canvases, oils and watercolors, and then you have surfers. They co-exist pretty well, because the painters usually stay up on the cliff and the surfers are down in the water.

The issue is parking.

Rockpile is in what is basically a ravine between two outlying points, so there is a narrow road down to it and a small parking lot along the actual beach. The small lot obviously has limited room for cars, which is the source of a lot of the recent trouble at Rockpile.

The locals know each other's rides, and if a strange car with a surf rack is parked there, that vehicle and its driver could have a problem. Cars *sans* racks are usually given a pass because the locies figure it's a painter who isn't going to try to take up valuable space out at the break. In fact, some of the artists have taken to leaving cardboard signs reading 'I'm An Artist' inside their windshields.

Boone doesn't do that. He parks the Deuce in the dirt along the side of the road, goes around to the back of the van and pulls out his old 9′3″ Balty longboard and leans it against the side of the van. As he peels down to his board trunks he checks out the other cars.

Despite the location, it seems to be a pretty working-class group.

There are a couple of Beemers and one Lexus, but for the most part it's Fords, Chevys and Toyotas. And relatively young, lots of decals for metal bands in the windshields. Other decals are less benign: 'If You Don't Live Here, Don't Surf Here;' 'This Is Protected Territory;' 'Rockpile Regulars Only.'

Nice, Boone thinks as he shoulders his board and then carries it down to the beach. Very broley.

Rockpile is beautiful, no question about it. Boone can see why anyone would want to paint it, surf it, or just hang out there. Just hanging out is about the only option for a surfer today, because there isn't much surf, but some of the boys are out there by the rocks, sitting on their boards and waiting for something to happen. And scoping the newbie walking into the water. There's about ten of them, all sitting up and watching Boone as he jumps on his board and paddles out.

Boone angles off to the right, toward what would be the shoulder of the break if anything were breaking. It's surf etiquette – he's headed toward the rear of the line-up and not crossing the path of a wave if anyone was lucky enough to get a ride. It shows he has manners and that he knows what he's doing, but that apparently isn't enough at Rockpile.

One of the surfers breaks out of the line and paddles toward him.

Boone stops paddling when the guy gets close, and nods in acknowledgment. The surfer looks to be in his mid-twenties, has a lot of tatts, short hair. One of the tattoos is a number '5,' which Boone doesn't get, but the rest are the usual Celtic knots, barbed wire, and the like.

"S'up?" Boone asks.

"S'up?" the surfer asks. "You new here, bro? I don't think I've seen you before."

Boone smiles. "Haven't been here for a while. I usually surf the pier at PB."

"How come you're not there now?"

"Thought I'd change it up a little."

"Think again, bro."

"What?"

"Think *again*, bro," the kid says louder, getting a little aggro. "This isn't your break."

Boone is careful to smile again. "Isn't *anyone's* break today, bro. There's nothing breaking."

He's truly amazed that the kid wants to start up over literally nothing. He can't get crowded out of a wave that doesn't exist.

The kid says, "Go home, dude."

Boone shakes his head and goes to paddle around him. The kid paddles into his way. Boone tries the other direction and the kid blocks him again.

"That's bad form, kid," Boone says. The 'kid' sounds strange coming out of his mouth. It doesn't seem like so long ago when *he* was the kid and the *veteranos* were gruffly teaching *him* good form. Jesus, Boone thinks, I'll be on the Gentlemen's Hour soon. Gumming my fish taco and telling tales about the good ole days.

The kid asks, "What are *you* going to do about it?"

Boone feels a flare of temper but squelches it. I am not going to get into a fight in the water, he tells himself. It's just too stupid. Push comes to shove . . . well, I won't let it come to shove, I'll back off first. But otherwise, kid, I'd knock you off that board and dunk you until some manners soak in and . . . Ego, Boone tells himself. Ego, testosterone and something else – jealousy of the kid's youth?

"Just get out of my line," Boone says. It sounds weak.

He sees another surfer paddling full-steam toward them. The guy is bigger, bulkier, older, his shoulder muscles huge as he paddles with easy strength.

I'm about to get my ass kicked, Boone thinks. Gang-jumped in the water.

Epic.

"Show some respect!" the new guy hollers as he comes up. "Don't you know who this is?!"

He glides and sits up on his board. He's huge – big, broad chest, heavy muscles, square forehead, thick brown hair greased straight back. Probably mid-thirties. Boone knows him from somewhere, but can't quite place it.

"This is Boone Daniels," he says to the younger surfer. "Boone freaking Daniels. *Mister* Daniels to you, pup, and you'll show him some respect."

"Sorry," the kid mutters. "I didn't know."

Because BD is a BFD, a Big Fucking Deal, and he has an all-rides pass to any break on the Great California Water Park from Brook Street in Laguna to Tijuana Straits. Messing with Boone means not only jerking with him, which is sketchy enough, but also taking on Dave the Love God, High Tide and Johnny Banzai.

Like that time at PB pier a couple of years back, when some dismo fishing dudes thought Johnny B had tangled up their lines and went down to front him about it. Yeah, four of these brave fuckers on Johnny – for about five seconds – then Boone, Dave and High Tide paddled in and it turned out that the fishermen didn't want to throw so bad after all.

You call the wolf, you get the pack.

"You're welcome here," the older guy says. "Always welcome."

"I appreciate it."

"Mike Boyd," he says, stretching out his hand. "I'm a karate buddy of Dave's."

"Right, right," Boone says, remembering. Dave took him to a few dojos and they messed around with it a little, and Boone went to one of Dave's tournaments a couple of years back and Mike was there.

"How's Dave?"

"He's Dave, he's good."

"Haven't seen him for a while," Boyd says. "You still hang with the PB Dawn Patrol?"

"Yeah, you know."

"Your crew is your crew."

"That's it."

"What brings you here?" Boyd asks. It's friendly, not a challenge, but there's a little edge to it. Boyd's clearly the sheriff here, and he wants to know what's going on at his beach.

"Checking it out," Boone says.

"Nothing on today."

"Same all over," Boone says. They talk bullshit – the flat surf, the heat, the usual crap – then Boone asks, "Hey, you know this kid Corey Blasingame? The Rockpile Crew?"

Boyd turns to the younger surfer and says, "Push off, alright?" When the kid is a few feet away, Boyd spits into the water, and then juts his chin toward the handful of surfers laying on the shoulder. "I'm a martial arts instructor. Brad's a dry-waller. Jerry's a roofing contractor. We don't live here but we've been surfing here forever. It's our place. Some of the kids? Yeah, they're local kids, some of them come from money, I guess. They live around, so it's their place, too."

"Corey, Trevor Bodin, Billy and Dean Knowles," says Boone, "they glossed themselves the Rockpile Crew.

"Rich, spoiled La Jolla kids playing at being something they're not," Boyd says. "There's no gang here, just a bunch of guys who surf."

"Did you know Corey? What can you tell me about him?"

"Corey's a strange kid," Boyd says. "He just wanted to belong somewhere."

"And he didn't?"

"Not really," Boyd says. "Just one of those kids who always seemed just one click behind the wheel, you know?"

"Got it," Boone says. "What about Bodin?"

"Tough boy."

"Real tough," Boone asks, "or gym tough?"

There's a difference. Boone hasn't seen a fighter yet who looks bad against a bag. And most look okay in sparring matches, where nobody is really trying to hurt anybody. But you put that same guy in a physical confrontation on the street, in a club or a bar, and maybe he doesn't look so good.

"A little of both," Boyd says, sounding kind of cagey.

"You've seen him in action?"

"Maybe."

59

Maybe nothing, Boone thinks. Maybe Trevor had helped Boyd keep the fatherland pure – a little law enforcement on the beach or in the parking lot. "And?"

"He does okay for himself," Boyd says. "He's got an edge to him, you know?"

No, I don't know, Boone thinks. Bodin backed down pretty quickly at The Sundowner that night, when he was four-on-three. Maybe his edge came out when the odds were a little better, like four-on-one.

"I guess," Boone says, "Hey, Mike, tell me something. If you'd paddled over here and I wasn't a buddy of Dave's and all that, what . . ."

Because that kid didn't paddle over here on his own. You sent him to check it out, chase away the interloper. Were you going to 'extort' me, Mike? Make a profit? Further a criminal activity?

"You would have been politely asked to find another place to surf," Boyd says.

"What if I said no?"

"You would have been politely asked to find another place to surf," Boyd repeats. "Why are you asking?"

"Curious."

Boyd nods, looks around at the flat sea. Then he says, "So, we're the bad guys now, I guess, huh? We're the Neanderthals, the animals who give surfing a bad name, just because this fucked-up kid connected with a punch?"

"I didn't say that."

"All I ever wanted," Boyd says, "all I want *now*, is one little stretch of water in this whole fucking world. I just want a place where I can come and surf. Is that so much to ask, Daniels? Huh?"

I dunno, Boone thinks.

Maybe it is.

23

Yeah, but he kind of gets Boyd.

He gets all the Mike Boyds and the Brads and the Jerrys.

A man works his ass off his whole life, putting up drywall on a house he could never afford, puts food on the table, clothes on his kids' backs, and all he asks in return is the chance to ride a few waves. Like, he made that deal and it was a good deal, but then it changed, as the water started to get clogged with yuppies, wannabes, dilettantes, and dot-com billionaires who can barely wax their own boards.

It's not that they're just taking his water, it's that they're taking his life. Without that Rockpile break, what he is is a drywaller, a roofer, a karate instructor in a strip mall. With that break, he's a surfer, a *Rockpile* surfer, and it means something.

It does.

So what about the kids, the next generation that Boyd needs to keep in line? They have everything, they live in the houses that the Brads and Jerrys work on. They have money, privilege and futures (or used to have futures, nix that for Corey), what the hell are they about?

Why do kids from Rockpile emulate gangstas?

And why are you so pissed off about it? he asks himself as he drives south on the PCH, back toward PB. Because they turned to surfing, like you did, and found something different than you did? An aggressive localism? A crew? A tribe?

You have your crew, he tells himself, you have your tribe.

Dave, Johnny, Tide, even Hang.

Sunny, in absentia.

And face it – it's everything to you. Probably more than it should be.

Yeah, but you don't go out killing people. You just go out and surf, talk some bullshit, have some laughs, bolt some fish tacos. Watch the sun set.

Good times.

So why didn't Corey find *that*?

Maybe because you find what you look for.

What Boyd said about Corey Blasingame? Even in his own circle, the kid didn't quite cut it. It was like he was trying to fill in this silhouette of what he thought he should be, but he couldn't color inside the lines.

Boone's cell phone rings.

Hang set it to play the first bar of Dick Dale's 'Miserlou.'

"S'Boone."

"Boone – Dan. I have those records you asked for."

"Cool," Boone says. "Meet me on the pier."

"Ten minutes?"

"Sounds right."

Boone makes the rest of the drive back to Crystal Pier, parks the Deuce in the narrow slot by his cottage and walks out to the end of the pier. Dan Nichols is already out there, leaning against the railing, staring out at the ocean. Something you probably do a lot, Boone thinks, if you suspect your wife is cheating on you.

Dan hands him the phone record and e-mail print-outs.

"Did you look at them?" Boone asks.

"Yeah."

"And?"

"Nothing jumps out," Dan says. "No repeated calls to the same number, except to Melissa."

"Who's—"

"Her best friend."

"Do me a favor?" Boone says. "Cross out *any* of these you can explain."

"You could run the numbers, couldn't you?"

"Yup," Boone says, "any you don't cross out. Trying to save me some time and you some cash."

"Money isn't my problem in life, Boone." Dan looks sad, really beat-down. He runs down the sheet of phone numbers, crossing out line after line.

Boone says, "Dan, maybe this means you're wrong about this. Which is, like, a *good* thing, you know?"

"I just *feel* it."

"Okay." He takes the records from Dan. "I'll shout you."

"Thanks."

"De nada."

Boone walks back to the office, hands the phone records to Hang. "Want to make a little extra jack?"

"Deeds."

Surfbonics for 'yes.'

"Run these phone numbers," Boone says. "Names and addresses."

"Moly."

Momentarily.

Boone goes upstairs. Hang Twelve can not only make a computer sing, he can make it perform Puccini arias standing on a basketball while juggling burning torches.

Cheerful is banging the adding machine.

"Didn't have a chance to tell you," Boone says. He shoves some old mags off his chair and sits down. "I took the Corey Blasingame gig."

Cheerful doesn't look happy. Which, of course, is his default setting anyway, but now he turns the color up on the unhappy dial. "I'm not sure that's such a smart move."

"It's a macking dumb move," Boone says. "Why I'm qualified."

"Petra talk you into it?"

"Sorta."

"It's not going to make you very popular around here," Cheerful says.

Boone shrugs. “Keep it to yourself for a while.”

Hang Twelve bounds up the stairs. “I zipped the Arabics, got tags and cribs for every sat reach-out – totally squeezy, tube blast – and went Amish for you. Foffed?”

Translation: I ran the numbers, Boone dude, and got names and addresses for every cell-phone call – it was really easy and very fast – and I printed out a hard copy for you. Happy?

“Mahalo.”

“Nurries.”

No worries.

“Late, yah?”

“Latrons.”

Hang bounces back down the stairs.

Boone looks at the print-out. It has nothing to offer – calls to grocery stores, her masseuse, a boutique in Solana Beach . . . routine stuff with very few repeats. So if Donna Nichols has a lover, she isn’t communicating with him over the phone.

Sucks.

Now he’ll have to wait for Dan to go out of town and then follow her.

24

Boone’s place is the last cottage on the north side of Crystal Pier.

It’s worth a freaking fortune and Boone couldn’t have come close to affording it, but Cheerful insisted on giving it to him as a reward for helping disentangle him from a marriage with a twenty-five-year-old alimony hunter.

Despite its more-than-prime location, it’s a simple place. A small living room with a kitchen area, one bedroom, one bath. All the plank boards painted white. The very cool thing for Boone is that it sits literally right over the water. He can even open a window, stick a pole out, and fish right from his bedroom.

Boone comes in, goes to the fridge for a cold Dos Equis and sits down at the kitchen table with a fresh notepad, a pen, and the Blasingame file.

The two remaining eyewitness statements are key. Alan Burke can knock some of the sting out of the Rockpile Crew testimony because the other members have something to gain, but two objective eyewitnesses are far more damaging.

Jill Thompson is twenty-one years old, a part-time student at SDSU and a *barista* at Starbucks. The night of the killing, she and a friend of hers, Marissa Lopez, had been club-hopping along Garnet Street.

Marissa hooked up with a guy, Jill didn't.

She was walking west on Garnet when she saw a man walk east and cross the street to the parking lot.

'Then these four guys came out of the alley. They seemed pretty drunk to me. One of them just walked up to the man and hit him. The man fell. The guys got in their car and drove away. I went over to the man. He was unconscious. I used my cell phone to dial 911, but I guess it was too late.'

Simple, straightforward, Boone thinks, and consistent with the other witness statements, as baked as they might be.

Jill Thompson gave the police a detailed, accurate description of Corey and what he was wearing, and later picked him out of a line-up as the man who had punched Kelly Kuhio.

The other witness is George Poptanich, a fifty-four-year-old cab driver who was parked in the lot that night. It was common for taxis to wait in that lot for their dispatchers to send them to bars to pick up fares too drunk to drive.

Poptanich was sitting in his cab when he heard the Rockpile Crew come out of the alley to his left. He noticed the pedestrian because he thought he might be a possible fare. Then he saw one of the 'punks' walk up to the pedestrian 'aggressively.' He started to get out to help but there wasn't time before one of the kids punched the pedestrian in the face. Poptanich yelled at them, but the punks jumped into a car. Poptanich noted the license number, jotted it down in his log, and called 911. Then he went to assist the girl who was with the pedestrian. By this time, people were coming out of the bars.

A police cruiser picked the Rockpile Crew up five minutes later on the PCH, ostensibly on their way to La Jolla.

Poptanich also picked Corey out of the line-up as the kid who threw the punch.

There's a knock at the door.

Boone opens it.

"You wanna get dinner?" Dave asks.

He has a speargun in his hand.

25

Forty-five minutes later they jump into the water of La Jolla Cove.

Boone has a mask with a lamp, a snorkel, duck fins and his Ogie speargun, and now he and Dave, similarly equipped, swim out toward underwater caves, the aforementioned 'holes' that gave the place, at least in Boone's mind, its name.

Caves and underwater holes are good, because that's where the fish are.

The swim feels good, just a little cold and refreshing on a soft night. Most of the year they'd wear wet suits because the deep current runs cold, but it's still warm enough in August to go with just trunks.

It's a fine thing to do, night spear-fishing, and they owe it all to a group of nonagenarians collectively called the Bottomscratcher's Club. These were a bunch of WWII vets who had crashed in planes, sank in ships and survived amphibious assault landings, and came home to San Diego to find that their adrenaline-hyped systems weren't being sufficiently fed. So they started free-diving in the underwater caves of La Jolla Cove.

If the tight caves, heavy surf and tricky currents weren't dangerous enough, it's worthwhile to note that the only creatures that previously hunted under these waters were the great white sharks attracted by the numerous sea lions, their favorite meal, and that a free-diver in a wet suit and fins looks an awful lot like a sea lion.

Actually, spear-fishing had been against the law in San Diego up until the formation of the Bottomscratcher's Club, when a lawmaker observed that if any man had light enough brains and heavy enough balls to tempt great whites in their home territory, he should damn well have the right to do it. The Bottomscratcher's Club recently disbanded, due to age, but Boone and Dave feel that they're upholding a fine tradition of courage and stupidity.

And free food.

'Free food tastes better,' is an article of faith in Dave's cosmology, and Boone can only agree. There is something about the taste of food that you haven't laid out bucks for that is just, well, *better*.

Now Boone and Dave swim over to the cave where they think they'll have the best luck. Boone spits into his mask, swishes some water around the glass, and fits it snugly onto his face. Then he lays out, swims around for a second, and dives.

They call it free-diving because you're free of most equipment – crucially, air tanks and regulators. What you're free to do is hold your breath for as long as you can and get as deep as you can, leaving yourself with enough reserve in your lungs to make it back up. Both Boone and Dave are certified scuba divers, and sometimes do that, but on a summer evening it's easier to just jump in and go.

Boone flicks on his lamp and dives down toward the mouth of a narrow cave. He moves his head to shine the light around but doesn't see anything but tiny fish, so he comes back up, grabs a breath and dives again.

He spots Dave about fifty feet away, treading above a small crack in a reef. You want to stay close enough for visual contact but far enough away for safety – the last thing you want is to shoot your buddy with a spear.

Some movement catches Boone's eye. Turning back to a crack in an underwater rock, he sees a 'swish' disappear into it, leaving a roil of bubbles that shine in the lantern light. Boone swims down to the crack and feels it. It's narrow, but wide enough, and he turns sideways and pushes himself through.

The crack opens into an underwater chamber and Boone sees the yellowtail tuna below him, flipping its tail back and forth, motoring away. Boone is almost out of breath – he feels that tightness in his chest and the slight physical panic that always comes with running out of air – but he relaxes and pushes through it, diving down closer to the tuna. He raises the speargun to his shoulder and squeezes the trigger. The spear shoots out and strikes the fish behind the gills. The tuna thrashes violently for a moment, then is still, as a cloud of blood billows into the water. Boone pulls in the cord and brings the fish closer to his body.

Time to get going.

Boone turns and heads up toward the narrow chamber.

Except he can't find it.

A slight problem.

It was perfectly obvious from above, but it must look different from below and in poor light, and as he gropes his way around the chamber for an opening he feels really stupid. This would be a bad, dumb way to go out, he thinks, trying to keep his movements steady and unhurried, fighting the physical reflex to hurry.

But he can't see it and he can't feel it.

So he listens for it.

Small waves are coming into the cove, against the cliffs, and the water will go out the chamber and make a sound. He stops still and listens, and then he hears a faint whooshing sound and heads toward it.

Then he sees the light.

Not the light that they say you see before you go to heaven, but Dave's lantern shining into the chamber from the other side.

Why you dive with a buddy.

Especially a buddy like Dave the Love God.

These guys are *tight*, they've hung together since grade school, ditching classes through junior high and high school to go surfing, diving or just roaming the beach. It was like they didn't have separate houses – if Boone was at Dave's at supper-time, that's where he ate; if Dave was at Boone's at night, that's where he crashed. They'd sit up half the night anyway, playing video games, watching surf videos, talking about their heroes – and, yeah, one of those was Kelly Kuhio.

Some of the old guys on the Gentlemen's Hour called them the 'Siamese Idiots,' a double-dose of gremmie obnoxiousness joined at the hip. (Yeah, but those men looked out for them, made sure that their stupidity didn't cost them their lives, made sure they never crossed the line.)

Boone and Dave pooled their cash to buy that first van, used it go cruising the coast together looking for the best waves, and took turns on a Friday/Saturday night rotation system for dates. The van died a natural death after two years (Johnny B opined that its suspension just gave up the will to live) and the boys sold it for scrap and used the money to buy scuba gear.

Diving, surfing, hougueing, chasing girls. Long days on the beach, long nights on the beach, it builds a friendship. You're in the ocean with a guy, you learn to trust that guy, trust his character and his capabilities. You know he's not going to jump your wave or do something kooky that would get you hurt or even killed. And you know – you *know* – that if you're ever lost in the dark deep water, that guy is coming to look for you, no matter what.

So Dave's down there with a lantern, showing him the way up and out.

Boone swims toward the light, then sees the crack and squeezes through, pulling his catch behind him. Then he plunges up to the surface and gets a deep breath of beautiful air.

Dave comes up beside him.

"Nice catch."

"Thanks."

"You're an idiot."

"It's been said."

"Accurately," Dave says. "We should head in."

Because there's blood in the water, and if there's anything more attractive to a shark than a sea lion, it's blood. If any sharks are within a hundred yard radius, they'll be coming. Best to be on shore when they do.

"Let me catch a little more air," Boone says.

"Weak unit."

Again, accurate, Boone thinks. He takes in a couple more lungfuls and then they swim to shore and climb out on a shelf of rock.

"Beautiful night," Dave says.

Too true.

26

The three decapitated bodies lie in a drainage ditch.

Johnny Banzai shines a flashlight on them, fights off the urge to vomit, and slides down into the ditch. From the relative lack of blood he can tell that the men were killed somewhere else and dumped out here to be seen.

What happens to people who fuck with Don Cruz Iglesias.

Steve Harrington slaps the back of his hand to his forehead and moans, *"Ohhh, mi cabeza!"*

Funny guy, Harrington.

Johnny checks one of the dead men's wrists for tattoos and finds just what he expected – a tattoo depicting a skull with wings coming out of each side. *Los Angeles Muertos*, the Death Angels, are an old-line Barrio Logan street gang who've been revived by hooking up with the Ortega drug cartel across the border. The Criminal Intelligence guys had given Homicide a heads-up that the Ortegas had taken a shot at Cruz Iglesias yesterday and missed.

The decapitations are his response, Johnny thinks.

"Any ID on the Juan Does?" Harrington asks.

"Death Angels."

"Well, they sure are now."

Johnny's no particular lover of gang bangers, but at the same time he's not happy that the cartels' war for Baja has spilled over into San Diego and threatens to start a full-blown gang war like they haven't seen since the nineties. The Ortegas recruited the Death Angels, Iglesias signed up *Los Niños Locos*, the Crazy Boys, and now it won't be long before stupid kids and innocent bystanders start getting killed. So he'd just as soon the Mexican cartels kept their shit in Mexico.

The border, he thinks.

What border?

"I guess we're going to have to start looking for the heads," Harrington says.

Johnny says, "My guess is that they're in dry ice and on their way to Luis Ortega in a UPS package."

"What Brown can do for you."

A gory, media-feeding triple is not what I need right now, Johnny thinks. Summer is the busy homicide season in San Diego. The heat shortens emotional fuses and then lights them. What would be arguments in the autumn become fights in the summer. What would have been simple assaults become murders. Johnny has a fatal stabbing over a disputed bottle of beer, a drive-by that happened after an argument at a taco stand, and a domestic killing that occurred in an apartment after the air-conditioning broke down.

Then there's the Blasingame case headed for trial and Mary Lou all over his ass to make sure his 'ducks are in a row.' Whose fucking ducks are ever in a row, anyway? Five eyewitnesses and little Corey clinging to his strong, silent type routine, Mary Lou should just relax. Then again, it's not Mary Lou's nature to relax.

I wouldn't relax either, he admits, with Alan Burke on the other sidc.

He makes himself focus on the case at hand, even though he knows they're never going to make an arrest on it. This was a professional hit, and the pros who did it are already down in Mexico, knocking back a few beers.

But we have to go through the motions, he thinks.

"Hey," Harrington says, "what do you call three Mexican gang bangers with no heads?"

"What?" Johnny asks only because it's required.

He already knows the tired punchline.

A good start.

27

Boone spreads some old newspaper out on the deck and lays the tuna down on it. Taking his fillet knife, kept honed to a fine edge, he slices down the underbelly. He pulls out the guts and throws them over the railing into the ocean. Then he slices up behind the gills on both sides, cuts off the head, and likewise gives it to the sea.

Then he takes the two fillets he sliced and cuts them into thick steaks and washes them under a spigot. He goes into the kitchen, puts two of the steaks into a Ziplock plastic bag and puts them in the freezer.

He takes the other two, sprinkles them with a little salt and pepper, rubs some olive oil on, and carries them outside to the little propane grill that is set beside the cottage. He turns the heat up high to get the fish a little crisp, then turns it down to low, goes back inside and slices up some red onion and a lime, then comes back outside, squeezes some lime juice on the fish, turns it, cooks it for just another minute, then takes it off the grill and goes back inside. He slides each piece of the fish into a flour tortilla, adds a thick slice of red onion on the fish, goes back outside and sits down in a deckchair beside Dave, handing him one of the tacos.

If, as Dave believes, free food tastes better; and if, as is Boone's motto, 'everything tastes better on a tortilla' – then free fish on a tortilla is out of this world. The truth is that if you've never eaten fish that has just been taken out of the ocean, you've never eaten.

Add a couple of ice-cold Dos Equis and two ravenous appetites to the mix and life doesn't get any better. Throw in a soft summer night with a yellow moon and the stars so close you could hit them with a slingshot, and you might be in paradise. Toss a lifelong friendship into that mix, and take the 'might' right out of it.

They both know it.

Sit silently and savor it.

When they finish eating Dave asks, "So how's it with Pete?"

"Yeah, good."

"You close the deal yet?"

Boone doesn't answer and they both laugh. It's an old joke between them. For all the line-up talk about sex, when it comes down to individual women, no one talks. It's just something you don't do.

"When and if you do close the deal," Dave says, "it's over anyway."

"Thanks for the good wishes."

"No," Dave says, "I mean, right now you have that whole opposites-attract, *Moonlighting* sexual tension thing going for you. Once that's released . . . *adios*, my friend."

"I don't know," Boone says.

"Get real," Dave says. "You and The Brit are totally SEI."

"SEI?"

"Socio-Economically Incompatible," Dave explains. "She's downtown, you're Pacific Beach. She likes to dine out in great restaurants, you hit Jeff's Burger or Wahoos. She's all foodie, the next-great-chef, tasting menu, fusion; you're fish tacos, grilled yellowtail and peanut-butter and jelly on a tortilla. She likes getting dressed up and going out, you like dressing down and staying in . . ."

"I get it."

"That's just the Socio, I haven't even hit the Economic," Dave says. "She makes more a day than you do a month."

"There are months when I make zero."

"There aren't months when *she* makes zero," Dave says. "You don't have the jack to take her to the places she likes to go, and you're not going to accept her picking up the check time after time, gender-enlightened as you like to think you are. Right now she thinks it's all liberated and post-fem, but shortly after the first time your board and her wave slap together she's going to start wondering – and all her professional friends are going to tell her to wonder – if you're SEI."

Boone pops open two more beers and hands one to Dave.

"Mahalo," Dave says. Then, "And I guarantee you that one night you're going to be lying there post-coit, she's going to gently bring up the possibility . . . No, I can't."

"Jump."

"She's going to ask if you wouldn't really be happier going to law school."

"Jesus, Dave."

"On that day, my friend," Dave says, "you bail. You don't even stop to get dressed or pick up your clothes – you can always get a new T-shirt. You back-paddle, flailing your arms like a drowning barney. We will all come racing to your rescue."

"Can't happen," Boone says.

"Uh-huh."

Law school? *Law school?* Boone thinks. The first step to becoming a *lawyer*? Show up at an office every day at 9 in a suit and tie? Spend your time shuffling documents and arguing with people. People who *like* to argue?

Hideous.

They sit quietly for a few minutes, drinking in the night and the warm salt air.

Summer was slowly coming to an end, and with it the torpid sea and the days of lassitude. The Santa Ana winds would be blowing in, with bigger surf-and-fire danger, and then the swells of autumn and the colder weather, and the air would be cool and clear again.

Still, there's a certain sadness to the coming end of summer.

The two friends sit and talk bullshit.

Boone doesn't tell Dave that he's working on the Corey Blasingame case.

28

The case that Boone *still* works on is the Rain Sweeny case.

Rain was six years old and Boone was a cop when she disappeared from the front yard of her house.

The chief suspect was a short-eyes named Russ Rasmussen. Boone and his then partner, Steve Harrington, found Rasmussen. Harrington wanted to beat the answers out of the suspect, but Boone hadn't let him do it. Boone left the force shortly after that but Harrington stayed and worked his way up to sergeant in the homicide division.

Rasmussen never told what he did with Rain Sweeny.

He walked and went off the radar.

Rain Sweeny was never found.

Boone became a pariah on the SDPD and pulled the pin shortly after.

That was five years ago, and Boone hasn't stopped trying to find Rain Sweeny, even though he knows that she's almost certainly dead.

Now he sits down at his computer and checks a special e-mail file for any updates on the list of Jane Does that would match Rain's age and description. He pays annually for computer constructions of what Rain would look like at her current age, and now he compares her eleven-year-old 'photo' with pictures from morgues in Oregon and Indiana.

Neither of the poor girls is Rain.

Boone's relieved. Every time a photo pops up, it stops his heart; every time it's not Rain, Boone feels a bittersweet contradiction of emotions. Glad, of course, that the girl has not been confirmed dead; sad that he can't give her parents closure.

Next he goes to another address and checks for messages about Russ Rasmussen.

Through Johnny Banzai and his own connections, Boone has reached out to the Sex Crimes units in most major cities and state police forces. Creeps like Rasmussen don't strike just once, and sooner or later he's going to get picked up strolling a park or a schoolyard.

When he does, Boone is going to be there soon after.

He keeps a .38 in a drawer just for the occasion.

Tonight, like all the other nights, there's nothing.

Rasmussen has disappeared.

With Rain.

Gone.

Nevertheless, Boone writes to three more police forces, e-mailing photos of Rain and Rasmussen, the latter in case the skell has managed to change identities and is in custody under a different name.

Then Boone hits the sack and tries to sleep.

It doesn't always come easy.

29

The next morning's Dawn Patrol is another dull session, surf-wise.

The sea is flat glass – any half-competent surgeon could do delicate brain surgery sitting on a longboard in this ocean. Michelangelo could lie on a board and paint the Sistine . . . ahh, you get the idea.

Johnny tries to bust up the monotony.

"Do ducks," he asks, "really line up in a row?"

"Ducks?" Dave asks. "In a row? Why?"

"Why do I ask, or why do they line up in a row?"

"We haven't established yet that they *do* line up in a row," Tide says, "so Dave is asking why you're asking. Is that what you're asking, Dave?"

"Yeah, I'm asking why JB wants to know whether ducks line up in a—"

Boone dips his head into the water. When he comes back up Johnny is saying, "You know the expression 'ducks in a row?' I'm seeking input whether that reflects a zoological reality, or it's just bullshit."

"It would be an 'ornithological' reality," Boone says, "not a 'zoological' reality."

"Good pick-up, B," Dave says. "We finally know the question that Banzai missed on his SATs."

"Let it go, Dave."

"So?' Johnny asks. "Has anyone actually ever seen ducks in a row?"

"I believe that ducks," Boone says, "are freshwater creatures. Hence, I don't know that I've actually ever seen *ducks*, in a row or otherwise."

"I've seen ducks in a row," Tide offers.

"You have?" Johnny asks.

"At the Del Mar Fair," Tide says. "At one of those booths where you shoot the BB guns. The ducks were all in a row."

"This is just what I mean," Johnny says. "Is that an imitation of actual nature, or the perpetuation of an ornithological myth?"

"An avian stereotype?" Boone asks. "Pelicans are gluttons, seagulls are filthy, ducks are anal retentive . . ."

"Can you be politically incorrect about birds?" Dave asks.

"Only birds of color," Tide says. "Or female birds. White male birds you can trash. This Irish seagull waddles past a bar and—"

Hang Twelve sits up on his board and in a tone of unusual authority pronounces, "When the mother duck has *baby* ducks, the baby ducks swim behind her in a precise row."

"You've personally witnessed this?" Johnny challenges.

"Yes."

"Where?"

"Where what?"

They stare at each other for a second, then Johnny says, "We have to get some waves."

"We really do."

"We're pathetic," High Tide says.

"We are," Boone agrees.

He's not sure whether it's the absence of waves or the absence of Sunny that is the main source of this malaise. Probably both, but Sunny would have put a quick and witty end to this idiot discussion with some deadly accurate barb.

"Maybe we need to recruit another female onto the Dawn Patrol," Boone suggests.

"A replacement Sunny?" Dave asks.

"We already have Not Sunny the Waitress," Tide says. "Do we also want Not Sunny the Surfer?"

"Recruiting a replacement Sunny," says Johnny, clearly non-plussed, "would be making a statement that the real Sunny isn't coming back."

She isn't, Boone thinks. She's moved on. To the professional, sponsored surfer ranks. Good for her, but we have to face the fact that we're mostly going to be seeing Sunny on magazine covers, not out here in the line-up.

Hang Twelve, mouth agape, stares at him.

"What?" Boone asks.

"Shame on you," Hang says.

The session drags on in desultory silence. Even the ocean doesn't make a pretence of showing up, just lies there lifeless and supine.

"It's like a big lake," Tide says.

"Lakes don't have salt," Hang says, still pouting over Boone's suggestion of replacing Sunny. "There's no such thing as a big, salt lake."

The other surfers look at each other for a second, then Johnny says, "No. Don't bother."

They don't. They don't bother to educate Hang about Utah, they don't bother to launch into another topic of conversation, the ocean doesn't bother to come up with waves. Boone is grateful when the Dawn Patrol drags to an end and the guys start to paddle in.

"You coming?" Dave asks him.

"Nah, I'm going to hang."

He looks toward the shore, where the veteran denizens of the Gentlemen's Hour are already gathering, pointing at non-existent waves, sipping coffee and sucking cigarettes, doubtless talking about flat Augusts past.

And Dan Nichols is paddling out.

30

Boone tells him that he didn't find anything suspicious in the phone records or e-mail files.

Dan looks almost disappointed.

"Could she have a phone I don't know about?" he asks.

Boone shrugs. "I dunno. Could she? Wouldn't the billing come to you?"

"Yeah," Dan says. "I'm going out of town tomorrow. That would be a good time to . . ."

He doesn't say to what.

Boone's always thought that if you don't want to say something, it's a pretty good indication that you shouldn't do the something, so he says, "Dan, are you sure, man? Are you sure you shouldn't just, like, talk to her? Upfront, ask her what's up?"

"What if she says nothing is?"

"Good."

"But what if she's lying?"

That's kind of that, Boone thinks. He knows now that he's going to have to follow Donna Nichols and hope like hell the route doesn't lead to some other man's bed. It would be a very skippy result, to come back to Dan and tell him he's a paranoid jerk, go buy some flowers and stop being dumb insecure.

"Okay," Boone says. "I'm on it."

"You're a gentleman and a scholar."

I'm neither, Boone thinks, but whatever. "I'll have to pick up some equipment."

"Whatever you need."

What he's going to need is a little unit that will fit under the bumper of Donna's car.

"What does Donna usually drive?" Boone asks.

"A white Lexus SUV," Dan said. "Birthday present."

Nice, Boone thinks. For his last birthday he got some sex wax from Hang, some two-fer coupons for Jeff's Burger from Tide, and a card from Dave expressing the sentiment 'Go Fuck Yourself.'

"Who's the car registered to?" Boone asks.

"Me," Dan answers. "Well, the corporation."

"Natch."

Tax stuff, Boone thinks. People with corporations don't buy anything personally if they can help it. Anything that even tangentially touches the business is a write-off. But your wife's birthday present?

Dan says, "Donna's an officer."

Doesn't matter, Boone thinks – it would still be perfectly kosher for Dan to put a tracking device on a car his corporation owns, and he wouldn't have to disclose it to Donna, even if she were an officer. Boone describes the little tracker device that's attached to a small but powerful magnet. "You just put it under the rear bumper."

"Without her seeing me," Dan says.

"That would be better, yeah."

And the tracking device would be better than following her because this could be a long job, and it would be too easy to get made.

"I'll pick up the stuff and meet you somewhere to hand it over," Boone says.

"Cool."

No, un-cool, Boone thinks, already feeling like a sleaze.

Very un-cool.

They paddle in.

Boone skips The Sundowner because he's in a hurry.

He now has one clear day to explore the life and times of Corey Blasingame.

31

He drives over to Corey's 'place of work,' as they say in the police reports.

Corey delivered pizzas.

Drove around in one of those little cars with the sign on top, carting twelve-dollar extra-large specials to college kids, slackers, and parents too busy on a given night to get supper together for the kids.

Yeah, okay, but what was rich kid Corey doing delivering pizzas for minimum wage and minimum tips? Tip money is good money if you're waiting tables at *Mille Fleurs* on a Saturday night, but not when you're pushing the pepperoni in dorms. Corey's daddy is slapping up half the luxury homes infesting the coastline, but the kid is driving around wearing a funny hat and taking shit for not getting there in twenty minutes?

Turns out Corey was about to lose even that job.

"Why?" Boone asks the franchise owner, Mr. McKay.

"The job was delivering pizzas," Mr. McKay says. "And he wasn't delivering them."

Worse, he was stealing them. McKay suspected that Corey had his friends call up, order pizzas, and then deny it when Corey went to 'deliver.' Then Corey ate the 'spoilage.' It got to the point where McKay insisted that Corey bring the spurned extra-large-with-everything-except-anchovies back to the store to be officially thrown away.

"Anyway, I think he was stoned," McKay says.

"On what?"

McKay shrugs. "I don't know anything about drugs, but he seemed like he was hopped up on speed or something. Really, I was about to terminate him when . . ."

He lets it trail off.

Nobody liked talking about the Kuhio killing.

Depressing, Boone thinks as he drives over to Corey's old high school. The guy had a gig hauling pizzas and jacks his own product. Like, if you were around pizza all the time, is that really what you'd want for dinner?

Boone checks himself. Are you feeling sorry for this kid now?

Yeah, sort of, especially after he leaves the school.

32

LJPA.

La Jolla Prep.

More properly, La Jolla Preparatory Academy.

Prep for what? Boone thinks as he approaches the security shack that flanks the gated driveway. The students were born on third base, so it must be prep for getting them that last ninety feet. Not that these kids start with a foot on the bag. No, they take a nice long lead, secure in the knowledge that no one is going to even try to pick them off.

The guard isn't too enthused about the Deuce.

It's a funny thing about security guys, Boone thinks as he sees the uniformed man step out of the shack with that 'Turn it around, buddy' look already on his face. They stay in one spot long enough, they get to thinking that they own the place. They actually take a protective pride in guarding a group of people who are very polite, even warm, as they're going in and out, but are never, ever going to ask them inside to the Christmas party. Boone can never understand why people will man the gates that keep them out.

And, since Columbine, getting into a school is hard, especially when the school is one of the most exclusive on the West Coast. Boone rolls down the window.

"Can I help you?" the guard asks, meaning, 'Can I help you *out*?'

Because the guard already knows. He takes one look inside the Deuce at the mess of wet suits, board trunks, fast-food wrappers, Styrofoam coffee cups, towels, blankets, and *knows* that Boone doesn't belong here. Now he has to make sure that Boone knows he doesn't belong here.

While the guard was checking out the van, Boone took a quick glance of the little nameplate pinned on his shirt pocket. "You're Jim Nerburn, right?"

"Yeah."

"Any relation to Ken Nerburn?"

"He's my kid."

"He's a good guy, Ken."

"You know him?"

"We've surfed together a little." Boone sticks his hand out the window. "Boone Daniels."

"Jim Nerburn."

"We met at a Padres game, didn't we?" Boone asks. "You were with Ken and some of his friends?"

"That's right," Nerburn says. "That Cardinal rookie threw a no-hitter."

"I remember that. Dollar hot dog night, too."

Nerburn pats his belly. “Yes, it was. What brings you here today, Boone?”

Boone takes out his PI card and shows it to Nerburn. “I’m on the clock. I need to talk to some folks about Corey Blasingame.”

Nerburn’s face darkens. Funny, Boone thinks, how faces tend to do that when you bring up Corey’s name. “They’d like to forget about Corey around here.”

I’ll bet they would, Boone thinks. LJPA students go on to Stanford, UCLA, Princeton and Duke, or maybe closer to home at UCSD. They don’t go to jail. Boone seriously doubts that Corey is going to make the holiday newsletter this year. *‘LJPA alum Corey Blasingame was admitted to San Quentin State Prison for the coming term, twenty-five-to-life. We wish Corey all the luck in the world as he starts his exciting new career . . .’*

“You knew him?” Boone asks.

“I knew him.”

“Trouble?”

Nerburn looks thoughtful. Then he says, “That’s the thing – no. God knows we got our rich kid chuckle-heads around here, think they can get away with anything, but the Blasingame kid wasn’t one of those. Never came blasting in or out of my gate.”

“What’d he drive?”

“Had a Lexus,” Nerburn says, “but he totaled it. Then his old man got him a pre-owned Honda.”

“Good cars.”

“Run forever.”

“He get hurt in the accident?”

Nerburn shakes his head. “Bumps and bruises.”

“Thank God, huh?”

“Truly,” Nerburn says. Then he asks, “The dad hired you?”

“Indirectly. The lawyer.”

“That’s the way it works?”

“Usually.”

“Maintains the privilege,” Nerburn says.

“I guess.”

Nerburn reaches inside the booth, pulls out a clipboard and scans it. "You have an appointment with anyone?"

"I could lie to you and say I did."

"You're supposed to have an appointment."

"You're right," Boone admits. "But, you know how it is, you let people know you're coming, they start to think about what they're going to say . . ."

"You get canned stuff?"

"Yup."

Nerburn thinks it over for a few seconds, and then says, "I'll give you a pass for an hour, Boone. That's it."

"I don't want to cause you any aggro."

"I can take care of myself."

"I get that."

Nerburn writes on a piece of paper and hands it to Boone. "I'm going to assume you're not carrying."

"I'm not," Boone says. Then he asks, "Hey, Ken didn't go here, did he?"

Nerburn shakes his head. "I could have sent him here – they have a program for long-term employees' kids – but I didn't."

"Can I ask why?"

"I didn't want him thinking he was someone he wasn't."

"Got it."

And so much, Boone thinks as he winds down the window, for my condescending, full-of-shit theory about loyal dogs guarding the gates.

Boone maneuvers the Deuce along the narrow, winding driveway, past pink stucco buildings and broad green soccer, football, baseball and lacrosse fields. Some boys are out playing lacrosse, and Boone is tempted to sit and watch, but he has work to do.

He parks in a slot marked 'Visitor' and finds the admin building.

33

The Head of School is real happy to see him.

The name Corey Blasingame is an automatic smile-killer.

"Come into my office," Dr. Hancock says. She's a tall woman, gray hair cut short. Khaki suit jacket over a matching skirt, white blouse with a rounded collar. Boone follows her into her office and takes the offered chair across from her desk.

Framed diplomas decorate the walls.

Harvard.

Princeton.

Oxford.

"How can I help you, Mr. Daniels?" she asks. Right down to business.

"I'm just trying to get a sense of the kid."

"Why?" Hancock asks. "How is your getting 'a sense of the kid' going to help him?"

Fair enough, Boone thinks. He says, "Because you can't know what you don't know, and you don't know what may or may not be useful until you find it out."

"For instance?"

"For instance," Boone says, "was Corey in a lot of fights in school? That's something the prosecution is going to ask, so we'd like to know it first. Was he popular, unpopular, maybe picked on? Did he have friends . . . a girlfriend, maybe? Or was he a loner? Did he do well in school? How were his grades? Why didn't he go to college, for instance?"

"Ninety-seven per cent of our graduates go on to a four-year institution," Hancock says.

Boone is tempted to say that Corey is also going on to an institution, probably for a lot longer than four years, but he keeps his mouth shut. She senses it anyway.

"You have an attitude, Mr. Daniels."

"No."

"Yes," she insists, "you do. You may or may not be aware of it – I suspect you are – but let me tell you what it is, just in case. You look down on these kids."

"Hard to do from where I stand, Dr. Hancock."

"That's just what I mean," she says. "You're a reverse snob. You believe that kids in a school like this shouldn't have any problems because they have money. And when they do have a problem, you sneer at them as spoiled and weak. How am I doing?"

Pretty damn well, Boone thinks. Why is every woman I sit down with lately using me like a dart board and hitting bull's-eyes?

"You're doing great, Dr. Hancock, but I'm here to talk about Corey Blasingame."

"You can call me Lee." She leans back in her chair and looks out the window at the immaculately groomed sports fields, where girls are out for soccer practice. "The problem with my giving you a sense of Corey is that, sadly, I never had one. I consider him one of my failures, in that I never really got to know him myself."

Getting a grasp of Corey Blasingame was like grabbing Jello, she told Boone. No teenager's personality is solidly formed by that age, but Corey's was unusually amorphous. He deflected attention, was particularly adept at finding cracks and slipping through them. He was neither exceptionally good nor exceptionally bad. He got Cs, not As or Fs, which might have called attention to him. He never ran for student office, joined no clubs, associated with no cliques. But neither was he your classic loner – he always sat with people in the lunch room, for instance, and seemed to join in their conversations.

No, he was not shunned or picked on, certainly not bullied.

Girlfriends? He had dates to dances and such, but there was no particular girl, certainly not one of those conspicuous high-school romances. But he was never a Homecoming King, or on the court, or anything like that.

He did play baseball in his sophomore year.

"And now you are wondering," Lee says, "why I don't know more. Yes, you are, and don't bother to deny it. I know because I've asked myself a few thousand times why I didn't know more, and the hard truth that I've had to tell myself is that I really didn't notice him. He wasn't a kid you *noticed*. He just wasn't, and I have spent many a sleepless night trying to convince myself that I didn't fail him by not noticing, that I didn't fail the man he killed as well. You just never imagine that . . ."

She trailed off and gazed out the window.

"No, you don't," Boone says. He wants to say something to take her off the hook but he can't think of anything that's not just stupid, and he also knows from experience that no one else can take you off the hook you made yourself.

Boone's in the parking lot when a guy trots up behind him.

"You were just in the office asking about Corey Blasingame?" the guy asks. He's pretty young, maybe in his late-twenties, and has that look of a teacher who's still excited about being a teacher.

"My name's Daniels," Boone says. "I'm working for Corey's lawyer. Do you remember him?"

"Ray Pedersen. I was the Jayvee baseball coach."

"I wondered about that one year," Boone says. "Was he any good?"

"No," Pedersen says. "He thought he was a pitcher on his way to the bigs. He had a decent slider, but his fastball never broke out of the seventies. A lot of his pitches went deep the other way."

"Did he get cut or did he quit?"

"He quit," Pedersen says.

"Because . . ."

"Have you met the dad?" Pedersen asks.

Boone shook his head.

"Meet the dad," Pedersen says. "It explains everything."

34

The dad, Boone learned from Pedersen, used to stand behind the backstop and scream at his son.

Not an uncommon type in SoCal schoolboy baseball, which does send some kids to the big leagues, but Corey's dad was a stereotype gone crazy.

"Way over the top," Pedersen says.

Every pitch, Bill Blasingame would yell his critique at the top of his lungs. Even while the kid was in his warm-up, Blasingame would shout instructions. It went beyond encouragement – Bill would berate his son about the inadequacies of the last pitch, question his nerve, his courage, his skill.

And harass the umpire. "It caught the corner! It caught the freaking corner! Come on, ump. Wake up!"

It got to the point where Pedersen talked to him about it, asked him to dial it down a little, sit in the stands where he wasn't such a distraction to the boy. Blasingame didn't take it well, said he was a taxpayer, had a right to stand where he wanted – as a parent, he had a right to talk to his own kid, and nobody was going to tell him different.

Yeah, except Pedersen did.

Pedersen banned him from the ball field.

It happened after one particularly brutal incident.

Pedersen had put Corey on the mound in the top half of the eighth with what looked to be a safe four-run lead. It was garbage time, really, but it was a chance to get Corey some playing time, and Pedersen was out of pitchers anyway.

The kid blew up.

First pitch was a fat fastball that got cracked for a double.

Bill went off. "Have you been watching the game! The kid can't hit a change-up! Why are you throwing him a fastball? Wake up! Wake up!"

Next batter, Corey opened up with two balls, his dad started pawing around behind the backstop like an enraged bull, and Corey followed with a slider that got hit clean into left field, brought in the runner and put the batter on first.

"You're throwing stupid! That was stupid!"

Pedersen got out of the dugout, walked over and said, "Take it easy. It's a game."

"Yeah, that's why you're losers, right there."

"You're not helping. Take it easy."

Corey's next pitch was a hanging curve that ended up over the right-field fence. Now the lead was down to two, with no outs, and Bill Blasingame started playing to the crowd. "Get him out of there! He sucks! He's my kid, for chrissakes and I want him out of there."

Pedersen remembered that people just sat there in embarrassed silence, it was that awful.

It got worse.

Corey hit the next kid with a pitch and put him on base. His next twelve pitches were balls. As his father screamed, ranted, threw his hands in the air, made a show of covering his eyes with his forearm. "Suck it up! Be a man, for chrissakes! Get it together! Man up!"

When the go-ahead run came across the plate, Bill totally lost it. "You dickless wonder! You worthless little piece of crap! I always wanted a daughter and I guess I got one!"

Pedersen trotted over. "That's it. You're gone. I want you out of here."

"You think I wanna be here?" Bill yelled. "Happy to go, my friend. Happy to go!"

But it was too late. Pedersen acknowledged that he should have got him gone weeks earlier. The damage was already done. Corey stood on the mound, fighting back tears. People in the stands looked at their feet. His own team mates couldn't figure out anything to say to him. Pedersen went out to the mound.

"He's something, your dad."

Corey just nodded.

"I don't think you have it today," Pedersen said. "Is your arm hurting?"

"Yeah, it's hurting."

"Let's call it a day."

Pedersen brought the second baseman in to pitch. Corey sat the rest of the game out in the dugout and never came back.

So Boone is prepared to hate Bill Blasingame when he meets him.

Bill doesn't disappoint.

35

First of all, Bill keeps him waiting for thirty-seven minutes.

Boone isn't all that big on watches, but he keeps time as he leafs through magazines in Bill's lobby because it *says* something, doesn't it? Your son is in the hole looking at a possible death penalty, and you're too busy to sit down with someone working for the guy you hired to get him off?

A little disconnect there?

The receptionist is actually embarrassed, keeps looking up from her desk at Boone with this look of, like, what, are we kidding here? But she's not about to say anything to nudge Bill along.

Nicole knows what she's there for. Long, shiny black hair, blouse cut just low enough to show the promise of the big boobs, heavy lip gloss – her presence says that Bill is a player and for the right kind of money you too can enter the fun world of prime real estate/money/sex. So she keeps reading *Vogue* and glancing up every few minutes to see if Boone is going to wait it out.

He is.

For one thing, he's on the meter, and Bill is ultimately picking up the tab. So if the man wants to waste his own money being a dick, it's cool with Boone. Usually there isn't a fine for that.

Second, patience is the single most necessary quality in a surfer and an investigator. Waves are going to come (or not, as the case may be) when they're going to come (ditto), just like developments in a file. The trick is to still be there when they do, and that requires lots of patient hanging in and/or around.

Third, Boone really wants to see if he can figure out Corey Blasingame via his dad.

When Bill finally comes out of his inner sanctum, he looks at Boone and says, "I called Alan's office. You check out."

"Lucky me."

Bill doesn't like that. His chin – which is just starting to turn double – comes up a little and he gives Boone one of those 'Who do you think you are?' looks, which Boone doesn't respond to. So Bill says, "Come on in, Lucky You."

And glares at Nicole as if to say, 'Who are you letting bug me like this?'

Nicole looks at her nails.

Not a bad idea, Boone thinks – they're nice nails.

"Shut the door behind you," Bill says.

Boone kicks it shut with the back of his foot. Bill notices. "You have an attitude, Daniels."

"You're the second person today to tell me that," Boone says, thinking, okay, maybe the third or fourth. The view from Bill's office is terrific, showing La Jolla Cove in all its glory, from the kiddy beach where the seals come to rest, all the way north to the curving stretch of La Jolla Shores, the home of Jeff's Burgers. Boone dismissed the thought of a burger and got down to business. "I'm here to talk about Corey."

"You have news to tell me?" Bill asks. He sits behind his desk and motions Boone to a chair.

"No. I was hoping you had something to tell *me*."

"I already talked to Alan and his girl," Bill says. "I can't think of her name – the attractive Brit . . ."

"Petra Hall."

"That's it," Bill says. "So I don't know what more I can tell you that I didn't already tell them. Or what the hell difference it makes. Corey hit that man, he killed that man. Now we're just shopping for the best deal, isn't that right?"

"The Rockpile Crew—'

"Look," Bill says, "I didn't know that even existed, okay, until I read it in the papers. I don't know, I guess the Bodin kid used to hang around the house a little, and the two brothers . . ."

"Do you know when—"

Bill just kooks out.

"No," he says. "I don't know when, I don't know why, I don't know shit. I'm a bad father, okay? Isn't that what you want to hear me say? Fine, I said it. I'm a bad father. 'I gave the kid everything he needed except what he needed most – love.' Isn't that what I'm supposed to say now? I was too busy with my work, I didn't give him time or attention, I showered him with material things because I felt guilty, right? Okay? Are we done now? You can drop your attitude?"

"You made all his baseball games," Boone says.

"Oh, they told you about that," Bill says. "Maybe I was a little over-intense. But Corey needed pushing, he wasn't exactly a self-starter. The kid lacked motivation, the kid was *lazy* . . . Maybe I took it too far, so it's my fault, okay? I yelled at the kid at a baseball game and that made him go out and kill someone. My bad."

"Okay."

"You have kids, Daniels?"

Boone shakes his head.

"So you don't know."

"Tell me."

Bill tells him.

He was a single dad. Corey's mom was killed in a car accident when the kid wasn't quite two years old. Some drunk careens off the

Ardath exit into her lane and Corey gets to grow up without a mother. It wasn't easy trying to raise a kid and build a business at the same time, and, okay, maybe Bill should have scaled things back, become a 9-to-5 wage slave and been home to bake cookies or whatever, but he just wasn't built that way and he wanted to give Corey every advantage, and that meant making money. A house in La Jolla is expensive, day care is expensive, private schools are expensive. The green fees at Torrey Pines are fairway robbery, but if you want to be making the kind of deals he wanted to be making, you'd better tee off there, and buy a few rounds in the clubhouse to boot.

If you don't have a kid you don't know how it is, but you blink and they're six, blink again and they're ten, then twelve, then fourteen, and then you have this stranger in the house and he's way past wanting to hang out with you anymore, he has friends of his own, and then you don't see him at all, you just see signs of him. Empty Coke cans, a magazine left on the couch, towels on the bathroom floor. You go into the kid's room and it's a disaster area – clothes everywhere, food, shoes – anything and everything but the kid himself. You inhabit the same space, but it's like you're in different dimensions, you don't see each other.

So when Corey decided he wanted to play baseball, Bill thought this was a chance to connect. He was thrilled, because Corey had never shown an interest in wanting to do anything but hang out, watch TV and play video games. The kid had no initiative, no competitive drive, none, so baseball was a good thing, something they might even possibly share. And he got thinking, maybe this is the kid's route, his shot at being good at something, his way of finding his manhood.

Except it wasn't.

The kid just gave up on himself, in every area. Dropped out of baseball, let his grades slip to the point where he couldn't get into a good college. The plan was that Corey would attend a community college for the first two years, do his general ed stuff, get his GPA up, find something he wanted to do . . . but Corey couldn't even cut it at East Loser Juco, or whatever it was. Bill found out that he was cutting classes to go surfing with Bodin and those other kids. Bill had busted his ass to surround Corey with the elite, the *crème de la crème*, but Corey sought out the lowest common denominator, three other spoiled, lazy rich bums who didn't have a clue.

The Rockpile Crew. Hooded sweatshirts and tattoos, talking like rappers . . . like they didn't have the best education that money could buy. It was ridiculous is what it was. Fucking ridiculous. They see this shit on MTV and they think they're what they see.

Bill told him, 'You're not going to go to class, get a job.' Maybe he'd learn what it was like in the minimum-wage world, it might inspire a little ambition. What kind of job did the kid get? Pizza delivery boy, so he could spend his days at the beach or in that dumbass gym, pumping iron and working on his six-pack.

Yeah, okay, maybe it wasn't such a dip into the real world – the kid was taking in eight bucks per plus tips, but going home to a three-mill house with a stocked fridge and a cleaning lady. Maybe Bill should have thrown Corey out, tough love and all that crap, and he thought about it, but, like he said, you blink and . . .

Your kid gets in a scrap. A stupid, drunken case of testosterone gone crazy. He throws a punch that kills someone and wrecks his own life. Because, let's be honest here, Corey's life is over. What do you think prison – even a few years of it, if Alan pulls the rabbit out of the hat –is going to do to Corey? You think he can hack that? The kid isn't tough, he isn't hard, he's just going to become . . .

Bill stops there and stares out the window. A lot of window gazing, Boone thinks, when you're talking about Corey. Then Bill chuckles bitterly and says, "That punch? First time in his life that Corey ever followed through on anything."

His phone buzzes and Bill hits a button. Over the speaker, Boone hears Nicole say, *"You wanted me to remind you that you have a meeting with Phil at the site?"*

"Got it," Bill says. "I have to go."

"What gym?" Boone asks.

"Huh?"

"You mentioned a gym," Boone says. "What gym?"

36

Team Domination.

What the gym is called.

Set next to a Korean hair-and-nails salon in a strip mall in the PB flats, Team Domination is your basic dojo, one of probably hundreds in southern California. It had started life as a karate studio, morphed into a franchise American *kenpo* school, then, when the mixed martial arts craze hit, shifted its emphasis to MMA.

Boone is sort of aware of MMA, having seen some of it on TV. He has his own informal, casual relationship with the martial arts from hanging with Dave – who is really into it – and going to some classes with him. He'd had to do self-defense and hand-to-hand at the Police Academy, of course, and with Dave he'd gotten the basics of *kenpo* and a little judo, a couple of the funner kung fu kicks, and a little *krav maga* when Dave was into that. But Boone was never really into the whole dojo scene, with the white or black *gis*, the incessant bowing, and the 'Master' this and 'Master' that routine. Besides, any time put into kicking bags or sparring is time that he isn't in the water, and priorities are priorities.

But Boone has a good sense of the San Diego martial arts scene because of its close relationship with surf society. A lot of the martial arts instructors are also surfers, a lot of surfers are martial artists. Guys go back and forth from the beach to the dojo, which makes the localism of certain breaks all the more edgy.

See, most surfers are hyperkinetic, adult ADD types who need constant movement – and all the better if the action has a little edge to it, like someone trying to put a fist through your nose or a foot upside your head. And as both sports rely mostly on balance, timing and instant risk assessment, there is some crossover effect.

All the more so because both began their American lives as Pacific phenomena. Surfing, of course, started in Hawaii, but so did the American martial arts scene, when Chinese and Japanese workers on the sugar and pineapple plantations brought their traditions with them and opened schools. They were pretty much an Asian-Hawaiian thing until the Vietnam War, when guys from the '48' had layovers in the islands, picked the sport up, and brought it home, a lot like their dads had with surfing during WWII.

Once that happened, a lot of Asians in California who had been teaching the arts secretly in the Chinatowns and Little Japans, pretty much thought, 'What the hell? The cat's out of the bag,' and opened schools of their own. Guys who might have taken up boxing started putting on *gis* and sandals, smattering their conversations with bits of Chinese, Japanese and Okinawan. Tournaments started everywhere.

That touched off the Great Debate.

What would happen if . . .

A boxer fought a *karatega*?

Yeah, but under what rules? Could the karate guy use his feet or only his hands? The Asian martial arts guys were pretty arrogant about the hypothetical match, sure that their guy, with his lightning, long range kicks and devastating punching power, would easily knock out the one-dimensional, plodding boxer.

Didn't happen.

First time someone got one of these apples-and-oranges matches into a ring, the karate guy got off his kick, the boxer took it on his shoulder, waded in and knocked the surprised *karatega* right out.

It sent the martial arts community reeling. All those guys who went to the dojo to learn the ultimate in self-defense were suddenly left wondering – is it really? Did you really need to spend all that time bowing and meditating and breathing and learning all those imported esoteric techniques, all the while feeling like a doofus in your robe and colored belt, or would you be better off hitting one of the old boxing gyms and learning how to throw a good old, round-eyed, American right cross that had been more than enough for John Wayne.

The dojos fell on hard times as the common wisdom dictated that the 'arts' were great for kids to learn discipline and women to tighten their glutes, but if you were planning on being in a street fight or the classic dark, empty parking lot confrontation, they were basically useless, the triumph of style over substance. The thinking was that if you got off a good kick and really landed it, fine, but once your attacker closed in and grabbed you, the Asian martials arts had nothing to help you.

You dropped by most dojos in the nineties, what you saw was boatloads of kids hopping up and throwing kicks, and chanting in unison, and the instructors became basically babysitters. The dojo as after-school day care center for the two-career family came into being. It was soccer all over again – good for kids, useless for adults.

A real fight was going to be won by the biggest guy.

It was the Rise Of Bubba, and the professional martial arts scene became dominated by the atavistic advent of 'cage fighting,' basically two jumbo-size crackers in a cage, beating the hell out of each other until one of them dropped. It was bloody, brutal, wildly popular enough to get banned in several states. Real martial artists watched appalled as fighting's center of gravity shifted from the West Coast to the Deep South, and guys with names like 'Butterball' became renowned champions and folk heroes.

But the 'art' had been taken out of the martial arts.

Salvation came from Asia, but through an unlikely conduit.

Brazil.

Enter the Gracies.

Here's what happened: The Japanese master who pretty much invented judo got fed up with his countrymen thinking of it as a game instead of real fighting. A prophet is not without honor save in his own land and all that, but anyway, he sent a group of disciples out to spread the word throughout the world. One of them, a cat named

Maeda, ended up in Brazil where he hooked up with two teenage brothers, Carlos and Helios Gracie.

The Gracie brothers took the judo and morphed it into something that came to be known as Brazilian *jiujitsu.* What Brazilian *jiujitsu* basically did was to take the fight to the ground. The Gracies would get their opponents on the mat and roll around until they got them into complicated, intricate arm-locks, joint-locks and chokes, and it was all about technique.

The 'art' was back in martial arts.

In the nineties, Helios' son, Royce, accepted an invitation from his older brother to move to California to help him teach the art. In an old California tradition (see Alter, Hobie) they started in their garage.

But it wasn't until the family issued the 'Gracie Challenge' that the form really took off. The Gracies offered $100K to anyone who could knock out the relatively slight, 175-pound Royce. Nobody could. He beat everybody, taking them to the ground and making them give up before he snapped their arms or ankles or choked them into unconsciousness.

Thus was born the UFC, the Ultimate Fighting Championship.

It was a revival of the old debate – which form of the martial arts was superior? The Gracies organized a single-elimination tournament and invited boxers, kickboxers, *muy thai* fighters, wrestlers, even the Neanderthal cage fighters.

Royce beat them all.

On television.

Everybody saw that you *could* do something when a three-bill gorilla got hold of you – Gracie *jiujitsu.* A lot of the fighters started to learn the system and incorporate it into their repertoire.

The UFC thrived as a television, DVD and internet empire. It got away from the cage-fighting image, established weight classes and rules, attracted serious martial artists.

But now there was a new question – could anything beat Gracie *jiujitsu*? Yeah, maybe, if you could keep the fight 'on its feet,' that is, knock out your *jiujitsu* opponent before he could take you to the ground.

The answer came with the generic term MMA – mixed martial arts.

"It makes sense," Dave the Love God said to Boone one night as they were watching a match on television. "Really, it's what the old Asian masters always said: 'You do whatever works at the moment.'"

So the dojos started teaching a little of everything. The new kids coming up wanted to get into the UFC – they wanted to study *jiujitsu*, boxing, wrestling, kickboxing, *muy thai*, in a combination that made sense. More and more studios that once offered only one discipline were changing over to MMA to survive.

Team Domination, for instance.

It seemed as if all the new dojos called themselves Team this or Team that, on the theory that it took a team of instructors, each with his own specialty, to train a mixed martial artist. Also, all the students trained with each other – a team of sorts for an individual sport, a 'band of brothers' out to conquer the other teams.

So Boone walks into Team Domination.

37

A real dojo smells.

Badly.

Mostly of sweat. Rank, stale sweat.

Team Domination reeks.

A circular ring dominates the center of the studio. As Boone walks in, two guys are rolling around on the mat in the ring, practicing their *jiujitsu*. Heavy bags hang from the ceiling, and three other guys are banging away at them, alternating punches with low kicks and knee strikes. Another two guys straddle heavy bags on the floor and slam elbows into their downed 'opponents.' In one corner, a student hefts kettle weights while another skips rope.

There are none of the trappings that Boone would recognize from the old-school Asian-type studio – no *gis*, no belts, Chinese paintings of tigers or dragons, no single white chrysanthemum in a vase. Instead, posters of UFC stars are pasted to the walls, and slogans like 'No Gain Without (Other People's) Pain.'

The students don't wear *gis* but are decked out in a variety of Gen X gear, mostly cammie trunks and T-shirts. Some sport black 'Team Dom' ball caps. A few are in plastic 'sweat' suits, trying to cut weight. Most of the guys have tattoos, lots of them, all over their arms, down their backs, on their legs. The guy supervising the *jiujitsu* practice looks up, sees Boone and walks over.

"Hey! What brings you here?"

It's Mike Boyd.

38

Which makes two points of contact.

Rockpile and the dojo.

And two points of contact always make a cop or investigator kind of edgy. Two points of contact is another way of saying 'coincidence,' which is another way of saying 'Easter Bunny.' You get the chocolate and the jelly beans and stuff, but much as you'd like to, you don't really believe that a rabbit brought them.

"Corey Blasingame," Boone answers. "Again. Funny you didn't mention this yesterday, Mike."

Funny and not so funny, Boone thinks. Pretty understandable: If you ran the place where the kid maybe learned how to throw a lethal punch, you might not like to talk about it either.

"You didn't ask," Boyd says.

"I'm asking now."

Boone says it with a smile and Mike smiles back, but the look in the man's eyes says he doesn't like it. Doesn't like Boone showing up here, doesn't like questions about Corey. Boone asks, "Aren't I welcome here, Mike?"

"You're welcome," Boyd says. "But it's not the water, you know?"

Boone gets it. This is Boyd telling him, *You may be the A Male out in the surf, but this is* my *world.*

"Corey was one of your students," Boone says.

"Not really," Boyd answers. "He hung out a little. Corey was . . . how should I say this . . . more about the 'about' than the 'the,' if that makes any sense?"

"Yeah, it does." You get it in surfing all the time – the dismos who like to put on the wet suit, carry the board around, paddle out, but don't like to take the wave when it comes. It's a good expression 'about the about,' Boone thinks.

"Corey didn't like to get hit," Boyd says. "And that's what you do in MMA. You get hit, you get cut, you get your nose busted. You gotta be kind of a freak to enjoy that kind of fun, and Corey wasn't that kind of a freak."

"I'm just trying to get a sense," Boone says, "of what this is all about."

" 'This?' "

"MMA."

Boyd goes into a speech that sounds practiced and a little defensive. MMA is a highly technical combat art that requires high levels of training, conditioning and practice. Although it can certainly look bloody, it has a fine safety record – unlike high-school football or professional boxing, there has never been a fatality in a sanctioned UFC bout.

"You wanna work out," Boyd says, "I'll show you a little. I know you can handle yourself."

"I don't know about that."

Boyd says, "You're the sheriff over at The Sundowner, right? I heard you can take care of business. You and your crew."

"I don't have a crew."

Boyd smirks at this. "There's that lifeguard, the big Sammy, the Jap cop."

The 'lifeguard' is okay, Boone thinks, but 'Sammy' and 'Jap?' He says, "I have a Samoan friend, who is, yes, big, and a Japanese friend."

"I didn't mean any offense," Boyd says, still smiling.

"See, it sounded like you did." Boone isn't smiling.

Some of the activity in the room stops as the students sense an impending conflict. They have a nose for this kind of thing, an unerring radar that tells them of imminent violence. They're into it, wanting to see what their teacher will do to this guy.

"Where are we going with this?" Boyd asks, feeling their eyes on him. He knows he can't even look like he's backing down. If he shies from a fight, or loses, half his devoted team will find a new school. The other half will stay and eat him alive – they're pack dogs.

Boone has no such worries. "We don't have to go anywhere with it."

He hears a guy in the back of the room mutter, "Pussy." A few of the others are smiling and shaking their heads. Boyd feels the momentum, and doesn't want to let it go. He says, "You came into *my* place, my friend."

"I'm not your friend."

"Tell you what," Boyd says. "Strap up, get into the ring with me, and I'll show you what MMA is all about."

Maybe because it's been a sad day, or because he's pissed off about a lot of things he can't do anything about, maybe even because he let that kid at Rockpile mouth off to him, Boone decides it might be a good time to throw a little.

39

Five minutes later, he's stripped down to just his jeans, is wrapping the MMA gloves around his hands, and one of the students is handing him a mouthpiece.

"This *is* new, right?" Boone asks.

"I think so."

"You *think* so?"

"I just took it out of the wrapper."

"Better."

The guy looks at him funny, and then says, "I'm Dan. I'm your corner."

"This is a circle."

"Huh?"

"There are no . . . Never mind," Boone says. "What does a corner do?"

"Coach," Dan says. "Yell out advice and encouragement. Help carry you out of the ring if you, like, can't walk."

"Great."

Dan explains the rules. They're going to fight one five-minute round. You can kick, punch, wrestle, grapple, but no kicking in the balls, eye-gouging, biting, or kicking or kneeing the opponent in the head when he's down.

"If he gets you in a joint lock or a chokehold," Dan says, "and you feel something about to pop or break, tap him three times and he'll stop."

"Okie-dokie."

"We have a saying."

"What's that?"

" 'Better to tap a second too soon,' " Dan recites, " 'than a second too late.' "

"Good saying."

If a guy were to have a crew, Boone thinks, this would be a most excellent time to have one. It would be really nice to see Dave, Tide or Johnny walk through that door. If I feel something about to pop or break . . .

"You ready?" Boyd shouts.

Boone already has his mouthpiece in, so he just gives a thumbs up and shuffles into the center of the ring, trying to remember some of the Wit and Wisdom of Dave the Love God, the chapter on fighting. If it's a big guy, Dave said, try to take his legs away from him early. Those pegs are holding up a lot of weight and wear out easily, especially with a little assistance from you.

So Boone comes in and shoots a quick, slapping low roundhouse kick that hits Boyd in the low left calf. It makes Boyd wince a little, so Boone does it again right away and then moves off to the side.

Boyd comes forward, shooting two left jabs that Boone sidesteps. The teacher looks a little surprised – Daniels has a few more skills than he thought. But he keeps coming forward – two more jabs followed by a right hook, then a straightforward kick to set up a spinning backfist that whizzes just past Boone's nose as he jumps back and gets a collective 'Whoo!' from the crowd.

No shit, whoo! Boone thinks. If that had connected I'd be on queer street until next week. He tries another low kick to the calf but Boyd is ready and moves his leg out of the way, throwing Boone off balance. Boone tries to recover with a straight right punch, but Boyd ducks under it, grabs him around the ribs, lifts him over his head, and walks him toward the edge of the ring.

Boone feels it coming, but even if he didn't, there's plenty of time to hear the onlookers groan in happy anticipation, and one of them narrates, "Slam!" Boone's being carried along like he's backwards on a wave and he looks down to see Dan looking up at him, wincing.

"Any advice?!" Boone asks.

"You're kind of fucked!"

"Encouragement?!"

"Uhhhh, hang in there!"

Yeah. Then Boone feels himself going over backwards, there's a second of that awful falling feeling, and he tries to remember what Dave told him. *Look at your belt, so you don't hit the back of your head.*

Boone looks at his belt.

A second later he slams onto the canvas a half second before Boyd drops all his weight on him. The air goes out of Boone's lungs, he feels like his back might be broken, and the world is doing this funny spinning thing.

Yeah, but he's been here before, at the bottom of a big wave that weighs a hell of a lot more and is even meaner than Mike Boyd, so he knows he can survive it. He hears a couple of the onlookers yell excitedly that Boyd is 'achieving full mount,' and is a little concerned what that might be, recalling the time that he and Dave attended Dave's little brother's high-school wrestling match and agreed that any sport that gave points for 'riding time' and didn't involve either a horse or a bull was at least a little homoerotic. And now Boyd is sitting upright on his chest, like the classic schoolyard bully – 'full mount' – and starts to rain elbow strikes down on Boone's face.

"Ground and pound!" Boone hears someone say, and that about sums it up as he tries to move his head to avoid the 'pound' component. It sort of works – Boyd's elbows glance off Boone's face instead of splitting it open and breaking his cheekbones. Boone gets his forearms up around his head and Boyd switches to roundhouse punches, trying to find an open spot to hit.

Boone waits until Boyd leans in to give his punch more leverage, then bucks up and throws Boyd forward, over his own head. Now Boone's face is jammed into Boyd's crotch, which isn't pleasant, but at least puts it out of punching range. He slithers out from under, rolls, gets to his feet and turns, just in time to see Boyd getting up. Timing his punch, Boone rolls his right shoulder and lets it go just as

Boyd turns. The punch connects hard on the jaw. Boyd sprawls backwards, bounces off the ring and slumps down on his ass, half out of it.

"Jump on him!" Dan screams from the 'corner.'

Boone doesn't. He just stands there sort of confused. Any other martial art he ever dicked around with – hell, in life itself – you don't hit a man when he's down. You just don't, and now he gets the diff between MMA and all the rest – in MMA, the whole point is to hit the dude when he's down.

Boyd gets up, shakes his head to clear it, and comes toward Boone.

"Three minutes!" Dan yells.

Three minutes?! Boone thinks. Three minutes left? He would have thought it was maybe twenty seconds. Anyone who doesn't believe Einstein's take on relativity has never gone a round in the ring. Time doesn't slow down or even stop, it slams it into reverse and goes backwards.

Now Boone totally gets it – he should have jumped on Boyd and pounded him into total unconsciousness. Boyd is coming toward him, the lights are back on in his eyes, and now – as the joke goes about Jesus' return – he's pissed.

But definitely more cautious, almost respectful. He's seen Boone survive the slam, the ground and pound, escape and rock him with a single punch. The surfer has heavy hands – one-punch hands – and he doesn't look tired or even winded.

He isn't – you want a cardio workout, paddle a surfboard. Boone launches two more low kicks, aiming one at the inside of Boyd's thigh to smack the femoral artery. Boyd winces at each one, but keeps coming forward. Boone moves backward, circling so as not to get trapped against the ropes. Shooting jabs to keep Boyd at a distance, he keeps moving, trying to gain space, trying to waste time.

"He's a pussy!" someone yells. "He don't want any part of you, Mike!"

True on both counts, Boone thinks. He goes in for another kick, but Boyd is ready and grabs Boone's leg, lifts it and throws him to the mat. Boone covers up to ward off the ground and pound, but it doesn't come. Boyd drops on to him, but rolls over so that Boone's on top, his back against Boyd's chest.

Boone feels Boyd's thick right forearm slide under his chin and tighten on his throat, then Boyd's left hand press against the back of his head. Boyd arches his back, stretching Boone out and tightening the grip like a noose.

"Tap out! Tap out!" Dan yells.

Boone twists to loosen the grip but it's in too tight. Boyd's forearm is locked onto his throat. Boone can see the thick muscles knotted, and, just above the wrist, a small tattoo.

The number '5.'

Boyd hisses, "Tap, Daniels."

Fuck that, Boone thinks.

Then he's out.

40

He's on the mat when he comes to.

Dan looks down at him with concern.

"What happened?" Boone asks.

"Rear-naked choke," Dan says.

Sounds ugly, Boone thinks, especially the 'rear' and 'naked' parts.

"Why didn't you tap out?" asks Dan.

After a little bit of thought, Boone remembers what 'tap out' means and what happened to put him in the position to do it. Or not, as the case may be. Dan and another student help him to his feet. His legs feel shaky. He looks across the ring and sees Boyd looking at him. Boone takes some small satisfaction that Boyd has an ice pack pressed against his jaw.

"Why didn't you tap?" Boyd asks.

It seems to be the question of the day.

"Didn't feel like it."

Boyd laughs. "You're no bitch, Daniels. Only a real freak would rather *black* out than *tap* out."

'Real freak' apparently being high praise.

"Thanks."

Boone walks toward the door on legs that are still objecting to being given so much responsibility. Then he stops, turns around and says, "There is something you can teach me."

"Shoot."

The Superman Punch.

41

You have to have your legs under you to do it, which Boone doesn't, but Boyd demonstrates on a heavy hanging bag.

It's basically simple, but it's harder to do than it looks. You jump off one foot, toward your opponent, then while in mid-air, execute a downward chopping punch with the opposite hand. The impact is incredible because of the momentum of the whole body being thrown into the punch.

Boyd does it and the heavy bag hops on its chain, comes back down, and shakes.

"It's not a move you want to try a lot," Boyd explains after he does it, "because both feet are off the ground and that leaves you vulnerable to any kind of counter. If you miss with it, you're truly fucked. But if you connect . . ."

"So you teach this," Boone says.

"Sure."

"Did you teach it to Corey Blasingame?"

"Maybe," Boyd says. "I don't know."

Yeah, maybe, Boone thinks. He takes two steps toward the bag then launches himself. Twisting his hip in mid-air, he throws everything into the punch and can feel the energy surge all the way up his arm as his fist makes contact.

A wild adrenaline surge.

Superman.

The heavy bag sags in the middle and pops back.

Mike Boyd seems impressed. "You can come train here any time," he says, then adds, "We need men like you."

Boone walks out of the dojo. After a day of dipping his spade in the sad, barren soil of Corey Blasingame's life, his question isn't how the kid could have beaten someone to death, but how it didn't happen sooner.

He gets into the Deuce and heads for the Spy Store.

42

The small shop is a creepy little place in a strip mall in Mira Mesa, its customer base being a few actual PIs, a lot of wannabes, hard-core paranoids, and not a few of the grassy-knoll, wrap-your-head-in-tin-foil-the-government-is-attacking-you-with-gamma-rays set who won't buy off the internet because the CIA, FBI, Homeland Security and Barbara Bush are all tracking their downloads. The store is usually filled with a lot of browsers who just like electronic gadgets and cool spy shit.

And there's a lot of cool spy shit in there – bugs, listening devices, cameras that look like anything other than cameras, computer cookie devices, computer anti-cookie devices, computer anti-anti-cookie devices . . .

Boone finds his first item: a LiveWire Fast Track Ultra-Thin Real

Time GPS tracking device. It's a black box about 2½″ square, with a magnet attachment. He picks up a ten-day battery to go with it, then looks for the next item on his mental list.

The Super Ear BEE 100 Parabolic is a nasty and effective piece of intrusive work, a cone-shape listening device capable of picking up a conversation from a good city block away. Boone picks out a compatible digital recorder with the appropriate cord and plug-in, and decides that he has what he needs for the job. He already has the camera – it came with the basic Private Investigator Starter Kit along with the cynicism, a manual of one-liners, and a saxophone soundtrack.

He walks up to the counter and says to the clerk, "You talk to me in Vulcan, I'm puking on your floor."

"Hey, Boone."

"Hey, Nick," Boone says. When Nick isn't working, he's playing Dungeons and Dragons. It's just the way it is. Boone hands Nick two credit cards, one his business, the other personal, and asks Nick to run the tracker and the listening device separately. He'll toss a little time onto his hourly billing to cover the cost of the 'Super Bee' and hopefully Dan will never have to find out about it.

It's a little sleazy, but it's really for Dan's protection. He hasn't asked Boone for audio evidence of his wife's alleged infidelity, but Boone's going to get it anyway, even though it creeps him out.

What usually happens is that the wronged party confronts the cheater ('I had you followed by a private investigator') and the guilty spouse just gives it up. But every once in a while the philandering partner goes the 'That's my story and I'm sticking to it' route, just stonewalls and denies it all, which puts both the PI and his client into a bad situation.

(Get a group of PIs in a bar after a few stiff pops and they'll tell you some beauties, the responses ranging from the simple *'Nu-unnnh'* – that is, it just didn't happen – all the way to Boone's personal favorite, 'She's an event planner and we were working on your birthday party. Surprise, honey!')

Most people don't want to believe that their loved one is cheating on them, some of them so desperately that they'll jump at any out. Even showing them photos or video of their beloved going in and out of a house or hotel room won't do it, because they'll cling to the flimsiest excuses. One that seems to be really popular lately is, 'We're just emotional friends.'

Emotional friends. You gotta love the phrase. The rationale is that the cheatee hasn't met the cheater's emotional needs, so he/she had to go 'outside the relationship' to feel 'emotionally validated.' So the cheatee is asked to believe that their loved one and the other man/woman spent the hour in the motel or the night in the house just talking about their feelings, and the desperate cheatee goes for it.

Unless you have a tape of the spouse working out more physical feelings. The grunts, the moans, the heavy breathing ('What, honey, you were planning my party at the *gym*?'), the sweet whispered nothings, are the collective, cliché smoking gun, but no decent PI wants to lay that on an already hurting spouse unless he has to.

So what you do is record the main event and stick it away somewhere unless or until you absolutely have to pull it out. You don't tell the client that you have it, because most of them can't resist the temptation to listen to it, even though you advise them against it.

But you have it if you need it. It's for your client's protection and your own.

So Boone puts the eavesdropping technology on his own card so Dan doesn't see the expense, ask about it, and end up with the sounds of his wife's illicit lovemaking on his mental play-list.

Nick runs the item across the scanner and says. "You got the software for this?"

"Hang hooked me up."

"Cool," Nick says. "This new version of this tracker? You can set it for one-, five- or ten-second blings, it has a motion alarm and a detachable motion alert. And it keeps a record of everyplace the vehicle goes. One-eighty-one and sixty-three cents, please."

Boone pays cash, takes the receipt, and gets out of there before he has to listen to a conversation about how the Venusians are systematically injecting truth serum into your Quaker instant oatmeal packages.

He's back in the parking lot when two guys come up to him and one of them sticks a gun in his ribs.

43

"Hello, Rabbit," Boone says.

"Howzit, Boone?" Rabbit says. "Red Eddie, he wants to see you."

"Wants to see you," Echo says.

The origin of Echo's name is pretty obvious. So is Rabbit's, actually, but no one likes to talk about it. Rabbit and Echo are sort of the Mutt and Jeff, the Abbott and Costello, the Cheney and Bush, of Red Eddie's squadron of thugs. Rabbit is tall and thin, Echo is short and thick. Both the Hawaiian gangsters wear flower-print shirts over baggy shorts and sandals. The shirts run about three bills each and come from a store in Lahaina. Red Eddie pays his muscle well.

"I don't want to see him," Boone says.

He knows it's useless to refuse, but he just feels he has to give them a little aggro anyway. Besides, his ribs already hurt from when Mike Boyd tried to enfossilize them into the canvas.

"We have our instructions," Rabbit says.

"Our instructions."

"That's *really* annoying, Echo."

"Get in the ride," Rabbit says.

"In the—"

"Shut up." But Boone goes with them and gets into the black Escalade. Rabbit gets behind the wheel and turns the ignition. Fijian surf reggae music comes blasting out of the speakers.

"You think you have enough bass?!" Boone yells.

"Not enough?!" Rabbit yells back. "I didn't think so!"

"Didn't think so!"

The Escalade goes throbbing down the street.

All the way to La Jolla.

44

Red Eddie stands on his skateboard, perched at the lip of the twenty-foot-high half-pipe he had built in his backyard.

One of the many reasons his stuffy La Jolla neighbors love having Eddie in the hood.

Red Eddie is shirtless over black *hui* board trunks, the black being a symbol of extreme localism back in the islands. If you're a *haole*, and you pull up to a break full of guys with black trunks on, pull out. What Eddie isn't wearing is a helmet, or elbow or knee pads, because he thinks they make him look stupid.

Now he points to the bracelet attached to his right ankle.

"You see this?" he says as Rabbit and Echo usher Boone into the backyard. "This is *your* bad."

Boone isn't exactly eaten up with guilt. For one thing, if you had to be under house arrest, Red Eddie's is a pretty nice crib to do it in. His little nest is 7,000 square feet overlooking Bird Rock Beach, with a horizon pool, Jacuzzi, skateboard half-pipe, four bedrooms, a living room with a 260-degree view of the Pacific, a state-of-the-art kitchen where Eddie's personal chef does new and progressive things with Spam, and the home-theater with its enormous flat-screen-plasma, Bose sound system, and every piece of video-game techno known to post-modern man.

Second, Eddie should be in an 8x7 hole in a FedMax facility on some cold rainy stretch of northern coast instead of his sunny mansion in La Jolla, because the Harvard-educated, Hawaiian-Japanese-Chinese-Portuguese-Anglo-Californian *pakololo* magnate was importing underage Mexican girls along with his usual marijuana shipments, and Boone is more than happy to accept responsibility for busting him.

Therefore, third, Red Eddie is damn lucky to be under house arrest as his lawyers drag out the criminal proceedings against him while persuading the judge that Red Eddie, who owns houses in Kauai, Honolulu, the Big Island, Puerto Vallarta, Costa Rica and Lucerne, is no flight risk because of his ties to the community. 'Ties to the community' no shit, Boone thinks – Eddie's ties to the community are stored in numbered accounts all over Switzerland and the Cooke Islands.

"Do you know, Boonedoggle," Eddie says, "that I can't go more than seventy-five feet from my house except to go to the doctor? And did you further know, Bonnie-boone, that I have developed a chronic condition that requires frequent medical attention?"

"You're a perpetual dickwad?" Boone asks.

Which indicates massive testosterone levels on his part.

Red Eddie just smiles at the insult, but his Doberman, Dahmer, likewise perched on the edge of the half-pipe, looks down at Boone and growls.

"You're starting to look alike," Boone says. "He has a collar, too."

They do kind of look alike – short hair, thin wiry bodies, long sharp noses. Except that Eddie's hair is orange while Dahmer's is jet black, and Eddie's body is festooned with tattoos whereas Dahmer has retained the natural look. The other big difference is internal – as a dog, albeit a vicious dog, Dahmer possesses a genetically encoded set of moral restraints.

Eddie launches himself off the platform, flies down the pipe, gets air, does a 180, lands on the opposite platform and asks, "You know what your problem is, Ba-Boone?"

"Why do I have a feeling that you're going to tell me?"

"You're *lolo*," Eddie says. "Stupid. You're a bus laugh, you really crack me up. Number the first – you had a chance to end my game and you passed on it. Stupid. Number the second – you thought I was guilty of child prostitution when I didn't know those sick taco fucks were sticking little girls in between my bales of healthful herbal products. Stupider, and, may I add, personally hurtful. Number the third – you actually had the temerity to try to put me into prison for this misapprehension. Stupidest. And just when I think you have achieved the summit of stupidity-ness, you surpass yourself."

He has a point, Boone thinks. I probably should have let him drown when I had the chance, and I *was* dumb enough to think that the justice system was going to exact justice. And even though Dave could and would testify that Red Eddie had hired him to bring shipments of weed in from the ocean, there was no physical evidence. And no evidence directly tying Eddie to the children, either. The sad fact is that Eddie will probably soon take off his ankle bracelet and walk. So how could I top that?

Eddie tells him.

"Boone, Boone, Boone," he says, "I keep an eye on my friends and a bigger eye on my enemies, and seeing as how you are simultaneously both, why'd you think you could intrude your stupidiosity into my business and it wouldn't reach my ear?"

The light comes on.

Boone says. "Corey Blasingame."

"Killed one of the *ohana*," Eddie says. "*Lolo* as you are, do you think for one moment I would let that slide? No can be."

"I didn't think about it at all."

"Exactly."

Check. A *haole* killed a native Hawaiian – not only a native Hawaiian, but a genuine *kamaaina*, a man of standing, a hero. Of course Eddie would consider himself honor-bound to avenge that, even if no one asked him to, or even wanted him to. It would have nothing to do with a simplistic sense of justice, or even his feeling for Kelly, it would be about Eddie's prestige.

Like any socio, Eddie is all about Eddie.

"Hey, Eddie," Boone says, "let's do a quick tally – how many Hawaiians Corey has killed versus how many Hawaiians you've killed."

Eddie looks at his boys and says, "Hurt him a little."

Before Boone can move, Rabbit slides in and jams a heavy fist into Boone's kidney. It hurts, a lot more than a little, and Boone finds himself on his knees.

Which was more or less the idea.

Eddie looks down with some satisfaction, launches himself, does another aerial maneuver and lands again.

"Don't you talk to me that way," he says. "Especially when I'm making you a favor. I'm only trying to save you a little sweat, *bruddah*, keep you from spinning in little Boondoggedness circles for absolutely nuttin'."

Eddie thinks he owes Boone because Boone pulled Eddie's little son out of the ocean once. Now he leans over and sticks his pointed nose right at Boone. "Whatevuhs you do or don't, whatevuhs Alan Burke do or don't, no boddah, garans – little Corey B be dead. Anyone gets in my line, including you, Boone, there'll be *koko*. Blood. Mo bettuh you paddle off, *bruddah*."

"You're right, Eddie," Boone answers. "I should have let you drown."

You at least deal dope and you probably dealt children, you take what you want by force, and your wealth is built on other people's pain.

"I talk to the shark," Eddie says, "and only the shark can tell me when it's my time. And he hasn't told me."

"I'll have a word with him."

Eddie laughs. "You do that, Boone-brah. Now get up and get out. My physical therapist is coming over. Five-five, an insta-woodie rack, and a Dyson mouth. Speaking of which, it must be a dry spell for you now that Sunny has flown, or are you tapping that little Brittita?"

He sees the dark look come across Boone's face. "Boddah you? You give me stink eye, you got bus nose like I smell, *da kine*? You wanna go, *bruddah*, let's go. Local-style, skin on skin."

"If you didn't have the dog and your boys—"

"But I do. Sucks for you."

He slides down the tube.

Sucks for me, Boone thinks as he gets to his feet and feels the resultant ache in his back where his kidney is protesting its ill treatment.

Eddie sucks for the whole world.

45

Rabbit and Echo drive Boone back to the Spy Store to pick up the Deuce.

Eddie will kill you but he won't inconvenience you, because it would violate his sense of aloha.

"I owe you a shot," Boone tells Rabbit.

"I shame, *bruddah*."

"I shame."

"Nothing personal."

"Personal."

"As awri," Boone says. That's alright.

"Ass why hard," Rabbit says.

"Ass why—"

"Shut up."

Rabbit and Echo are actually kind of fond of Boone, who's always treated them pretty nicely, not to mention the fact that Eddie is protective of Boone, even though he now officially hates his *haole* guts.

"Never trust a *haole*," has become Eddie's new mantra.

He'll actually sit cross-legged on his half-pipe platform first thing every morning – which for him is about eleven o'clock – and chant, "*Om mane padme hung*, never trust a *haole*," one hundred times or until he gets sick of doing it, which is usually about six reps. Then he smokes a big bowl of *pakololo* to enhance his aloha, which it massively does.

By this time the chef has the Spam fired up.

Then Eddie has to figure out how to kill the whole day without going more than seventy-five feet from his house. This usually involves numerous business meetings, his physical therapist, his masseuse, constant refreshment of Maui Wowie, sunbathing, skateboarding, thousand-dollar-a-throw call girls, and dozens of video games with Rabbit and Echo, none of which they'd better come close to winning.

His other pastime is surfing medical websites because he's allowed necessary visits to consult with a physician. So Eddie has developed a staggering variety of physical symptoms that would arouse the envy of the most ambitious hypochondriac. Since his arrest, Eddie has been tested for lupus, fibermyalgia, cholera and an elusive yet persistent recurrence of 'Raratonga Fever,' for which he is even now seeking permission to travel to Lucerne to consult with the world's only, and therefore pre-eminent, specialist – a *haole*.

Anyway, Rabbit feels a little bad about punching Boone and Echo . . . uhhh . . . echoes the sentiment. They drop him off back at the Deuce.

"You take care, eh, Boone?"

"Care."

"Bumbye," Boone says.

By and by, later.

He climbs into the Deuce and heads for The Sundowner.

On the way, he calls Dan Nichols, and then Johnny Banzai.

46

Boone takes a shower in the office and changes out of his sweaty clothes.

The hot water helps, but *just*. His face is puffy from the 'ground and pound,' and his neck bears a rough red splotch from the choke-out that looks like he tried to hang himself and changed his mind. His whole back hurts from the body slam and the kidney punch, and Boone begins to think that there might be better ways of earning a living.

He could be a lifeguard – Dave's offered many times to get him on – or he could become a . . .

A . . .

Okay, a lifeguard.

That's about it.

Cheerful is just about ready to leave for the day, as he has Stouffer's and Alex Trebek waiting for him. To say that Cheerful is a creature of habit is akin to opining that a sloth is a creature of leisure. His life is measured by strict routine and ritual.

Every Saturday he goes to Ralph's and buys seven Stouffer's Lean Cuisine microwave dinners, one, obviously, for each night of the week. (Saturday is Swiss Steak, Sunday is Turkey Tetrazzini, Monday spaghetti Bolognese, Tuesday chicken and rice, Wednesday . . . you get the idea.) He dines (okay, go with it) at precisely 6 p.m. as he watches the local news, then the NBC Evening News, then *Jeopardy*, at which he keeps his own score in his head and usually wins. In the half-hour that it takes for *Wheel of Fortune* to spin, he showers, shaves and changes into his pajamas and a robe. He's back in front of the television to watch the rerun of *7th Heaven* that Hang Twelve programmed to Tivo for him, and then he goes to bed. Saturday and Sunday were a bit of a problem, as there is no *Jeopardy* nor reruns of *7th Heave*n, but Hang solved this dilemma by banking episodes of *Gilmore Girls* and taking a blood oath of secrecy.

At 9, Cheerful goes to bed.

He gets up at 4 to have a cup of tea, a slice of unbuttered rye toast, and check the Asian markets. At 8, half his working day over, he rewards himself with another slice of toast, which fuels him for a half-mile walk. Then he goes to Boone's office, fusses with the books and waits impatiently for Boone to show up from the Dawn Patrol. He has lunch at 11 a.m. when Hang runs across to The Sundowner and brings back half a tuna salad sandwich and a cup of tomato soup.

Every day, no variation.

Cheerful is a billionaire and this is his blissfully miserable life.

But now he stays long enough for Boone to fill him in on his day of fun and adventure.

"Blasingame sounds like a piece of work," Cheerful says.

"Which one?" Boone asks.

"The dad," Cheerful grumbles.

"I'm beginning to wonder about the kid," Boone says.

"How so?"

Boone shrugs. He doesn't quite have his finger on it, but there's something sketchy about the whole story. He starts to explain when he hears Dan Nichols' voice downstairs: *"I'm looking for Boone Daniels?"*

"Up here!" Boone yells down the stairs.

Dan comes up.

"Dan, Ben Carruthers," Boone says, introducing Cheerful. "Ben, Dan Nichols."

"Pleasure," Dan says. "Any relation to the Ben Carruthers of Carruthers Holding?"

"That's me," Cheerful says.

"I've always wanted to meet you," Dan says. "You're kind of a recluse."

Cheerful nods. "I have an appointment. Nice to meet you."

He goes down the stairs.

"I'm impressed," Dan says. "I won't ask if he's a client."

"A friend."

"Then I'm even more impressed," Dan says. "Your friend is an investment genius. His company owns about half the world, I think."

"He's a good guy."

Dan looks at Boone's face and neck. "You been in a fight?"

"Working out in the gym."

"Sort of PI stuff, huh?"

Not really, Boone thinks. The few other PIs he knows do their work-outs in bars, lifting shots and beers. "I have the equipment."

"Good."

"One last time, Dan. You sure you want to know?"

Because some things are better left unknown. Ignorance may not be bliss, but knowledge isn't always a chocolate cone with sprinkles, either. And if something's in the past, it might just be better to leave it there – not everything you bring up from the bottom of the ocean is treasure.

"I'm committed to this, Boone."

Famous last words. Like guys who commit to the wrong line on a wave – once you're in it you might realize that you made the wrong choice, but it's too late. You're going to ride that line all the way to the wipeout.

"Just put it under the bumper," Boone says, "onto anything metal. I can track her movements from my van."

"007 kind of thing."

"Yeah, okay," Boone says. "How long are you out of town?"

"Two or three days. Depends."

"I have your cell?"

"Yup."

"I'll be in touch."

"Thanks for this, Boone."

Thanks for nothing, Boone thinks as Dan heads out.

And speaking of thanks for nothing . . .

47

Boone meets Johnny at The Sundowner.

Now, Boone has met Johnny at The Sundowner, like, a lot. You wanna run the numbers, Boone has probably met Johnny at The Sundowner more days than he *hasn't*. And he usually looks forward to it. Why not? The Sundowner is cool, Johnny is cool, it's all skippy.

Not gonna be this time.

So Boone is the opposite of stoked about it.

"You rang?" Johnny asks as he sits down at the table across from Boone. Johnny has his summer homicide detective uniform on – blue cotton blazer, blue shirt, khaki pants. He takes one look at Boone and says, "You've been in a fight."

"A couple of them."

"Did you win anyway?"

"Neither one."

"Then it hurts worse, huh?"

Boone doesn't know if it hurts worse, but it definitely *hurts*. As does what he's about to tell Johnny.

"You want a beer?" Boone asks.

"Oh, yes, I want a beer," Johnny says. The G2 on the street is that Cruz Iglesias has slipped into San Dog to escape the heat in TJ, and if that's true, it's alcohol-motivating news. It means that the Death Angels will be on the hunt, and they're not exactly SEAL-like in their target selection process. It could get sloppy ugly bloody. So Johnny would like a lot of beers. "Most definitely I want a beer, but I'm going on duty so I can't *have* a beer."

Boone signals the waiter and orders a couple of Cokes.

Johnny says, "You wanted to see me about something?"

"Yeah. Thanks for coming."

"Are we in the business or personal realm here?"

"Business," Boone says, although he's worried it's going to get personal. Murky border there, as easy to cross as the one with Mexico just a few miles to the south, and, just like that border, hard to cross back from.

"Shoot," Johnny says.

"Red Eddie told me he's going to kill Corey Blasingame," Boone says.

"Okay," Johnny says, taking it in. "How did you come by this information? You and Eddie don't exactly hang."

"He sent a gunpoint invitation."

"And how could you say no?"

"How could I say no?"

Johnny nods then gives Boone a long look. 'So here's the big question – why does Eddie give you the word? Let me rephrase that, why does Eddie give *you* the word?"

Boone takes a deep breath and then says, "I'm working on the Blasingame defense team."

Johnny stares at him. "Tell me you're kidding."

Boone shrugs.

"Putting my Sherlock Holmes hat on here," Johnny says, "let me deduce: Alan Burke is representing Corey. Burke's second-chair is a certain British woman you've been dating. Hence . . . and it's elementary, my dear Watson . . . you're whipped."

"It's not that." It's hard to be whipped by something you haven't . . . he doesn't finish the thought. Let Johnny think what he wants. There are tougher topics to take on and you might as well get it over with and jump. So he says, "You coached the Rockpile boys to write their statements, J."

Johnny looks at him for what seems like an hour. Then he says, "That Blasingame bitch is guilty. You know it, I know it, he knows it, Burke knows it, even that tea-bag you're banging knows it."

"Easy, now."

"*You* go easy," Johnny says. "You back *way* off. Unless, that is, you're going to choose a betty over your friends."

"It isn't about her," Boone says.

"Then what's it about?"

"The first-degree charge is jacked up."

"You want Mary Lou's number?"

"The witness statements—"

"—say what they say," Johnny insists. "Did I let them know how the system works? You bet I did. Did that change what happened out there that night? Not even a little."

"Come on, J – you have Trevor Bodin putting intent in Corey's mouth."

"He *had* intent in his mouth!" Johnny yells. "He said what he said, and he wrote it down. What are *you* saying, Boone?"

"What do you mean?"

"Are you saying that I cooked the statements? The confession?" Johnny asks. "Is that the tack that you and your new best friends are going to take? You can't try the facts so try the cop?"

"Johnny—"

"You know what that would do to my career?" Johnny asks.

Boone knows. As fast as his own descent in the force was, Johnny had been that fast in the upward direction. Johnny's rising with a rocket, there's talk of Chief of Detectives someday, and Banzai takes his career very seriously.

"I'm not trying to hurt you," Boone says.

"Yeah?" Johnny says. "Well, I don't want to be collateral damage when your do-gooder, misplaced, pussy-whipped meddling goes off."

He walks over to the bar and sits down, his back to Boone.

A shaft of sunlight pierces the room as the door opens and High Tide comes in for his End Of the Workday Beer, a ritual that he practices with religious devotion. He sits down at the table with Boone and then notices Johnny sitting by himself at the bar.

"What's with Johnny B?" Tide asks.

"We had a spat."

"Over a boy?" Tide asks, raising a fat finger to the waiter. "Tell you what, why don't you girls come over tonight, we'll make popcorn, put on a nice, goopy movie, and the two of you can have a good cry and make up. We could even make brownies."

"I'm helping defend Corey Blasingame."

Tide looks at him in disbelief, sees he's serious, and then says, "Maybe I'll have my beer at the bar."

"You know where it is."

"Late."

"Late."

Tide lifts his bulk out of the chair, shakes his head, walks away and settles himself on a stool next to Johnny.

Well, Boone thinks, this has been a good day.

48

Well, it has been for Jones.

Nothing not to like, moving from one fine hotel to another, checking in twice a day to see if they want him to interview someone, with or without a terminal conclusion.

Jones prefers to be active. He enjoys his work, but a little leisure doesn't go down so hard, either. Apparently his employer and the powers that be are trying to work this particular problem out 'amicably.' If so, Jones gets a free vacation in San Diego; if not, he does a job of work and takes a fatter envelope home with him.

In the meantime he strolls the beach boardwalk, slathers himself with sun block, observes the lovely young ladies in their swimsuits, and imagines them grimacing in pain.

All in all, a good day.

49

Boone goes home.

Pulls a yellowtail steak out of the fridge, gets it ready and tosses it on the grill.

Sunny used to always bust him for his ability to eat the same thing over and over again, day after day, but Boone never got what the problem was. His logic was simple: If something is good on Tuesday, why isn't it good on Wednesday? All that's changed is the day, not the food.

"But what about variety?" Sunny pressed.

"Over-rated," Boone answered. "We surf every day, don't we?"

"Yeah, but we change up the place sometimes."

He steps outside, turns the fish over, and sees High Tide coming up the pier. Boone goes outside to meet him.

"Big man," Boone says. "S'up?"

"We need to talk."

Boone unlocks his door and says, "Come on in."

He's known Tide since college days, when the big man was a star lineman at SDSU, headed for the pros. He was there to pick him back up when a knee injury ended that career. Boone didn't know him in his gang banging days, when Tide was the lord of the Samoan gangs in O'Side, before he found Jesus and gave all that up. He'd heard the stories, though – not from Tide but from other people.

They go into Boone's. Tide gently lets himself down on the sofa.

"You want anything?' Boone asks.

Tide shakes his big head. "I'm good."

Boone sits in a chair across from him. "What's up?"

High Tide is usually a pretty funny guy. Not now. Now he's dead serious. "You're on the wrong side of this, Boone."

"The Blasingame case."

"See, we don't look at it as 'the Blasingame case,' " Tide says. "We look at it as the 'Kuhio murder.' "

" 'We' being the island community?" Bundling together the Hawaiians, Samoans, Fijians and Tongans who have moved in greater numbers to California.

Tide nods. "We fight amongst ourselves, but when an outsider attacks the *calabash*, the community, we bond together."

"I get that."

"No," Tide says, "if you got that, you wouldn't be lining up on the other side. We're talking about Kelly Kuhio . . . K2. You know how many islanders the kids have to look up to? A few football players, a couple of surfers. You remember when the Samoan gangs were going at each other?"

"Sure."

"K2 went street to street, block to block, with me," Tide says. "He put himself on the line to bring the peace."

"He was a hero, Tide, I'm not arguing that."

Tide looks bewildered. "Then . . ."

"They're out to lynch that kid," Boone says. "It's not right."

"Let the system work it out."

"That's what I'm doing."

"*Without* you," Tide says. "Burke can hire any PI he wants. It doesn't have to be you. I'm telling you, it's personally hurtful to me that you took this case. I'm asking you, as your friend, to step out of it."

High Tide is not only a friend, but one of the most fundamentally decent people that Boone has ever known. He's a man who rebuilt his life – not once, but twice – a family man whose view of family extends to his whole community. He's gone back and worked with the gangs that he used to lead in fights, he's created peace and a little hope. An intelligent, sensitive man who wouldn't have come with this request unless he'd given it a lot of thought.

But he's wrong, Boone thinks. Every lawyer, every investigator in town, could take a pass on this case on the same basis, and even the Coreys of the world – especially the Coreys of the world – need help. If Kelly taught us anything, he taught us that.

"I'm sorry, Joshua, I can't do that."

Tide gets up.

Boone says, "We're still friends, right?"

"I don't know, B," Tide says. "I'll have to think about that."

First Johnny, now Tide, Boone thinks after the big man has left. How many friendships do I have to put on the line for piece-of-shit Corey Blasingame?

Then he smells his fish burning.

He runs outside but the tuna has already gone Cajun-style on him. He brings it back in, lays it in a tortilla with the red onion, finds some hot sauce in the fridge, pours it all over the fish and then scarfs down the whole mess in a few big bites.

Food is food.

Then he calls Pete.

She's still at the office, of course.

You don't make partner working 9-to-5, or even 9-to-9.

"Hall," she says.

"Daniels."

"Hi, Boone, what's up?"

He fills her in on his day looking for the soul of Corey Blasingame, leaving out his fight at the dojo, Red Eddie's threat, and the fact that he's pissing off half his friends. There'd be time to tell her about that later.

When he's finished his account she says, "There's really not a lot there we can use. The father is an alternately overbearing and neglectful horror show, and Corey was a mediocre surfer and a poor martial artist. Unfortunately, not poor enough. I think it does knock the 'gang' thing back a bit, though."

"There is no Rockpile 'gang' outside the four of them," Boone says. "And their only criminal activity seems to be going around trying to start fights."

Yeah, except, he thinks. There's always a freaking 'except,' isn't there? The 'except' in this case being the two points of contact. Corey and the other Mouseketeers surf at Rockpile, a spot notorious for its localism, and the sheriff there is Mike Boyd. Corey and the boys trained at Boyd's gym, where Corey learned the punch that killed Kelly Kuhio. The freaking Superman Punch.

". . . a late dinner or something?" she's saying.

"Uhh, Pete, yeah, I'd like to, but I have to work."

"The 'w' word?" she asks. "From the self-proclaimed surf bum?"

She keeps it light, but he can hear that she doesn't quite believe him, thinks it's payback from last night.

"Yeah, you never know, huh?" Boone says. "But, listen, another night . . ."

"Another night. Well, I won't keep you."

He punches out.

50

Dan Nichols is also on the phone.

Saying, ". . . I understand . . . I understand . . . No, I understand."

Dan understands.

51

Bill Blasingame sets down the phone.

His hand is shaking.

He looks at it, surprised. Tells himself to quit being a pussy and stop his hand from quivering.

It doesn't.

Bill's *freaked*.

52

Well, he paid me back, Petra thinks. She gets out of the elevator and walks into the parking structure of the office building. Apparently an appreciation for subtlety is too much to expect from a man whose idea of sophistication is a shirt with buttons.

Petra hits the 'unlock' button on her remote key, flinches at the responding honk of the horn, and reminds herself again to take it into the dealer to have that particularly annoying 'feature' removed.

She gets in, turns the ignition, and heads toward the exit, driving down level after level of switchback turns until she comes to the gate, rolls down the window, and touches her card to the little machine.

What passes for human contact, she thinks.

Well done, girl, she tells herself. Another evening of dining alone over a microwave 'dinner' or a take-out Chinese, and *God*, would that there were a decent Indian in downtown San Diego that delivered, just to mix it up a little.

She steers the car onto the street.

I should start walking to work, she thinks. The streets are relatively safe at night, it's foolish going to the gym and hitting the treadmill, and God knows I'm not in a particular hurry to get home. Where I usually do the same things I do in the office, only with my shoes off and the television on for background noise. Read documents, take notes . . . go to bed.

Alone.

Again.

Yes, well done, girl.

She goes down the ramp into the parking structure of her building.

Damn him, damn him, *damn* him.

53

A few students are hanging out in Team Domination, sparring, getting in a little bag work, lifting weights.

One of them is Boone's 'corner,' Dan.

"Hey," Boone says. "Mike around?"

"He took off."

"Any idea where?"

Dan has this funny little look on his face, like he knows where Boyd is but also knows that he shouldn't say. The other gym rats have their ears pricked up, too. So apparently *'Where is Mike?'* is an interesting question.

"I say something funny?" Boone asks.

A guy yanking kettle weights in the corner sets them down and comes over. Boone recognizes him from this afternoon. The guy says, "Mike said you might come around."

"And here I am."

"He said we could use a guy like you."

"Well, I'm a useful guy."

I can surf, I can burn fish . . .

"Mike's out in Lakeside," the guy says. " 'The 14 Club.' "

'The 14 Club?' Boone thinks. He remembers the '5' tattoo on Mike's thick forearm. The boy has this number thing going.

"I'll go check it out," Boone says.

"You go check it out," the kettle-weight guy says with this weird, smarmy smile.

So I guess we agree on that, Boone thinks.

I'll go check it out.

54

It's an article of faith among surfers in SoCal that you journey east of Interstate 5 at your own risk.

Nowhere is this more true than in San Diego County.

In fact, a lot of people make a clear distinction between 'San Diego' and 'East County,' the latter, rightly or wrongly, having a rep for crystal meth, biker bars, and the Southern California version of rednecks. Sticking with the stereotypes for the moment, west of the 5 you have stoned out surfers smoking weed, east of the 5 you got jacked-up gearheads spitting tobacco.

Boone drives *way* east, like forty miles out to the town of Lakeside, up in the barren hills just north of Interstate 8.

Lakeside is cowboy country.

No, actual, real cowboys – hats, boots, big belt buckle cowboys – forty-five minutes from downtown San Diego. The bars out here have pick-up trucks in the gravel parking lots, built-in tool-boxes in the beds, and dogs chained to eyebolts to keep people from lifting the tools while the owner's inside having a few beers.

The 14 Club is your classic cinder-block bunker. The small windows have been painted black to keep cops, wives and girlfriends from peeking in. The small '14' sign is hand-lettered, red on black. There's dozens of these joints in East County – hard-drinking caves for hard-working guys looking to blow off a little steam at the end of the day.

Yeah, except—

Boone walks through the door and the music is *blasting*.

Bass like resuscitation paddles.

And it ain't Merle Haggard, either, or Toby or Travis or who the hell ever. It's slamming heavy-metal 'punk,' for lack of a better description, and the clientele aren't cowboys, they're skinheads. Doc Martens, suspenders, T-shirts, tatts, the whole nine.

Which is surprising to Boone because he thought that scene died a well-deserved death years ago. Great, he thinks, now we have *retro*-skinheads. I guess everything comes back in style sooner or later.

Boone, in his faded Bullhead jeans, black Hurley T-shirt and an old pair of Skechers, feels distinctly out of place.

SEI.

The skins are slamming to the music and they are *jacked* on beer and speed. This scene could get ugly – ugli*er*, Boone reconsiders – in a heartbeat. He looks around and spots Mike Boyd leaning backward on the bar, a bottle of beer in his hand, watching the scene and nodding with approval.

Boone pushes his way through the crowd and makes his way to Boyd.

"Hey!" Boone shouts over the music.

Boyd looks only a little surprised to see him, but then again, he also looks about half shit-faced. "Three times in one day! To what do I owe the honor?! And how's your neck?!"

"Still attached to my head!" Boone answers. "Just barely!"

"Tap out next time!"

Yeah, 'next time,' Boone thinks. Ain't gonna be no next time, Mikey.

"How'd you find me?!" Mike yells.

"Your boys clued me! I hope that's cool!"

"You're welcome here!" Mike says, tapping his fist to Boone's. "*Very* welcome!"

"What *is* here?!" Boone asks. "What is this?!"

"You know '14?!' " Boyd asks.

Boone shakes his head.

"You will!" Boyd says. "When you find yourself, who you really are, your identity!"

Okay, Boone thinks, this is getting seriously weird.

"Why did you come here, Boone?!"

Good question, Boone thinks, his head already throbbing from the concussive noise. Boone's musical tastes run to Jack Johnson, Common Sense, Dick Dale, maybe a little surf reggae or some good Hawaiian slack key. This shit is killing him. I must be getting old, he thinks, grousing about how loud the kids play their so-called music.

Next stop, the Gentlemen's Hour.

He doesn't know how to answer Boyd's question. Like, what's he supposed to say – that he's hinky Boyd has shown up twice in the same case? That he wonders what the nexus is between the Rockpile Break, Team Domination, and Corey Blasingame?

As it turns out, Boyd answers his own question.

"You came here," he says, "for the same reason that salmon swim upstream!"

"To spawn?!" Boone asks. "I don't *think* so, Mike!"

There are some girls here, but they're way too young and not at all Boone's type. Pale, skinny blonde East County chicks, wearing black jeans over boots and hanging all over their skinhead boyfriends? No spawning for me, Mike.

"To fulfill your natural destiny!" Boyd answers.

Seriously, seriously, *grim* weird.

Anyway, Boone thinks, my natural destiny is to surf until I have to gum my fish tacos and hopefully topple over in a wave.

West of the 5.

Speaking of 5, what's the tatt about?

And what's up with this '14' shit?

The music picks up – picks *up* – in intensity and the skins start slamming each other, chest-bumping, head-butting – retro, retro, retro – as the lead guitar wails the same chord over and over again, and then Boone picks up on the lyrics.

Wham!
Show 'em who I am!
Wipe the mud off my feet,
Hose the mud off the street
So I can walk again
Like a white man!

Okaaaay, Boone thinks. Rhymes, anyway. Boyd leans over and yells into Boone's ear. "Fourteen! Fourteen *words*!"

Which turn out to be, "We must secure the existence of our people and a future for white children."

Boone counts them up – fourteen words alright.

"The man who said that," Boyd hollers, "died in prison!"

Good idea, Boone thinks.

Wham!
The taco's head goes bam!
What do I see?
Another block is free!
Where I can walk again
Like a white man!

"He gave his *life* for the cause!" Boyd yells. He has fucking *tears* in his eyes. "We all have to be prepared to give our lives for the cause!"

Yeah, no, Boone thinks.

Not me.

Not for *this* cause.

White supremacist, neo-Nazi, needle-dick, double-digit-IQ, mouth-breathing, bottom-feeding, off-the-chart dismo, sick bullshit.

The skins are rocking out now – the adrenaline is pumping, the blood is flowing.

Good, Boone thinks.

Bleed out.

55

As Boone drives away, his ears are still ringing from the music and Boyd's parting words.

"You'll be back, Daniels! When you figure it all out, you'll be back!"

Yeah.

Boone drives west until he spots a Starbucks sign – no big trick there – and pulls off. He digs out the laptop and Googles.

The fourteen words – 'We must secure the existence of our people and a future for white children' – was the Nathan Hale of one David

Lane, founder of neo-Nazi group The Order, who was sentenced to a buck ninety in prison for murder, bank robbery and other happy crap. He tapped out in the joint in 1997.

So good things *do* happen in prison, Boone thinks.

He types in '5 + white supremacist.'

What comes up makes him sick to his stomach.

In white-supremo code, '5' stands for 'The Five Words . . .'

I have nothing to say.

56

Turns out to be a white supremacist slogan coined by a local San Diego buttplug, Alex Curtis, at his trial for violating people's civil rights. Boone sort of remembers the whole thing. Curtis was a young creep from East County who had a website and a streaming podcast to spew his drool. Was a big proponent of the 'lone wolf' tactic – which said that the racists should act alone to foil law enforcement – go out solo to kill Jews and blacks and the rest of the 'mud people.'

Curtis went to jail back in – was it 2006? – and became kind of a cult hero-martyr for the knuckle-dragger set, and according to the story on the website, his words in court, 'I have nothing to say,' became a slogan.

Encoded in the number '5.'

Good, Corey, Boone thinks.

Real good.

I guess you found something you could belong to.

57

Regarding the next morning's Dawn Patrol, there's dawn . . .

. . . but not much of a patrol.

Boone, Dave and Hang are out there, but Johnny and Tide are 404.

"Johnny must have got hung on a case," Dave observes.

"Probably," Boone says.

"Yeah, but where's Tide?" Hang asks.

"He was at The Sundowner last night," Dave says.

"He say anything?" Boone asks.

"About what?"

"I dunno," Boone says. "Anything."

Great, he thinks. Lie to the friends you have left.

"He was quiet," Dave says. "A big Buddha statue sitting at the bar, banging beers. I left early, had a date with a nurse from Frankfurt. The Euros are here in force, man. The beach is like the freaking UN."

"Weak dollar," Boone says.

"I guess." Dave looks at Boone funny, like: What aren't you telling me?

Boone sees it and ignores it. Can't tell you what I can't tell you, bro, and you'll find out about it soon enough anyway.

58

Corey Blasingame sits slumped across the table from Boone.

"I have noth—"

"Save it."

Corey shrugs and reaches for the plastic bottle of water by his right hand. Boone gets to it first and moves it out of reach. When Corey stretches his arm out to get the bottle, Boone grabs his wrist and holds it down on the table.

Then he reaches over and slides Corey's sleeve up.

Sees the '5' tattoo.

He lets Corey's wrist go. The kid jerks his arm back and smirks at Boone.

"I killed him," Corey says, "because I thought he was a nigger."

59

Corey freaking Blasingame.

Total loser.

Even when he tries to do something hatefully stupid and stupidly hateful, he fucks it up. Sees a dark-skinned man come out of a bar, thinks he's African American, kills him, and then finds out his victim is Hawaiian.

Well done, C. Good job.

You killed one of the finest men I've ever known because you 'thought he was a "nigger." '

Excellent.

The rest of the scenario is easy to put together – Corey originally confessed to the crime but, realizing that he'd fucked up, didn't cop to his real motive. Then the Aryan Brotherhood boys got to him in the lock-up and let him know that he could do his time in one of two ways – as a snitch or a race hero. Even a fucking idiot like Corey figured out he'd better take Door Number Two. So he fell back on the 'I have nothing to say' mantra, which made him more of a hero. But then he just couldn't keep it inside – something forced him to make himself look as bad as possible.

'I killed him because I thought he was a nigger.'

Hateful *and* stupid.

Boone goes down the ramp below the big office building on Broadway and 6th, takes a ticket from the machine and makes several orbits of the parking structure before he finds a vacant space. He locks up the Deuce, gets into the elevator and goes up to the fourteenth floor, to the door marked 'Law Offices of Burke, Spitz and Culver,' and goes inside.

He's known Becky Hager for years. Middle-aged, very attractive, long curly red hair, she's the sentinel at Alan's castle gate. If Becky doesn't want you to get in to see Alan, you're not getting in to see Alan.

"Daniels," she says. "Long time no."

"Busy, Becky."

"Surf up?"

"Not lately," Boone says.

"You here to see Mary Poppins? Blasingame?"

"Yup."

Becky gives just enough of a smirk to inform him that she knows there's a little more between him and Petra than a purely professional relationship, then pushes a couple of buttons and says into her mouthpiece, "Petra? There's a 'Boone Daniels' here for you?"

She listens, then looks up at Boone and says, "She'll be out in a minute. The new *Surfer* arrived."

Boone sits down and looks at the magazine. Petra comes out two minutes later, looking cool and lovely in a white lawn self-stripe blouse over a light tan skirt.

"This is a surprise," she says.

"Sorry I didn't call."

"That's quite alright," she says. "Come on back."

"Nice to see you, Daniels."

"And you, Becky."

Petra's office is midway down the hall. It has a nice view of the city, dominated by the aircraft carriers docked at the Navy Base with Point Loma as a backdrop, but Boone knows that she covets a corner office that comes with being made partner.

She sits behind her desk, which is as neat and tight as she is.

"I have motive for Corey," Boone says.

"Do tell."

"He was making his bones with the white supremacist movement," Boone says, "and went after Kelly because he thought he was black."

"How do you know this?"

"He told me."

"You *asked* him if he did it?"

"Of course not," Boone says. "He volunteered it."

"Why?"

"Because he's a fuck-up, Pete," says Boone. "A total loser. I hate him. Anyway, that's what I was doing last night when you called, checking it out. I didn't mean to. . ."

"No, I'm sorry for the last minute invitation. It was presumptuous of me."

"Look, you can presume . . . what you want to . . . presume."

"I don't know *what* to presume about us, Boone," she says. "Are we colleagues, or friends, or *more* than friends, or—"

Before he knows what he's doing he's standing up, leaning over her desk and kissing her on the mouth. Her lips flutter under his, something he's never experienced before, and they're fuller and softer than he would have thought. He pulls her out of her chair, and papers spill off the desk onto the floor.

He lets her go.

"So that would be more than friends?" she says, smoothing her skirt. "I presume?"

What the hell are you doing? he asks himself. One second you're ready to take her head off, the next second you're kissing her.

"I'd better go tell Alan the good news," she says.

"Right."

Boone has felt awkward, uncomfortable and indecisive before, but never anything like this. Do I just leave? he wonders. Or shake her hand? Or kiss her? On the lips? Or the cheek, or . . .

She comes around the desk, puts her hand behind his neck, closes her eyes and kisses him, warmly.

"I'll go with you," Boone says.

"That would be nice."

On his way out of the office he passes by Becky who says, "Wipe the lipstick off, idiot."

"Thanks."

"*Nada*."

He goes into the lobby, turns around and comes back. Hands Becky the parking ticket. "I forgot to get validated."

"I think you got plenty validated," Becky says. Then, her eyes wide with mock surprise, adds, "Oh, you want me to stamp the *ticket*."

She takes the ticket from him, stamps it and hands it back. "Cheerio, old chap."

Becky, Boone thinks, is the whole barrel of monkeys.

60

"Let me share a concept with you, Boone," Alan Burke says, staring out his window at San Diego Harbor. "I hired you to make our case better, not work it up from involuntary manslaughter to a *hate crime*!"

He turns to look at Boone. His face is all red and his eyes look as if they might pop out on springs like they do in the cartoons.

"You were never going to get 'invol man,' " Boone says.

"We don't know that!"

"Yeah, we do."

Petra says, "I think what Boone is trying to say—"

"I know what Boone is trying to say!" Alan yells. "Boone is trying to say that I'd better crawl on my hands and knees into Mary Lou's office and accept any deal she offers short of the needle. Is that what you're trying to say, Boone?"

"Pretty much," Boone answers. "If I found this out, I can guarantee that John Kodani will find it out, too. And when he does—"

"—Mary Lou re-files on the hate crime statutes and Corey gets life," Alan says. He punches a button on his phone. "Becky, get Mary Lou Baker for me."

Alan looks at Petra and Boone and says, "I'd better get with Mary Lou before Boone *helps* us anymore and puts Corey on the Grassy Knoll. You don't have him on the Grassy Knoll, do you? Or anywhere in the vicinity of the Lindbergh baby? You got him nailing Christ up, too, Daniels?"

"I'm guessing Corey's not crazy about Jews, Alan."

"Funny," Alan says. "Funny stuff from a guy who just harpooned my case."

"I didn't harpoon your case," Boone says. "Your client is guilty. Deal with it. Get the little shit the best deal you can and move on to the next one. Just leave me out of it."

Boone walks out of the office.

Petra follows him, grabs him by the elbow and hauls him into the law library. "Why are you so angry?"

"I'm not."

"You are."

"Okay," Boone says, "I'm *angry* because I'm helping you get this sub-hominid a deal he shouldn't get. I'm *angry* because you're going to do it. I'm *angry* because Corey *should* get life-without-parole instead of the sixteen-to-twenty you're going to plead him out for. I'm *angry* because—"

"Or maybe you're just angry," Petra says. "Maybe mister cool, laid-back surfer is seething with rage about the . . ."

"Back off, Pete."

". . . injustices in the world," Petra continues, "that he can't do anything about, which he masks with this 'Surf's up dude' persona, when in actual fact . . ."

"I said, back off."

"Rain Sweeny was not your fault, Boone!"

He looks stunned. "Who told you about that?"

"Sunny."

"She shouldn't have."

"Well, she did." But Petra's sorry she said it. He looks so hurt, so vulnerable. "I'm sorry. I'm very sorry . . . I had no right . . ."

Boone walks out.

61

It's good being Donna Nichols.

What Boone thinks after he drives over to the Nichols' neighborhood south of La Jolla, parks a couple of blocks away from the house, and waits with a paper-wrapped breakfast burrito, a go-cup of coffee and his laptop computer.

Donna comes out of the house a little after 10.30. She's hot, no question about it, her blonde hair done in a pony-tail under a white visor, and her tight frame tucked into a white sleeveless blouse and designer jeans. Boone watches her little red icon ping – he's set it for one-second intervals – on his laptop screen and makes a correct assumption about where she's headed: an upscale mall called Fashion Valley.

Boone gets there first and hangs out around a central point. Sure enough, Donna shows up a few minutes later. He watches her go into Vertigo, an expensive spa, then goes back out to the parking lot, finds her car and parks the Deuce on the other side where he can still watch, and sits. Now he remembers why he hates any kind of surveillance work – it's boring as hell – especially on an August morning where it's already getting hot. He rolls the window down on the van, sits back and tries to grab some sleep.

Yeah, good luck with that.

He's too pissed off to sleep.

What, I'm this subterranean well of rage threatening to go off like a volcano or something? Boone asks himself. I'm this earthquake waiting to happen? Just because I think it's a shitty thing that a racist creep decides to kill someone and won't end up paying the full tab? Yeah, well, he may not in the court system, but in the Red Eddie System he's going to get the max, and there won't be twenty years of appeals and people doing candlelight vigils, either.

So chill, he tells himself. All this happy legalistic horseshit is irrelevant, 'moot' as they might say, a card game trumped by Eddie's willingness to come in and play 52-Pickup. But are you happy about that? Boone asks himself. Are you a vigilante now? Then he realizes that it isn't his own voice he's hearing, it's K-2's, asking those gentle questions, doing his Socratic Buddha thing.

Boone doesn't want to hear it right now so instead he gets mad at Pete all over again. Where the hell does she get off fronting me with Rain Sweeny? And on the topic of what the hell, what the hell was Sunny doing telling her about it? Is this some sort of sistuh-chick thing, ganging up on the guy? Get him to talk about his *feelings*?

Donna's in the spa for a little over an hour and comes out looking even better, if that's possible. Some kind of new make-up look or skin treatment or something. He waits for her to pull out of the lot and then watches the screen to see where she's headed.

Downtown.

She heads south on the 163, gets off on Park Boulevard and turns left into Balboa Park. Slowly wends her way around the narrow, curving streets and then parks in the lot just south of the Spreckels Amphitheater.

Boone hits the gas to catch up and pulls into a slot just in time to see her walking north up the Prado, the main street in Balboa Park. Following her up past the zen garden to the Prado restaurant, where she meets three other women and goes inside.

Ladies who lunch, Boone thinks. He buys a newspaper, finds a bench over near the Botanical Garden across the street, and waits. He's sweaty and hungry, so he breaks the monotony by walking back to a kiosk outside the Prado and buying a pretzel and a bottle of mango juice, then goes back and sits down, just another unemployed slacker killing an afternoon in Balboa Park.

62

Mary Lou Baker is skippy.

But then again, she always is.

The happy warrior.

Now she looks across the table at Alan Burke and says, "Oh, please, Alan. Save the cat-with-the-canary cryptic smile for some young pup who's impressed with your resumé. I have your client's confession, I have five witnesses, I have the medical examiner's report that Kelly's death was consistent with a severe blow to the head. You have . . . let me think . . . right, that would be nothing."

Alan maintains the feline smile, if only to get her more jacked up. "Mary Lou," he says as if addressing a first-year law student in class, "I'll get the ME to testify that the severe blow to the head could have come from striking the curb. I'll get three of your witnesses to admit that they pled to reduced charges in exchange for their testimony. As for the so-called 'confession,' come on, ML, you might as well tear it up right now and put it into the office john, because that's about all it's good for."

"Detective Sergeant Kodani has a sterling reputation . . ."

"Not when I'm done with him," Alan says.

"Nice," Mary Lou answers. She leans back in her chair, puts her hands behind her head and says, "We'll drop 'special circumstances.' "

"The judge will drop the 'special' before we go to motions," Alan says.

"You're going to roll the dice on that?"

"Seven come eleven."

Mary Lou laughs. "Okay, what do you want?"

"You go manslaughter, we have something to talk about."

Mary Lou jumps out of the chair, throws her hands up into the air and says, "What do I look like to you . . . *Santa Claus?!* Christmas comes in *August* now?! Look, we're wasting our time here. Let's just go to trial, let the jury hear the case and hand your client life-without-parole because you want to come in here and joke around."

Alan looks wide-eyed and innocent. "We can certainly go in front of a jury, Mary Lou. It would be an honor and pleasure to try a case with you. And no one is going to blame you for an acquittal. You were handcuffed by a shoddy investigation and a rush to judgment, what could you do? I'm sure Marcia Clark would—"

"I'd go second-degree," Mary Lou says. "My best and final offer."

"That's fifteen-to-life."

"Yeah, I've read the statute," she says.

"Sentence recommendation?"

She sits back down. "It would have to be somewhere in the mid-range, Alan. I won't push for max, but I can't go minimum, I just can't."

Alan nods. "He serves ten-on-sixteen?"

"We're in the same ballpark."

"I'll have to take it to my client," Alan says.

"Of course."

Alan stands up and shakes her hand. "Pleasure doing business with you, Mary Lou."

"Always, Alan."

The Gentlemen's Hour.

63

The women finally come out of the restaurant. Kisses on the cheek all around, promises to do this again 'sooner,' and then Donna starts walking back toward the parking lot. Boone gives her a good head start, then catches up, passes her, and is in his van waiting when she pulls out of the lot. He gives her a lot of time, watching her progress on the screen as she drives west on Laurel Street through the park, down toward the airport, then gets on the 5 north.

She could be heading home, but she takes the exit for Solana Beach and parks on Cedros Street. Boone is just a couple of minutes behind her as she parks and then walks from store to store on this block of expensive furniture stores. Then she goes into a clothing boutique and spends forty-five minutes. And some money, apparently, because she comes out with a couple of dresses on hangers and goes back to her car.

Now she drives home and pulls into the garage.

Boone sits a block away. Ten minutes later, a car pulls into the driveway. A young man in a tight-fitting black T-shirt, bicycling shorts and *muscles* gets out and rings the bell. Donna lets him in.

She wouldn't, Boone thinks. She wouldn't have the nerve or the bad taste to do this right in her own home. Doesn't happen. He takes his binoculars, scopes the license plate and calls Dan.

"That's Tony," Dan says. "Personal trainer."

"Uhhh, Dan, I know this would be really cliché, but . . .'

"Tony also dances in an all-boy nude dance review in Hillcrest," Dan says, naming San Diego's pre-eminent gay neighborhood.

"Unless he's swapped jerseys . . ."

"Okay, then."

Tony comes out an hour later. Donna, red-faced and sweating, waves goodbye and goes back in.

So it's good being Donna Nichols, Boone decides. A little spa treatment, a nice lunch, some high-end shopping, a customized workout, hopefully a quiet dinner at home. And, just as hopefully, Dan is wrong about his wife's infidelity. Just a little premature mid-life insecurity on his part. Has probably happened to half the guys on the Gentlemen's Hour.

Yeah, no.

Because it's August and August blows.

There's no surf, K2 is gone because some stupid kid has to belong to something, women reach into your insides and rip them out, and Donna Nichols comes out of her house dressed to kill.

64

Boone watches the little pings head toward Del Mar.

His route takes him past Torrey Pines Beach and that beautiful stretch of the Pacific Coast Highway that he loves so dearly. It's just summertime dusk, with the sun setting fat and hot over the horizon, and plenty of people are still lazing on the beach.

Boone never drives this stretch without feeling this little tug at his heart. The place is just ineffably beautiful, and he feels lucky to live there. It cheers him up a bit, makes him forget for a moment that he's about to do something that he really doesn't want to do.

North on Torrey Pines Road, then up Camino Del Mar – the town of Del Mar's re-christening of the Pacific Coast Highway – then a left up the steep hill away from the ocean. Donna passes 'Go,' collects $200, and lands on the square marked 1457 Cuchara Drive.

Her car is parked in the driveway when Boone catches up to the flashing red dots on the GPS screen and slowly drives down the expensive suburban street. You have to have bucks to live in this neighborhood – not necessarily Dan Nichols' kind of bucks, but bucks. Not a lot of on-street parking here, and Boone doesn't want Donna to notice the van, so he's happy to find a spot about halfway down the block and across the street.

He can see Donna through the living-room window, sitting on a sofa having a drink. A guy sits next to her, but Boone doesn't get a good view of him. Boone slouches in his seat and points the listening cone toward the house.

Checking the monitor on the recorder to make sure he's getting sound, he sits back and waits. No point in listening in on the small talk – it will all be on the tape anyway. A few minutes later she gets up. The lights in the living room go off, then a light in what's probably the bedroom comes on.

Boone slips the headset on to make sure he's getting a clear signal.

He is.

It's horrible.

Really horrible.

Boone feels like a total, low-life, bottom-feeding, mouth-breather as he listens to the sounds of their lovemaking. Donna likes to talk dirty – or at least she thinks that her squeeze likes to hear her talk dirty – so her voice is all over the tape. There's no doubt it's her – and Boone is grateful that Dan isn't hearing this.

He's sorry that he has to hear it, but he does. It's a potential intermediate step to having to share the tape with Dan. He knows how that conversation goes:

"Boone, are you sure?"

"I'm sure."

"They couldn't have been doing something else?"

Like knitting, watching The Bachelor, *building cabinetry . . .*

"Dan, I heard them. It's unmistakable."

So he listens.

The guy is pretty verbal himself, uses her name over and over again, and Boone takes the headset off after there's no doubt what they're doing. He doesn't want to be any more a part of this than he has to.

He sits back, vividly remembering why he hates matrimonial work.

His cell phone rings. It's Petra.

"Hello, what are you doing?"

"Working." You know us deceptively laid-back surfer dudes – we're always on the job. Our anger keeps us going.

With a rare tone of uncertainty in her voice, Petra says, *"Listen, I'm really sorry about this morning. I was completely out of line, and it wasn't my place to—"*

"Forget about it."

Awkward silence, then Petra says, *"Well, if you'd like to take a break or something? We could grab a coffee or . . ."*

"I'm kind of on a stakeout."

"Oh. Right."

"Yeah. I'm pretty stuck."

"Well, I could join you," Petra says. *"Bring something over to where you are."*

"That sounds really nice," Boone says. "But, Pete, there's a reason it's called *private* investigation work?"

"Oh, of course. Sorry. Stupid of me."

"No, no. It's just that it's *that* kind of case."

"Right."

Quit being a dick, Boone tells himself. She said she was sorry, what more do you want? Stop being such a big relationship baby. So he says, "How about tomorrow night? I think this thing is wrapping up, I'd probably be loose."

"Well, why don't we just see?" Petra says. *"I'm not exactly sure what my schedule's going to be. Actually, now that I think about it, I might be committed to get together with some friends. Foodies . . . dinner in the Gaslamp, that sort of thing."*

That is, Boone thinks, not the sort of 'thing' *you'd* be interested in.

SEI.

"Sure," he says. "Why don't we play it by ear?"

"That sounds like a good idea," Petra says. *"Well . . . sorry to have bothered you."*

"No, you didn't. It was nice to have a break."

"Always glad to be of service."

That went well, Boone thinks. 'Foodies.' Foodies should be lined up against a wall, read that day's specials, then machine-gunned.

Around 1 a.m. Boone sets the GPS tracker to alert him if the car moves, finds his portable alarm clock in the back and sets it for 6:30, tilts the seat back and goes to sleep.

Donna Nichols comes out at 6:37 a.m.

An overnight bag slung over her shoulder.

A middle-aged, burly white guy with curly sandy-colored hair and a red goatee, wearing just a silk bathrobe, stands in the doorway and kisses her goodbye. Then he bends over, picks up the newspaper and goes back inside.

Donna opens her car door, tosses the bag into the front passenger seat, gets in and backs out of the driveway. Boone waits for a minute, the blips on the screen telling him that she's headed home, then pulls up and checks out the name on the mailbox: 'Schering.' Then he pulls ahead and finds a different parking spot.

At 8:20, Boone looks into his rearview mirror and sees Schering's garage door open. A tan Mercedes 501 backs out and heads down the hill. Boone gives it a second, then follows. He doesn't want to tail him too closely and get made, and he can always reverse Schering's full identity through the address and the license plate, but it would be easier to find out where the man works and do it that way. He catches up with Schering as he takes a right onto Camino Del Mar, heading south. Schering turns onto Torrey Pines Road, and for a second Boone wonders if he's going to Nichols' house on a when-the-cat's-away theory, but then Schering drives past the golf course and takes a left into a business park of small, two-story office buildings.

The Mercedes pulls into a slot marked 'Reserved.'

Schering gets out of the car. Boone notices that he's dressed

SoCal Summer Professional – blue blazer, khaki slacks, white shirt open at the collar. Expensive brown Oxford shoes, highly shined. No wedding ring. Schering grabs his Haliburton briefcase from the passenger seat, walks to the building behind the parking spot, and climbs a set of exterior stairs to the second floor. Boone waits a minute, gets out and walks up the same stairs. He reads on the signboard that three offices share the floor – a lawyer, a title company, and 'Philip M. Schering, Geological Engineering Consultant.'

Schering does dirt.

65

That is to say he's a 'soils engineer.'

We always think of houses or any buildings being constructed from the foundation up, but that's not really true. The real 'foundation' is the earth beneath the foundation. At the end of the day, all buildings are constructed on dirt, in one form or the other. If that dirt isn't solid, then it doesn't matter how strong a foundation you build, in reality there is no foundation.

But dirt isn't just dirt. Because it's made up of broken-down rock and decomposed vegetation, there's an infinite variety of types of dirt – depending on the type of stone and vegetation, its moisture content or lack thereof, its compaction and stability.

It goes deeper than that, literally. Dirt always sits on something – either water or rock – and again, depending on the depth of the soil, its humidity, the angle or 'slope' at which it sits, it rests in various degrees of stability or, in the negative case, instability.

Same with the rock or water it sits on. The rock might be whole and stable, or cracked – in the most severe instance, for example, by earthquake – and resettling, shifting, moving. Any of this instability will likewise affect subterranean pools of water, which further impacts surrounding rock and the soil that sits on top of it.

So when we look at soil, it appears to be inert, but that is often anything but the truth. In reality, the subsurface soil is in a state of flux, either rapid – in the case of a landslide – or imperceptibly slow, as is the case of the world's evolution over billions of years. The truth is that the soil is always changing.

Which would be a gigantic so-what, except that we build things on it, most notably our houses, and it's the job of soils engineers such as Phil Schering to tell us whether the soil can sustain the building, or whether we need to do some work on it, if such work is even feasible or effective.

Southern California has a lot of soils engineers because a lot of people want houses there, and because it's basically a desert that happens to roll up to an ocean. Which is just fine until you start building houses and subdivisions, office buildings, hotels, streets and roads on those bluffs, because the bluffs are made mostly of sandy soil and loose clay.

Take, for instance, Boone's beloved Pacific Coast Highway. The civil engineers who built it basically cut away the bottoms of bluffs, triggering huge internal landslides farther up the slopes. Drive the PCH now, and you'll see lots of big, concrete retaining walls to keep those bluffs from becoming part of the Pacific Ocean.

But the highway was built decades before the big housing boom in Southern California, and the bluffs could withstand and recover from the pressure of the cutaway. What happened, though, was that more and more people wanted to live on those bluffs. Houses and huge subdivisions were built, often too quickly, and the people moved in.

People need water. To drink, cook, bathe, launder, flush. Most of that water makes it into drains and has little effect on the soil stability. But people also wanted lawns. Lawns are composed of grass, which, unlike the cactus, requires water. Lots of it. So the same people who were drinking cooking, bathing, laundering and flushing, started to water their lawns, and that water doesn't go into drains, it seeps into the soil of loose sand and clay. Because water is a lubricant, and the most patient, pernicious and powerful destructive force in the physical world, it further loosens the already loose subsurface soil until the housing developments sit on what is basically a toboggan run, the buildings themselves being the toboggans.

They are going to slide.

As they do, foundations crack, driveways crack, sidewalks crack, stucco cracks, floors buckle, ceilings sag, roof tiles pop for no (apparent) reason. And, occasionally, houses and condos just slide off the edge, or fall into sink-holes that magically appear and swallow up houses.

Which brings out another Southern Californian phenomenon.

Litigation.

People sue – insurance companies, contractors, architects, the city, the county, each other. And when they sue, both sides require the services of engineering consultants such as Phil Schering to testify why the soil under their houses, condos, offices or hotels 'failed,' and whose fault it was, i.e. somebody else's.

Basically, Phil Schering is a professional expert witness. You can make a very nice living charging five bills an hour as an expert witness. The time on the stand is the least of it – a consulting engineer like Phil Schering also bills for the time he spends evaluating the case, time spent preparing his testimony, meetings with lawyers – the meter is running, my friend.

Hence the house on Cuchara Lane in Del Mar.

And social proximity to women like Donna Nichols.

Boone drives back to Pacific Beach.

It's too late for the Dawn Patrol.

66

Boone paddles out past the other surfers on the Gentlemen's Hour, rips the leash off his ankle and rolls off his board into the water, letting it cleanse the dirt and fatigue of a depressing all-night stake-out.

The ocean is timeless and therefore a great holder of memories and they wash over Boone with the cool water as he dives.

Sunny.

When Boone was helping her train to bust into the professional ranks, they used to do this – free-dive as deep as they could go. She was like an arrow shot into the water, a long, sleek dart of energy and strength. They'd stay down until they felt their lungs about to burst, then stay down a little longer before plunging to the surface for that beautiful breath of air. Then they'd do it again, challenging each other, pushing each other, Sunny so stubborn and determined that she'd never give in before Boone.

After a few dives, they'd swim beside each other to find their boards where they'd drifted, then go on a long paddle parallel to the beach until their shoulders ached and their arm muscles burned with fatigue. Or they'd race – short, sharp dashes as if trying to beat each other into a wave, because he knew that's what she'd need to break it on the tour: to get into that winning wave before the competition.

So he pushed her, never gave her a break or edge for being a 'girl.' Not that she needed one – Sunny was as strong and quick as any guy, stronger and quicker than most, her long frame and wide shoulders perfect for the water. She was ripped, in killer shape from a strict vegetarian diet supplemented with some fish. The diet, the yoga, the weight-lifting, the brutal workouts she put herself through, the endless hours in the water – Sunny was a dedicated animal.

It was K2 who turned her onto yoga.

More memories as Boone touches the bottom, then arches up and shoots for the surface. He comes up and looks back at the shore.

All the boys laughed when Kelly brought that yoga shit to the beach. It didn't bother K2, he just unrolled his mat on the sand and started doing those slow moves, furling, unfurling and stretching his body into the funny, impossible shapes as he ignored the chuckles and witticisms around him.

He just smiled and did his routines.

Then tore it apart in the water.

Yeah, laugh all you want, boys – call him 'guru,' 'swami,' do your best George Harrison imitations – he's tearing your *hearts* out in the surf. He gets any wave he wants, finds the perfect line and *shreds* it, with a grace and pure athleticism you can only dream about, and that old man can do it to you all day long.

Boone treads water, looks at the beach, remembers and laughs.

Recalls the day that Sunny joined K2 in his yoga session. She strode up, laid her mat beside his and started to copy his moves. He didn't say anything, just smiled and kept going through his routine, and now the boys were really watching because this babe was putting herself through these contortions and it was, uhhh, compelling. Like, no one was *not* going to watch that, and then one of the dudes joined in to get next to Sunny, and then a few more, and it wasn't long before K2 had a yoga class going on the beach.

Not for Boone – he did his workouts in the water – but Sunny was a devotee, totally aware that K2 was a father figure to her. Sunny's own dad split when she was three, and she was totally open about the fact that she always wanted a dad.

"Basic psychology," she told Boone during one of their training sessions. "I want to stay aware of it so I don't do the stereotypical thing of trying to get the love I didn't get from my father from my boyfriend."

Which is a good thing, Boone thought, because he was her boyfriend at the time. So it was perfect when Sunny made her yoga hook-up with K2.

"It's almost better than having a real father," she told Boone.

"How so?"

"Because I'm choosing my father figure," she answered, "so I can look for all the qualities I want in a father instead of having to settle for whatever my real father was."

"Got it."

So did K2.

He was so cool about it. It didn't freak him out, he never talked about it, never came close to doing that creepy 'You can call me Daddy, daughter' thing. He just kept on being himself – kind, gentle, wise and open.

All the qualities you'd want in a father.

Anyway, Sunny had her grandmother, Evelyn, and her father-figure, K2, and her own package of DNA, and self-reliance, and a love for the ocean, so she never became the neurotic fucked-up SoCal broken family girl who careens around for love and ends up creating another generation of fucked-up SoCal broken family girls.

She became a great surfer instead.

A great lover and then a great friend.

He remembers that night on the beach. Low tide and deep fog, and him and her under the pier, making love with the water washing over them. Her long sleek neck tasted like salt, her hands were firm on his back, her long strong legs pushed him deeper into her.

After, they wrapped up in a blanket together and listened to the sound of the small waves slapping the pylons, and talked about their lives, what they wanted, what they didn't, and they just talked bullshit and made each other laugh.

Boone misses her.

He swims over, gets on his board, sits up and looks at the beach.

No less than the water itself, the beach is a place of memories.

Stand on it, you look out at the ocean and remember certain waves, awesome rides, bad wipe-outs, hysterical conversations, great times. Sit off it and look back and you remember lying around talking, you remember volleyball games and cookouts, your memory makes it night instead of day and you remember bonfires, pulling on sweatshirts against the cold, guitars and ukuleles and quiet talks.

Now he remembers a talk he had with K2.

They were sitting a little away from the fire, listening to someone strum 'Kuhio Bay' on the uke, when K2 said, "The secret of life . . ."

He paused and then added, ". . . *Grasshopper* . . ." because he liked to make fun of his status as a local guru, ". . . is to do the right things, big or small, one after the other after the other."

Boone had just returned to the surf and the beach after months of self-imposed isolation following the Rain Sweeny case. He'd quit the force, laid on Sunny's sofa until she booted him out, then hid in his own place feeling sorry for himself.

Now he was back and it was only Sunny, his now ex, who knew that he wasn't fully back. Sunny and, it seemed, K2.

Who just said that and left it there for Boone to pick up or not.

But they both knew what he meant:

You did the right thing.

Now, will you keep doing it?

Yeah, K, Boone thinks, watching the beach change from the night of his memory to the harsh sunlight of an August day, but what's the right thing?

You know.

In your gut, you know.

Shit, K.

Shit indeed, Grasshopper.

67

Boone goes to Starbucks.

Which doesn't happen very often.

It's not like he's some sort of anti-globalization, anti-franchise freak, it's just that he gets his coffee at The Sundowner and pretty much leaves it at that. Like, Boone could probably distinguish between Kenya AA and root beer, but that's about it.

Anyway, he goes, and endures the skepticism that results from his order of a 'medium black coffee.'

"You want an *Americano grande*," the *barista* asks him.

"A medium black coffee."

"*Grande*."

"Medium," Boone says, gesturing to the cups. "The size between large and small."

"That's a *grande*."

"There we go."

"Your name?" the *barista* asks.

"My name?"

"So we can call you?"

"For what?"

"For when your *Americano grande* is ready."

"I thought you'd just pour it."

"We have to make it," the *barista* says. "Then we'll call you."

"Boone."

"Boo?"

"Just use Daniels."

"Thank you, Daniel."

He stands there waiting for his coffee. She looks at him kind of funny, then points to her right and says, "It will be over there. They'll call you."

"Got it."

He slides over to his left and waits behind another couple of caffeine communicants who receive their *cappuccinos* and *macchiatos* with appropriate reverence, then hears, "Daniel."

"Thanks."

"You got it."

He takes his coffee into the main part of the place and sits down in an over-stuffed easy chair. About the only one there without a laptop computer, he feels like an old man going to the newspaper rack and taking a physical copy of the *New York Times*, printed on something called paper, and goes back to his chair. People look up, slightly annoyed, when he turns the page and makes a rustling noise.

To Boone's mild surprise, the New York paper is actually pretty good, even though it lacks a surf report. He knows there are waves on the East Coast because he's read about it in *Surfer*, but apparently even the local rag doesn't think it's important enough to write about. Anyway, he kind of gets into the reports on world news and books and the time passes pretty quickly until Jill Thompson takes her break.

That is, she goes out back to smoke.

Boone slots the paper on a rack apparently put there for that purpose and walks around out back. She's pretty – slight build, short, spiky blonde hair, a little stud in her right nostril. Soft blue eyes, thin lips sucking on a thin brown cigarette.

"Jill?"

"Yeah?" She points at her name tag. Like she really doesn't feel like being hit on by another customer.

"My name is Boone Daniels. I'm a private investigator."

Her lips get thinner. "I already told the police what I saw."

"See," Boone says, "I think the police may have told *you* what you saw."

My gut tells me, he thinks. My gut says that there's something sketchy about this whole thing. Because it's too neat, too wrapped-up, and neither murder nor life is that clean.

"What do you mean?" Jill asks.

"You know what I mean."

He sees the slight expression of self-doubt. "I don't think I should be talking to you."

"You seem like a nice person," Boone says. "Let me tell you what I think happened. You were walking down the street, probably a little less than completely sober yourself. You saw or heard something, then you saw a man on the ground. You tried to help him but it was too late and you felt terrible about that. It's an awful feeling, someone dying on you. You feel helpless, even guilty that there was nothing you could do."

Boone looks in her eyes and sees the hurt still there. "You wait quite a while for the detectives to get there. While you're waiting, you play the thing over and over again in your mind, wondering what you could have done. Then the detective comes to question you and he suggests what you can do now – you can help put the guy who did it behind bars. You can get justice for the victim."

Jill's eyes tear up.

"See," Boone continues, "the police had already picked up a suspect. They already thought they had their guy. So the detective who interviewed you asked his questions in a certain way, didn't he? 'Did you see this guy?' 'He was sort of thin, wiry, had a shaved head?' 'He was wearing a hoodie with the sleeves cut off?' 'He walked up and hit the victim?'

"And by the time you get to the precinct, Jill, you believe you saw Corey Blasingame throw that punch. You really think so, because that's what you want to think, because a man died in your arms and you couldn't help him then, but now you could. You could walk in and identify his killer."

She's tough, though, and tries to brave it out. "I saw that piece of shit kill him."

"Yeah?"

"Yeah."

He likes her, even though he doesn't believe her. This girl wants to do the right thing. He says, "Show me."

"What?"

"Show me how Corey hit him."

"I don't have to do that."

"Absolutely you don't," Boone says.

She glares at him, takes a drag of the cigarette and snuffs it out. Then she takes a stance, cocks her right hand, and throws a pretty wicked cross.

With her feet planted solidly on the ground.

Boone takes a card out his shirt pocket and offers it to her.

"Kelly Kuhio's death was a tragedy," he says. "A stupid, ugly, unforgivable thing that never should have happened. The only thing worse would be answering it with another stupid tragedy. Kelly would tell you the same thing."

She takes the card.

68

Boone goes into Pacific Surf where Hang Twelve is trying to cope with a busload of German tourists who are bustling around the shop, trying on anything that isn't chained down, asking him a zillion questions about wet suits, fins and boogie-board hydro-dynamics.

"It doesn't matter!" Hang is pleading. "There's no surf anyway! No waves! Get it? No waves! *Nein* waves! Waves *verboten*! Can't ride the Maxi-Pads. Boone, what's German for 'flat?' "

"Vlat," Boone says, making it up.

"Vlat," Hang is saying as Boone goes up the stairs to his office.

Cheerful looks up from the old-fashioned adding machine, one of those dinosaurs that still has the little loop of paper coming out of it, usually stained with red ink. The old man is actually smiling. Boone has to look twice to make sure it's not a heart attack or something, but it sure looks like a smile.

Awkward, however, because Cheerful is way out of practice. Boone's a little afraid he might pull a face muscle. Maybe he should warm up first, do some cheek stretches or something.

"This is a big day in your life," Cheerful says.

"They're bringing *Baywatch* back?" Boone asks.

Cheerful holds up a slip of adding-machine paper. "Boone Daniels Investigation Services is in the black."

"Wow."

"I thought you'd be happier," Cheerful says.

"The surf sucks," Boone says, "and I have some bad news for a friend."

"The Nichols thing?"

Boone nods.

"She cheating on him?"

"Yup."

"But that's not all that's bugging you," Cheerful says.

"Nope."

"Spill."

"I think I got it wrong on the Blasingame case."

He walks Cheerful through it, then the old man says, "So maybe you were a little blinded by your anger. It happens. But you have to remember that the kid confessed in the station, he confessed to you, and you still have another objective eyewitness."

George Poptanich, Boone thinks.

The cab driver.

There's something about him skitting around the edge of Boone's consciousness. He yells down to Hang, "Yo! Is the *Kriegsmarine* still down there?"

"The what?!"

"Never mind," Boone says. "You got a minute to do some work for me?"

"Dude."

"Run a criminal check on a George Poptanich?" He spells the name and hears Hang slapping the keyboard even before he finishes.

The phone rings.

It's Dan Nichols. *"Anything?"*

"Dan, maybe it would be better to talk about this in person," Boone says.

Pause. *"That's not good, huh?"*

"No," Boone says.

"I'll be back this afternoon," Dan says. *"We'll talk."*

"Sounds good."

As good as that conversation can be, which is, like, *not*.

Hang comes bounding up the stairs. "Dude."

"Dude."

"Yabba-dabba-doo!" He hands Boone a print-out.

Georgie has a sheet.

69

George Poptanich lives in PB.

Boone rings the doorbell of his little bungalow. They must have built a thousand of these places on the PB flats back during WWII to house the aircraft workers. They mostly look alike – the living rooms are in the front, the kitchens in back on the left, two bedrooms in back on the other side. They have small front yards and a small rectangular yard in the back.

George looks like the doorbell woke him up – his gray hair is tousled, he's wearing a wife-beater, plaid Bermuda shorts, and sandals. He's in his mid-fifties – fifty-three, Boone knows from his sheet – heavy, sloped shoulders and a pot belly.

He looks real happy to see Boone.

"Georgie Pop," Boone says. "Do you remember me?"

"No. Should I?"

"About five years ago," Boone says. "I arrested you."

"That don't exactly make you special," Georgie says, that tired look in his eyes that comes from a life of being hassled by cops.

"You going to invite me in," Boone asks, "or should we do this on the street in front of the neighbors?"

Georgie lets him in.

The place is a dump, which is too bad, Boone thinks, because the other people in this neighborhood took pride in keeping their places up. Georgie points to an old sofa, disappears into the kitchen and comes out with a bottle of beer.

One bottle of beer.

He plops down in an easy chair and asks, "Who are you and what do you want? You don't look like a cop."

"I used to be."

"We all used to be something."

"True that," Boone says. He identifies himself and tells Poptanich that he's working on the Corey Blasingame case. "I read your statement."

"So?"

Georgie's sheet is for B&E. He did two stretches, walked on two other charges. It's not uncommon for burglars to moonlight as cab drivers. What they really love are bookings to the airport. Chat with the fare: 'So where are you off to?' 'Long trip?' 'Give me a call when you get back – I'll pick you up.' Sometimes the fare comes back to a house that has been denuded of stereo equipment, televisions, cash and jewelry. Or they pick up a drunk from a bar – drunks are notoriously chatty, they'll tell you anything. Who they live with, where they work, what their hours are, all the great stuff they own . . .

"So," Boone says, "what do you want to bet that you don't have a cab license?"

Because a two-time felon isn't going to get one. The idea is to put them in the hole for a while, let them out, and then make sure they can't make honest livings.

"I gotta make a living," Georgie says. "So I moonlight for a buddy. He keeps his cab busy, I make a buck. You wanna bust my balls for that, go ahead."

No, Boone thinks, but I'll bet Steve Harrington did. I'll bet he took one look at Poptanich, one look at the photo on the taxi license, and knew that he had a live one. A major fine at least, and the buddy loses his card and his living.

Harrington has a memory like a beefed-up Mac. He probably made Poptanich right away. And maybe . . .

"Steve Harrington looking at you for a job?"

"Harrington don't do B&E."

"No shit," Boone says. "But he talks to the guys who do. Maybe he mentions to them that he found Georgie Pop out on the prowl again so they might want to come around and ask you your whereabouts on certain nights, or take a look at cab bookings, unless . . ."

"You fuckin' guys are all the same," Georgie says. "Always twisting the arm."

"Yeah, boo-hoo, Georgie."

"So what do you want from me?"

"I dunno, the truth?"

"Already told it."

There's that look in his eye that Boone's seen a thousand times from skells. That little glint of feral cunning that they just can't help from flashing when they think they've done something cute.

Boone laughs. "I get it. I had it backwards. You were *already* in the line of fire and you saw a chance to do yourself some good. So you write down the license number because you know you can trade up on a murder beef."

Georgie shrugs.

"Except Harrington drives a tough bargain," Boone says, "especially since he knows you're looking at three-time-loser status. You want a solid from him, you're going to have to give him more than a license plate. You're going to have to wrap up Corey Blasingame for him."

"I heard the kid confessed anyway."

"So what's the harm, right?"

Georgie shrugs again. Like, yeah, what's the harm? A man's dead, the kid's going down for it anyway, someone might as well get some good out of it.

Someone like Georgie Poptanich.

Boone is faced with the hard truth that most career criminals are sociopaths. It's no use appealing to their consciences because they don't have them. You can only appeal to their self-interest.

Or their fear.

"Let me tell you what the harm is," Boone says. He pauses for a little dramatic effect, and then says, "Red Eddie."

Georgie goes white. "What's Eddie got to do with it?"

"Eddie is going to clip the guy who killed his *calabash* cousin," Boone says. "And if he finds out that he didn't because certain people like you deliberately misled him . . . well, that would be the harm, Georgie. And he will find out."

"Because you'll tell him."

"Bingo."

"You son-of-a-bitch cocksucker!"

Boone gets up from the chair. "Just tell the truth, Georgie, all I'm asking. If you saw what you said you saw, fair enough. But if you didn't . . . I'd think about that, if I were you."

"Harrington *told* me the kid confessed."

"He didn't lie," Boone says. "The question is, did you?"

"Fuck you."

Yeah, Boone thinks.

Fuck me.

70

The jailer brings Corey into the room.

The kid looks thin in the baggy orange jumpsuit, but the fact is that he probably has been losing weight on the awful jail food. He plops down in the chair across from Boone and stares down at the metal table.

"Hi," Boone says. "I have a few more questions for you."

"I have nothing to say."

Great, Boone thinks. We're back to that.

"First question," Boone says. "You didn't throw that punch, did you?"

Corey looks up.

71

"Yes, I did."

"I don't think so," Boone says.

"I did," Corey insists. "I told the cops I did."

It's the first time Boone sees any animation, any emotion, from him. He says, "Yeah, I know – you killed him because you thought . . . blah-blah. I know what you told the cops, what you wrote. I think it's all fucking bullshit."

"That girl saw me do it," Corey says hotly. "The cab driver saw me do it."

"No, they didn't."

Corey drops his head again. "I don't have to talk to you."

"I think," Boone says, "you claimed that punch before you knew that it killed Kelly, and now you're trapped in that lie, and it's attached to your balls. I think that you want to be a man so badly, you'd fuck up the rest of your life for it."

"What are you, some kind of shrink?"

"Maybe," Boone says, "you were just so high you don't remember, so you swallowed whatever bullshit the cops fed you. Or maybe Trevor Bodin told you that you threw that punch, and you liked what that did for you so much you held onto it, I don't know. But I'm telling you right now, Corey – knowing a little bit about you, looking at you, there's no fucking way you killed that kid. You're not Superman."

Corey shifts his stare from the table to the floor. He shuffles his feet a little bit, then mumbles. "Too late anyway."

"What is?"

"I confessed."

Yeah, it's a problem, Boone thinks. A real close-out wave, but I've paddled through close-outs before. This one is a matter of making my good friend Johnny Banzai eat that confession piece by piece on the stand.

Humiliating him.

Calling into doubt his ethics and credibility.

Shredding his career.

For this punk kid who *wants* to claim the murder.

And who Red Eddie will probably kill anyway.

"What if it isn't?" Boone asks. "Too late."

Corey thinks about this for a few seconds, then shakes his head. Then he gets to his feet and calls for the guard to take him out. He turns in the doorway and says to Boone, "I killed him. I killed him, alright?"

Alright, Boone thinks.

Alright, maybe we should just let it go down that way. Sometimes a wave just breaks bad and you get caught in the bad break and that's the way it is.

So leave it be.

Make everybody happy.

72

Okay, not Dan Nichols.

He catches Boone outside Pacific Surf and they go for a walk along the boardwalk.

"Tell," Dan says.

Boone tells him everything he observed with Donna and Phil Schering. Her driving straight to his house, spending the night, kissing him goodbye in the morning.

"So, you're sure about this?"

"Dan, what do you need?" Boone asks. "She spent the night. No offense, but I don't think they were baking cookies and watching chick flicks."

"Yeah, I know."

"I'm sorry. I really am."

"I wanted to be wrong," Dan says.

"I know you did. I wish it broke that way."

"Fuck," Dan says. "I mean, you think you're happy, right? You think *she's* happy. You give her everything . . ."

Boone doesn't say anything because there's nothing to say. He could go the whole *women are greedy bitches, nothing's ever enough* route, but it's too easy a line. All he can do is walk with the guy and let him blow off steam.

Matrimonial sucks.

"I don't know what to do now," Dan says.

"Don't do anything in a hurry," Boone says. "Take your time, think about it. A lot of marriages make it through this kind of thing . . ."

Great, Boone thinks, now I'm Dr. Phil.

"I don't know," Dan says.

"You don't need to know right now," Boone says. "Chill for a spell, lay out, don't act from anger."

'Don't act from anger?' I sound like K2.

Which is another difficult conversation on the horizon.

73

"Take the deal," Bill Blasingame says.

Boone sits at the table in the main conference room at Burke, Spitz and Culver. The door is shut, but the picture windows provide a view of the harbor where an aircraft carrier is currently docked, dominating the scene, looking impossibly large and lethal.

"Don't we want to ask Corey about it?" Petra asks. "It's his life."

Boone sees Alan shoot her a don't-speak-unless-spoken-to look but she stares right back at him. Good for you, Pete, Boone thinks.

"Corey will do what I tell him to do," Bill says. "I think we've seen what happens when Corey takes charge of his own life."

Keep your mouth shut, Boone thinks. Sit there, look at the nice harbor and keep your stupid surf-bum mouth shut. Let this go the way everyone wants it to go.

"Still," Alan says, "I'm obligated to consult Corey. He's the defendant. He has to explicitly agree to any deal."

"He'll agree," Bill says. "It's best for him, best for everyone, to get this over with."

And off the front pages of the papers, Boone thinks. With real-estate prices already crashing, it's tough enough, right, Bill? And how many players want to tee off with the murderer's father? Sweep it under the rug, sweep Corey into the hole.

"He'll have to serve at least ten years," Alan warns, "on the sixteen-to-twenty."

Bill says, "He'll be twenty-nine when he gets out, still a young man with his whole life in front of him.

Right, Boone thinks. A weak unit like Corey in the State Pen for ten years? What's he going to be like when he gets out . . . if he gets out . . . if someone doesn't pick up Red Eddie's contract first? And suppose he does make it through, what kind of life is he going to have as a convicted killer?

But let it slide, Boone thinks. Keep your pie-hole closed. Bill's right – it'd be better for everyone. Corey gets his cheap manhood, Johnny gets to keep his rep and his career, you get to go back to the Dawn Patrol.

Forgotten and forgiven.

Over.

Out.

Alan stands up. "Okay, I guess that's it," he says. "I'll go talk to Corey and we'll get this done. Given the facts, I really don't think it's a bad result."

"Turn it down," Boone says.

74

"What?!"

Bill's all red in the face.

"Turn it down," Boone repeats. "He didn't do it, he didn't throw that punch."

"How do you know?" Bill asks. "How do you know he didn't throw it?"

"I asked him," Boone says. "I saw it in his eyes."

"You saw it in his *eyes*?!"

"I think we'll need a little more than that for a jury, Boone," Alan says softly, although Boone notices a little flush on his cheeks.

Boone makes his case: The testimony of Corey's three Rockpile buddies is suspect from the get-go; Jill Thompson couldn't demonstrate the distinctive punch that she allegedly saw; George Poptanich's statement came fresh from Steve Harrington's EZ Bake Oven. Add to that the fact that Corey is a crappy martial artist without the strength, mass or co-ordination to throw that punch. And Boone saw it in his eyes.

"He told you he did it," Alan says.

A confused kid, Boone tells them. Drunk and high. Scared. In the tank with sharks who smell blood and know how to go in for the quick kill. It happens more than you'd think.

"If Corey didn't do it," Alan says, "who did?"

"My money would be on Trevor Bodin," Boone says. "He has the size, the athleticism and the temperament. He's another one of Mike Boyd's disciples. If we do a little digging, I'll bet we'll find that he's also mixed up in this white supremacist stuff."

"Then why does it get laid on Corey?" Petra asks.

"Because – no offense, Mr. Blasingame – he's the weakest unit," Boone says. He lays out a possible scenario for them. The Rockpile Crew confronted Kelly. Let's say it was Bodin who threw the lethal punch. They got away in the car. Corey was so blasted that maybe he even passed out. The other three made an agreement to throw Corey under the bus. It sounds just like Bodin, and the Knowles brothers would have been too afraid to have gone against him. When the cops pulled them over, they pointed the finger at Corey.

So when Harrington interviewed Thompson and Poptanich, he already had Corey down as the killer and communicated that knowledge to the witnesses, fairly forcefully in Georgie Pop's case. John Kodani had all those statements when he went in to work Corey. He confronted him with them and got him to confess.

Corey probably doesn't even know what did or didn't happen. But he does know that he's a hero in the idiot racist set. Add to that the probability that the Aryan Brotherhood boys in the lock-up tell him to be a stand-up guy. He still thinks his dad's money's going to get him off, but the longer he sits in the hold, the harder it is to stick with the 'I've got nothing to say' mantra. One more tap, Boone tells them, and that wall cracks.

Corey's confession is the foundation of Mary Lou's case. Once it cracks, the whole thing could come sliding down.

"But can we crack it?" Alan asks. "How good a witness will Kodani be?"

"Very good," Boone admits.

"There you go," Bill says.

"You can make him look bad," says Petra.

"Don't stroke my ego, I don't like it."

"Sorry," Petra says. "But you could also throw reasonable doubt on the case against Corey by casting suspicion onto Bodin."

"As much as the judge will let me."

"You'd get it in," Petra says.

"Again—"

"Sorry, but if either Thompson or Poptanich recants—"

Bill leans across the table and stares at Boone. "Can you truthfully say that you are one hundred per cent certain that my son didn't kill that man?"

"No."

"Then this is crazy," Bill says. "We have a good deal, we should take it. I'll make that clear to Corey and you, Alan, will do the same. Let's not forget here who's paying your bill."

"I know who's paying my bill," Alan says, "but I will put the options in front of Corey, accurately and equally, and then he can decide. And Bill, if that means you stop paying my bill, fuck you and I'll do it *pro bono*."

When Shakespeare wrote we should kill all the lawyers, Boone thought, he didn't know Alan Burke.

75

"Boone," Alan says after Bill slams the door behind him, "you're giving me whiplash. One second you want the kid strung up, then you jump the case from manslaughter to a hate crime, now you're saying he's innocent."

"I didn't say he was innocent," Boone argues. "I said he didn't throw the punch. If he was part of a gang that assaulted Kelly, he should do time. But he doesn't deserve the death penalty."

"Who said anything about the death penalty?"

"Red Eddie."

"Oh?"

Boone tells them about Eddie's threats against Corey.

Alan takes this in, then says, "I will present young Mr. Blasingame with his options in an even-handed way. And if he chooses to go to trial, God help the both of you! But you, Petra, can help both him and yourself by lining up the best causal biomechanics expert in the universe, and you, Boone, had better go back to digging like a dog on crank. It wouldn't hurt if you found Nazi paraphernalia and KKK robes in Mr. Bodin's closet, for instance."

"Right away, Alan."

"Got it."

"Thank you," Alan says.

He leaves the room.

"He certainly seemed in a hurry," Petra says.

"He's pissed off."

"Not Alan," she says. "Blasingame. He seemed in a terrible hurry to accept a deal that would put his son in prison for ten years."

"He doesn't want to roll the dice on a jury," Boone says. "I get it."

He does and he doesn't. If I were in his place, Boone thinks, and someone told me that there was a good chance my kid didn't do it, I'd leap at that hook. Blasingame couldn't push it away fast or hard enough.

And on the topic of confessions . . .

"Look," Boone says, "about the other day—"

"I was completely out of line," Petra says. "I assumed an intimacy that simply doesn't exist and—"

"I was an immature, hyper-sensitive jerk."

"Yes, alright."

"So you're busy tonight?" Boone asks.

"I have that thing," Petra says. "But I should be free and clear by . . . tennish."

"Tennish."

"Around ten."

"No, I knew what you meant," Boone says. "I just . . . yeah. Ten . . . around tennish . . . should I call you?"

"Or just come over."

"To your place," Boone says.

"Well, yes," says Petra. "Not to the restaurant, I meant."

"No."

To her place, Boone thinks.

To close the deal?

76

"Either there is a deal in place or there is not," Cruz Iglesias snaps.

The cartel boss is in an ugly mood, cooped up in the modest house in Point Loma, on the run from Ortega's assassination squads and the American police. He's bored, edgy and irritated that his business is not being conducted the way that he expects.

"It just might take a little longer than . . ."

"No, we're done."

"I really think . . ."

"I don't care what you think anymore," Iglesias says. "We've tried your way. We'll do it my way now."

Iglesias snaps the phone shut. He doesn't want to hear any more excuses or any further pleas for more time. He's given these *gueros* ample opportunity to work out their problems, he's been more than generous. He has tried to act like a gentleman, and expected that they would do the same, but it just hasn't happened.

At the end of the day it's about money. Gentlemen or no gentlemen, these *yanqui* buffoons are messing with his money, a lot of it, and that is something that he simply cannot tolerate.

He yells for Santiago to come out of the kitchen. His lieutenant is whipping up his deservedly famous *albondigas*, and it smells wonderful, but Iglesias has more urgent business than homemade cuisine.

"You look ridiculous in that apron," he says when Santiago comes in.

"This is a new shirt," Santiago protests. "Three hundred dollars, Fashion Valley. I don't want to get it . . ."

"That thing we talked about," Iglesias says. "It's time to make it happen."

"Los Niños Locos?"

"No," Iglesias says. He doesn't want a gruesome execution to send a message, he just wants to get it done. "Give it to that man . . ."

"Jones?"

"Yes." After all, they're paying his daily fee in addition to expenses, they might as well get some work out of him. "Just tell him to keep it simple."

The man Jones has a tendency to get flamboyant.

But he does dress like a gentleman.

77

Dan Nichols feels a strange sense of relief.

It's odd, the calm that comes over you from just knowing.

Knowing what's happened, and knowing what you have to do now.

78

Boone tries to work out what to wear.

To a booty call.

Well, not exactly a booty call. You can't really call it a booty call when you've been putting it off for over three months and you have genuine, if confused, feelings for the person. And is it really a booty call? Boone wonders. Or just the continuation of a kiss? Or a conversation about the 'relationship' and where it's going? What do you wear to a conversation about a relationship? Usually body armor, although he hasn't owned a Kevlar vest since he left the police force.

Not that Boone has a lot from which to choose. He has a winter wedding and funeral suit and a summer wedding and funeral suit, one white and one blue dress shirt, and a single pair of khaki 'trousers' that Cheerful ordered for him from the Land's End catalogue and have never been off the hanger. Otherwise, his wardrobe, such as it is, consists of five pairs of jeans in various states of disrepair, T-shirts, long-sleeve pullovers from O'Neill, Ripcurl, Hobie and Pacific Surf, and a staggering collection of boardshorts. Hooded sweaties make up a large part of his wardrobe, but it's too hot for them anyway. As for footwear, he owns the black dress shoes that go with the wedding and funeral suits, three pairs of Reef sandals, and one pair of black Skecher tennis shoes, because the Skecher store is just a block from his office.

Boone decides on the white dress shirt and his least faded jeans and then sits there in mental paralysis over the choice of the tennis or dress shoes. Petra might infer from the tennis shoes that he's taking this too casually – which would piss her off and which he's certainly not – but the dress shoes might signal her that he expects that they're going to have sex, which he sort of does, but isn't really all that sure, and he doesn't want her to think that he's taking that for granted, but on the other hand he does want her to think that . . .

Sandals are probably out of the question, Boone thinks.

He's mulling this over when his cell phone rings.

It's Sunny.

79

Phil Schering opens the door.

And says, "Oh, shit."

No shit, oh shit.

80

Johnny Banzai gets the call.

Truth be told, he's almost relieved that it's not another gang slaying, more fall-out from the Baja Cartel reorganization. On the other hand, the murder of a middle-aged white guy in a nice Del Mar neighborhood brings a lot more heat than some dead teenage Mexican gang bangers in Barrio Logan.

He pulls up to 1457 Cuchara Drive.

The neighbors are out on the sidewalk, looking concerned. They have those 'this kind of thing just doesn't happen here' looks on their faces. Yeah, but it does, Johnny thinks as he gets out of the car. Gang bangers lop each other's heads off, surfers beat another surfer to death, men get shot in 'nice' neighborhoods, and it all happens here.

"This is going to be a major pain in the ass," Harrington mutters as they walk up to the house.

Yes, it is, Johnny thinks. The recent killing spree in San Diego is bad for a town that depends on tourism. The City Council rags on the Mayor, the Mayor passes it down to Mary Lou, Mary Lou hands it off to the Chief, and then the shit flows downhill to me. Why, he wonders with rare self-pity, do people have to kill each other on *my* shift?

The victim lies on his back in the living room.

One entry wound square in the forehead from close range.

Harrington's examining the front door. He looks down where Johnny's squatting beside the body and shakes his head. They've worked together for a while now so Johnny knows what he means – there are no marks on the door around the lock.

The victim opened the door for the shooter.

"Stop 'N' Pop," Harrington says.

Sure looks like it, Johnny speculates from the placement of the body. The victim opened the door, the shooter pulled the gun walked the victim back a few steps, then shot him. Not your hot August night sudden flaring of violence, but a premeditated, 'cold-blooded' murder.

Still, it doesn't have the look or feel of a professional hit. Contract killers don't normally do the job at the target's home, but more often at their place of business or on the way to or from it. And they usually take the body, dump it somewhere, or destroy it.

So what you have here is probably an amateur, most likely a first-time killer angry enough to make a decision and then act on it.

The Crime Scene boys arrive so Johnny gets out of their way and goes out on the street to help Harrington with the canvas. There are certainly plenty of neighbors standing around to interview, but most of them have nothing useful to offer.

Some heard the shot and called 911.

No one saw anybody come to the door or leave.

One older guy, from across the street one door down, says that he's noticed a 'weird' vehicle hanging around the neighborhood lately.

An old Dodge van.

Wary of burglars, he even jotted down the license plate.

Johnny recognizes it.

Boonemobile II.

Aka the Deuce.

81

"Sunny! Hey!"

"Hey yourself! S'up?"

"Nuch," Boone says. "Where are you?"

"Bondi Beach, Oz," she says. "Thought I'd give you a shout."

It's great to hear her voice. "What time is it there?"

"I dunno," Sunny says. "Listen, did I catch you at a bad time? You going out or something?"

Women are amazing, Boone thinks. Talk about high-tech spy stuff – she's on the other side of the freaking world and can smell over the phone that I have a date. He'd tell her no, but they have a long-standing deal never to lie to each other, so he doesn't say anything.

"You do, don't you?" she asks. "At . . . ten at night? Boone, baby, that's a booty call."

"I don't know."

"Who is it?" she asks. "Is it the British betty? What's her name?"

Boone knows that Sunny knows her name. But he says, "Petra."

"You charmingly call her 'Pete,' " Sunny laughs. "I'll bet she loves that. Makes her feel all girlie and stuff. It's her, right?"

"Look, this must be costing you a—"

"It is, isn't it?" Sunny says. "It's cool, my Boone. She's a good chick. I like her. Kinda tightly wound, but . . . Okay, what are you going to wear?"

"Jesus, Sunny."

"I know you, Boone," she says. "I don't want you to blow this. So what are you wearing?"

This is both sick and wrong, Boone thinks. But he says, "White dress shirt, jeans."

"Tennis or dress shoes?"

"I dunno. What do you think?"

"*Where* are you meeting her?" Sunny asks. "Bar or club?"

"Her place," Boone.

Sunny laughs. "If you are meeting a woman at ten p.m. at her place, it doesn't matter what you're wearing." Her implication being that, whatever you're wearing, you won't be wearing it for long. Then she adds, "By the way, congratulations."

"Tennis or dress?" Boone insists.

"Black or brown?"

"Black."

"Dress."

"Thanks."

"De nada."

"The shirt. In or out?"

"Jeans?"

"Yeah."

"Is this the, uhhh, first . . ."

"Yes."

"Aww, he's shy," she says. "In."

"Thanks."

"No worries."

They talk about her surf tour, how well it's going, how she's getting in shape for the big wave season in Hawaii, Pipeline and all that. Boone fills her in a little on what he's been up to, skipping the Blasingame case, and tells her that the gang is doing well.

"Tell them I miss them," Sunny says. "I miss you, too, Boone."

"Yeah, me too."

"Love you, B."

"Love you, Sunny."

Boone hangs up. Five seconds later the phone rings and Sunny asks, “Do you have any cologne or after-shave?”

“No.”

“Good.”

She hangs up.

Feeling weirder than weird – he will never understand women and neither will anyone else, even Dave – Boone goes to his closet, takes out the black dress shoes, then finds a pair of white gym socks and wipes the dust off them. This leads him to the unhappy quandary of what color socks to wear, and again, he has limited choices.

White or white.

He decides on white and then checks his watch – 9:25. Almost time to leave if he wants to be at Petra’s apartment downtown by ten. But the date isn’t for ten, it’s for ‘tennish’ so he sits and debates with himself about when to actually arrive. Ten? Five-past? Ten-past? What’s ‘ish,’ anyway? And is ‘ish’ different in England than in the US?

He heads out the door at 9:40, to get there around 10:10.

When he opens his door, Johnny Banzai is standing there.

Which is good.

“Johnny,” says Boone. “Look, I’m glad you came by. I’m—”

Then he sees Sergeant Steve Harrington walk up behind Johnny.

Which is bad.

82

They hate each other.

Boone and Harrington.

No, they don’t hate each other, they fucking *hate* each other. Go to your thesaurus, look up every synonym for hatred, add them together, multiply them by ten, and you still don’t come up to the level of malice that these two guys hold for each other.

"Good evening, piece of shit," Harrington says.

"Johnny, what the hell?" Boone says, ignoring him and turning to Johnny Banzai. If they're here to bust my chops about Blasingame, Boone thinks, nine-something on a Friday night is way out of bounds.

"Can we come in?" Johnny says, looking grim. "Have a talk?"

"Now?"

"Yeah, 'now,' asshole," Harrington says. "We're here 'now,' aren't we? We want to come inside 'now.' We want to talk 'now.' "

Boone shines him on. He looks only at Johnny and asks, "You have a warrant?"

Johnny shakes his head.

"Then, 'no,' " Boone says. "Anyway, I'm going out."

"Got a date?" Harrington asks.

"As a matter of fact."

"Where you taking her?" Harrington asks, checking his watch. "Lego-Land's closed for the night."

The last time Boone punched Harrington he ended up in jail, so he keeps his hands down. It's what Harrington wants, anyway, an excuse to roust him. Johnny steps in and says, "Boone, it's better you come to the house so we can record the interview."

"What are you talking about?" Boone asks.

"You want to tell us where you were tonight?" Harrington asks.

"Here."

"You got anyone who can verify that?"

"No."

Harrington looks at Johnny and smiles. Steve Harrington has a face like razor-wire and the smile doesn't help. "The neighbors noticed a suspicious vehicle lurking around the neighborhood and one of them jotted down the plate. Guess who the vehicle belongs to, surf bum? I almost thought it was my birthday."

"What neighbors? What are you yapping about?"

"Do you know a Philip Schering?" Johnny asks Boone.

Boone doesn't say anything.

"S'what I thought," Harrington says. "Can we just take him in now?"

"Take me in for what?"

"You're a person of interest," Johnny says.

"In what?"

"In Schering's murder," says Johnny.

This is macking messed up, Boone thinks.

Dan Nichols used me to bird dog his wife's lover.

Then he killed him.

83

The interview room is small.

It was designed that way so the suspect feels tight, trapped, suffocated – the detective can get right in his face without necessarily being accused of deliberately trying to intimidate him, which, of course, he is.

Puke-green walls, a metal table, two chairs. A video camera bolted into a corner on the ceiling. The classic one-way mirror on one wall, which everybody and his dog knows from television is a window onto the facing observation room.

Johnny sits across the table from Boone. Harrington leans against the wall in the corner, his entire purpose apparently to keep a smirk trained on Boone like a gun.

"You were at the scene," Johnny says. "The neighbor wrote down your plate and described your van accurately."

"Not tonight."

"So do you want to tell me what you were doing there?" Johnny asks. "On *any* night?"

"No."

Not now, anyway, Boone thinks.

He's not going to cover for Dan Nichols indefinitely. If he did this, screw him, but he wants a chance to talk to him first. He looks up as Harrington gives out a disgusted little snort of laughter – like, of course he doesn't want to tell you what he was doing there, he was there killing Philip Schering.

"If it's professional," Johnny says, "I'll get it anyway. I'll pull your phone records, e-mail, billing records. I'll bring in Ben Carruthers if I have to."

"Leave Cheerful out of it," Boone says.

"Up to you, not me," Johnny says. "If you were there on a job related to your activities as a private investigator, just tell me. I understand that you might think you have a client's interests to protect, but I'm sure you're also aware that it's not a privileged relationship."

Boone nods. There's no 'PI-client' privilege, as there is between a lawyer and his client. The only time the attorney-client privilege would apply to Boone is when he's working directly for a law firm, in which case his communications to the lawyer would be protected. But in this case he was working directly for Dan Nichols, so he's . . . fucked.

"What was your relationship to Philip Schering?" Johnny asks.

"There was no relationship."

"He wasn't your client," Johnny says.

"No."

Johnny asks, "Was he the target of an investigation?"

Fucking Johnny Banzai, Boone thinks. Don't ever play chess with him. Or poker. At least not for money. He interrogates like he surfs – finds a clean, direct line down the wave and never gets off it. My man can read a wave – and he can read me.

"I think I'm done here," Boone says.

"Please," Harrington breaks in. He steps up to the table, sets his hands on it, and leans across at Boone. "Please keep stonewalling, Daniels. I'm begging you. Keep it up. We've put you at the scene, and we'll put you in the house. We have 'opportunity' and we'll have 'means.' That just leaves 'motive,' and we'll get that, too. So you just keep your mouth shut all the way through the trial and really piss the jury off. *Please.*"

Just like Harrington, Boone thinks, to way overplay his hand. He might have 'opportunity' – he can put Boone at Schering's place. But 'means,' no. He doesn't have a murder weapon, and even if he does, he can't possibly tie it to me. As for 'motive,' there is no motive, so he can kiss that goodbye, too. No, Harrington really jumped the gun, and Boone can read annoyance even on Johnny B's poker face. They're nowhere near having me as a suspect, and they know it.

Johnny plays the best card he has.

"If you're covering for somebody," he says, "you're impeding a homicide investigation, which will at least get your PI card pulled even if it doesn't result in a felony charge. Keep it up, Boone, and you're edging toward 'accessory.' "

"Accessory, my ass," Harrington says.

"If you have enough to hold me," Boone replies, "hold me. In that case, I want a lawyer. If not, I'm leaving now."

Johnny shakes his head.

"Late," Boone says.

84

Boone walks out into the street, then over to the US Grant Hotel to get a taxi.

Boone gets in, leans his head back, and takes a deep breath. It was one thing to eavesdrop and tape people having sex, that was bad enough, but to set someone up for murder? Completely different deal, something he never thought he'd be involved with. It makes him sad and furious at the same time.

It only takes him a few minutes to drive to Nichols' house that time of night. Boone pays the driver, gets out, and rings the doorbell. Dan comes to the door looking sleepy in a T-shirt and sweatpants.

"Boone, it's a little—"

Boone grabs him by the front of the shirt and pushes him inside, kicking the door shut behind him. He backs Dan into the huge living room, pushes him over the arm of a sofa and asks, "Where were you tonight, Dan?"

"What the—"

"Where *were* you tonight, Dan?"

"Here," Dan says. "I was here."

"Can you prove that?"

"Let me up, Boone."

Boone releases his grip. Dan sits up on the couch, rubs his chest, and looks at Boone with a little anger in his eyes. "Who the fuck do you think you are?"

"I'm the guy the cops just rousted," Boone says, "because they think I had something to do with killing Phil Schering."

"What?"

Boone watches him closely, looking for legitimate surprise in his eyes. But he can't tell whether Dan is shocked that Schering is dead or that Boone knows about it. But the guy is shook, no question about that.

"Somebody murdered Schering," Boone says. "Was it you?"

"No!"

"You used me to find your wife's lover so you could kill him," Boone says.

"I wouldn't do that, Boone."

"Which?"

"Neither."

Right, Boone thinks. On the same day that he confirms Schering is Donna's lover, Schering gets murdered and Dan had nothing to do with it?

"Bullshit," Boone says. "I called you, you went off your nut, you drove over there and you shot him. Where's the gun, Dan? What did you do with it?"

"Nothing!" Dan yells. "I've never even owned a fucking gun!"

"Get some shoes on."

"What for?"

"I'm taking you in," Boone says. "You can tell the *cops* you've never even owned a fucking gun."

Dan tells Boone his story.

After Boone called him, Dan went out and had a couple of drinks. Brooded and thought things over. Then he went home. Donna was there. He confronted her with what he knew. She admitted everything.

She met Schering at a lunch she was having with her friend, Renee, at Jake's On the Beach in Del Mar. He was sitting at another table with some business associates and they noticed each other. At first it was just a look, then she returned his smile. Before the lunch was over it seemed as if they were always stealing glances. As she was waiting for the valet to bring her car, he came up to her and gave her his card.

She never intended to call him, she never did. She just stuck the card into her purse and forgot about it. Until Dan canceled their third 'date' in a row. They were supposed to go out to dinner. She had dressed special and gone out and bought a new perfume. She was sitting in the house, ready and waiting for him to come home, but then he called and said he was tied up in a meeting he couldn't get out of.

Donna was pissed. They had planned this evening because they had already talked about not having enough time together lately. It had been weeks and weeks since they'd been out just on their own – not some business-social or charity event – a couple of weeks since they'd made love, and lately even that hadn't been so good. It was like they were becoming disconnected, so they had each set aside this evening to . . . well . . . reconnect.

So she was hurt and angry, and she remembered the guy at the restaurant, and she dug into her purse and found his card. She was only going to meet him for a drink . . . okay, maybe dinner. Meet him and apologize and tell him exactly what she was doing. She even sort of hoped he wouldn't answer when she called, but he did.

Of course he remembered her, he said, who wouldn't remember

her? And, yes, he had plans for that evening but he would cheerfully cancel them. They met at Jake's because, obviously, they both knew where it was and he was a regular and could always get a table. He lived just up the hill. Phil made a point of saying that and, of course, she knew why.

She didn't intend to go to bed with him. Just dinner, drinks and maybe a few laughs with a man who wanted to give her some attention. But one thing led to another, and she ended up at his place, in his bed, in his arms.

Donna felt horrible the next morning. Horrible. But then Dan didn't even ask her where she'd been. He was on the phone all morning, sealing some deal, and when Phil called she answered. They'd been seeing each other ever since, for the past few months.

She told Dan the whole story.

They fought, they yelled, they talked, for the first real time in years. He told her how angry he was, how hurt. She told him she was sorry for what she had done, but he spent so much time with his work, his business, she felt bored and lonely.

He apologized for neglecting her, and asked her if she loved Schering. She said she didn't, she loved *him*.

"We cried together, Boone," Dan says. "We held each other and cried."

Yeah, that's beautiful, Boone thinks.

"It was beautiful, Boone."

There you go.

Dan left only one thing out of the story, Boone thinks. Between drinking and brooding and coming home, he swung by Schering's house and blew him up. The only question is, where did a citizen like Dan Nichols get a gun, and what did he do with it?

Don't know, don't want to know. It's Johnny B's problem.

"Get your shoes, Dan."

"What's going on?"

The woman's voice comes from the stairs.

85

Boone looks up to see Donna Nichols, in a blue nightgown, her hair tousled, her eyes dull with sleep. Even so, she's intensely beautiful, and Boone feels like a creepy voyeur, seeing her in person after he's listened in on her having sex.

"Honey," Dan says. "This is Boone Daniels. The private investigator I was telling you about."

"Oh." She walks across the living room and extends her hand. "I'm Donna Nichols. I don't think we've met. Formally, that is. Apparently, you know a lot more about me than I know about you."

"I'm not here on a social call, Mrs. Nichols."

"Please – Donna."

"Donna."

"Why *are* you here, Mr. Daniels?"

Boone looks at Dan, like, *you* do it, dude. Anyway, he wants to watch her reaction. Dan stands up and walks to her. Holds her hands and gently says, "Honey, Phil Schering was murdered tonight."

"Oh, my God."

She puts her face into his shoulder. When she lifts it up again, Boone sees that her cheeks are wet with tears. "Oh, my God. Dan, tell me you didn't . . ."

"No."

"The police are going to want to talk to both of you," Boone says.

Dan turns and looks at him. "Did you—"

"No," Boone says. "I kept you out of it, but it's only a matter of time. They'll subpoena my records, get your name, Dan, and they'll come talk to you. It would really be better if you got ahead of the curve and talked to them first. Do you have a good lawyer?"

"Oh, my God, Dan." Donna sits down on the couch. She looks shaky.

"Sure," Dan says, "but only for business. I have squads of corporate lawyers, but . . . for something like this. . . I mean, I've never even had a DUI."

Boone digs in his wallet, comes out with Alan Burke's card, and hands it to Dan. Why not? he thinks. Dan can afford his hourly and this is right in Burke's wheelhouse. Alan apparently doesn't mind defending guilty clients, and this is just his kind of case. Are you kidding? A celebrity billionaire on trial for murder? Beautiful, socialite wife? Sordid love affair? The media will eat it up, and Alan does like to see himself on TV.

Nichols looks at the card and says, "Oh, sure, I've heard of him. I mean, I know him from social events and . . . he gets out on the Gentlemen's Hour sometimes, doesn't he?"

"Yeah," Boone says. "We can call him now, he'll meet us at the precinct."

"At this time of night?"

"He owes me a solid."

Dan looks at the card and asks, "Can't this wait until morning, Boone? I mean, they probably won't get your records until then and, you know, with a little sleep . . ."

"Trust me, Dan, neither of you are going to sleep," Boone says.

And I don't trust you, Dan, Boone thinks. With your money, you could be on a private jet tonight, then on a beach in Croatia somewhere, buying your way out of an extradition. The cops will claim that I tipped you off so you could run, and then I am looking at an accessory rap. Even if I beat it, I lose my card.

So, no thanks.

"Dan," says Donna, "let's get this over with. The sooner we face up to this the better."

"But you'll—"

"I'll take ownership of what I've done," Donna says.

That's nice, Boone thinks. Somewhere in Donna Nichols' busy days, she's found time to DVR *Oprah*. 'Take ownership . . .'

Dan hands him back the card. "Could you call him, please? We'll get dressed."

"Sure," Boone says.

Donna nods. "I think that would be good."

They go back upstairs to get dressed.

86

Petra is *très* pissed off.

No man has ever stood her up before, ever, certainly never under these circumstances. Now she's sitting on her sofa dressed in a lovely blue satin negligee ready to give herself to a man who has apparently, in the California vernacular, 'spaced her off.'

It's humiliating.

Completely, totally, utterly humiliating.

She feels like the second lead in a bad romance novel, or a modern, sexually loose Jane Austen character, vainly waiting for a man to come and take her away from her mundane existence. Pity the apartment lacks a harpsichord. A hovering mother, a dotty father, an earnest sister in whom to confide her heartbreak.

Heartbreak? she thinks.

Over *Boone Daniels*?

Please.

She is furious, though. I invited him here, she thinks, for what was obviously going to be our first sexual encounter, and the man *forgets*, doesn't even have the common courtesy to ring and apologize? A flaw in character or a failure of nerve? she wonders. Either way it doesn't bode well for a relationship. Do you really want a man who's afraid to have sex with you?

Or, she thinks, does he just not fancy you? Not in 'that way,' as they say. Fair enough, but what about that kiss? That took you totally unprepared. He certainly seemed to fancy you then, didn't he?

A bottle of good red wine sits open on the coffee table, flanked by two long-stemmed glasses. She picks up one, pours herself a long drink, then changes her mind and goes to her liquor cabinet for some whisky. God, she thinks, first I make myself into a slut – albeit rejected – for him, now he's turning me into an alcoholic.

She takes her Scotch neat, sits down and turns on the television.

Damn Boone Daniels.

87

Johnny Banzai is not exactly crazy about Boone either when he walks into the precinct house with Dan and Donna Nichols in tow.

Not to mention Alan Burke.

It's sort of like giving with one hand and taking back with the other. Here, Johnny my bro, here's a suspect for you. And, oh, here's someone who won't let the suspect talk to you.

Thanks, Boone, *por nada*.

"Are these the clients you were protecting?" Johnny asks Boone.

"Pretty much, yeah."

"Swell."

"Indeed."

"Don't say anything more, Boone," Alan Burke says. He doesn't look his usual dapper self, in a pair of jeans and an old sweatshirt that he pulled on when he got Dan Nichols' call. His hair is tousled and he's unshaved.

"Are you representing Mr. Daniels?" Johnny asks him.

"No."

"Then don't instruct him," Johnny says.

"Am I out of here?" Boone asks.

"For now," Johnny answers.

"I never thought I'd hear myself say this," Harrington says, "but, Daniels, don't leave town."

Boone nods and walks out the door. Technically, they could still jam him up on obstruction charges but it won't go far seeing as how he brought Dan Nichols in to be interviewed. So he's free and clear. As for Dan and Donna, their problems are their problems. You got Dan a good lawyer, you're out of this.

Forget about it.

Forget . . .

Oh, shit.

Petra.

He gets on his phone.

It rings and rings and rings.

Clearly, she has caller ID.

88

Yeah, but he has one of the all-time great excuses, right?

'Honey, I was arrested on suspicion of murder.'

Has to be good for a hall pass, doesn't it? Has to be, Boone thinks, if I can get her to listen to it.

He debates with himself what to do next. Part of him says to let it slide until morning – he looks at his watch, okay, *later* in the morning – and let her cool down. Another part of him says he should drive over there right now and ring her doorbell.

What to do, what to do?

He calls Dave.

Who is, after all, the Love God.

"Oh, this better be *prime*," Dave says when he answers the phone.

"You busy?"

"I was getting busy," Dave answers. "What is it, you forgot the lyrics to *The Jetsons*? For the last time, it's 'His boy, Elroy. Jane, his wife.'"

Boone explains his situation, without specific reference to the Nichols. Dave just lets it slide that Boone was picked up on suspicion of homicide and that Johnny B was the picker-upper. He gets right to the problem at hand. "Go over there."

"Really?"

"*Hell*, yes," Dave says. "Dude, do you have any idea how pissed she is? Chick sets up a booty call and you don't get your booty over there?"

"Uhh, murder charge?"

"Doesn't matter to a woman," Dave says.

"Has to. Come on."

"Hold on," Dave says. Boone hears him talking softly to someone, then Dave gets back on and says, "No. Doesn't matter."

"Shit."

"Shit indeed," Dave says. "Listen to your Uncle Dave, who has himself been in this same doleful situation . . . I just said that to make him feel like a little less of an idiot, babe . . . What you do is, you go over there, ring her bell, and beg forgiveness over the intercom. She won't let you in, but she'll feel better that you made the effort."

"Then flowers . . . candy?"

"A little cliché," Dave says, "and knowing the woman in question, she'd be happier with a DVD of your ritual disembowelment. No, this goes to Defcon 4 – you might be looking at jewelry."

"Yikes."

"You fucked up, bro."

"I was detained for—"

"Again . . ."

". . . doesn't matter?"

"The beginning of wisdom, Boone."

Dave hangs up.

Boone drives over to Petra's building.

89

Nichols admits everything.

Except the murder.

Johnny Banzai sits and listens as Dan Nichols, closely monitored by Alan Burke, admits that his wife was having an affair with Phil Schering, admits that he hired Boone Daniels to uncover the infidelity, even admits that he shared part of the responsibility for his wife's adultery.

"I work so many hours," he says.

Johnny isn't buying it. Hell, he and his wife each have full-time jobs, and kids, and they don't play around on each other. You make time for what's important to you. It's the simplest way of learning what really matters to a person – just look at how he spends his time.

Besides, Johnny doesn't give a stale tortilla *why* Donna Nichols cheated, only *that* Donna Nichols cheated, and he wouldn't care about that either except that the guy she cheated with turned up dead. He wouldn't really care about that, either, except he turned up dead on Johnny's shift.

So now Johnny has two high-profile cases – the Kelly Kuhio murder, with all its tourist and surf culture implications, and now a billionaire socialite adultery/murder that will have the media coming in its collective shorts and the Chief buzzing around his head like an annoying but powerful fly.

And his ex-buddy Boone has managed to turn up in both cases.

"Where were you last night?" Johnny asks.

Burke nods to his client, allowing him to answer.

"Home with my wife," Nichols says, with a trace of self-righteousness that annoys Johnny. "We talked. About everything. Our thoughts, our feelings . . ."

"That's fine," Burke says.

Beautiful, Johnny thinks. The cuckolded husband's alibi is his cheating wife. You have to love the symmetry. "And did you confront her with your knowledge of her infidelity?"

"I wouldn't call it exactly a confrontation," Nichols says. "I just told her that I knew she was having an affair and asked her—"

"That's enough," says Burke.

"What did you ask her?" Johnny says.

Burke shoots his client an I-told-you-so look.

"How could she do that to me," Nichols says.

"And what did she say?"

"Don't answer that," Burke snaps. "Irrelevant."

"This isn't a courtroom, counselor," Johnny says.

"But it could end up in one, couldn't it?" Burke asks. "Her response to him regarding her motivation is immaterial. What you want to know—"

"Don't tell me what I want to know."

"What you *should* want to know—"

"Ditto," Johnny says, realizing that he's falling into Burke's game. The lawyer is distracting him, breaking up his rhythm, turning his interrogation of the witness into a skirmish between cop and lawyer. He leans across the table to focus on Nichols. "How long did the conversation last?"

"I don't know," Nichols says. "I didn't look at my watch. Until we went to bed. Eleven o'clock?"

"Are you asking me or telling me?"

"He told you he didn't know, Detective," Burke says, "and I'm not going to allow him to speculate."

Of course you're not, Johnny thinks, because it's a critical issue.

The 911 call from the neighbor had come in at 8:17; the black-and-white responding to a 'shot-fired' called at 8:24. The responding officers kicked in the door and found Schering, in a bathrobe, already dead on his living-room floor.

Johnny got the call at 8:31; logged on to the scene at 8:47. He interviewed the neighbor and had Boone's van at the scene, but the neighbor couldn't recall if it left before or after he heard the shot, just that this van had been 'lurking' around the neighborhood recently.

The ME hasn't established time of death yet, and it would be nice to pin Nichols down to a time after which his wife's testimony won't help him. Personally, Johnny thinks Nichols shot his wife's lover *before* this heart-to-heart talk ever happened, if it happened at all, but it's possible that he slipped out afterward, and wants to leave that door open.

Burke isn't going to let him narrow it down, so Johnny has to press the offensive a little harder. "Is this possible, Mr. Nichols? Let me run this scenario for you, and you tell me if it's possible. Daniels calls you, tells you he has definitive proof that your wife is sleeping with Schering. You go over to confront your wife's lover. I get it, I totally get how you'd be angry. . . hell, furious . . . the guy has been doing your wife . . ."

"That's enough, Detective," Burke says.

". . . and you get into an argument. I mean, who wouldn't? I know I would, Harrington here certainly would . . ."

Harrington nods sympathetically. "Hell, yes."

". . . any man who calls himself a man would, and you argue and things get out of hand and maybe you pull the gun. Just to threaten him, scare him, I don't know, mess with his head. Maybe he reaches for it and it goes off."

"Don't respond to this fiction," Burke says.

Which pisses Johnny off, because he's using the 'fiction' to lure Nichols into putting himself at the scene. Once he does that, Johnny will use the gunshot forensics to jerk the 'self-defense' rug out from under him.

He keeps at it.

"You're freaked out," Johnny says. "You never meant for anything like this to happen. You panic and drive away. You drive straight home and when you get there you're so shook up you can't hide it from your wife. She asks you what's going on and you tell her. Just like you said, you tell her you know about the affair. You tell her about the terrible thing that happened when you went to Schering's house. She says it's going to be alright, you'll both say you were home the whole evening, working on saving your marriage. Is that possible, Dan? Is it just possible it happened that way?"

He looks closely into Nichols' eyes to see if he can discern the flicker of recognition.

"No," Nichols says. "It didn't happen that way."

"How *did* it happen?" Johnny asks. Softly. Empathetically. Like a therapist instead of a cop.

"I don't know," Nichols says. "I wasn't there. I was home with my wife."

Burke looks at Johnny and smiles.

90

"Boone who?"

It's a little scratchy over the cheap intercom speaker, but clear enough.

"I'm sorr—"

The intercom clicks off.

He hits the button again.

"I'm about to call the police."

"Funny thing," Boone says. "Speaking of the police—"

Dead.

He hits it again.

"Go away, Boone."

"I was picked up on suspicion of murder."

A pause, then she buzzes him in.

91

The wife's story matches.

Almost too well.

Her husband came home, she doesn't remember the time, and was clearly upset. He told her he knew about her affair with Philip Schering. She admitted it. They sat and talked for hours, but she doesn't recall what time it was when they went to bed. The next thing she remembers is hearing a discussion and going downstairs to find Mr. Daniels there. That's when she learned about Phil's death.

"This is awkward, Mrs. Nichols," says Johnny, "but were you seeing Mr. Schering?"

"You already know that I was."

"I'm asking you."

"Yes," she says. "I was."

"And did you have sexual relations?"

"We did."

"When was the last time you saw him?"

"Last night," Donna says. "No, I guess it was the night before. I don't know, what time is it now?"

"It's early in the morning," Johnny answers. "Where were you last night?"

"At home."

"Alone?"

"No, my husband was with me."

Johnny asks, "When did he get home?"

"Early," Donna says. "Seven, maybe?"

Nice, Johnny thinks. She has him home by 7, the shot isn't heard until shortly before 8:17. While someone is pumping a bullet into Schering's chest, the Nicholses are at home doing Dr. Phil's Relationship Rescue. Funny how life works.

"You said your husband confronted you with the evidence of your infidelity," Johnny says.

"I didn't say that," Donna snaps. "I said that he told me he knew. There was no 'confrontation.' "

"Did you ask him how he knew?"

"Yes."

"What did he tell you?"

"That he had hired a private investigator who had me under surveillance," Donna said. "Who had tracked me to Philip's house."

"Did you deny it?"

"There didn't seem to be a point," she said. "Obviously, he knew."

"So your husband had Schering's address."

"I suppose so, yes," Donna says. "But my husband isn't a violent man. He couldn't have done this."

Yeah, but he did, thinks Johnny, who's not a big believer in coincidence. On the same day a man finds out his wife is fucking around, the fucker gets killed. That's motive, not coincidence. And now the wife, guilty as hell about the affair, colludes with the alibi.

"Do you know what an accessory is?" he asks.

"Don't patronize me, Detective Kodani."

"Your husband is not a practiced criminal," Johnny says. "Sooner or later – I'm betting sooner – he's going to confess to this killing. When he does – not 'if,' Mrs. Nichols, 'when' – your lying about this alibi will make you an accessory. You can write each other from your respective cells."

"Should I retain an attorney?"

"That's entirely your choice, Mrs. Nichols," Johnny says. "Shall we break off this interview so that you can make a phone call?"

"Not just now, thank you."

"You're welcome."

She'll fucking kill on the witness stand, Johnny thinks. Cool, beautiful, sympathetic. Contrite about her affair. Burke will lead her through her testimony and the jury will believe her. Then women will want to be her and the men will want to do her. She'll pull her husband right out of the shit.

It's good to be Dan Nichols, he thinks.

If you can afford to marry a Donna and hire an Alan Burke, you get away with murder.

92

Petra, an uncharacteristically ratty, terry-cloth robe wrapped around her, is standing in the open doorway of her condo when Boone gets off the elevator.

"Murder?"

"I didn't do it."

She ushers him into her apartment. It's nice, one of those old warehouse conversions that came along with downtown urban renewal when the new ballpark was built. It's the new, hip, trendy area – which suits her, Boone thinks, because she's hip and trendy.

Except for that robe. Maybe I got the booty call thing wrong.

"Murder?"

Boone looks out the window. "Hey, you have a view of the park."

"I hate baseball. Murder?"

"Right. Cricket is probably more your—"

"I hate sport. Murder?"

"Hot dogs taste better at the ballpark," Boone says. "You have to put a lot of mustard—"

"Boone!"

She'd fallen asleep on the sofa, waking up only when he buzzed her number. When she heard 'murder' she let him in and then ran into the bathroom for the robe to disguise the sexy negligee. The right side of her hair is all mushed from the sofa, but the make-up that she had put on so carefully is intact.

He sits down on the sofa, she sits beside him, and he tells her about the whole Nichols thing. There's no confidentiality issue because as an associate at Burke, Spitz and Culver, she's also Dan Nichols' lawyer.

"So the police put you at the murder scene," she says.

"It wasn't a murder scene when I was there," Boone says. "It was more of a porno scene."

"Right," she says. "And you were never in the house."

"Right," Boone says. "Look, I'm really sorry. I thought of calling you when they first picked me up, but calling a lawyer would have looked bad, and then I got all torqued and then going to see Nichols . . ."

"I understand."

"You do?"

"Of course," she says. "Look, can I get you something? Coffee, a drink, something to eat?"

Dave the Love God is a false god, Boone thinks. A mere wooden idol, a Wizard of Oz. He knows nothing of women. At least, not this woman. "You know, I am a little hungry."

"Right."

She gets up and walks into the kitchen. He follows and looks over her shoulder as she opens the refrigerator, which is virtually empty.

"Let me see," she says, "I have yogurt . . . and . . . some more yogurt . . . and . . . Oh! Cottage cheese."

"How about just some coffee?" he asks.

"Good, right," she says. "Except that I don't have any, actually. I have tea. A very nice herbal tea I get at this special shop down on Island. Imported from Sichuan."

Drinking herbal tea is like sucking dew off a lawn, Boone thinks. Which he has done, after a Mai Tai Tuesday at The Sundowner, but it doesn't sound so good when you're not horribly drunk and desperately dehydrated. Besides, herbal tea is one small step removed from yoga, leg-warmers and spa treatments. Boone says, "Maybe just some water."

She gets him a glass of water and then says, "Crackers! I have crackers."

Petra had hosted a little pre-dinner wine and *hors d'oeuvres* thing a few weeks ago and had some crackers left over. She searches the cabinets and finds the box, then looks for an appropriate plate on which to set them.

"The box is just fine," Boone says.

"Really?"

"Sure."

She hands him the box and sits down on the counter. He stands beside her and they eat crackers and drink water as Petra starts breaking down Boone's situation. Boone was at the house but not in the house, but at what point in time? And has the Medical Examiner established a time of death? Obviously, that would be key.

Boone's listening but not *really* listening. He's not all that concerned with being a 'person of interest' in the Schering murder anymore, as he's been willingly bumped off that platform by Dan Nichols. He looks at the little crumbs that cling to the corner of Petra's mouth, which, with her tousled hair, give her a very attractive air of imperfection. And the robe has slipped a little on her left shoulder, revealing the spaghetti thin strap of something blue and silky and . . .

How do you kiss someone with crackers in your mouth? Is it 'how,' he wonders, or 'should,' as he casually takes a drink of water and tries to swish it around his mouth nonchalantly to clear it of the cracker yuck.

Petra's going on about . . . something . . . when Boone leans over, brushes a crumb off her lips with his finger, and then kisses her. If she's surprised, she's pleasantly surprised, because her lips do that fluttery, butterfly-wing thing and she brings her hands to the back of his neck and pulls him in a little closer.

Her lips are freaking incredible, Boone thinks, so soft and surprisingly full, and the kiss lasts a long time before he breaks it off to kiss her neck, where her skin is so white and delicate it seems almost fragile, and he likes it when she turns her head a little to open more of her neck to him.

Her perfume is unreal. Sunny was never a perfume girl. She was more of a sun-salt-and-air-are-nature's-perfume girl (which certainly worked, salt and sun being aphrodisiacal to him) but Petra is definitely a girlie-girl, with the negligee and the perfume, and he finds he likes it, really *likes* it as he works his way down her neck and then back up and then gently nudges a strand of her black hair out of the way and kisses her ear.

"If you do that," she says, "I can't stop you."

"I don't want you to stop me," he says.

"Good. Neither do I."

So he keeps kissing her ear, and she starts to kiss his neck, and Boone feels like he's happily drowning in her perfume and she doesn't stop him when he reaches down and pulls the knot on her thick terry-cloth robe, and it slides open and he feels the smooth satin and her flat stomach and starts kissing his way down her chest when he hears her say, "Kitchen-counter sex."

"Uhhhh . . ."

"I don't want our first time to be kitchen-counter sex," she says, kissing along his collarbone. "Can we go to the bedroom, please?"

Oh, yeah, Boone thinks, we can go to the bedroom, please. We can totally, absolutely go to the bedroom please. He lifts her off the counter. If he'd tried to lift Sunny in anything but a fireman's carry, he'd be on the way to the E-Room, but Petra is petite, light as air, as he swings her off the counter and walks toward the living room.

"Are you going to carry me into the bedroom?" she asks, laughing.

"Uhhh . . . yeah."

"It's a tad Neanderthal, isn't it?"

He pushes the bedroom door open with his foot. "You don't approve."

"No, I approve."

He sets her on the bed and lies on top of her. Her negligee rides up on her thighs and he feels her against him. So does she, because she murmurs, "Hmmm, nice," and reaches down and fumbles with his belt. He lifts his hips to give her an easier time and she gets his belt loose and then pushes his jeans over his hips and they're kissing again, she darting just the tip of her tongue in and out of his mouth as she feels for him, finds him and . . .

The phone rings.

"Ignore it," he says.

"I am."

They both try to ignore it as it jangles three times, her crisp British tone on the answering machine announces that she can't come to the phone just now but please leave a message, and Alan Burke's voice comes over the speaker: "*Petra! I'm at the police station. Get your ass out of bed and get it down here.* Now."

She tries to go back to kissing Boone, but it doesn't work and she sighs and says, "I have to go."

"No, you don't," he says, but it's a feeble try at best because they both know the moment is over. Some waves are like that – they build and build and you think you're in for the ride of your life and then they just . . . flatten.

'Wavus interruptus' is what Dave calls it.

"Yes, I do," she says.

"Yes, you do," Boone says, rolling off her.

"I am so sorry."

"Nothing to be sorry about."

"For me as well, I mean."

She gets up, slides open a closet door and starts taking down clothes. Then she disappears into the bathroom, to emerge a few minutes later the Petra Hall that he's familiar with – cool, professional, efficient.

"Do I look," she asks, "as if I just got up from a bed of passion?"

"Only to me," Boone says.

"That was the perfect response," she says. "Listen, could I have . . . what do they call it in baseball games?"

"A rain check."

"One of those?"

"Absolutely."

"It was very nice," she says. "What we did, as far as we got."

"It was great."

He gets up and walks to her car in the subterranean garage. A quick kiss on the lips and she drives off to join the campaign to save Dan Nichols.

I hate matrimonial, Boone thinks.

93

"I like Daniels for it," Harrington says after they've kicked the Nicholses loose with the usual warnings about staying available.

Well, there's a shocker, Johnny thinks. Harrington would like Boone for both Kennedy assassinations, the Lindbergh kidnapping, and the crucifixion of Jesus Christ.

"His AA test came up negative," Johnny says.

"So what?" Harrington says. "They come up with a lot of false negatives."

Harrington walks him through it. First, they have Daniels at the scene, while they don't have Nichols. Second, rich people rarely, if ever, do their own killing – they hire other people to do it for them. Third, Daniels is just the kind of low-life, perpetually broke surf bum who would do something like this.

"He bird dogs Schering for Nichols," Harrington says. "Then Nichols says there's money in it for him if he finishes the job. Shit, it was probably Daniels who made the offer. As a former cop – which I'm ashamed to say – Daniels knows how to use a gun. But he's such a dumb asshole he drives his own vehicle to the scene. What we do now is squeeze his balls into a confession then get the DA to offer him a reduced sentence to roll on Nichols. Job done, we go get breakfast, home to bed."

But Johnny doesn't like Boone for it. Pissed off as he is about Boone jumping into the Corey Blasingame wave, he doesn't buy Boone as a killer. Neither should Harrington. Hell, their whole beef started when Boone refused to help him tune up a child kidnapping suspect and the guy walked.

Boone is a lot of things – overly laid-back, irresponsible, immature – but a killer for hire? Granted, Boone always needs money, but this? No way, no how. He's probably kicking himself for his unintentional role in Schering's death.

No, if Nichols hired this out, he found someone other than Boone Daniels.

Okay, so what was Boone doing at Schering's? Obviously, he tracked Donna Nichols there. But the neighbor's statement had Boone parked right outside the house and that's bad technique. Boone wouldn't go in that close unless . . .

. . . he needed proximity.

For what?

Johnny waits for Harrington to sign off the shift, then gets his own car and drives to Crystal Pier.

94

"Where is it?" Johnny asks him.

"Where's what?" Boone asks.

He's half-asleep, having just woken up from a very short night in time to go out on the Dawn Patrol, when the doorbell rings and it's Johnny Banzai. He leaves the door open and walks into the kitchen to put the water on for a badly needed pot of coffee.

Johnny follows him in.

"The tape," Johnny says. "You have video or audio of Donna Nichols getting horizontal with the late Phil Schering."

"I do?" Boone asks. He pours Kona beans into the grinder and the whir drowns out Johnny's response, making him say it again.

"You parked out in front of Schering's house with a camera or a sound-capturing device and you made a tape," Johnny repeats. "I'm hoping it's a video so it has a time track on it."

"Sorry," Boone says. "Audio only."

"Goddamnit," Johnny says. "Anyway, I want it."

"Why?" Boone asks. "The boys at the house want a dirty chuckle?"

"You know why."

Boone leans against the counter and looks out the window at the ocean, barely lit by the lamps on the pier. "There's no surf again today. August blows. Look, you don't need the tape. You already know that she had sex with Schering. If you don't already know, I'll tell you – she had sex with Schering. There's nothing on that tape that's going to help you, J."

"They might have said something."

"They didn't."

"Nichols hear the tape?"

Boone shakes his head.

"You were there from when to when?"

"I wasn't there last night, J," Boone says.

"The neighbor says differently."

Boone shrugs. "The neighbor is mixed up. I was there the night *before*. All night. I left in the morning when Schering went to work."

"Did you go back to Schering's last night?"

"One last time," Boone says. "I was here until you and Fuckwad came by to visit."

The pot whistles. Boone pours a little water on the coffee, waits a few seconds, then pours the rest. He doesn't wait the recommended four minutes, but presses the plunger down and pours himself a cup.

Johnny asks, "Do you have anyone that can put you here before we came?"

Boone shakes his head, then says, "I talked with Sunny on the phone."

"Landline or cell?"

"Since when do I have a landline?"

"Yeah, I forgot," Johnny said. So Boone's phone would show a record of him talking to Sunny, but wouldn't say where he was. "What time did you talk to her?"

"I dunno. After nine."

So it doesn't help him anyway, Johnny thinks."I want that tape."

"Get a warrant," Boone says, "and you can have it."

"I will."

There's a slight lightening of the sky outside the window, the faintest touch of gold on the water.

"Sun's coming up, Johnny."

It's time for the Dawn Patrol.

"You take it," Boone says. "I'm dead tired, and, anyway, I don't go to parties where I'm not welcome."

"You're making your own choices, Boone," Johnny says. "I don't feel like I even know you anymore. Worse, I don't think you know yourself."

"Knock off the pop-pyscho-babble and go surf," Boone says.

Words to live by.

95

Boone catches the Gentlemen's Hour instead.

To his considerable surprise, Dan is out on the line.

"I didn't do it," Dan says when he paddles up next to Boone.

"Yeah, you said that."

"You don't believe me," Dan says.

"It doesn't matter what I believe," Boone says. "Look, I hooked you up with a good lawyer, I'm out of this."

Yeah, except I'm not, he thinks. At the very least, I'll be giving a statement and probably testifying about my role in the whole thing. And one cop wants to make it out that you paid me to kill your wife's lover.

And a man is dead.

For no good reason.

A lot of that going around in San Diego these days.

96

Okay, maybe Dan didn't do it, Boone thinks, as he paddles in.

Maybe Dan is telling the truth, and he had nothing to do with Schering's murder. There's always that possibility. But if Dan didn't, who did?

If Schering was fucking around with another's guy wife, maybe Donna Nichols wasn't the only one. Maybe there was another jealous husband or boyfriend out there. Maybe Schering was a real player, and someone else wanted him off the field.

Doubtful, but possible.

So worth checking out.

For several reasons, Boone thinks as he walks to the office. If Dan goes down, he takes me with him. I'm the guy that fingered the guy he killed. Worse, the suspicion that I did it, or helped, will always be out there. And fuck the suspicion – if I had anything to do with Schering's murder, *I* want to know about it.

Hang is behind the counter.

"Hey, Hang."

Hang doesn't answer.

"Hey, Hang. S'up?"

Hang just looks at him. With a baleful expression.

"What?" Boone asks. "They stop making Pop Tarts or something?"

"I heard something," Hang says.

Boone has a sneaking suspicion what he heard, but he asks, "What?"

"That you're helping get Corey Blasingame off."

"I'm working on his defense team, yes."

Hang looks dumbstruck. Shakes his head like he just bottom-smacked and is trying to clear the wuzzies out. Looks at Boone like Boone just shot his puppy and ate it in front of him.

"You have something to say," Boone says, "say it."

"You're wrong."

No Surfbonics now. Just plain English.

"What do you know about it?" Boone says, more sharply than he'd intended. "Seriously Hang, the fuck you know about anything?"

Hang turns away.

"Cool with me," Boone says. He feels a little bad as he goes up the stairs but his anger washes it away. Screw it, Boone thinks, I don't need his hero-worship. It's a drag anyway. I'm not who he thinks I am? Cool. I'm not who he thinks I am.

Maybe I'm not what anyone thinks I am. Or what they want me to be.

Cheerful is hunched over the adding machine as usual. He doesn't look up but waves his hand and says, "Up bright and early, I see."

"I was up most of the night," Boone says. He walks through the office and gets into the shower. He comes out, wraps a towel around his waist and tells Cheerful all about the events of the night – the cops picking him up, Dan Nichols being a (probably worthy) murder suspect.

"Send his check back," Boone says.

"I already deposited it."

"Then send him a refund," Boone says. "I don't want blood money."

"You're so sure he did it?"

"I have some doubts."

Cheerful gets up from his chair and stands over Boone. No, he *looms* over Boone, and asks, "So are you going to sit there on your ass being pissy and feeling sorry for yourself, or are you going to do something about it?"

"I've already done—"

"Bullshit," Cheerful says. "You're an investigator, right? You think Nichols might not be the real killer? Then go out and *find* the real killer. *Investigate*."

Yup.

Boone throws some clothes on and heads out.

Refund, Cheerful thinks.

No wonder he's always broke.

97

Boone hops into the Deuce and drives up to Del Mar. If Schering picked up one woman at Jake's, maybe he picked up others. Maybe it was his happy hunting ground.

Jake's is an icon.

The restaurant, just across the street from the old Del Mar train station, sits on the beach. Actually *on* the beach. You get one of the front tables at Jake's during high tide, you're practically in the water. You sit there and watch kids play out in front of you, and just to the south there's a tasty little break below the bluffs where the surfers hang. You ever get tired of living in San Diego – the traffic, the prices – you go to Jake's for lunch and you aren't tired of living in San Dog anymore.

You wouldn't live anywhere else.

Boone doesn't go to one of the front tables today, he goes to the bar. Orders himself a beer, sits and checks out the surf, then strikes up a conversation with the bartender. Lauren's a pretty young woman, tanned with sun-bleached hair, who took the job because it keeps her on the beach. It takes two slow beers to get around to the subject of Phil Schering.

"I knew him," she says.

"No kidding?"

"He used to hang out here a lot," she says. "It was sort of his place. His out-of-office office. He did a lot of business lunches here."

"What kind of business was he in?"

"Some kind of engineer?"

With that upward, Southern Californian inflection that turns every sentence into a question. Boone's always thought it was a reaction to the transience of Californian life, like – it is . . . isn't it?

"He hang out at the bar a lot?"

"Sometimes, not a lot," Lauren says. "He wasn't a big drinker and this isn't exactly a pick-up joint."

"No," Boone says, "but was that what he was looking for?"

"Aren't we all?" Lauren asks. "I mean, looking for love?"

"I guess."

Boone lets a good minute pass, looks past the bar out the window where the ankle high surf curls onto the sand. He gets up, leaves the change from a twenty on the bar, and asks, "So, did he find it? Schering, I mean. Love?"

"Not that I noticed," Lauren says. "I mean, he wasn't really the player type. You know what I mean?"

"I do."

"You do," she says, scooping up the change, "because you're not the player type either. I can always tell."

Off Boone's quizzical look she adds, "I gave you a big opening and you didn't walk through it."

"I'm sort of seeing someone."

"Tell her she has a good guy."

Yeah, Boone thinks – I'll let her know.

98

So the Phil Schering as playboy theory looks shot, Boone thinks as he hands his ticket to the valet and waits for the kid to bring the Deuce around. We're probably not looking for a jealous husband – who else would have a capital grudge against a soils engineer?

The valet hops down from the Deuce and looks surprised when Boone hands him three dollar bills. Based on the vehicle, he was probably hoping for a quarter. But the kid looks enthused.

"Are you Boone Daniels?"

"Yeah."

"Dude, you're a legend."

Great, Boone thinks as he gets behind the wheel. I'm a legend. Legends are either dead or old. He pulls out onto the PCH and moves his mind from the topic of being old back to the topic of a motive for killing Phil Schering.

Motives are like colors – there are really very few basic ones, but they have a thousand subtle shades.

Your primary motive colors are crazy, sex and money.

Boone doesn't linger on the first. Crazy is crazy, so there's no line of logic you can pursue. It's too random. Of course, there are shades of crazy: You have your basic, organic, Chuck Manson or Mark Chapman crazy. There's also the 'temporary insanity' crazy, aka 'rage' – a tsunami of anger that washes away normal restraint or inhibition – a person 'sees red' and just goes off. A sub-category of rage is drug- or alcohol-induced rage – the booze, pills, meth, ice, steroids, whatever, make a person commit violence they otherwise would never do.

None of these apply to what facts Boone knows about the Schering murder.

Boone goes on to the next major motive, sex. Murder over sex is closely related to rage as it's usually provoked by jealousy. So if sex was the motive, Dan Nichols is the number-one suspect, as it doesn't appear as if there were other jealous husbands or boyfriends. Yeah, Boone thinks, but for the moment anyway you're looking for someone other than Dan, so move on.

On to money.

People will kill for the jack, sad but true. But what kind of money hassle could Schering have been involved in? A business deal gone south? A bad debt? Did he have a gambling jones he couldn't keep up with? Even if he did, pop culture notwithstanding, bookies and loan sharks rarely kill their deadbeats – it's a guarantee of never getting paid.

No, you usually kill someone so you can *get* your money.

But what kind of a payday could Schering offer? Wasn't anything he had in the house, because Johnny never brought robbery up as a possibility. So if Schering didn't have something, maybe he was in the way of something.

Whose payday could Schering have been cockblocking?

Boone drives to the dead man's office.

No crime tape up. The cops haven't sealed the scene and why should they? Schering wasn't killed here, plus they have a suspect they like and they're fixated on him.

Good, Boone thinks.

For the time being, better.

Still, you can't bust into the office in what they like to call 'broad daylight,' so it will have to wait.

He occupies his mind with something else.

Dumbass Corey Blasingame.

Boone wonders if Alan has had the time to go see him and offer him the deal, and whether Corey will take it or not.

His phone goes off.

It's Jill Thompson.

99

"Will I be in trouble?" she asks.

She sits in the passenger seat next to Boone in Starbucks parking lot and chews on a strand of hair in her mouth. She looks young to Boone. Awfully young.

"For what?" he asks.

"Lying to the police."

"You didn't exactly lie," Boone says. "I think it can be worked out."

She chews the hair more vigorously then breaks it down for him. She didn't see Corey throw that punch. She heard the punch, she thinks, looked around and saw the man on the sidewalk. Some guys were getting in their car and driving away. She cradled the injured man in her arms and called 911.

"I had blood all over me," she says.

Later, when the cop was talking to her, he asked her if she saw Corey hit Kelly – the cop told her that was the man's name – and she said yes. She thought that's what happened, she did, and she just wanted to help Kelly.

"But you'll tell the truth now?" Boone asks. "It might not be necessary, but if it is, you'll tell the police what you told me just now?"

She lowers her head, but she nods.

"Thanks, Jill."

She opens the door. "Do you want something? A *latte* or something? I can get you a free *latte* if you want."

"I'm good."

"Okay."

He waits for her to get inside, then calls Pete and arranges for her and Alan to meet him at the jail.

100

One question a defense attorney will never ask his or her client:

'Did you do it?'

Most clients are going to answer 'no,' but if the client answers 'yes,' the attorney is in a bad jam. He can't violate the attorney-client privilege, but, as an officer of the court, he can't go into a trial and commit or suborn perjury.

In Alan Burke's case, though, he already has an answer in the form of Corey Blasingame's confession. Now he spends long moments pretending to peruse it as Corey shifts around anxiously in his seat.

Boone sits back and watches as Alan reads out loud, " *'We were outside the bar waiting because we were pissed that they threw us out of there earlier. So I saw the guy coming out of the bar and decided to mess him up. I walked up to him and hit him with a Superman Punch. I saw his lights go out before he hit the ground. Other than that, I have nothing to say.'* "

He looks up at Corey and raises an eyebrow.

"What?" Corey asks.

"What, what?" Alan answers back. "You want to say something about this?"

"No."

"Jill Thompson didn't really see you throw the punch," Alan says. "Did you know that?"

"No."

"But the cops told you she did, right?"

"I guess so, yeah."

"We don't think the cab driver saw you throw it, either," Alan says. "But again, the cops told you that he did?"

"I guess."

Alan nods.

Corey quickly says, "But Trev and Billy and Dean all saw me hit him."

"That's what they say."

"They wouldn't lie."

"They wouldn't?" Alan asks. "They're about to close a deal that would put them in jail for eighteen months. That bargain is based on them testifying that you threw the punch that killed Kelly."

"Okay . . ."

"Okay if they're telling the truth," Alan says. "Not so okay if they're lying."

Christ, kid, Boone thinks, he's holding the door wide open. Walk through it, Corey. Take one single step on your own behalf.

Not happening.

Alan Burke didn't get where he is in life by giving up easily. So now he asks, "Is it possible, Corey, is it just possible that in all the chaos . . . remember, you'd been drinking . . . someone else threw that punch and you just got confused when you talked to the police?"

Corey looks at the floor, looks at his shoes, the wall, his hands.

"Is that possible?" Alan asks.

No answer.

"Possible or probable?" Alan asks, almost as if he were cross-examining him on the stand, nudging him toward the edge of the cliff.

Corey won't go.

Instead, he straightens up and announces, "I have nothing to say."

"White supremacist garbage you picked up from Mike Boyd?" Boone asks. "You're just going to take the pipe because you finally found something so shitty even *you* could belong to it?"

Petra warns, "Boone—"

Boone ignores her. "You couldn't deliver a pitch or a pizza, you couldn't really surf and you couldn't really fight, but you could sign on to this filth, and when you finally thought you'd succeeded at something, you killed a 'nigger,' you just hold on to it because that's all you have. A stupid, dirty slogan, 'I have nothing to say.'"

"For God's sake . . ."

"I don't think you threw that punch," Boone says. "I think Trevor did. Except he's too smart to take the weight so he lays it on you. I hope you *do* keep your mouth shut, Corey, I hope they do give you the needle, so maybe you can finally *be* something. Maybe some other racist piece of shit will tattoo your name on his wrist and—"

"I don't know, alright?" Corey yells. "I don't fucking remember what happened, okay!"

He slams his fists on the table, then raises them and starts hitting his own head as he repeats, "I don't fucking know! I don't fucking know! I don't . . ."

The guard rushes in, grabs him in a bear hug, pinning his arms.

"I don't fucking know. . . I don't . . ."

He breaks down into sobs.

Alan turns to the guard.

"Can you get DA Baker down here. *Now*?"

101

Here's the story that Corey tells, on the record.

He started surfing with Trevor and the Knowles brothers. Something to do and it was fun, you know. At first, the older guys there didn't really want them around, but Trevor made their bones by chasing some foreigners away. Then Mike said they should swing by his gym, check it out.

They were all, like, why not? MMA is cool, and it was, so they started spending most of their time at the gym and at Rockpile.

So they, like, hung around the break and the gym, and they helped keep it pure at Rockpile, you know. It was their water, their turf, and they tagged themselves the Rockpile Crew, and they were hanging in the gym one night and Mike asked if they'd like to check out some websites and they said sure, they thought he was talking about porn or something, but then he logged on and it was all about the white race and how they had to fight to preserve it, and Mike asked what they thought and they said they thought it was cool.

Mike said it was like the white race was their tribe and they were warriors, and warriors fight to protect their tribe, and were they willing to fight? And they said they were, and Mike said that's what they were all about, training as warriors to protect their tribe. He told them about Alex Curtis going to prison and what Alex said and the number '5' and Corey went out after a few beers one night and got that ink and Mike said he was becoming a warrior . . .

And a warrior fights for his people.

'San Diego used to be white,' Mike said, *'now it's mud. They're crowding us out. Pretty soon there won't be room for white guys anymore on our street , at our beaches, in our own waves.'*

And Trev said, *'Somebody should do something about it.'*

That night, *that* night, they were cruising that night, club-hopping, looking for trouble. If you wanted to be a fighter, okay, you had to fight, and you just couldn't get enough fights in the gym, not unless you were one of the stars, which Corey wasn't. But a lot of MMA guys had a lot of street fights, beach fights . . . man, they just kicked asses wherever they could find asses to kick.

So they went out.

Corey, Trevor, Billy and Dean.

The Rockpile Crew.

They hit a bunch of bars but couldn't get anything going. Then they rolled up on The Sundowner. By this time they'd had a lot of beers, and downed some speed, so they were torqued, ready to go, and that's when that lifeguard guy came and threw them out.

Like we didn't belong, Corey said. There was all kinds of mud in there – tacos and slants and even niggers – and they wouldn't let white men stay?

That was bullshit.

So they went riding around, high and stoked, adrenaline pumping, and Trev just wouldn't let it go, wouldn't let it go, just kept at it, like: *'We have to take care of this, we can't let them disrespect us like that.*

'It ain't right.'

So they went back and waited outside, across the street, in the alley. They got themselves worked up, started duking with each other, really throwing down, and that's when Trev spotted the nigger coming out of The Sundowner.

And Trev was all, like, 'Let's go show him, let's mess him up a little, fuck with him, sweep the mud off our street.' So they went up to the guy, and they didn't know it was K2 – he had on this hooded poncho and it was dark and there was like blood in the back of Corey's eyes, sloshing around inside his head, boiling hot . . . all he could see was that red. And then there was yelling. The next thing he knew he was sitting in the back of the car, and they were all stoked and shit, and Trev was slapping him on the back, yelling, 'You got him good, man. You took him out! Did you guys see our boy Corey hit him with that Superman?' And then Billy and Dean were saying, like, 'Yeah, we saw you, Corey. We saw you do him.'

And Corey was like . . .

Proud.

Like, proud that he'd defended his turf, you know? Stood up and fought like a warrior for his tribe.

They drove around some more, and then the cops found them. Put them in cuffs and took them down to the station, and that's when Corey confessed.

'I hit him with a Superman Punch.'

102

"Come *on*, Mary Lou!" Alan says in her office.

"I don't," she says. "I don't see how this really changes things. Except that your client has now confessed to a hate crime."

Alan tries to blow right through that little problem."He hasn't confessed to anything. This wipes out his prior so-called confession."

"Not necessarily," she says. "It's a new story he tells now that he's closer to the reality of prison, but the original confession has immediacy."

"I'll put him on the stand," Alan says, "and the jury will believe him."

Yes, they will, she tells herself. Because even you think you believe him. Face it, you like Trevor Bodin for the killing now. It's like Alan's living in her head because he says, "Reduce Corey to manslaughter, rip up Bodin's deal on the basis that he lied to you, and raise the charge on him."

Right, she can hear the defense attorney cross-examine her already. *'You originally charged Corey Blasingame with the killing, didn't you? And you charged him because you were confident that he did it. Just as you say you're confident now that my client did it?'* She looks at Alan and says, "You know I can't do that."

"I know you can't hold this charge on a kid you know is not guilty," Alan says softly. "Isn't in you, Mary Lou."

"Don't push it," she snaps. "Your kid isn't exactly a martyred innocent, is he? He went out looking for a fight, he found one, he went over in a gang and they beat a man to death because the man wasn't white. He has to do some time for that, Alan."

"I agree," Alan says. "But not life-without-parole."

"Let me think about it."

"Hours," Alan says. "Not days."

When he leaves, Mary Lou stands in the window and looks out at downtown San Diego, a city that will not react well to a reduction of the charges against Corey Blasingame. She's already heard the refrains in reference to the other three: 'Rich white kids get slapped on the wrist.' 'If it had been Mexicans or Samoans who did this, they'd be under the jail.' Maybe they're right, she thinks. And maybe Alan's right when he implies that we're making a scapegoat of Corey Blasingame.

But explaining the reduction to the powers will be brutal. She has to tell them something, give them some reason, and the only one she can give is that the confession was bogus, the witness statements hinky, and the investigation botched. Rush to judgment and all that. It's Harrington and Kodani who'll take the fall.

She couldn't give a shit about Harrington, a loose cannon who has it coming, but John Kodani is a good detective, smart, ethical, hard-working. He had a suspect who confessed and he believed the confession, that's all. Now it could cost him an otherwise brilliant career.

It's a shame.

Then again, it's all a shame, isn't it?

Her intercom buzzes.

"Yes?"

"There's a George Poptanich to see you?"

103

Dave the Love God climbs down from the tower.

Another uneventful day of watching tourists not drown. And tourists not drowning, as has been amply explained to him by the Chamber of Commerce, is a very good thing. Earlier in the year, a swimmer had been killed by a great white, which is a very bad thing – obviously for the swimmer but also for business, and also explained to the lifeguards by the Chamber.

Short of getting Robert Shaw and Richard Dreyfuss and heading out in a boat, Dave's not sure what he's supposed to do about shark attacks, although he did actually foil a great white one time by kicking it in the nose. The fact is that the ocean does have sharks – and riptides and big waves – and people are going to be attacked, just as they're going to drown; but statistically the most dangerous activity *by far* that people do in connection with the beach is to drive to it.

Anyway, he decides to grab a beer at The Sundowner. Johnny B might be there on his way to the night shift, High Tide is coming off his day, and Boone . . .

Who knows where Boone might be?

Boone is on some kind of strange, weird trip. Maybe it's Sunny being gone, or his infatuation with the British Betty – who is definitely, unquestionably, *hot* – or maybe it's just that he's tired of surfbumdom, but the Boone he knows is 404.

It's funny because Boone, more than any of them, could always find the through-line of a wave, and would hold that line like he was laser–guided. Now he's flapping around all over the water like some newbie kook, headed for a bad wipeout.

Sure enough, Johnny Banzai and Tide are holding the bar in place, although JB is nursing a Diet Coke.

"S'news?" Dave asks.

"Nuttin'," Tide says.

"S'up, Johnny?"

"S'up, Dave?"

There's nothin' up in August, man – not the surf, not their spirits. Only thing that's up is the temp.

And the tension, because Johnny B looks *worked.*

"Boone is helping Alan Burke fuck me," Johnny explains.

"What?" Dave asks. Boone fucking over a friend? Not poss.

"It's true," Tide says. He tells Dave about Boone joining the Blasingame defense team.

"Back-paddle," Dave says. "You're telling me that Boone is trying to rescue the little bastard who killed K2? No freaking way."

Johnny shrugs, like, it's true, go figure.

"Whoa," Dave says. What the crud is happening to us? he wonders. What's happening to the Dawn Patrol?

It's shrinking for one thing, he thinks.

Sunny is gone.

And, face it, Boone may be on his way out, if he's not *adios* already.

What's that old cliché about (shudder) marriages – 'We just drifted apart?' Are we just drifting apart, Dave wonders, or is it more than that?

Too bummed for a beer, Dave just heads home.

104

Boone goes back to Schering's office at 10 p.m.

Parks the van down the road and walks up to the office complex. The lock is easy – it only takes him a couple of minutes to get in.

He turns the little flashlight on, sticks it in his mouth, and hits Schering's desk. The computer is on 'sleep,' and, to Boone's relief, Schering was still logged on. Boone double-clicks on an icon marked 'Billings' and is soon scrolling through Schering's recent time records. Boone sticks a thumb-drive in the port in back of the hard drive, drags and clicks, then removes the thumb, peeks out the window, and goes out the door.

Thanks to technology, he thinks, rifling records is so much easier than it used to be.

105

Back in his own office, Boone switches on his computer, sticks in the thumb-drive, and peruses Schering's billing records.

He seems to have been working on four cases at the time of his death.

One of them is a multi-million-dollar house on the ridge in Del Mar that appears to have developed a serious 'slab crack' in the foundation, with further cracking in the driveway. The second apparently involves major stucco cracking throughout a strip mall in Solana Beach. The third features a condo complex on the bluffs overlooking the beach. The bluff, as far as Boone can discern, appears to be sliding away.

The fourth is the infamous La Jolla sinkhole.

106

What spices were to the early Portuguese navigators, what gold was to the Spanish conquistadors, tobacco to Virginian plantation owners, opium to Afghani warlords, real estate is to Southern California business people.

Real estate – land, houses, and business parks – is the bottom-line source of wealth on the golden, coastal strip. It's the basis for investment, lending, exchange, retail, money-laundering, you name it.

So when eighteen expensive homes suddenly drop into a hole, the symbolic value is enormous.

The bottom, literally and metaphorically, falls out.

Someone is going to pay.

The question is, who?

Which, Boone thinks, is a very pertinent question when you want to know who had a motive for wanting Phil Schering in the past tense, because the late Phil was a soils engineer, not only a soils engineer but an expert witness soils engineer, not only an expert witness soils engineer but a very effective expert witness soils engineer who could potentially have a big say in determining . . .

. . . who pays.

Phil was billing an insurance company.

107

"Insurance companies don't generally kill people," Cheerful says, "in the physical sense. They hire lawyers who kill people in the financial sense."

At first, Cheerful wasn't, well, cheerful about Boone waking him up late at night, which for him is anything after 9 p.m. So when Boone rang his bell at the unheard of hour of 11:23, Cheerful expected that someone had better be dead. Well, yeah, and someone was, but it was Phil Schering and Cheerful didn't give a damn about that, except for how it might affect Boone.

Cheerful has a very simple philosophy about humanity. He loves his few friends – basically the Dawn Patrol – and would do anything to help them. The rest of the human race exists solely to make him money.

Which it does.

And money is the topic that Boone came to seek his advice about. Cheerful looks at the copy of Schering's bill and says, "Technically, Hefley's is not an insurance company. It's a reinsurer."

"Meaning that it insures again?"

Correct, Cheerful instructs him. Sometimes a primary insurance company takes on a risk that is too large for it to cover on its own, so it mitigates some of that risk by insuring it with a 'reinsurer.'

"Kind of like a small bookie laying off a piece of a large bet?" Boone says.

"That's a rough but adept analogy," Cheerful admits.

"So, a bunch of expensive homes drop into a hole," Boone says.

"The insurance company can't handle the whole loss, so they turn to the reinsurer to pick up the bill."

It's not that simple, Cheerful explains. For one thing, it's highly unlikely that all the homes, or even a majority of them, would have the same insurance company, and even less likely that each of those carriers would reinsure with Hefley's. The company probably had one or more of the destroyed homes, which, as total losses, would stack up into the tens of millions of dollars, and hired Schering to determine the cause of the loss.

"But the cause of the loss is simple," Boone says. "The landslide."

"That's ignoring the question," Cheerful grumbles, "of what caused the landslide? What was the cause of the cause?"

"Why does that matter?"

"It matters a lot," Cheerful says.

Insurance companies do not write coverage for earth movement. It's right there in the small print under 'Excluded Coverages.' What the underwriting gurus would tell you is that insurance is meant to protect you from accidental, sudden events – storms, floods, fires – and that earth movement is neither sudden nor accidental. It takes a long time and it's no accident. The earth is always moving – that's what dirt does.

"So Hefley's is off the hook anyway. The earth moved."

"Not so fast," Cheerful says. "You can't just look to the cause of the loss, you have to find the 'proximate cause.' "

"You mean, what sort of caused it?"

"Not the *ap*proximate cause, surf bum," Cheerful says. "The *proximate* cause."

"What's that?"

"Go to the library," Cheerful says. "Preferably a law library. You know any good law firms?"

"Yes."

"Goodnight."

"Goodnight," Boone says. "Are those baby hippos on your pajamas?"

"Yes. So what?"

"Nothing. It's just funny, that's all."

"Is it?"

"No."

"I didn't think so. Get out."

Boone gets out.

108

Petra was amazed at how quickly Boone became adept at researching case law.

He'd phoned her and asked her to meet him at her office, saying that he needed her help, and she'd come. Without saying how he'd come about the information, which might have compromised her as an officer of the court, he told her what he'd learned about Phil Schering and why he needed to research something called 'proximate cause.'

She showed him how to use the search vehicle on the computerized case law, and he was at it like a Supreme Court clerk. Truly impressive. They worked at it all night. By the time a pink sky snuck through the east-facing window, Boone had for himself a good grasp of the existing California case law regarding earth movement and coverage.

"There's a chain of events leading up to any loss," he says. "Some causes of loss are either implicitly or explicitly covered under the insurance contract, and some are specifically excluded. California case law states that if a cause of loss isn't specifically excluded by the contract, then that cause is covered and the insurance company has to pay for the damages.

" 'Proximate cause' doctrine – which is basically an amalgam of a number of decisions in cases – states that the insurance company, in analyzing coverage, has to determine the nearest, most important cause of the loss, the 'proximate cause,' if you will. Unless the 'proximate cause' of the loss is specifically excluded, the loss is covered."

"So," Petra says, "in the case of houses that were destroyed by falling into the sinkhole, the 'proximate cause' is earth movement, which is specifically excluded, so the insurance company is not liable."

"Not so fast, counselor," Boone says. " 'Proximate cause' doctrine used to be the precedent, but in more recent cases, such as Neeley *v.* Firemen's, the law has evolved to now state that, while the proximate cause of the loss must be decided, if any event in the chain of events leading to the loss is not specifically excluded, then the loss is covered and the insurance company has to pay."

Christ, that's sexy, Petra thinks. She leans in a little closer and asks, "So, what impact does that have on your analysis of these cases?"

"The real issue seems to be negligence."

"Negligence?"

"Negligence," Boone repeats. And what is that perfume? Because it's really affecting his concentration. But he pushes through it and says, "Negligence is not specifically excluded as a cause of loss. But 'weak link' doctrine, if you will, holds that if negligence is found *anywhere* in the chain of events, then the loss is covered."

"Is that what it holds?"

"Yes, it is."

"I see."

"No, I don't think you do," Boone says, looking into those amazing violet eyes. "See, if negligence occurs in the chain of events, the insurance company must pay the insured even if it intends to pursue subrogation . . ."

"What's subrogation?"

"Subrogation . . ." Boone says. "Subrogation is when an insurance company sues the negligent party to recover the money it paid the insured."

"That's right. You've got it."

"I do?"

"Oh, yes," she says. "You know, you might want to think about law school."

"Do you feel the same way about desktop sex as you do kitchen-counter sex?" he asks.

"No," she says, "they are two entirely separate entities in my mind."

"That's good."

"That's very good."

He has one leg of his jeans off when they hear a door open, then footsteps come down the hall. Boone hops over and closes the door.

"Is someone here?"

"Becky?"

Petra gets up and straightens her clothes as Boone does the same. Then she rearranges her hair and opens the door.

"Well," Becky says, "it's nice to know that someone gets in before me from time to time. Good morning, Boone."

"Good morning, Becky."

"We were doing some research," Petra says.

"Well, there you go."

"We're almost finished."

"I'm sorry I interrupted."

"Boone," Petra says, "I think that's about as far as we can get on this, for the moment anyway. I think I'll just go splash a little water on my face and track down a coffee."

She walks past Becky.

"Yeah," Boone says, "I think I'll . . ."

"Fly?"

"Yeah, you know, take off."

"*Your* fly, idiot," Becky says with a smile. "Zip your fly?"

"Thanks."

"Don't mention it."

It's a long drive to Pacific Beach.

He doesn't bother to catch the end of the Dawn Patrol.

109

Cheerful looks up from the desk as Boone comes in.

"You're in early."

"Yeah, well," Boone says, "you gotta grow up sometime."

"You look like hell."

"And feel worse," Boone says. "But I do know about negligence."

"You've *always* known about negligence," Cheerful says.

"No, I know about capital N negligence," Boone says. He runs down what he learned in the all-nighter session with Petra, leaving out the *coitus interruptus* part. Or, more accurately, he thinks, the Becky *interruptus*.

"We don't know," Cheerful says, "what Schering's report was going to say, because he didn't live long enough to produce it. But if he was billing for the insurance company, it probably meant that they hired him to produce a certain result, and that result would be that there was no negligence involved in the chain of events, which would get them off the hook."

"Maybe," Boone says, "or that there was clear negligence that they could successfully subrogate."

"If Schering was killed over this," Cheerful says, "somebody knew what his report was going to say, and it was dangerous enough that they killed to prevent him from testifying to it."

But how would anyone know? Boone wondered. Did Schering talk about it? Telegraph it somehow? Write a preliminary report? Or . . .

"Was he putting himself up for auction?" Boone asks.

"His opinion for sale to the highest bidder?"

"Which could mean that the losing bidder might have decided he didn't want to lose," Boone says.

"Or," Cheerful offers, "the highest bidder decided that he didn't want to pay."

110

"You're saying that Phil Schering was a whore?" Alan Burke asks, a little out of breath because he and Boone have just paddled out to the break and Alan hasn't hit the Gentlemen's Hour in a while.

You want to know what kind of cardio condition you're in, paddle a surfboard, even in a mild sea. It will tell you all you need to know. It tells Alan he needs to hit the Gentlemen's Hour more often, or maybe get one of those roller boards and put it in the office.

"A whore?" Boone asks.

"A geo-whore," Alan says cheerfully. "Listen, I cut my teeth on all those dirt cases back in the eighties and nineties, and there was a geo-whore on every corner. They knew what opinion you wanted without you having to tell them, and they delivered it. You got to court, it was pretty much a battle between your geo-whore and their geo-whore. You get a whore who gives good testimony, you usually win."

"Did you know Schering?"

"No," Burke says. "He's newer to the game. But I'll have Petra run a search and grab his testimony transcripts, and that should give us an idea of what his *schtick* was. So you don't think Dan Nichols did it?"

"No. Do you?"

"I don't," Alan says. "It's too retro. People don't kill over adultery anymore, they just divorce. Did you know they had a pre-nup?"

"Nope."

"Yup," Alan says. "So Dan loses a little money and goes out shopping for the next trophy wife. Big deal. She's done him a favor by leaving on her own before her sell-by date."

"Cynical."

"SoCal," Alan shrugs. "So, Boone . . ."

"So Alan."

"Look," Alan says, "a good investigator is hard to find, so much as I'd hate to lose one . . . you don't want to do this the rest of your life. It's a living, but there's no up-side. So here's my offer – I'll finance your way through law school, you have a job in my firm when you pass the exam."

Whoa.

Speaking of SoCal, in other places offers like this are made on the golf course; here it's out in the surf, or absence thereof.

"Alan, I don't know—"

"Don't answer now," Alan says. "Think about it. But really *think* about it, Boone. It would be a big change for you, but change can be a good thing."

"Sure."

"Let me know."

"Okay."

"Son of a bitch."

"What?"

Alan points outside. "A wave."

Boone looks. Sure enough, a ripple about a hundred yards out breaks the otherwise flat surface of the sea. Then it appears as a small ridge, then it builds into an actually rideable wave. Nothing to make the cover of *Surfer*, to be sure, but definitely a wave.

"It's yours," Alan says.

"No, you take it."

"You sure?"

"Positive."

"You're a gentleman."

Alan starts paddling. Boone watches him catch the wave, then gets up, and feels the wave pass beneath him.

I'm a gentleman, he thinks.

Dave is waiting for him on the beach.

111

"What's up?" Boone asks.

"I heard."

From the steely look on Dave's face, Boone knows what he's talking about. "You have a problem with it?"

"You don't?"

"Of course I do," Boone says. He hesitates, then adds, "Look, weird as this sounds, I think it's what Kelly would have wanted."

"What are you *smoking*?"

"Anyway, I'm not convinced that Corey did it."

"Johnny's pretty convinced," Dave says. "He took the confession. You're going to jam him up, B?"

"I don't want to."

"Then don't." Because you don't fuck a friend. They both know this. You just don't do it. "How many times has JB stood up for you?"

"A lot."

"So? That doesn't mean anything?"

"He's wrong on this one," Boone says.

"And you're right," Dave says.

"I think I am."

Dave shakes his head. "Dude, I don't even know if I know you anymore. Maybe you should just climb into a suit and tie and become one of them."

"One of them?"

"You know what I mean."

"Yeah, I do," Boone says, starting to get mad. "And, yeah, maybe I should. Maybe I don't want to be a surf bum all my life."

Dave nods. Looks way out toward the water and then back again at Boone. "You go ahead, bro. Us bums will try to get by without you."

"I didn't mean—"

"Sure you did," Dave says. "At least stand by your words, leave me with some respect for you. It's been a ride, B. Late."

He walks away.

Late, Boone thinks.

112

Winners and losers.

Start with the potential losers, Boone tells himself as he walks over to The Sundowner. Potential losers are more likely to kill out of desperation than potential winners are for profit. People tend to dread their losses more than they hope for their wins.

So, list the losers.

Hefley Insurance.

Could be a big loser. What if Schering wasn't giving them the answer they wanted, or was holding them up for more money? But, as Cheerful says, insurance companies don't actually, physically kill people . . . do they?

Keep them on the list, but unlikely.

He walks into The Sundowner where Not Sunny is caught off-guard by his uncharacteristically early appearance. She's leaning against the bar, catching a standing nap, when the door opening wakes her. She sees Boone and signals the cook to get his usual going on the grill. Then she walks over and pours him a cup of coffee.

"Thank you," Boone says.

"You're welcome."

"Uhhhh, what's your name?"

"Not Sunny."

"No, I mean, what's your real name?" Boone asks. "Not the one we glossed you with."

The question takes her by surprise. Having been called Not Sunny during working hours for several months now, she actually has to think about it for a second. "Jennifer."

"Thank you, Jennifer."

"Okay," she says. "Your usual?"

"Yeah. No," Boone says. "It might be time to change things up a little, Not— Jennifer. I'll have . . . the, uhhhh . . . blueberry pancakes."

"Blueberry pancakes?" Not Sunny Jennifer asks.

"Are the blueberries fresh?"

"No."

"I'll take them anyway."

"Okay."

She goes to piss off the cook, who already has the eggs working.

Boone goes back to contemplating losers.

If Schering kept faith with Hefley's, Boone thinks, the next possible losers would be the homeowners. So you'd have to have a homeowner with a lot of bucks to lose having an uninsured house fall into the rabbit hole, or a homeowners' association.

Now, homeowners' associations in SoCal are known for their brutality and utter ruthlessness in enforcing their codes, but Boone can't quite envision one commissioning a contract murder, although he'd loved to have sat in on that meeting.

'All in favor of snuffing Phil Schering, please indicate by saying "aye." Motion carried. There's coffee and cookies . . .'

He doesn't even know if there is a homeowners' association for the neighborhood, so decides that his first task after consuming the pancakes is to go down to the County Building and start researching ownership records. Come up with a list of the homeowners and try to see if any of them are likely candidates.

Not Sunny Jennifer brings him the pancakes.

And a bill.

"Will there be anything else?" she asks as if she worked hard to memorize the line.

Boone's a little startled. As an unofficial bouncer and keeper-of-the-peace at The Sundowner, he hasn't received a bill for breakfast in years. Not Sunny Jennifer sees the surprised look on his face. Anxiety overwhelms her and she gives it straight up. "Chuck said to next time you came in. Charge you. Like, you're not family."

"Relax. It's cool."

"I feel weird."

"Don't," Boone says. He gets up, digs out his wallet and leaves enough cash to pay the bill, plus a generous tip. "Just tell Chuck for me that someone else can keep things cool around here from now on. I don't go where I'm not invited."

Not Sunny Jennifer frowns – it's a lot to remember.

"Just tell him *adios*," Boone says.

" 'Adios,' " she repeats.

Adios.

113

Searching real-estate records at the County Administration Building is a sure antidote to any genre-inspired desire to be a private investigator.

The (sad) truth is that a real PI does a hell of a lot more paper-chasing than sitting around the office slugging bourbon while some long-legged blonde drapes herself across his lap and begs for sexual penance for her sins and a tenor saxophone wails in the background.

Most of the work is a slog through records and Boone hasn't heard a Coltrane riff yet.

The County Administration Building is an enormous edifice that takes up three blocks on the east side of Harbor Drive, smack in the middle of the tourist district. Across the street, visitors come to see the old sailboats that are now maritime museums, or the decommissioned aircraft carrier, or go on harbor cruises, or grub down at Anthony's Fish Grotto. Farther down Harbor Drive are the enormous docks where the big cruise ships come, spilling tourists out to hit the bars and clubs a few blocks away in the Gaslamp District, or to take a pedicab ride, or just stroll the long promenade that curves around the harbor, where hundreds of small, private sailboats moor.

But the CAB is a monument of mundane bureaucracy set in the middle of all the good times, like a stern librarian with a finger to her lips.

It's a busy place, with people coming in to file records, take exams for various professional licenses, get married, all manner of happy crap. Boone has to take the Deuce for several orbits around the huge parking lot before he finds a spot.

So now he sits at a computer station and sifts through real-estate transfer notices, tax records, building permits, and cross-references them against street maps, utility plots and newspaper accounts of the sinkhole episode. It takes him well into the afternoon, but by then he has a list of the eighteen owners whose homes were destroyed.

Then he runs the list of names through his own mental file-card tray of local bad guys. The truth is that very few people will kill for money, even lots of it. Very few people will kill at all, even in the 'heat of passion,' and fewer still will kill in the fabled 'cold blood.'

But those that will, do, and if you're looking at San Diego – the busiest corridor for illegal substances trafficking since Satan slipped Eve the apple – you have to think about drug money and the expensive houses it can buy in a town like La Jolla. The big drug barons – most of them from Tijuana – are, of course, multi-millionaires, and multi-millionaires invest their multi-millions in the most exclusive neighborhoods. Now you're talking about people who can and have killed over a nickel, so offing someone to protect a three- or four-million-dollar investment is a no-brainer.

But Boone's mental search comes up with no matches. None of the owners listed is a drug lord, mob guy or otherwise sketchy, although Boone is aware that some of the homes might have ghost owners behind the recorded names. But that would be a dead-end street anyway, so he asks himself about more potential losers in the game of negligence hot potato.

If Hefley's were to subrogate, he reasons, who would it sue? And if a homeowner were left with a destroyed home and couldn't collect from the insurance company, who would he sue?

Either the builder or the county.

The builder for some kind of negligence, or the county for issuing a permit for that builder to construct a house on unsafe ground.

You can cross off the county – it has no budget line for contract killings – so you're left with the builders.

Boone leaves the CAB and drives up to Mira Mesa.

114

The San Diego County Building Permits office sits on a very nondescript street in a nondescript suburban neighborhood in North County, and is generally known not by its name but its location.

'Ruffin Road.'

Ruffin Road is limbo. Building plans have been held up for *years* by the bureaucrats at Ruffin Road, or just lost, misplaced, misfiled, never to be seen again. Contractors will explain interminable delays simply by saying, "I've been at Ruffin Road," or "It's held up at Ruffin Road," and those excuses will be accepted.

San Diegans have opined that Amelia Earhart, Jimmy Hoffa and the Holy Grail are all to be found at Ruffin Road, if only you could get a clerk to search, and the more waggish insist that Osama bin-Laden is not hiding in Bora Bora or Waziristan, but is safely filed as 'vin-Laden, Osama' somewhere in the bowels of Ruffin Road.

Ruffin Road makes the DMV look like the drive-through window at In 'N' Out Burger. Anyone who has ever built a new home, remodeled an old one, or rebuilt after a fire or landslide pronounces 'Ruffin Road' in the same hushed tone that was once used for the Bridge Of Sighs, the Tower of London, the Inquisition.

'I have to go to Ruffin Road' is a phrase met with sympathy not unmixed with relief that it's the other guy, not you.

Burly roofing-contractors – hard-drinking brawlers who work the highest buildings with a scornful laugh – stand trembling before the counter at Ruffin Road, metaphorical hat in hand, waiting hopefully, plaintively, for an inspector to give their plans, literally, the stamp of approval. Desperate homeowners on their fifth or sixth try to get that addition approved stand in tortured suspense as one of the bureaucratic Torquemadas pores over the latest version of their proposed plans.

It is to this dire place that Boone repairs to get the names of the contractors who built the homes that now sit at the bottom of the La Jolla sinkhole. He goes up to the inaptly named 'Reception Counter' where a middle-aged woman, her hair dyed a color not found in nature, her glasses actually hanging from her neck on a beaded chain, sits on guard.

"Shirley."

"Oh, God, what the cat dragged in?"

"How's your daughter, Shirley?"

"Out again," Shirley says. "Third time."

"Is a charm," Boone answers.

"Your lips, God's ears," Shirley says. "Anyway, thanks for what you did."

Elise had a meth problem and missed a court date, to boot. Shirley called Boone to try to find her before the bail bondsman or police could take her into jail. Boone did and took her to the hospital so at least she could detox in a bed instead of a cell, and the judge ended up suspending sentence and allowing her to go directly into rehab.

"No worries. Is Monkey in?"

"Where else would he be?"

Nowhere, Boone thinks, it was a rhetorical question. Monkey Monroe ran the records room of Ruffin Road and rarely came out. The records were his personal treasure that he hoarded and protected like Gollum. Some people thought that Monkey was part-vampire because he never came out in the light of day.

"You think he'd see me?"

Shirley shrugs. "He's in one of his moods."

"Just ask?"

She gets on the phone. "Marvin? Boone Daniels would like to see you . . . I don't know what for, he just wants to see you . . . Act like an actual human being for a change, would you, Marvin?" She holds the receiver into her bosom and says, "He wants to know if you brought anything."

"Cupcakes."

"Cupcakes, Marvin." She listens for a second then says to Boone, "He wants to know if they're the good kind or some cheap supermarket shit."

"The good stuff," Boone says. "I went to Griswald's."

He holds up the bag to show her.

"He went to *Griswald's*, Marvin . . . Okay. Okay." She smiles at Boone. "You can go down."

"You want a cupcake?"

"You brought extra?"

"Of course."

"Thank you, Boone."

He takes a cupcake – chocolate frosting – out of the bag and sets it on her desk. "Tell Elise I said hi."

"Why don't you date her?"

"No."

He gets in the elevator and goes down to the records room.

As usual, it's colder than a loan shark's blood – Monkey keeps the

AC cranked up because it's better for the computers. And noisy – the air conditioners are blasting, the bank of computers humming. Monkey crouches on one of those weird, posture-improving chairs that you half-kneel on, rolls toward Boone and reaches for the Griswald's bag.

"Vanilla. Did you get me vanilla?"

"Is the Pope German?"

One look at Monkey, you know why he's called Monkey. His arms are unnaturally long, especially next to his short-waisted, small body, and he's quite possibly the most hirsute human being in the world: tendrils of curly hair popping up over his shirt collar and around the back, thick hair on his arms, and hairy knuckles. The scraggly hair on his head is starting to thin and show a few unkempt strands of silver, but his eyebrows are thick, and his beard, which comes up high on his cheekbones, almost to his deep-set simian eye sockets shaded by bottle-thick glasses, is black.

He grabs at the bag like a monkey reaching through the bars and snatching popcorn from a kid at the zoo, and his hands dig greedily into it. Within seconds his mouth is full of cupcake, his lips crusted with white frosting and crumbs.

Another reason he's called Monkey is that he's a true computer monkey. What Monkey's hairy little fingers can't do on a keyboard can't be done. They can make his bank of computers cough up data about any part of any building ever constructed (legally, anyway) in San Diego County.

But the real reason he's called Monkey stems from an unfortunate incident when the director of Ruffin Road urgently needed a copy of an old building permit, couldn't remember Marvin's name and asked Shirley to summon, "That guy in the basement, you know, the records monkey." Monkey has tried many times to get his nickname shortened to 'Monk,' which he thinks is more distinguished and more apt, given his role as a scribe of sorts, but it ain't gonna happen.

"What do you want, Boone?" Monkey asks. Gratitude or expressions of simple courtesy aren't in Monkey's nature – he sees the world pretty much as a constant quid pro quo, so why say 'thank you' for the quo when the request for the quid is doubtless on the way.

Boone hands him the list of properties. "I need to know who built these houses."

"*You* do. *I* don't."

"Alright, Monkey, how much?"

"There are eighteen properties listed here," Monkey says. "Twenty each."

"Dollars?"

"No, cat turds, you moron. Yes, dollars."

"I'll give you ten."

Monkey digs in the bag for the next cupcake and shoves it into his mouth. "Round it up to two hundred, you cheap piece of surf trash."

"Yeah, alright, but I need it now."

"You don't ask for a lot, do you?" Monkey says, rolling back to the computer. "Bring a couple cupcakes, think you own me."

"Griswald's."

"Whatever." He starts banging keys.

"This is on the down low, Monkey," Boone says.

"Who am I going to tell, idiot?"

True, Boone thinks. Monkey rarely leaves the record room and has no known friends. No one can stand him. Actually, Boone has developed almost a fondness for Monkey, although he doesn't know why. Maybe it's the sheer persistence of his unpleasantness, his refusal to let his standards down, or raise them, whichever.

Now he types away, moaning in pleasure from the cupcakes and/or professional interest at what he's seeing on the screen, which he keeps carefully tilted away from Boone. "Ummmm . . . ohhhhh . . . unnnnnn . . . this is interesting."

"What's interesting?"

"Nothing *yet*, asshole," Monkey answers. "Ummmm . . . ohhhhh . . . unnnnnn . . ."

It goes on for a good ten minutes.

"Are you looking up my stuff or giving yourself a happy ending?" Boone asks. Shirley, for one, believes that Monkey's dedication to masturbation comes only behind his obsession with his records and greed for pastry items. ("If you handed him a file, a girlie magazine and a cheese Danish, he'd have a heart attack.")

"If I wanted to jerk off, limp dick," Monkey answers, "I'd think about that girlfriend of yours. The little Brit with the tight rack."

"Nice." Boone and Pete had run into Monkey on the street down in the Lamp one night. It was startling – and disturbing – to see him out of his natural element. Anyway, Monkey had looked Pete up and down as if she was a stack of cupcakes he couldn't wait to devour.

"She's three-Kleenex material," Monkey says, the lips hidden in his beard twisting into a lascivious leer.

"*God*, Monkey."

Ummmm . . . ohhhhh . . . unnnnnn . . .

An interminable hour later, during which Boone has seriously considered suicide several times, Monkey swivels in his weird chair and says. "This *is* sort of interesting, beach bum."

"Okay, can I ask *now* what's interesting?"

"Money."

"What about money?"

"*My* money, retard," Monkey snaps.

Boone takes two bills out of his wallet. Monkey snatches them and shoves them into the front pocket of his stained khaki trousers.

"*What's interesting* is that all your houses were built by one company. It was part of a single development owned by an LLC called Paradise Homes." He hits a couple of buttons and hands Boone a sheaf of print-outs. "Paper for the big dumb Luddite."

"Thanks."

"So, Boone," Monkey asks. "You still seeing her?"

"Yes."

"What about the other one?" Monkey asks. "The tall blonde surfer chick?"

"Sunny and I are pretty much done."

"Can I have her number?" Monkey asks.

"She's out of the country."

"God fucking dammit!" Monkey grabs the Griswald's bag and digs around for some crumbs, which he shoves into his mouth.

Boone sighs. "I'm going to regret this, I know, but she has a website."

Monkey's eyes light up. "She does?"

"Sunnydaysurf.com."

"Photos?"

"Yes."

"Video?"

"Enough, Monkey."

Monkey rolls his chair to another computer and starts banging on the keys.

It's nothing Boone wants to see. Neither Sunny's site, with photos of her shredding it at Bondi or Indo, or the onanistic use that Monkey is going to make of it. He takes his records, gets back in the elevator, waves a goodbye to Shirley, and goes out to the Deuce.

Paradise Homes, he thinks.

Eighteen times a couple of mill each?

Money to kill for.

115

"Hello, lover boy," Becky says, grinning at Boone.

"Hello, Becky."

"Who did you come to see?" she asks. "Do you have an appointment, or is this a spontaneous booty—"

"Okay, okay. Is she in?"

"This is your lucky day." She buzzes Petra, who comes out to the front desk. He follows her to her office and tells what he's learned about Paradise Homes, LLC. She says, "So Paradise Homes could be on the hook for all that money?"

"And the next question is – who are Paradise Homes?" Boone asks. "It's a limited partnership, who are the partners?"

"I can track that down from here," she says.

"Aren't you busy on the Blasingame case?"

"Nichols is our client, too," says Petra. "Besides, there's nothing much to do now except wait for Mary Lou to decide how she wants to go."

Turns out she's quite a keyboard jockey. Sits with a cup of tea in one hand, the mouse in another and rocks. It takes three hours, but she comes up with the answer. She leans back and points to the monitor.

"To coin a phrase," she says, "Jesus Christ."

It jogs Boone's memory.

In Blasingame's office, when he was interviewing him about Corey.

'That punch? First time in his life that Corey ever followed through on anything.'

The phone buzzed and it was the pretty receptionist, Nicole: *'You wanted me to remind you that you have a meeting with Phil at the site?'*

No, Boone thinks. It couldn't be.

Could it?

Bill Blasingame is the chief partner in Paradise Homes.

116

Boone sits in the Deuce outside Blasingame's office building.

Nicole comes out at 6:05 and heads straight for Happy Hour at a bar across the street. Not surprising given who she works for, Boone thinks. If I worked for Blasingame, which sort of I do, Happy Hour would be about 10 a.m.

Boone waits a few minutes and then goes in.

The bar is like a convention of local receptionists, most of them sitting at one long table, drinking, blowing off a little steam, bitching about their bosses, unwilling to go home yet to the lonely condo or the marriage that's gotten boring sooner than hoped.

Boone takes a seat at the bar and orders a beer. He pretty much keeps his eye on a baseball game playing on the wall-mounted television as Nicole finishes her first drink, then a second. When she's in the middle of the third she gets up to use the ladies and walks past him, but if she notices him she doesn't let on.

She comes back out, finishes her drink, drops some money with her friends and leaves the bar. Boone catches up with her in the parking lot as she digs in her purse for her car keys.

"Nicole?"

"Do I know you?"

"My name's Boone Daniels," he says. "We met the other day in your office. You shouldn't be driving right now."

"I'll be fine, thanks."

"I don't want to see you get a DUI," he says. "Hurt yourself, somebody else."

"Who do you think you are?"

"I'd like to be your friend," he says.

"I bet you would." She laughs, but it has no humor. It's a harsh and bitter sound. Which is a real shame, Boone thinks.

"Friends don't let friends blah-blah-blah," he says. "Let me buy you a cup of coffee."

"The MADD pick-up is original, anyway," she says. She drops her keys back in her purse. "There's a Starbucks across the street."

They walk over to Bucky's and he orders her a tall iced *latte*, himself an iced green tea with lemonade. She looks at his drink and laughs, "You some sort of health freak?"

"I'm coffee'd out."

"Burning it at both ends, huh?"

"You could say that." Two murder cases – one in which I'm a suspect. Yeah, that's both ends and more, if you could have more than two ends. Which would make a great inter-wave topic for the

Dawn Patrol – then he remembers that he's not on the Dawn Patrol anymore, and the guys at the Gentlemen's Hour wouldn't go for it. "So how is it, working for Bill?"

"You wanna guess?"

"Kind of a pain?"

"More than kind of. He's a real son-of-a-bitch." Then she remembers herself and adds quickly, "You're not, like, a friend or a business partner, are you?"

"Neither."

"How do you know Bill?"

"I'm working on his kid's case."

"Oh."

"Oh," Boone says. "What makes him a son-of-a-bitch?"

"You don't know?"

"I'm interested in what *you* think," Boone says.

"Well, that would make you the first," Nicole says. "Bill, for instance, isn't very interested in what I *think*. Unless I thought with my boobs."

"Which you don't."

"No." She looks down at her chest and asks, "Hey, what do you guys think?"

She listens for a second and then says, "Nothin'."

They both laugh. Then Boone starts to push the river a little. "Hey, when I was in with Bill a few days ago, you buzzed him to say something about an appointment he had?"

But you don't push the river, just like you don't get out in front of a wave. It's usually a bad idea. It sure is this time. She looks at him and says, "You bastard."

"I—"

"Yeah, you want to be my 'friend.' Well, fuck you, *friend*."

She slams her cup down and walks out. Boone follows her outside, where she's steaming back toward her car. "Nicole, come on."

"Fuck you."

Boone gets ahead of her. He doesn't grab her or even touch her, but keeps his hands up as he says, "Was it Phil Schering?"

One look in her eyes and he knows it was. And that she knows that Schering was murdered.

"Get out of my way."

"Sure."

Passers-by on the street look at them and smile. Lovers' spat. She has to wait for the light to turn to cross the street and Boone stands beside her and says, "Nicole, what was Bill doing with Schering?"

"Get away from me."

The light turns and she crosses the street, Boone right beside her. He stays with her until she gets to her car, and then as she takes her keys from her bag, she looks up at her office and says, "Jesus, if he sees me with you . . ."

"Let's get out of here, then."

She hesitates but gives him the keys. He opens the passenger door for her and she slides in. Boone gets behind the wheel and pulls out. Takes a right onto La Jolla Boulevard, heads north and asks, "What was Bill doing with Schering?"

"I need this job."

"You could get a job in any one of a hundred offices, Nicole."

She shakes her head. "He won't let me leave – won't give me a reference."

"Tell him to go fuck himself." Boone turns left onto Torrey Pines.

"You don't understand," she says. "He's blackmailing me to stay."

"What are you talking about?"

She looks away from him, out the passenger window. "Three years ago . . . I had a drug problem. I took some money from him to buy coke . . ."

"And now you pay him back or he goes to the police," Boone says.

Nicole nods.

She probably hasn't had a raise in those three years either, Boone thinks. Works overtime without compensation, and who knows what other services she performs? And he won't call the cops – he knows they won't give a shit about a three-year-old case – but she doesn't know that, and if she tries to leave, he'll hang the drug tag around her neck. In the closed world of La Jolla, that will bar every door for her.

Nice.

She's crying now. In the reflection of the window glass he can see mascara running down her face.

"Nicole," he says, "someone killed Schering and an innocent man is getting blamed. If you know anything, you need to tell it."

She shakes her head.

"I'll get you started," he says. "Phil was what you call a geo-whore. Bill used his services. They were going to meet the other day at the La Jolla sinkhole."

She nods.

He plays a hunch. "Does Paradise Homes mean anything to you?"

She keeps looking out the window.

Then she nods again.

117

Monkey sits at his computer at home and looks at Sunny's website.

It's a satisfying encounter, but all it does in the end is piss him off. Why should guys like Boone Daniels get all the hot women?

Monkey goes through the checklist of possible answers.

Looks.

Okay, nothing he can do about that. Well, he could shave, get a haircut, brush his teeth, eat something other than processed sugar and pastry items, and hit the personal hygiene section at Save-On every once in a while, but it isn't going to make him look like Boone, so fuck it.

Sexy job.

A brainless PI? Forget it.

Become a surfer.

Involves deep, cold, moving water and physical exertion beyond the . . . never mind.

What else attracts women?

Money.

But you don't have money, he tells himself, looking around his shit hole one bedroom east of the Lamp, a building which will soon go condo, which he can't afford.

But you could *get* money, couldn't you?

What was Neanderthal Daniels sniffing after?

Paradise Homes?

Monkey wipes the keyboard off, logs into his database and goes hunting. I may not have looks, a sexy job, a surfboard or money (yet), but I have access to information, and information is power, and power is money and . . .

An hour later he has his answer.

Picks up the phone, waits for someone to answer and says, "You don't know me, asshole, but my name is Marvin. You have a problem, and I'm the solution."

Thinking . . . How do you turn Monkey into money?

Just drop the k, baby.

Invigorated, he goes back to Sunny's website.

118

Boone turns on La Jolla Shores Drive, then takes a left on La Playa, then a right, and pulls into the parking lot at La Jolla Shores beach.

Nicole looks at him funny.

"You want to take a walk on the beach?" he asks.

"A walk on the beach?"

"Great time of day for it." Well, any time is a great time for it. But early-evening on a hot August day, with the sky just starting to soften into a gentle pink and the temperature starting to drop: perfection. And dusk is a great time for confession – give your sins to the setting sun and watch them go over the horizon together. Put your past in the past.

So why don't *you* do it? he asks himself.

No answer.

She flips down the sunshade and looks at herself in the mirror. "I'm a mess."

"It's the beach, nobody cares. Come on."

"You're nuts." But she goes with him.

They don't say anything for a long time, just walk and watch the sky change color, and think about what she told him.

Bill used Schering as a geo-engineer on a lot of development projects over the years. Schering would go out, do a report on the suitability of a site for construction, and Bill would use that report to take to the county for approval. Most of Schering's reports were legitimate but sometimes . . .

Sometimes he would shade the report a little, maybe overlook a weakness, a flaw, a potential danger. And usually the county would accept Schering's report, but sometimes the inspectors needed a little . . . persuasion . . . to pass on a piece of land.

"Phil was the bagman," Boone said.

"I guess so."

It made sense. As a geo-engineer, Schering had relationships with the county engineers. He could go to breakfast or lunch, arrive with an envelope, leave without it. A week or so later, the permits would get issued. They did it a bunch of times.

"I was no blushing virgin either," Nicole said. She took the bonuses, the gifts, the vacations, all the little perqs that came with flowing money. Schering took the payments to the geo-engineers; she took them to the politicians.

"What about Paradise Homes?" Boone asked.

It was Bill's really big shot, Nicole told him. His chance to go from Triple A to the major leagues. He got a group of investors together, called the company 'Paradise Homes' and put everything he had into buying the land. But . . .

. . . the land was no good. Bill got pretty drunk one night in the office after they'd . . . after she'd given him what he needed to relieve the stress . . . and he told her. She didn't understand all of it – she wasn't sure he did, either – but the land sat over some kind of geological problem. Sandy soil over rock, and there was a shifting plate or something underneath . . .

Schering tried to tell him, to warn him, but Bill begged him . . . *begged* him . . . to write a different report. For the county, for the investors.

"Hold on," Boone said, "the *investors* didn't know about the land problem?"

No, because Bill knew that if *they* knew, they'd never put their money into it. Schering argued that it was a time bomb, but Bill argued what was time when you're talking about earth movement? The earth is always moving. The problem could be hundreds or even thousands of years away. And they were talking millions and millions of dollars . . .

Schering wrote a clean report. Did what he had to do to get it through the county. A lot of envelopes went out . . . vacation homes were sold under market value. Ski places in Big Bear, weekend desert spots out in Borrego . . .

The site was approved.

"How do you know all of this?" Boone said. "I know Bill talked a little when he was 'comfortable,' but—"

"I dug in the files," she says. "I kept copies of Schering's original reports and compared them to the new ones he wrote."

"Why?"

Bill was blackmailing her, she thought she'd turn it around and blackmail him. Win her freedom, maybe take a little of all that money with her on the way out.

"But you didn't," Boone said.

"Well, I haven't," she said.

Maybe she just got lazy, or complacent. Maybe it was all too difficult, too hard to understand. Maybe she just didn't have the confidence to think she could actually pull it off. And maybe . . . maybe her feelings for Bill were. . . complicated.

Then the whole thing with Corey happened and she didn't have the heart to 'pile on,' and Bill hadn't demanded anything of her lately, and she just kind of forgot about it, then . . .

Paradise Homes collapsed.

Bill freaked out, just freaked out. He was on the phone to Phil all the time. He was calling lawyers, insurance people . . . it was horrible. Bill was a mess – first the thing with his kid, then this. He was sure he was going to lose everything. Especially if Phil got weak-kneed and couldn't keep his mouth shut.

Or if he sold himself to the higher bidder, Boone thought. And Blasingame was right – he could lose everything. If a criminal conspiracy were even alleged, a plaintiff could walk right through his corporation and sue him personally. Take his bank account, his investments, his real property . . . his house, his cars, his clothes.

And no wonder he's in a hurry to get his son's case out of the newspapers. The longer the spotlight stays on the Blasingame name, the more digging people do, the more likely someone is to connect him to Paradise Homes and the landslide disaster. He had all this shit going on . . .

Then Schering was killed and Nicole got scared.

Bill said apparently it was some kind of jealousy thing – Phil was banging another guy's wife, was the rumor – and that it had *nothing* to do with them, nothing to do with *him*, but there was no point in taking chances. He told her to dump appointment books, eighty-six phone records, bills, anything that could connect him to Schering.

"But you didn't," Boone said.

She didn't.

She didn't keep them all, but she kept the really tasty ones.

119

"It's beautiful," she says, watching the sun go down. "Just beautiful. I'm usually still at work . . ."

"It has a way of putting things in perspective," Boone says. He lets a few seconds go by before he says, "I need those records, Nicole."

"They're my safety net."

"Until he knows you have them. Then they're a danger." Rule of thumb: If you know where the bodies are buried, sooner or later you're going to be one of them.

"You think he killed Schering?"

"You don't?" Boone asks. "You of all people know what he's capable of. Nicole, he might already be thinking about what he told you when he was drunk."

"I know."

"If I have the records, I can help you," Boone says. "I'll take you to a cop I know—"

"I don't want to go to jail."

"You won't," Boone assures her. "Once your story is on the record, it's done. You're safe. There's no point in anyone doing you harm. But the records prove your story. Without them . . ."

". . . I'm just a bimbo secretary with a nose-candy problem."

He doesn't say anything. There's no response to that – she's dead on.

Nicole scans the view, the long curving stretch of coastline from La Jolla Point to the south, all the way down past Scripps Pier toward

Oceanside. Some of the most valuable real estate on earth, some of it built on land that never should have been built on. She says, "So I'm supposed to trust you."

He gets it, totally. Why should she trust him? Or some cop she doesn't know? Why should she trust any public official? She's seen them bribed and bought – helped to do it herself.

A new idea, a fresh fear, hits her. "How do I know Bill didn't send you? You work for him. How do I know he didn't send you to find out what I know, get what I have?"

She's on the edge of panic. Boone has seen it before, not just on cases but with inexperienced swimmers in the deep water. They feel overwhelmed, outmatched, exhausted – then they see the next wave coming and it's too much, too frightening. They panic, and unless someone is there to pull them out, they drown.

"You don't," Boone says. "All I can tell you is, at the end of the day, you have to trust someone."

Because the ocean is too big to cross alone.

120

Bill Blasingame gets on the horn to Nicole.

Calls her at home.

NA.

Calls her on her cell.

NA – the bitch has it turned off.

He's freaking. First Phil Schering gets shot, then Bill gets the phone call. He remembers what was said, pretty much word for word. *'This can't go any further. You can't let this go any further. Do you understand?'*

Bill understands. He knows the people he's dealing with.

But I can contain it, he thought after the phone call. With Schering dead, the only other person who could really blow this open is Nicole. And she knows what side her bread is buttered.

Except what if the stupid twat doesn't? What if she panics? Or gets greedy?

And now she won't answer her phone. She's looking at caller ID and blowing me off. Where the fuck is she? he wonders. Okay, where is she usually this time of the day? Out getting shit-faced with her buddies.

He leaves the building, crosses the street and goes into the bar.

Sure enough, the nightly bitch session of the Aggrieved Secretaries' Club is in full swing. They're not all that happy to see him when he approaches the table. Fuck them, he thinks, and asks, "Have you seen Nicole?"

"She's off the clock," one of them answers.

Mouthy bitch.

"I know," Bill says, "but have you seen her?"

The mouthy one giggles. "Have you looked between the sheets? There was this really cute guy giving her the eye and he followed her out of here, and I think girlfriend was open to a hook-up."

Bill goes back to his office building, looks in the parking lot, and doesn't see Nicole's car. Calls her cell again, then her home, but she doesn't answer. Great, he thinks, I'm dying here and the bitch is out getting laid.

121

Monkey hangs by his arms from chains thrown over the steam pipe.

The man gives him another gentle nudge in the chest and Monkey swings back and forth. It's hot down in the building's boiler room but the man wears a suit, button-down shirt and tie, and doesn't sweat at all.

Monkey does. He's dripping all over the floor and the man is careful not to let it get on his leather shoes as he steps close, shakes his head and says, "Marvin, Marvin, Marvin. They call you 'Monkey,' don't they?"

"How do you know that?"

Jones smiles and shakes his head. "Monkey, I need you to talk to me."

His voice is soft. Cultured and gentle, with the slightest hint of an accent.

"I did everything you wanted," Monkey says.

True enough. After he arranged the meeting they came to his place – this gentleman and some Mexican gang bangers – put a gun to his head, sat him down and had him erase all the records pertaining to Paradise Homes from the data bank. Then they took him down to the basement, hung him from the steam pipe and asked him how he came to be so interested.

"You haven't told me what I want to know."

"I did," Monkey says. "I told you all about what Blasingame did. I told you all about Daniels."

"But you haven't told me with whom Mr. Daniels is working," Jones says. "You seemed to indicate that he is a rather stupid man, unlike yourself. *He* could not have put this all together the way you did."

"He works alone."

"Oh, dear, Monkey." Jones shakes his head again, then reaches into his trouser pocket, pulls out a pair of surgical gloves, and carefully fits them on. "You are very clever with records, Monkey, and very thorough. You made one tragic error, though, in placing your faith entirely in them. You didn't realize there are people whose names never appear in records."

Then he reaches inside his jacket pocket and removes a thin, metallic rod, flicks his wrist, and the telescopic baton slides out to its full, one-foot length. "I believe it's more or less a commonplace for a person in my situation to say something along the lines of, 'I don't want to hurt you.' Bad luck for you, Monkey. You see, I *do* want to hurt you."

He does.

122

Mary Lou Baker goes off on Johnny B.

"Did your boy Steve run the witnesses through the microwave?" she asks Johnny after summoning him to her office.

"What—"

"One of my star witnesses, George Poptanich, otherwise known as 'Georgie Pop,' came to see me," Mary Lou says. "He says Harrington twisted his arm to identify Corey."

"What, he had an attack of conscience?"

"He had an attack of terror-induced constipation!" Mary Lou yells. "It now seems he's scared shitless about having maybe fingered the wrong guy. Yeah, he's going to make a great witness, John – a two-time loser who goes back on his story."

"You still have Jill Thompson," Johnny says.

"Burke doesn't think so," Mary Lou says. "Burke says she'll recant. Who interviewed her? You or Harrington?"

"Steve did."

"He gets fucking cute with me," Mary Lou says, "he'll take you down with him."

Johnny nods. About all he can do. Harrington has a reputation for taking the straightest line between two points.

"What about you?" Mary Lou asks. "Did you tune Corey up on the confession?"

It pisses Johnny off. Mary Lou is no fresh-faced kid, but an experienced, many laps around the pool prosecutor who knows how things work. Knows that all confessions are orchestrated to some extent or another.

"I played nice with him," Johnny says. "Look at the tape, there are no gaps."

"I didn't ask if you hit him. I asked if you tricked him . . . led him in any way."

Of course I tricked him, Johnny thinks. I grabbed him by the nose and I led him. That's what we do, Mary Lou. That's what you pay us for. He didn't say that, though. What he said was, "The confession will stand up, ML."

"He's going back on it."

"Fuck him. Too late."

"What about *your* witness statements?"

"What about them?" Just to buy a little time and pay back some of the annoyance.

"Are they finessed?"

I should hope so, Johnny thought. Finesse is a job requirement. But he says, "Did I show Trevor, Billy and Dean a crystal ball of what their futures would look like if they didn't come to Jesus? Sure. Do they have ample motive for throwing Corey under the bus to salvation? You bet. But this decribes, what, eighty-five percent of our witness statements in a good year."

Mary Lou stares at him and taps her pencil on the desk. It's amazingly annoying. Then she says, "I'm going to cut a deal."

"Oh, come on, Mary Lou!"

"Don't give me the hurt, indignant shit!" she yells back. She calms down and says, "It's for your sake, too, Johnny. Alan threatened to nail you to the cross on the stand."

"I'm not afraid of Alan Burke."

"Put your dick back in your pants," Mary Lou said. "I'm only asking, does he know something I should know?"

"If he does, I don't know what it would be," Johnny said.

"You took Blasingame straight to the house, right?" Mary Lou asked.

Johnny heard the implied question. They both knew Steve

Harrington's reputation for tuning suspects up before they sing on tape. But this wasn't some Mexican from Barrio Logan or a black kid from Golden Hill; this was a rich white boy from La Jolla and Steve knew better than to mess with that potential lawsuit.

"It was all by the book, Mary Lou."

She stares at him again and decides he's telling the truth. Kodani's reputation is straight-up. "Alan has Daniels working for him on this, doesn't he?"

"What I hear."

"Daniels was a good cop," Mary Lou said. "What happened to him wasn't right."

"No, it wasn't."

"You're surfing buddies or something, aren't you?"

"Not so much anymore," Johnny says.

Since Boone went to the Dark Side.

"So I don't have to worry," Mary Lou asked, "about leaks coming out of the detective division?"

"I resent that, Mary Lou."

"Just checking, John," she said. "Don't get your back up. There are eyes on you, you know. The powers wouldn't mind an Asian Chief of Detectives. The diversity thing. I just don't want to see you fuck yourself up out of a misguided sense of friendship."

Johnny knew that a public spectacle, like Burke going *Deliverance* on him in court, would definitely fuck him up. Add to that the potential of a high-profile murder case involving Dan and Donna Nichols . . . the rest of Johnny's career is on the line over the next few weeks.

Make those cases, he thinks as he drives over toward The Sundowner and looks for a place to park, and I'm on my way to Chief of Division. And, admit it, that's what I want. Do a bad public wipeout on those cases and the old glass ceiling is going to come down on my yellow skin and slanted eyes like a bad, angry wave, and I will be Sergeant Kodani for the rest of my derailed career.

So he isn't all that thrilled when his cellie rings and he sees it's Boone.

123

"Fuck you," Johnny says.

Boone's not too surprised – he knows that Johnny's royally pissed about the Blasingame case and probably shouldn't even be talking to him outside the office about the Schering murder. "Johnny, I—"

"Save it, friend,*" Johnny says. "I hear you put me square into Burke's sights for the Blasingame trial. It's going to be about me now? Just for the record, Boone,* friend, *in case you guys are planning to turn me into Mark Furman, I've never used the word 'cracker' or 'whitey' in my life. Late."*

"Don't," Boone says. "I have a break in the Schering murder."

"Bring it to the house."

"Can't."

"Of course not."

"Johnny, this will make the case for you."

"On Nichols?"

"No."

" 'Bye, Boone."

The line goes dead. He walks back over to Nicole.

"Is your cop friend going to meet us?" she asks him.

"Not yet," Boone says. "You hungry?"

"I could eat."

He walks her over to Jeff's Burgers.

They've spruced the tiny place up a little bit. Its two long narrow rooms have a fresh coat of white paint and murals of the Coronado Bridge with little sailboats gliding underneath. Nicole stands at the counter and looks up at the menu printed on the board above.

"What's good?" she asks.

"At Jeff's Burgers?"

"Well, yes."

"A Jeff's Burger," he says.

She asks for a Jeff's with everything, fries and a chocolate shake. Boone doubles the order, then they go sit in a booth. The food is ready in a couple of minutes and she digs into it like it might be her last meal.

"S'good," she says.

"Stick with me," Boone answers. "I know all the good places."

She keeps wolfing it down. Doesn't say a word until she's finished the whole thing and then says to him, "Okay."

"Okay, you're done?"

"Okay, I trust you."

"Because of a *burger*?"

She nods and tells him that's pretty much it. If he was a slime bucket on Bill's payroll he would have taken her to the nearby Marine Room, bought her an expensive meal and plied her with wine. Only a genuine surf bum chump would be dumb enough to take her to Jeff's Burgers.

Well, Boone thinks, you work with what you got.

124

"He has a girlfriend," Monkey gasps. "British."

"Name?" Jones asks.

"Pete."

"Come again?"

"Petra, I think."

"Surname?"

Monkey shakes his head.

"Oh, dear."

"Hall," Monkey says quickly.

"Good," Jones says. He turns to the Crazy Boys. "Wrap this up and take him with you. We might have more questions to ask him later."

They take Monkey down from the pipe.

125

Nicole drives Boone to a storage locker in Solana Beach and tells him to wait in the car. Comes out five minutes later with a box and puts it on his lap, then drives him back to her office parking lot and drops him off at the Deuce.

"That's quite some ride you have there," she says. "The PI business booming?"

"Like real estate," he says. "What are you going to do now?"

"Go home, I guess."

"You have a friend or a relative you could stay with?" Boone asks. "Someone Bill doesn't know about?"

She has her grandmother up in Escondido, and Boone suggests she stay there for a few days. She gets it, tells him she will, and they exchange cell-phone numbers.

"You did the right thing," Boone says.

"The right thing," she says, "won't pay my mortgage."

Too true, Boone thinks.

126

They have the papers spread out all over Petra's living-room floor as they create piles of related records and documents that link one to another.

"Do you know what we have here?" Petra asks him.

Boone knows. Freaking dynamite, enough to blow the lid off the city and shake it to its foundations. Bribes to city, county and state officials for approvals for building projects on dangerous ground; cover-ups of shoddy construction practices; real-estate development partnerships that connect to half the big business people in the county. And this is from just one developer, Bill Blasingame. He can't be the only pitcher working the corners of the plate, there must be dozens. Where would those connections lead?

Yeah, Boone knows what they have there.

"This might be more wave than we want," he says.

"What do you mean?" she asks.

Boone explains that sometimes you get into a wave that's too big for you to handle. It isn't a matter of pride or ego or even your skill level, it's just physics – the wave is too tall, heavy and fast for your board and your body, and it will crush you.

He has that sense here. The individuals and businesses listed in Nicole's records are connected, and the connections are connected, and it's not just linear – each line reaches out in multiple directions to other lines – it's what that old yuppie concept of 'networking' is all about, and in a city as small and tight as San Diego, the network is close and dense.

Where in that network do you bring this information? he asks her. You bring it to the DA's office – where is the district attorney in that matrix? Bring it to the cops – same thing. A judge – ditto ditto.

"Certainly we can take this to Alan," Petra says. "I mean, we have to take it to Alan, it's potentially exculpatory evidence for a client. For you, as well."

She sees the look on his face and says, "Good lord, Boone, you don't suspect Alan?"

He doesn't suspect that Burke is involved in any sketchy real-estate deal, but Alan is definitely woven into the San Diego power network. And Petra doesn't know the leverage that can be worked on a guy like Alan – all of a sudden the wiring in his office building is out-of-code, a slam-dunk motion in court goes the other way, a guy he defended five years ago claims that Alan suborned him to perjury . . .

It's Chinatown, Pete. It's Chinatown.

"So what do you want to do?" Petra asks.

"We'll turn it over to Alan in the morning," Boone says. "In the meantime, let me lay a little pipe."

"Really, Boone, these metaphors."

If you take the info to one source, he explains, it might get buried. Take it to two or three, you improve your chances.

"But to whom do you take it?" she asks.

Depends in 'whom' you trust.

127

Nicole finally calls him back.

"Where the fuck," Bill asks, "have you been?"

"Out," she says. "Listen, I wasn't even going to call you . . . I . . ."

She starts crying, for Chrissakes.

"Nicole," Bill says, "why don't you come over and we'll talk about this? We can work it out. You can have anything you want, I swear. Come on, we've meant a lot to each other. Do this for me, come over."

There's a long hesitation, and then she says, "Okay. I'm on my way."

Ten minutes later his bell rings and he opens the door.

It isn't Nicole.

"Hello," Jones says.

128

"I shouldn't be meeting you," Johnny says, "outside the house."

Yeah, but he does. He meets Boone beneath the pylons under Crystal Pier. Meets him because old habits die hard and old friendships are hard to let go, even when the old friend planted a blade somewhere around your lumbar vertebrae.

"I appreciate it," Boone says.

"You burned me, Boone."

"I did your homework for you," Boone answers. "If you'd done it first—"

"Fuck you," Johnny says. "That kid is guilty as sin and now he's boo-hooing you and you're all buying his act. So why am I here?"

"That break on the Schering case . . ."

"Did Dan Nichols pay for it?"

"It had nothing to do with Nichols," Boone says. He tells Johnny about Nicole, Bill Blasingame and Paradise Homes.

When he's done, Johnny says, "So you're telling me that Phil Schering banging Donna Nichols is just a coincidence."

"There's no coincidence," Boone says. "Donna Nichols was having an affair with a guy who was involved in a real-estate scandal gone bad. The guy got killed, probably by Blasingame. Billy Boy has at least as much motive, Johnny. Bring him in and make him give you an alibi for that night."

"I know my job, Boone," Johnny says. "How do I know this story isn't total bullshit, seeing as how you've gone all gullible these days? Let me get this right – Junior isn't a murderer, but Senior is? I love it."

"I have the records."

"Rewind?"

"I have the records," Boone says. "Nicole gave them to me."

"And you didn't bring them along because . . ."

This occasions one of those awkward silences. Which Johnny breaks by saying, "Because you trust me, sort of."

"It's not you, JB."

"*Noooo*," Johnny says, "it's the *baaaad* department, right? Boone Daniels was the one shining light of purity and he had to leave, lest he be corrupted by the rest of us. Fuck you, Boone, you think you're the only honest man in the world?"

Boone names three names he saw in Nicole's papers.

"You take those names in to your lieutenant," he says, "what happens?"

"Then why come to me at all?" Johnny asks.

"Because you're taking the wrong angle on the Schering murder."

"Just like the Kuhio case."

Boone shrugs.

"You're unfreaking believable lately," Johnny says. "Everyone's wrong but you. We have the wrong guy for Kuhio. We have the wrong guy for Schering . . . Hey, Boone, there couldn't be a little self-interest involved here, could there? I mean, you get Dan Nichols off the hook, you wiggle free too, don't you? You don't have to try to sleep at night knowing that you fingered a guy to get murdered."

Boone's fingers curl into fists.

Johnny sees it.

"God, would I like to, Boone," he says. "But my career is already fucked enough without a fight with a civilian in my jacket. But back off, before I realize I don't give a fuck."

Boone unclenches his hands and steps back.

"Smart, B."

"You'll pick up Blasingame?"

"I'll think about it."

They both know he'll do more than think about it, because they both know that Boone has maneuvered him into doing more than thinking about it. Johnny Banzai is a good cop, and now that he knows he has another suspect, he can't act as if he doesn't.

"Be careful on this one, Johnny," Boone says.

"Ride your own wave," Johnny says. "I'll ride mine."

Boone watches him walk away.

129

"Is she coming?" Jones asks.

Bill Burlingame, his wrists and ankles duct-taped to a dining-room chair, shakes his head. "I don't know. I guess not."

Jones smiles.

"Oh, dear," he says, "my employer is not going to like that."

130

Donna Nichols looks especially radiant as she moves through the crowd, working the room, making small talk. The crowd is lively and happy, munching on expensive finger food, sipping champagne, laughing and chatty. The lantern light makes her shine particularly golden.

Balboa Park is beautiful.

On this soft summer evening, yielding to the night-time cool, with the glow of lanterns lighting the courtyard of the Prado – bathing the old stone and grillwork in an amber light, and sparkling on the water in the fountain – the effect is magical.

The people are beautiful, too.

San Diego's beautiful people – the women in plunging white dresses and the men in white jackets and ties. Beautiful tans, beautiful smiles, beautiful hair. A beautiful event, this fundraiser for the museum, and Boone feels out-of-place in the summer wedding and funeral suit he'd climbed into to come over here.

He stands in the shadow of an archway, at the perimeter of the gathering, and scans the crowd to find Dan. He admires the Nicholses for not hiding in their house but confronting the Schering scandal head-on, and proceeding with an evening like this. He knows there must be sidelong glances, behind-the-back whispers and jokes, but the Nicholses seem unaffected. Finally he makes eye contact. Dan excuses himself and walks over to Boone. "Hey, what's up?"

"Can we go out and talk?"

"Yeah, yeah," Dan says.

He follows Boone outside onto the Prado. A few strollers are out, and a couple of San Diego police watch the entrance to the courtyard, to keep the public away from the glittering party inside.

"You didn't kill Phil Schering," Boone says.

Dan's smile is totally charming. "I guess I already knew that, Boone. But I'd sure like to know why you know it now."

Over his shoulder, Boone sees Donna come out from the courtyard. She walks up and puts her hand on Dan's shoulder. "What is it?"

She looks alarmed.

Dan smiles and says, "Boone's about to explain, darling, why he doesn't think I killed your lover. We speak openly about these things, Boone. Our counselor said that was a healthy thing."

Boone tells them about Bill Blasingame, Paradise Homes and Nicole's documents that prove it.

"Thank God," Donna says when he finishes. She wraps her arms around her husband and puts her face into his neck. When she raises her head, her cheeks are wet with tears. She looks across at Boone and says, "Thank you. Thank you, Boone."

"Is this over now?" Dan asks.

Boone shakes his head. "No, there's a ways to go, but I doubt they'll even charge you now, and if they do, with your alibi and the other potential suspect . . ."

"We owe you, Boone," Dan says. "More than we can say."

Donna nods.

"I did it as much for myself," Boone says.

"I don't know what Alan's paying you," Dan says, "but there'll be a big bonus, I can tell you that."

Boone shakes his head. "Not necessary. Or wanted."

"Okay," Dan says. "Tell you what. I think it's time that Nichols had a Chief of Security, and I think that's you. Mid-six-figure yearly salary, benefits, profit-sharing, stock down the road if you choose."

"That's generous, Dan," Boone says. "I'll think about it, I really will. I'm also thinking about law school, though."

"Law school?" Dan asks. "I could see that."

"I don't know if I can."

"We're going to be okay, Boone," Dan says. He holds Donna a little tighter. "We've talked a lot, we've been really open. We're committed to each other, and we're going to be okay."

"I'm glad," Boone says.

Dan turns to Donna, "Well, honey, we'd better go back in before everyone thinks we're involved in another murder."

Donna kisses him on the cheek, extends her hand to Boone and says, "Thank you. Truly."

"You're welcome."

Dan says, "Well, see you at the Gentlemen's Hour?"

"Sure."

That's where he surfs now.

With the gentlemen.

131

Cruz Iglesias gets on the phone.

Not a lot of people have Red Eddie's backdoor number, but Iglesias is one of the privileged few.

Eddie answers on the third ring. "W'asup?"

"Eddie," Iglesias says, "I have a favor to ask of you."

Gentleman to gentleman.

132

They hit him as soon as he steps through the door.

One pistol shoved into his face, then the other slammed into the back of his head.

Boone drops to his knees, not out but wobbly. Even with the world tilting he can see that the gang bangers have wrecked his place, gone through it like a hurricane. But he's too out of it anyway to stop them wrapping the duct-tape around his mouth, then over his eyes. They jerk his arms behind him, wrap more tape around his wrists and push him to the floor.

He kicks out, but there are at least three of them, and they hold his legs and tape his ankles together, then pick him up and carry him into this bedroom. He feels the air of the open window as they lift him, then push him out.

Into the water.

Into the dark sea.

133

Shut it down.

What Johnny's lieutenant told him.

His shift commander listened patiently to Johnny's rendition of Boone's Paradise Homes story, nodded vigorously at the salient points, whistled appreciatively when Johnny mentioned some of the names allegedly involved, then told him . . .

Shut it down

Actually, shut it the *fuck* down.

"You came in here," Lieutenant Romero said, "and we talked about baseball. The Pads have no middle relief, I'm glad we agree on that. You left."

"But—"

"But fucking nothing, Kodani," Romero said. "You push on that, you know what pushes back? Weight comes from *above*, my ambitious friend, and do you know who's between you and the above? That would be me. Shut it the fuck down."

"Burke will pursue it," Johnny argued, "even if we don't. One way or the other."

"Don't be so sure about that," the lieutenant said. "Far as I'm concerned, this is one multi-millionaire against another. Let them rip each other to shreds and we'll pick up the pieces. But you don't, repeat for emphasis, you do *not* go anywhere near Bill Blasingame. People are going to think you have some kind of hard-on for that family, John."

So now Johnny is on his way to roust Bill Blasingame.

He finds him at home.

With dirt in his mouth.

134

"We found the bitch."

Jones sighs. The young gangsters that his client provided – what is their collective moniker? The Crazy Boys – are efficient and suitably cold-blooded, but must they always be so vulgar? And vague.

"*Which* bitch?" he asks into the phone, "given that we are looking for not one, but two, women."

"The British bitch, no se, *Petra."*

"Pick her up," Jones says. "Bring her to me."

A woman, he thinks.

And a man.

Conceivably a couple?

The possibilities are tantalizing.

135

Boone feels the water embrace him.

Not scary, not scary at all.

He doesn't struggle but lets himself sink until he feels the bottom, then uses it to push off. Then he 'seals' it, flaps his bound legs back and forth, propelling himself up until he breaks the surface and gets a breath of air.

He kicks gently to keep himself from sinking and listens.

The shore break is behind him.

If anyone could make it to shore blind, with his arms and legs tied, it's Boone freaking Daniels.

Except . . .

There's a boat right there where he comes up.

He hears the water hit the hull.

Then he feels a hand grab him by the hair, hold him, and push him back under. But not before he hears the guy say, "Let's see how long you can hold your breath."

136

A long time as it turns out.

A long time, over and over again, as the hand holds Boone down until his lungs are about to explode, then lifts him above the water while Boone gets as much air as he can through his nose, then pushes him down again.

They do several cycles of this before the guy asks, "Where are they?"

Doesn't wait for an answer before shoving him down again.

When he pulls Boone back up, he asks again, "Where are the records that she gave to you?"

He leans down and rips the tape off Boone's mouth. "Tell me, and we can stop all this."

As soon as I do tell, Boone thinks, I'm a dead man, so he shakes his head, and opens his mouth to swallow a lungful of air before the guy pushes him down again. Boone struggles and thrashes to shake himself loose of the grip, but can't do it, and then stops, knowing that he's burning up precious air. So he stays still and tries to relax, knowing that they'll pull him up before he actually drowns.

They can't get what they want if I'm dead, he tells himself.

And they don't know who they're playing with here.

The Breath-holding Champion of the Dawn Patrol, that's who.

We practice for this, asshole. We go to the bottom, pick up heavy rocks and walk.

I beat Johnny Banzai . . .

High Tide . . .

Dave the Goddamn Love God . . .

Even Sunny Day . . .

Then his body overrules his mind and his feet start jerking like a hanged man's and they lift him up again. He gasps for air as Jones says, "You're being very foolish."

And pushes him down again.

They say that drowning is a peaceful death.

137

They'd tortured him.

Blasingame is duct-taped to a chair by the wrists and ankles. The fingers of his neatly severed hands, laying on the floor, are all broken. So are the bones in his feet.

His dead eyes are wide with horror and pain.

Johnny can't tell if they'd stuffed the dirt in his mouth before or after planting the two bullets in his forehead, but maybe the ME will be able to establish that.

Two victims shot in the forehead, he thinks. Unusual for a pro, who would usually shoot his marks in the back of the head. But this one was no crime of passion, it was a professional job. So maybe this pro is a sicko – likes to see the look on the victim's face before he dies.

The dirt is odd, though. He's seen the severed hands bit before – a Mexican drug cartel punishment for someone who got greedy and put his hands where they shouldn't be. They broke his fingers first to get information, then punished him as a lesson to others, then finished him off.

But the dirt?

What is that about?

Like he got greedy and built Paradise Homes on bad dirt, and certain people are going to lose a lot of money, so they decided to make him accountable?

Fucking Boone, Johnny thinks.

138

Boone starts to go to sleep.

When he stops thrashing the world gets very still and peaceful like Mother Ocean has him in her lap, singing him a lullaby, a pulsing hum like the sounds of whales or dolphins. He feels warm, almost cocooned, and he remembers that he has often said that he would like to die in the ocean instead of in a bed with tubes sticking out of him. Many times said in those conversations on the Dawn Patrol that when his time came, he would just swim out until he was exhausted and couldn't swim anymore and let the ocean take care of the rest. And maybe this is a little sooner than he hoped for but it's like getting into a wave, better too early than too late.

Remembers now his mother telling him that she surfed when she was pregnant with him, took him out with her in the gentler waves, dove under water so he could feel the pulse and pull, he in the water of his mother, she in the water of hers. They say this is where we came from anyway, crawled from brackish waters onto land, and maybe all of living is a quest to go back, not from dust to dust but from salt to salt. The tide comes and goes out and one day it takes us with it people say they are going up into the sky that's where heaven is up there with the father but maybe you don't go up but down not into hell but into the deep belly of your mother, the deep impossibly deep blue and that would be okay that would be good a world away from air because you are so tired of holding your breath hoping for air a world beyond struggle and hope, a world of perfect silence you've had good times and good friends it's been a good ride on this wave let it go . . .

Except he hears K2 say:

Not yet.

139

Johnny Banzai's eating shit.

From Steve Harrington, for starters.

"You just stumble onto this?" he asks Johnny. "Decided you'd take a ride over to a perp's father's house and . . . bingo-bango! 'Look, Ma, no hands?' "

"I had a lead," Johnny admits.

"Partners?" Harrington asks. "We're 'partners,' remember? You ever seen any movies? Cop shows on TV? We're closer than brothers . . . than married couples. *Starsky and Hutch*? Any of this ring a bell?"

The ME is doing his thing on Blasingame's body. A rookie uniform is puking into a white plastic bag. Johnny wants to get the hell out of there, not because of the puke or catching shit from Harrington, but to get to Boone and tell him a Mexican drug cartel might be looking for him.

Just because he hates the guy doesn't mean he wants him tortured to death.

Johnny really wants to get out of there when Lieutenant Romero arrives, takes one look at the scene and pulls him out on the street.

"Tell me you're deaf," Romero says.

"Lieutenant—"

"Because you must not have heard me say, 'Do not go anywhere near Bill Blasingame,'" Romero says. "Or you did hear me say 'Do not go anywhere near Bill Blasingame,' and interpret it to mean, 'Do go near Bill Blasingame.' Which is it?"

Johnny ignores what he assumes to be a rhetorical question and, seeing how his career is swirling around the toilet anyway, says, "It looks like Mexican drug stuff to me. The severed hand, the . . ."

"Why do my people," Romero asks, "catch the blame for every nasty, violent, sick activity that happens in this city? A guy gets his hands sliced off and you just assume the beaners did it?"

"I said, it *looks* like . . ."

Romero gets right up in his face and hisses, "I told you to stay away from this. I told you to keep some distance so we could duck and cover, and you put me right into it. You want my job, Kodani, is that it? I swear, I'll take you right down with me."

"I already figured that, sir."

"Yeah, you're a smart bastard, aren't you?" Romero asks. "See how smart you feel checking up on paroled pedophiles the rest of your career."

"Am I off this case, Lieutenant?"

"You're fucking right. Get out of here."

Johnny gets in his car and heads for Boone's.

140

Boone comes to on the deck of the boat.

Water gushes out of his mouth and he takes a deep breath of air.

Someone says quietly, "Did you think you had died?"

Boone nods.

"You're going to wish you had," Jones says.

141

On the way to Boone's place, Johnny hits him on the cell a few times, but the asshole doesn't answer.

Classic Boone anyway – he goes into his crib-slash-cave and forgets the rest of the world exists, doesn't answer his phone. Johnny just drives over to Crystal Pier. The Deuce is there, so Johnny goes to the door and knocks. Boone doesn't answer. Johnny walks around and bangs on the windows.

No Boone.

Johnny calls Dave.

"You seen Boone around?"

"Man, I haven't seen Boone in a long time."

"I hear that," Johnny says. "But do you know where he might be?"

"Try the Brit's place."

Johnny heads over to Petra's.

142

Boone bounces on the bottom of the boat like a gaffed fish.

Exhausted and scared, he forces himself to think. First try to gauge the boat's speed and direction. It's moving fast for its size, maybe twenty . . . as for direction, it's beating upwind, and the last he remembers, the wind was coming out of the south. Which scares him worse. If they're headed south for Mexico, that's a one-way trip. If it's somewhere north of the border, he still has a slim chance.

He keeps time by counting the seconds in his head, and then multiplying by the estimated speed. Shivering from his enforced dives, he tries to force himself to relax and concentrate. The constant monologue from what he's come to call The Voice doesn't help.

"Let me tell you what you're thinking," The Voice says. "You are thinking that you know something that we want to know, and as long as you don't give us that information, we have no choice but to keep you alive. That is correct thinking, as far as it goes. As soon as you tell us what we want to know, your usefulness to us ends and we will kill you.

"But here is the flaw in that thinking – it makes the assumption that life is a desirable state of being. I grant you, that assumption is valid – the instinct to survive, the inability to imagine the state of non-existence, is common to all sensate species – except in the most extraordinary of circumstances. But you are about to experience the most extraordinary of circumstances. That is, a state of being in which life is an intolerable burden, and your one wish will be for it to cease. When that condition is reached, as it will be, you will no longer wish to withhold your precious information. Rather, you will seek to release it, as in its release you will find your own.

"The only question for us now is, do you believe me when I tell you this, or will you force me to prove it to you? In the interest of fairness I should perhaps tell you that I derive no small amount of pleasure – both intellectual and sensual – from reducing beings to a state where they no longer wish to exist.

"Interestingly, we shall each occupy a counter-intuitive position at polar opposites: You will yearn for death instead of life; I will hope that you prolong your life as your suffering prolongs my pleasure.

"And you do present a particular challenge – most men, when faced with drowning, quickly beg to tell what we wish to know. You, on the other hand, seem quite adapted to a state that reduces other subjects to abject panic. Clearly, water is not a reductive element for you, so we must turn to other things. I assure you, there is no shortage of options, and I am keen to try them all.

"But in the interest of professionalism, as I have been retained to procure this information from you, I put it to you now – will you tell me what I want to know? Gentleman to gentleman: Where are the records?"

Petra has them, Boone thinks. I left them with Petra. He says, "What records?"

"Oh, good," says The Voice. "I was *so* hoping for that answer."

Boone hears the engine throttle down, and feels the boat slow as it turns port, toward land. A few minutes later, he feels it bump into something solid and then the scrape of metal against wood.

We haven't gone nearly far enough, he thinks, to be in Mexico.

They lift him out of the boat, and start dragging him along the dock – he can feel the slightly swaying wood under his feet, then up a slope.

Boone feels a hand above each of his elbows, but they have a loose grip, as if confident that he's been totally cowed. A reasonable assumption, he thinks, seeing as how his wrists are taped behind him and his ankles taped together.

He asks, "Where are we going?"

"To a place," The Voice says, "of serene quiet and exquisite pain."

Boone gauges the angle and distance of the voice, then jerks up out of the grasp at his elbows and throws his body as horizontally as he can get into the air, bends his knees, and then kicks out. He feels his feet make contact and hears The Voice grunt, "Ooof" before there's the sound of something heavy hitting the dock. Then he hears The Voice scream, "My knee! My knee!"

Boone tucks his chin into his chest as they start beating him.

Gun butts, boots and fists – but on the shoulders, the ribs, the legs, not in the head. They don't want to kill him and they don't want him to lose consciousness, so he lies there and focuses on The Voice's whimpers.

"Get him in the van," The Voice says eventually.

He hears a van door slide open and they lift him up and push him inside.

The door closes.

143

Petra sits on her living-room floor with her laptop set between her splayed legs, a mug of tea at her right hand, and does what she knows best how to do.

Organize.

Entering data from Nicole's blackmail material, she cross-references every entry until the program starts to create a spider diagram of names, companies, properties, inspectors, geologists, politicians, city council members, judges and prominent citizens.

The software program assigns a discrete color to each linear connection, and within a couple of hours the screen is a dense, motley web – a Jackson Pollock canvas of corruption with Bill Blasingame and Paradise Homes at its center.

She pushes a command button and the web starts to create webs of its own, spinning out, as it were, multiple webs within webs. Switching imagery, she feels as if she's looking through a high-resolution microscope, watching a cancer spread at hyper-speed.

The intercom buzzer startles her.

Who could be here so late at night?

"Boone?" she says into the speaker.

"Yeah."

She buzzes him in.

144

The psychology of the early hours of a kidnapping is amazingly consistent.

After the initial shock comes a short period of disbelief, followed by despair. Then the survival instinct kicks in and forces a sense of hope, predicated on the same question:

Is anyone looking for me?

Then the kidnapped person goes through a checklist of his or her day, all the mundane little details that make up an average life, the routines that define daily living, with a now crucial emphasis on habitual human contact.

Who will miss me?

And when?

At what point in the day will someone not see me and wonder why not? A spouse, certainly, a friend, a co-worker, a boss, a subordinate. Or would it be the lady who sells you the morning cup of coffee, a parking lot attendant, a security guard, a receptionist?

For most people, in most jobs, there's a long list of daily, routine human contacts whose concern would be triggered by the simple fact that you didn't show up for work, or school, that you didn't come home.

But for the person who works alone, with no routine schedule; who lives alone, without family; whose work takes him different places at different times, day or night, often secretly, there are no expectations, the failure of which would cause anxiety and launch a search.

These thoughts run through Boone's mind as he lies on the floor of the van, this enforced examination of his life in relation to other lives.

Who'll miss me? he asks himself.

What is the first point in time that I will be expected somewhere?

The Dawn Patrol.

Virtually every day since I was fifteen years old, he thinks, I've shown up on the Dawn Patrol. So, normally, if I didn't make it, someone would ask, 'Where the hell is Boone?'

Except that's over. My others-encouraged, self-imposed exile from the Dawn Patrol will make my no-show, not my absence, the expectation. They won't know, they won't care, they'll just assume that I'm still on my long strange trip.

So, what's next?

The Gentlemen's Hour.

The next phase of the daily surf clock, my new surf home.

I told Dan Nichols I'd see him at the Gentlemen's Hour, but will he remember that? Will he care? Like, so what if I don't show? He won't trip to something being wrong, he'll just think I'm busy doing something else, that's all. And if the old boys talking story on the beach notice I'm not there, it's a huge so-what. A nothing.

Next.

Well, that would be The Sundowner for breakfast. Who's going to miss me there?

Not Not Sunny.

Not Sunny Jennifer.

Most days, but not all days, I go into the office. So there's Hang Twelve downstairs in the surf shop. But Hang is pissed at me, sees me as a traitor and probably doesn't care if I show or not, if he even notices – observation of the real world not being Hang's strongest suit.

So then there's Cheerful.

Who sits up there like a buzzard, waiting for me to come in, most happily miserable when I'm really late. Cheerful, my last friend, would know, but would he think anything of it? Or just believe that I flaked again, or that a case has taken me elsewhere?

Sunny would miss me.

But Sunny's not here. Sunny's surfing and having her picture taken somewhere across the world.

Pete.

Petra Hall.

Pete knows what we're into, but she doesn't *know what we're into*. She has no freaking clue that this has taken us into realms we didn't imagine, and that's the point: No one is going to miss me for a long time, and during that long time I have to keep Petra's name from coming out of my pie-hole, or else I have to make them kill me before it does.

A hand reaches down and rips off the tape and The Voice asks, "Did you really think you could escape?"

The Voice is casual, but Boone can hear the edge of pain beneath it.

"No, I just wanted to hurt you," Boone says. "It gives me pleasure."

"I'll make you live an additional hour for that," The Voice says.

"Thanks."

"Don't mention it," The Voice says. "You know, you are remarkably calm for a man who is facing what you are. Let me tell you why you shouldn't be."

He starts telling Boone.

145

Petra opens the door.

John Kodani is standing there.

"Cute," she says.

"I take it," he says, "Boone isn't here?"

"You take it correctly," she answers. "And, as a lady, I should take umbrage at your assumption that he is, at this late hour."

"It's the middle of the day for me," Johnny says. "Well, do you know where he is?"

"I assume he's at home."

Johnny shakes his head.

"Then I haven't a clue."

"May I come in?"

"Why?"

"I think you might be in possession of some material germane to a murder investigation," he says. "Boone told me all about Blasingame and Paradise. About some records . . . what's it . . . Nicole gave him? I didn't believe him."

"And now?"

"I might believe him."

That's interesting, she thinks. Boone didn't ring me to tell me of any new developments. "May I enquire what has occurred to change your mind?"

"No," Johnny says. "May I come in?"

"No, I don't think so."

"I can get a warrant."

"Off you go, then."

He smiles. "I could just take you in, you know."

"For about five minutes," she says, calling his bluff. "Is it chilly out? Should I get a wrap?"

Johnny blows a puff of air out of his mouth and says, "Look, I'm worried about Boone."

"I thought you were no longer friends."

"We're not," Johnny says. "That doesn't mean I want to see him dead. You neither, for that matter."

Petra feels a sharp stab of fear, more for Boone than for herself. He left her to talk to Johnny and Dan Nichols, he didn't come back, now something new has clearly occurred and Johnny is worried about his life? She's tempted to let him in, give him Nicole's papers, show him the computer screen with its interwoven networks, but . . .

Can I trust him? she wonders. Boone didn't trust him enough to actually give him the records. If he'd wanted Johnny to have them, he would have given them to him already. But what's new? What's happened? Where is Boone? She asks, "What do you mean?"

"Alright, look," Johnny says. "Shall we both get undressed here?"

"Why, *Sergeant* . . ."

Johnny takes out his cell phone, flips it open, and shows her the photo of Bill Blasingame he took at the house.

She gets dizzy, feels like she might vomit, but controls it and listens as he says, "Bill Blasingame. They broke his fingers and every bone in his feet before they cut off his hands, and then killed him. I think they were looking for the records that Boone has . . . or maybe he gave them to you? I don't think they know you have them or they'd already have been here, but it's just a matter of time. I'm concerned that Boone's time may have already run out. So do you want to talk to me now?"

146

The Voice drones on.

His name is Jones, his professional name that is, and he was trained as a physician, a neurologist, in fact, so he knows every nerve in the human body. Early on, even as a boy, he was fascinated by the phenomenon of pain. What was it? How did it register in the brain? Could the brain be chemically influenced to block the perception of pain, and if so, did pain exist independent of the perception?

Somewhat similar to the old conundrum about a tree falling in the forest with no one present to hear it – if pain occurred and the brain did not perceive it, was it still pain? In any case, his early work all involved the reduction or elimination of pain; noble effort, truly, but as he continued his research, he could not help but notice that, on the visceral as opposed to intellectual level, he was likewise interested in the affliction of pain.

He first observed in a sexual manifestation (As is so often the case, wouldn't you agree, Mr. Daniels?) that he began to take pleasure from pain. Not his own, of course, but other people's. At first, he found willing participants among the submissive, masochistic community, women who found that the endorphin release triggered by mild to moderate pain allowed or enhanced orgasmic pleasure. This was the perfect symbiotic relationship, as the inflicting of said pain produced intense physical sensations for him.

Boone feels the van take a sharp right.

Alas, these sensations, similar to drug or alcohol use, were subject to the similar effect of diminishing returns; it would take a higher and higher degree of pain to produce an ever-lessening, unsatisfactory result, and he soon ran out of partners willing to endure that level of suffering. He turned to prostitutes, of course – fortunately there are any number of brothels, especially in Europe, that specialize in sadism – and this proved satisfactory for several years until his addiction required ever-increasing dosages and he became unwelcome at even the most tolerant of establishments. He found the answer in Asia and Africa for some time, where the desperation of poverty provided subjects for sale, but alas, one is not made of money.

Boone feels the rattle of an unpaved road beneath him. Wherever they're going, they must be nearly there, and he feels real fear, feels himself start to tremble.

It therefore became necessary to make his avocation a vocation, if Mr. Daniels would forgive the cliché, and he was pleasantly surprised to find a large number of clients eager, in fact, to retain his services at a more than reasonable fee.

It was the perfect match of personality to profession, of expertise to exigency. It has provided him with moderate wealth, material comfort, international travel, and pure physical pleasure beyond the imagination of those bound by the strictures of mundane morality. That is the reward, Mr. Daniels, for those rare individuals willing to confront and acknowledge their true natures and live their lives based upon that hard-acquired self-realization. Once he'd endured the agonies of self-hatred and recrimination, he fairly burst into the rarified ether of pure action.

He goes on and on.

War stories.

The rebel soldiers in the Congo, the diamond dealers in Burkina Faso, the Communist nun in Guatemala, the kidnappers in Colombia, the female student in Argentina whose cries for mercy produced . . .

The van slows down and comes to a stop.

"Ah, well. Now the drug cartels . . . the drug cartels are a boon to business. A guarantee of full employment, if you will. Their conflicts, rivalries, power struggles – the sheer intensity and duration of their hatreds, the uninformed barbarism of their rough-hewn viciousness – produce a demand for pain that is apparently limitless. It is a sellers' market.

"The geologist, Mr. Schering, was a disappointment. A simple 'hit' as they called it, for it had to be disguised as something else, as you know, Mr. Daniels.

"But Mr. Blasingame . . . Ahhhhh! The bones in the foot, as perhaps you know, are keenly sensitive . . . *acutely*, shall we say, sensitive to pain . . . and the application of a simple blunt-force object such as a hammer produced an impressive reaction. Snapping his digits was a second-act amusement, a superfluous frisson when you consider the denouement, the sawing off of his hands without benefit of anesthesia. A bit *sharia* law, admittedly, but it's what the Mexicans wanted: sending a message, *pour encourager les autres* sort of thing. The look of sheer incredulity on his face was delightful.

"There are, you know, some people in this world of ours who believe that bad things simply cannot happen to them, so when the blade first went in, his scream was as much from indignation as physical suffering. Of course, that didn't last, not throughout the amputation, much less the cauterization, which led the man to suffer through the agony in the belief that we had done with him – a belief I did nothing to discourage, I'm afraid. He screamed and sobbed and lost consciousness, but when we brought him round he thanked me for sparing his life. Then I started in on the other hand.

"I think the sheer disappointment quite crushed him, even when I assured him that 'this was it,' his punishment was almost over, if he could live through it, and that many men have lived useful lives, et cetera . . . He was quite shocked when the dirt was shoved into his mouth – another mandate from my Mexican employers – but I think somewhat relieved when I shot him.

"Which brings us to you, Mr. Daniels," Jones says.

"How foolish, how *careless* of you, to allow yourself to become somehow enmeshed with people who would cost the Baja Cartel multiple millions of dollars. Mr. Daniels, I have inflicted unspeakable agony on people who have cost them petty change. Do you have any idea what I have in my imagination for you?"

Jones reaches down and tears the tape from around Boone's eyes.

Boone blinks, momentarily blinded, then sees the spectacled eyes looking down at him. Pale blue, bright, and alive with ferocious sexual energy. Jones is a man in late-middle age, light brown hair thin at the top, wrinkles around his eyes. He's close-shaven, and even in this August heat wears a knotted knit tie, button-down white shirt, and a linen sports-coat.

A real gentleman.

"You look at me oddly," Jones says. "Why?"

Maybe because he has a bright red dot on his forehead.

147

Johnny is looking through the documents when he hears something in the hallway.

"You have a bathtub?" he asks Petra.

"I beg your pardon?"

"Go lie down in it," Johnny says as he unlatches the holster at his waist.

"I will *not*."

The doorbell rings.

A man's voice says, "Petra? Boone sent me to see if you're okay."

"One second," she says. "I'm just getting dressed."

Johnny juts his chin toward the bathroom. She gets up from the sofa and starts to go.

The door comes in.

There are three of them.

Los Niños Locos.

Crazy Boys.

The first one through the door sees Johnny, the badge he's holding up, and the pistol he has in his other hand, and makes a snap decision.

He raises the gun in his hand and fires.

Johnny fires back – two shots in rapid succession – and the Crazy Boy goes down.

The other two come in over him.

148

The right lens of the spectacles shatters, one bright blue eye disappears in a spray of red, and then Jones drops from Boone's view.

Two more shots follow, each into the brain of one of the narco-thugs. The driver slumps dead over the wheel. The last thug reaches for his gun but the bullet catches him mid-motion and then it's quiet.

The van door slides open.

"You good, *bruddah*?"

"Good, *bruddah*?"

149

Johnny's next two shots take out the Crazy Boy who comes in first, but the next one – the one they call Chainsaw – hits the floor, rolls to the right, and comes up shooting.

Diving to the floor himself, Johnny tips the coffee table in front of him, but it's not much cover and the little machine pistol blasts a swath across the top, sending splinters of glass and wood spraying across the room.

When Johnny comes up, he can't find the shooter.

Chainsaw finds him, though, and is about to squeeze off another burst when his heart blows up instead.

Petra stands against the wall.

Pistol gripped in both hands.

150

Boone asks for a phone, and Rabbit gives him one. "Who you calling, the Brittita?"

"He's calling the Brittita."

"Boone's in love."

"In *looooooove*."

She answers on the first ring.

"Pete?" Boone says. "Get out of there. *Now*."

"It's alright, Boone," she says. "Johnny's here. Just, please, meet me at the police precinct. I need you, please."

Boone hears sirens in the background.

151

Boone stands beside the van.

Three bodies inside – two Crazy Boys and Jones.

Rabbit tosses Boone a set of sweats. "You should get out of those wet clothes, *bruddah*."

"Wet clothes."

"Eddie wouldn't want you catching cold, *da kine*," Rabbit says.

"Da kine."

Boone peels off the wet clothes and crawls into the sweatsuit. It fits – Red Eddie is a big-on-the-details, Triple A-personality, micro-manager kind of guy. Which is all the more impressive given the quantities of dope he smokes.

"You're slipping, Boone," Rabbit says, "walking easy into your crib like that."

"Slipping," Echo agrees. "Advancing age."

They're both pretty casual about the corpses in the van. Why not? Boone thinks. With the warfare going on for control of the cartels, three bodies in a van is a sub-average day on the body count.

"I didn't know they were looking for me," he says, knowing how weak it sounds.

But a good thing that Red Eddie did.

Rabbit explains that Iglesias asked his permission to pick up Boone, knowing that Eddie had an interest and it was on his turf. Eddie didn't give his good, his word was 'hands-off Boone.' But

Iglesias did it anyway, which put Eddie in a bad position. He couldn't let himself be disrespected like that.

So Eddie sent his boys to keep an eye out. They were surprised when Boone went out the window, and the boat was a little hard to track, but as soon as it pulled into the little marina in National City, they knew just where the van was headed.

"They used this place before."

"Used it before. Habits kill."

"*Speed* kills."

"Speed kills," Echo says. "Then habits."

Boone hears yelling from inside the steel building. He opens the door and sees Monkey, hog-tied on the floor.

He looks in pretty tough shape, badly beaten.

"Monkey," Boone says. "Oh, shit, Marvin, are you . . ."

"Fuck you, asswipe."

Boone thinks Monkey's probably going to make it.

152

Harrington takes her statement, and for once he's respectful.

It's a no-brainer self-defense shooting, just as Johnny's is a righteous double-shoot. Two of the Crazy Boys are DOA, the other might make it. Harrington has mixed feelings about that – on the one hand it would be good to question him; on the other, it's always convenient when one of them checks out the hotel.

So he's nice with the British chick.

For one, she's a looker, even with the shock blanket wrapped around her shoulders. And she apparently saved his partner's life. So even if it wasn't pure self-defense, it's going to go down that way. He pitches the questions to get those answers.

"You clearly thought that your life was in danger, didn't you?"

"Clearly."

"And you had no possible avenue of retreat?"

"None."

"And you saw that Detective Sergeant Kodani's life was also in immediate jeopardy?"

"That's correct."

"Where did you learn to shoot?" he asks her, just out of curiosity.

"My father insisted," Petra tells him, still clutching the laptop computer she brought with her and will not let go. "He started me off on clays and rough shooting, and we were lucky enough to go on a friend's shoot occasionally. When I moved to San Diego, as a single woman living alone, I decided to acquire a handgun – licensed, of course. I go to the indoor range from time to time."

"It shows," Harrington says, smiling.

"I took no pleasure in killing that man," she says.

"Of course not."

"Is Sergeant Kodani . . ."

"John's in the E-Room getting some glass and splinters taken out," Harrington answers. "He's fine."

"I'm glad."

Harrington's about to ask her out when Boone Daniels comes into the room.

Petra gets out of the chair, sets the computer down, and throws her arms around him.

Harrington hates Daniels.

153

Boone takes her to Crystal Pier.

Her place is a yellow-taped crime scene and she probably shouldn't go back there soon anyway. For a change, she doesn't argue, just gets into a cab with him, and then lets him escort her into his home.

"Would you like a drink, Pete?"

She sits on the couch. "What do you have?"

"I have some wine in here somewhere," he says, rooting through the cabinet under the kitchen sink. "I have beer and maybe some tequila."

"A beer would be lovely, thanks."

Boone pops open a beer, sits beside her on the couch, and hands her the bottle. She lifts it to her lips and takes a long drink, looking at him with wide eyes. He's a little concerned that she's in shock. "You want to talk about it, Pete?"

"There's not a lot to say, really. I did what I had to do, that's all."

"You saved Johnny's life."

"Not before he saved mine," she says. "I owe him a great deal."

We both do, Boone thinks, and it makes him sad. They'd seen Johnny as they were leaving the precinct and he was coming in. He asked if Petra was alright, then thanked her, then looked at Boone and said, "None of this changes things between you and me."

Boone didn't answer him, just wrapped his arm around Pete's shoulders and walked her out. But he'll always be grateful to Johnny for going over to Pete's. If he hadn't . . . Boone doesn't want to think about that 'if.'

"Pete," he says gently, "I'm going to assume this is the first time you've ever . . ."

"Killed someone?" she asks. "You can say it."

"It isn't an easy thing to deal with," Boone says. "Even when you didn't have a choice. You might want to think about . . . seeing someone . . . you know, to talk it out."

"Why do I think you've been on the receiving end of that speech?" she asks.

"If I'd known," Boone says, "that the cartels were in this, I'd have never involved you. And I'm really sorry."

"I'm not," she says. "I'm not sorry at all."

Her remarkable violet eyes are wide and wet.

He leans over, takes the bottle from her hand and sets it down. Then he pulls her close and wraps his arms around her.

She puts her face into his chest and sobs.

154

It seems like an hour later when she pulls away from him, sits up, and says, "Thank you for that."

"No worries."

"You're a good man, Boone Daniels," she says. She gets up. "I'm just going to splash a little water on my face and freshen up."

"Are you hungry?" he asks. "You want some tea . . . something to eat?"

"Thank you, no," she answers. "I think I'd just like to turn in."

"You take the bedroom," Boone says. "I'll take the couch."

She goes into the bathroom.

Boone picks up the beer bottle, pours the remnant into the sink, and looks out the window. There's something that still doesn't make sense. The big money behind Paradise Homes came from the Baja Cartel, fine, but . . .

Petra comes out clad only in one of his T-shirts. She's brushed her hair to a shine, put on fresh make-up, and looks beautiful.

She reaches her hand out and says, "I wanted this to be with a lovely, filmy negligee I bought for the occasion, and perfume and soft music and scented sheets, but I've done the best I could with what was to hand."

"You're beautiful."

"Come to bed."

He hesitates.

"Pete," he says, "you've been in shock, maybe you still are. You're emotionally vulnerable . . . I don't want to take advantage."

She nods. "I've been terrified, I've seen horrible things, I've taken a life and I don't know how that's going to work out, but right now I need life, Boone. I want you inside me and I want to move under you like that ocean you love so much. Now come to bed."

He takes her hand and she walks him into the bedroom.

155

Petra sleeps the sleep of the dead.

Which, fortunately, Boone thinks, is just a metaphor, thanks to Johnny B.

That brings up another troublesome question. Who fingered me for the cartel? Johnny B was one of the few people who knew what I had on Paradise Homes.

No, Boone thinks. Couldn't be.

So run it back, barney. Who else knew about Paradise Homes?

Bill Blasingame, of course.

Nicole. But it wasn't her. Boone called her from the police station and she was alright. She'd almost gone to Blasingame's house, and changed her mind.

Johnny and . . .

Dan and Donna.

The Perfect Couple.

He remembers his conversation with Johnny B the morning after the Schering murder.

'There's nothing on that tape that's going to help you, J.'

'They might have said something . . .'

'They didn't.'

'Nichols hear the tape?'

No, Boone thinks, he didn't. He didn't even know about the tape.

Boone goes out to the Deuce, digs around in the back, and reaches into the flipper where he hid the tape he'd made of Phil Schering and Donna Nichols. He pops the cassette into the tape player, fast forwards past their lovemaking and watches the timer until it hits the morning before she left the house.

'You have to,' Donna says.

'I'm not going to prison for you.'

Silence, then, *'If you don't change your report, Dan and I are ruined. How could you do that to me? After—'*

'Is that *why you fucked me, Donna?'*

'I'm begging you, Phil.'

'And I thought you loved me.' A short, cynical laugh.

'If it's money,' Donna says, *'we can pay you whatever . . .'*

The nifty LiveWire Fast Track Ultra-Thin Real Time GPS tracking device keeps a record of every place that the target vehicle went. Boone types in the command for the program to do just that and watches it for the night that Schering was murdered.

You didn't follow Donna Nichols that morning, Boone tells himself. You followed Phil. You assumed Donna went straight home, but . . .

The record says she didn't. The record says that she went to a house down in Point Loma, was there for an hour, and *then* she went home.

Boone scrolls the tracking record. Donna Nichols made three more visits to the same house over the past two days. She – or at least her cool white Lexus – went to that house just after you left her at the party at the Prado. Just a little while before you were bagged and thrown into the water, then interrogated.

To find out what you did with the records.

He turns the GPS device onto 'active' and watches the screen.

Donna Nichols is at the same house now.

156

It's a modest house at the end of a cul-de-sac on a nondescript street.

There's nothing special about it, if you don't know what you are seeing.

Boone does.

He spots the two cars – a soccer mom-style van and a pre-owned sedan – parked out on the street with men sitting in them. *Sicarios*, as they're known in the narcotics trade. Gunmen, bodyguards.

Donna's car is in the driveway.

Boone knows he can't get closer – the *sicarios* in the cars would be watching and they'd shake him down before he got anywhere near the house where Cruz Iglesias is hiding. He turns around in the shallow opening of the street and does a U-turn, goes back down the avenue and turns into the parallel street.

The rear of the house is visible, set behind a high stone wall. *Sicarios* will be on guard in the backyard, but he doesn't see any on this street so he parks the Deuce a house away, turns off the motor and gets out the parabolic sound detector. He trains it at Iglesias' safe house, praying that it has the range advertised.

It takes a few minutes, but he picks up the sound of her voice.

Begging for her husband's future, begging for his life. Telling Iglesias that Dan knew nothing, *nothing* about Blasingame's scam originally, and that he told the drug lord as soon as he found out. He wouldn't cheat his partners that way, Don Iglesias. Their families have been in business together for generations.

"We came to you, didn't we?" she says. *"We came to you."*

"But what," Iglesias asks, *"if this scandal reaches you? How long before it reaches the rest of us?"*

"It won't," she says. *"Please,* por favor, *please. I beg you. What can I do?"*

He tells her.

Boone listens to the sound of their lovemaking, if it can be called that, for only a minute or so, and then he drives away.

157

The Dawn Patrol, or what's left of it, is already out, paddling toward the small break, their bodies silver in the gathering light. They are mercurial and fluid, timeless and of the moment. Boone watches, admiring their strength and grace, then turns away and walks outside.

He opens the stand-up locker and takes out a long paddle board and a paddle, walks to the edge of the pier opposite the Dawn Patrol, tosses the board over and jumps in behind it. He climbs up onto the board, balances the paddle, stands up and rows out, to give himself distance from his former friends, before he turns north and rows parallel to the coast.

Boone has always loved this coastline, each of its distinctive beaches and coves, points and cliffs and bluffs, its black rock, red earth and green chaparral, but now, as he takes it in, he sees it differently.

It's his home, will always be his home, but is it fundamentally flawed, built on cracks and faults, on shifting ground that will fall and slide and collapse? And the culture built on top of this unstable earth – the Southern California free, easy, casual, rich, poor, crazy, beautiful life – is it also fundamentally corrupt? Will its cracks and rifts widen to the point where it can no longer stand, its own weight pulling it down?

Boone feels strong, standing and rowing. It's good to stand on a board, instead of lying or sitting, it gives him literally a different perspective, a longer view. He looks back to where his old friends sit on the line, small now in the vast ocean, dots against the pylons of the pier. What about those friends, the Dawn Patrol? Were those friendships, too, built on a cracked and flawed foundation? Was it inevitable that the fissures of race and sex, ambitions and dreams, would separate them like continents that were once joined and now are oceans apart?

And what about you? he asks himself as he rows on, sweating with the fine exertion of powerful strokes against the current. What's your life been built on? Uncertain, shifting ground . . . unsteady tides? Has it all come apart now? And if so, can you rebuild it?

Has your life always been based on shaky foundations? Everything you believed been false?

He keeps rowing and only turns around when he has just enough strength to make it back to shore.

By that time, the Dawn Patrol has ended.

It's the Gentlemen's Hour.

158

He waits on the beach for Dan Nichols to come in.

Dan looks good, strong and refreshed and a little out of breath as he picks his board up from the water, walks onto the sand, and gives Boone a big wave.

"Boone!" he says. "I thought you were coming out."

"Changed my mind."

"Have you had a chance to think about my offer?"

"Yeah?"

"And?"

"You set me up, Dan."

Boone lays it out.

How Dan was a silent partner in Paradise Homes, partners with Cruz Iglesias and his Baja Cartel. When the homes fell into the sinkhole, Dan told Blasingame to fix it, gin up the geo reports, but he couldn't get it done.

"So you sent your wife," Boone says now, "you pimped her out to seduce Schering and get him to change his reports, but he wouldn't do it. Then Blasingame's son was arrested for killing Kelly Kuhio and it's all over the papers and people are digging into Blasingame's life and you got really scared the connection would come out."

So Dan hired Boone to 'follow' Donna, knowing where it would lead, knowing it would provide a motive for Schering's murder that would point an inquiry away from Paradise Homes. Dan and Donna were so desperate, so afraid of losing their money – or worse, if Iglesias found out how they'd put him in jeopardy – that they were willing for Dan to become a murder suspect.

"Boone . . ."

"Shut up," Boone says. "You sent your wife to lay her body out, then you tried a bribe, and when that didn't work, you had your cartel partners kill him before he could talk."

"That's outrageous!"

"Yeah, it is," Boone says. "And then you set *me* up. Used me to set a false trail so it would look like an act of jealousy. You knew you had an alibi, and you were willing to take the risk because you were that desperate. Otherwise, your partners down in TJ would do to you what they did to Bill Blasingame."

"Boone, we can talk about this," Dan says. "There's no need for this to go any further, we can settle this like gentlemen—"

"When I told you I had Nicole's records, you knew you were in trouble," Boone says, "so you sent your financial backers to get them back, whatever it took. Blasingame's life, Petra's . . . you didn't care."

"You can't prove this," Dan says. "I'll destroy you in court. I'll tell them *you* were having the affair with Donna, that you killed Schering out of jealousy. She'll back me, Boone, you know she will."

"Probably," Boone says.

Dan smiles a little. "It doesn't have to go there. How much do you want? Give me a figure, it will be in a numbered account end of business today."

Boone takes the tape cassette player out of his pocket and hits 'Play.'

"We came to you, didn't we? We came to you."

"But what if this scandal reaches you? How long before it reaches the rest of us?"

"It won't. Please, por favor, *please. I beg you. What can I do?"*

"It's a copy," Boone says. "John Kodani has the original. He's waiting up on the boardwalk now."

"You're making a mistake, Daniels."

"I met some of your partners," Boone says. "I'm betting the legal process is the least of your worries. Have a good life, Dan."

Boone walks away.

Passes Johnny Banzai on the way in.

159

Later that morning, Petra watches Alan Burke peruse the flow chart that she created on her computer.

He's dead silent for a good, long minute, then asks, "You have documentation of all this?"

"Yes."

Alan walks over to the window and looks out at the city. "Do you have any idea how many friends, colleagues and business associates of mine could be implicated by this?"

"I would expect quite a few," she says.

She is, as usual, polite and proper, but he notices that the deferential tone that she normally adopts is missing. Its absence is simultaneously alarming and promising. "Well, you expect correctly."

Petra hears the gentle mockery and wonders what it means. Is its import that Alan will fire her, run for cover and pull the lid down over his head? That would be the smart thing to do, and Alan has built his career on doing the smart thing.

"I'm glad you're alright," he says.

"Thank you."

"That must have been very frightening."

"It was."

Yeah, he thinks, looking at her, you were so terrified that you found the pistol in your bureau drawer and calmly gunned down a professional hit man. How can I let talent like that walk out my door? "You realize that there are going to be about eight zillion lawsuits coming out of your chart here? And that many of them will be politically difficult for me, and for the firm? Do you know the pressure that's going to come down on us from on high?"

"Absolutely."

Alan turns away and looks out at the city again. Maybe, he thinks, it needs shaking to the core, maybe it's time to take it apart and rebuild it again, and maybe there are worse things to do in the last phase of your career.

He turns back to Petra and says, "Okay, start contacting homeowners and signing them up. Do an assets search on Paradise and its related companies with an eye to freezing them, and . . . why aren't you already moving?"

"I want to be made partner," she says.

"Or maybe I should just fire you," Alan answers.

"I'll require a corner office, of course."

He trains his plea-bargaining, settlement-negotiating evil stare on her.

She doesn't blink.

Alan laughs. "Okay, gunslinger. Partner. Call maintenance and make it thus. But Petra—"

"Yes?"

"We'd better win."

"Oh, we'll win," she says. "Alan, what about Corey Blasingame?"

"We have a meeting with Mary Lou in thirty," he says.

"Did she give any hint?"

He shakes his head.

160

As does Mary Lou Baker.

At John Kodani.

She looks up from the stack of documents that he dropped on her desk, shakes her head again, sighs, and says, "You've been a busy boy, Sergeant. First the arrest of Dan Nichols, then a raid that nets Cruz Iglesias, then this . . . dirty bomb. Anything else you want to drop on me today?"

"That ought to do it."

"Oh, it ought to 'do it,' alright."

Johnny picked Mary Lou Baker to bring the records to because (a) she'd been busting his chops on the Blasingame case; and (b) she was the one prosecutor he knew with the integrity and stones to take this up and start filing charges.

"You do know you're ruining my career, don't you?" she asks him as she looks at the papers and winces.

"Or making it," he says.

"Same for you, chum," Mary Lou says. "Romero wanted you strung up by the *cojones*, but he can't do that now that you're the hero of a shootout, and Iglesias and all. But did you have to save a *defense* attorney, John? Bad taste."

"She was the only lawyer in the room," Johnny answers. "Besides, she pulled me out of the soup."

"We should recruit her for the good guys' team," Mary Lou says.

"We could do worse," Johnny says. "What about Corey Blasingame?"

"What about him?"

"What are you going to do?"

Her intercom buzzes. *"Alan Burke and partner here for you."*

"I'll be right out," Mary Lou says. Then, to Johnny. "I don't know yet. Let's go find out."

Johnny follows her into the conference room.

161

Boone, Petra and Alan are already seated at the table.

Mary Lou and Johnny sit down across from them.

Alan smiles and opens, "I'm taking it to trial."

"You'll lose," Mary Lou says.

"The fuck I will," Alan answers. "Your first three witnesses are garbage, the next two have recanted, which will make clowns of your investigating officers."

Boone glances at Johnny.

Face set in stone, but his cheeks turn red.

Boone looks away.

"We still have the confession," Mary Lou says.

"Yeah, go with that," Alan says. "I can't wait to feed it piece by piece to Sergeant Kodani here. How do you like your crow, Detective? A little salt and pepper?"

Johnny doesn't say anything.

Boone can't look at him, and Petra stares at the table.

Mary Lou stands up. "If there's nothing else . . ."

Johnny stands up too.

Looks at Boone with disgust.

"Come on, sit down, Mary Lou," Alan says. "We don't want it to end this way."

Mary Lou sits back down. "Neither Harrington's borderline subornation of perjury nor Kodani's assertive interview of the defendants changes the fact that your client, at least partially motivated by racial hatred, at least participated in a beating that cost a human life."

"Agreed."

"He has to do some serious time for that, Alan."

"Also agreed," Alan says. "But he didn't throw the fatal punch, Mary Lou. That was Bodin. And he wasn't the ringleader, that was Bodin too."

"There are practical reasons why I can't go after Bodin."

"That doesn't mean you should single Corey out for special punishment," Alan responds. "There's an issue of justice here."

"There's an issue of justice for Kelly, too."

"I share that view," Alan says. "My client participated in a disgusting act with a tragic result, and he should face the consequences. I'll go vol man.

"With max sentencing – eleven years."

"Minimum – three."

It's kabuki theater – they both know the next step in this ritual.

"Fine," Mary Lou says. "Medium-range. Six."

"Done."

They shake hands – Alan and Mary Lou, Alan and Johnny, Petra and Mary Lou, Petra and Johnny, Boone and Mary Lou, not Boone and Johnny.

They avoid each other.

162

Boone drives to La Jolla.

The Hole.

Rabbit and Echo are on duty in front of the house. Rabbit pats Boone down while Echo gets on the horn and then comes back and says it's okay for Boone to go in.

Or out.

Red Eddie's lying on a floatie in the pool, sipping some fruity drink with an umbrella in it. His ankle bracelet is wrapped in a plastic baggie. Dahmer's stretched out on a floating cushion nearby. Eddie cranes his neck up, squints into the sun and says, "Boonie, an unexpected pleasure! You could have just sent a card."

Red Eddie's pidgin Hawaiian comes in and out like the tide. It depends on his mood and intent. Today, he's all Wharton Business.

"Fuck you, Eddie."

"Not exactly the Hallmark sentiment I was expecting," Eddie says, "but pithy, nevertheless."

"Stay out of my life."

"Even to save it, Boone?" Eddie asks. "It's not just a past tense question – the Cartel is very upset with you, costing them all this money and trouble. They're not so happy with me, either, wiping out two of their boys and one of their best interrogators. When things settle for them, they'll be coming for both of us."

"Look out for yourself," Boone says. "Not me."

Eddie paddles to the edge of the pool and sets his drink down. Then he rolls off the floatie into the water, dives down to cool himself, comes back up and says, "This is the problem with that, Boone: I owe you. My son's life. My life, too. How can I ever stop repaying that? I can't. So you will just have to learn to accept my care and largesse – a little more graciously, please."

"I just came to tell you that Corey Blasingame didn't kill . . ."

"I already heard," Eddie says. "Do you think that I'm without resources in the hallways of power? I am informed that it was Trevor Bodin who murdered my *calabash* cousin. Is that correct?"

Boone doesn't answer, but says, "I suppose it's useless to ask you to refrain from doing what you're going to do."

"Supposition correct."

"Even if Kelly wouldn't want you to do it?"

"I never respond to 'even ifs,' " Eddie says. "Aloha, Boone."

"Drown."

Boone walks away.

"Nice," Eddie says. He dives again, comes up and yells at Rabbit, "What, you think my drink is going to swim over here by itself, *da kine*?"

Rabbit hustles for the drink.

163

Corey Blasingame goes before the judge that afternoon and pleads guilty to voluntary manslaughter.

The judge accepts the plea and sets sentencing for two months down the road, but as pre-agreed he's going to give Corey the medium-range sentence of 72 months, with credit for time served.

In the normal course of things, Corey will be out in less than three years.

The judge gives him a few minutes to say goodbye to people before the sheriffs take him away, but there really isn't anyone to say goodbye *to.* Both parents are dead, he has no siblings, and no real friends. Boone notes that none of the surfers from Rockpile or the fighters from Team Domination bothered to show up.

Banzai is there, almost as if he wants to take responsibility for blowing the murder case.

A lot of surfers show up, too, as many as the gallery can hold, more outside the courthouse, a bunch of 'human rights' groups holding signs reading 'Justice For Kelly,' 'Stop Hate Now' and 'Racism' with that diagonal line through it. Their disgust at the plea arrangement is palpable, and, inside the courtroom, Boone can feel their eyes burning through the back of his head.

So it's just the defense team – Alan, Petra, and Boone – that's there for Corey. If any of them was expecting gratitude, they'd have been disappointed. Corey just looks at them with his stupid, conflicted 'I just got away with something' smile.

Alan feels that he has to say something. "You'll probably be out in three years, maybe less. You'll have your whole life in front of you."

Sort of, Boone thinks. Corey probably hasn't figured out yet that his father's estate will be tied up in litigation and then sold off to pay lawsuits. So Corey will get out of the hole without a home or a dime in the bank, with a felony sheet, in a city that hates him, and not a friend in the world. Boone doesn't bother to enlighten him to that, nor to the fact that he saved the kid from a jailhouse shanking or worse.

Corey looks at Alan, then at Petra, then Boone, and mutters, "I have nothing to say."

Me neither, Boone thinks.

Nothing at all.

5.

164

He doesn't have anything to say, either, when he walks outside the courthouse through a mob of protesting surfers.

Some of whom shout his name and couple it with 'Traitor' and 'Sellout.'

He just puts a protective arm around Petra and helps her into the waiting car that takes them back to the law office.

165

They lie in bed at his place that night.

After a little while she asks, "Are you alright?"

"Yeah."

"Really? Because you seem sad."

He thinks about it. "Yeah, kind of, I am."

"Your friends?"

"That's part of it," he says. "But only part. It's the whole thing, you know? It's made me question . . . who I am. I never saw the ugliness until it was too late, until it killed someone like Kelly. Maybe I didn't see it because I didn't want to see it. I only wanted to see . . . paradise."

"You're being too hard on yourself."

"No, I'm not," Boone says. "If you don't see something, you don't have to do anything about it. And I didn't do a damn thing."

"You're not responsible for the whole world."

"Just my piece of it."

Petra kisses his neck, then his shoulder and his chest, and slides down his body gently, because he's bruised and sore and aching, but she does soft, loving things until he cries out. Much later, her head in the crook of his neck, she asks, "Have you had a chance to think about Alan's offer?"

Boone smiles. "He told you about that?"

"Yes."

"Before or after he made it?"

"Before," she says. "Does that matter?"

"Yeah, it does."

"Ah. I see. I didn't ask him, Boone. It was his idea."

"But he ran it by you first."

"I'm sure just to see if I'd be comfortable with the idea of you being around the office," she says.

"Are you?" Boone asks. " 'Comfortable?' "

She rolls over and puts her head on his chest. "Much, *much* more than comfortable. I'm ecstatic."

He holds her tight. "Why don't you stay here until you're ready to move back in to your place?"

"Yes?" she asks. "Yes, thank you, I'd love that, but it wasn't an answer."

"Yeah, Pete," he says, "I think I'll do it, the law school thing."

She smiles and settles closer into him. A few minutes later Boone feels her breathing deepen and he looks down to see that she's fallen asleep. He loves the smell of her, the feel of her, her hair splayed against his chest.

He doesn't sleep.

Lies there and thinks.

166

Boone beats the sun out of bed.

He carefully disentangles himself from Petra, so as not to wake her, pulls the sheet back up around her neck, then throws on a sweatshirt, jeans and sandals and walks into the kitchen to write her a note.

He steps outside into the still-dark morning, gets into the Deuce, and pulls off the pier onto the PCH. His route takes him right past the spot where the Dawn Patrol goes out, and in the faint light that is just now gathering, he can see their forms on the beach, performing the morning ritual of waxing and stretching and quiet conversation.

He doesn't stop, but keeps driving north.

167

The lightness in the bed wakes Petra up.

She misses his weight and warmth, but she's glad he's going back out on the Dawn Patrol, and then she thinks how nice it would be to have a morning cup with him before he goes out, maybe look out the window and watch him surf before she goes in to work.

She gets up and goes into the kitchen but he's already gone.

A note is propped against a cup on the table.

Pete,

I'm sorry, I love you, but I can't do it. The lawyer thing, I mean. It just isn't who I am. I guess I'm just not a gentleman.

I have something I have to take care of – my piece of the world – right now, but when I get back we'll talk about it. There's tea in the third cupboard to the right.

Boone

Of course you can't do it, she thinks. The lawyer thing.

Of course you can't, and of course it isn't who you are. It's not the man that I love, nor the man who apparently loves me. My God, she thinks – a simple, uncomplicated declaration of love. Subject, verb, object. I love you. Something you've never had before in your life.

Well, I love you, too, Boone.

And don't be sorry, please don't be sorry. I wouldn't change you, I was wrong to try, and as for not being a gentleman, you couldn't be more wrong about that, and when you get back . . .

She looks at the note again.

'I have something I have to take care of – my piece of the world – right now.'

Feeling a horrible pang of alarm, Petra hurriedly dresses and rushes out.

She catches the Dawn Patrol just as they're headed out.

Paddling in the shallow water.

Petra stands on the sand, waves her arms above her head and hollers, "Help! I need you! Come back! Help!"

Dave the Love God is more used to distress calls coming from the opposite direction, but a lifeguard is a lifeguard, so he turns around and paddles back in. He's not real thrilled to see that it's the Brit.

"It's about Boone," she says.

"What about him?"

"I think he's gone to do something stupid," Petra says.

"I can almost guarantee that," Dave answers.

She hands him the note.

168

Boone drives all the way up the PCH to Oceanside on that road that he loves so much.

Up through Pacific Beach and La Jolla, then down along Shores, then up to Torrey Pines and back down again along that incredible stretch of open beach, then up the steep hill to Del Mar. He goes down past Jake's, and the old train station, then drives up into Solana Beach, Leucadia, then down again past the long open coast at Cardiff and Carlsbad.

When he reaches the power station at the south edge of O'Side, he turns around and drives the whole thing again.

This road of memories and dreams.

He pulls off the road at Rockpile.

169

Boone pulls into the little parking lot.

Hard to find a spot, because the boys are really out.

Or not quite – most are still on the beach, getting ready to hit the water. Ten or twelve guys, Boone estimates, all of them white.

One of them is Mike Boyd.

Boone gets out of the van, walks up to him and says, "You're gone."

"What?"

"You filled those stupid kids with your garbage," Boone says, "and pumped them full of your shit, and you're guiltier than any of them. I don't want you in my ocean, or on my beach – here or anywhere, anytime. I don't want you in my world. You and all your buddies, you're gone."

Boyd smirks, looks behind him at his crew, and then says, "You're going to throw us all out, Daniels? Just you? You're believing your own legend there, dude."

"I'm going to start with you, Mike," Boone says. "Then I'm going to work my way through the rest of them."

Boyd laughs. "Check yourself, Daniels. You're a fucking mess. You won't last five seconds against me, never mind the rest of the boys. Walk away while I still let you. You know what? Better yet, don't. Stay right where you are so we can stomp the shit out of you."

His crew has gathered around him, eager to back him up.

No compunction.

Boyd smiles at Boone again, then the smile disappears from his face and his eyes widen as he focuses over Boone's shoulder at:

Dave, Johnny, High Tide, Hang Twelve, Petra, even Cheerful.

The Dawn Patrol.

170

The Battle of Rockpile becomes a legend among the surfing community of San Diego.

By that afternoon, the story gets told at The Sundowner and every other bar, burger place, taco joint and hangout on the coast.

The Dawn Patrol *v*. The Rockpile Crew.

It was a beat-down.

An ass-kicking.

A balls-to-the-walls, all-out, no-mercy *epic*.

The tale gets told how the PB Dawn Patrol slashed through the Rockpile like a tsunami wave through a pier. How Boone freaking Daniels, Dave the Love and War God, Johnny Absolutely Banzai, High Rolling Tide, and Hang Tough Twelve threw down, fists and feet, until the beach looked like a Tijuana bullfight – blood in the sand, baby. Even the chick got into it, man – punching, kicking, clawing – while that crazy ancient dude went around keying cars and smashing in windshields and headlights.

Alarmed artists on the bluffs (concerned citizens they) dialed 911 but the kookiest thing happened – the cops rolled up alright, but then they parked on the bluffs and never got out of their cruisers until it was time to buzz the EMTs to carry out the wounded.

Of which there were many, because DtLG went dervish, like that was the dude who once punched a *shark*, yeah, so he just went *off* on the Rockpile, and JB was all judo and shit so that Brazilian crap just couldn't cut it, and Tide, he grabbed three of those Pilers and banged their melons together like, well, okay, coconuts, and the squirrely little soul surfer rasta dude totally foffed energizer bunny, man, he just took the hits and kept on coming.

And would you like to have been there (and, much later, many would claim that they were), the beach denizens asked each other, when Mike Boyd launched himself into a Superman Punch to take out BD, and Boone stepped back, cocked his right knee, and cracked that surfing-strengthened-to-steel leg straight into Boyd's junk? They say you could hear that bang from the bluffs, like a board crashing into the rocks. Like . . . *whump!*

The beach-bongo telegram system spreads the story, and by sundown it's made it all the way to Oz where Sunny Day looks at her text message and smiles.

The Battle of Rockpile.

The 'Fivers,' as they get glossed, expelled from the beach.

Which was re-christened 'K2's.'

Paradise Found.
Epic.
Macking.
Crunchy.

171

"Violence on the beach," Dave intones through a swollen lip, "is very uncool."

"Completely inappropriate," Johnny agrees.

"No place for it," High Tide concurs.

"East of the 5," Hang Twelve says.

Boone just nods. He's too busy grilling fish to engage in conversation, he doesn't want to burn the fillets, and the drop-dead, you've-got-to-be-kidding-me, there-has-to-be-a-god show of a sunset is already distracting enough. Besides, his jaw throbs, as does his almost certainly broken nose, so it's just easier to keep his pie-hole shut.

And enjoy the resumption of the sundown cookout on the beach.

Even Cheerful showed up for the party, though he stays carefully on the boardwalk away from the sand and will have nothing to do with a fish taco. Boone has a Stouffer's in the micro-wave inside all set to go for him.

Pete looks good with a black eye.

She sure doesn't think so, and she's 'horribly embarrassed' at her 'unprofessional' behavior at Rockpile, but Boone knows that she got a rush from it. Even better, by virtue of her participation in The Battle of Rockpile – even if she never gets on a board – Pete is now and forever a fully accredited, completely accepted member of the Dawn Patrol.

As witnessed by the fact that they came up with a nickname for her.

Loco Ono.

It's sarcastic, and rough, but she's smart enough to know that they're poking more fun at themselves than they are at her. So that's a good thing, good for her and good for their relationship.

Because I guess that's what we have now, thinks Boone, a relationship. Wow. Even though we're still going to be SEI. I'm not going to law school, and Head of Security at Nichols' is out, so what next?

Nothing, I guess.

Nothing *new*, anyway, and that's just fine. The summer is coming to an end, and the more serious seasons will start. It's going to be plenty, just dealing with what's on its way. The Paradise Homes conspiracy is already unraveling, people are scrambling for cover or racing to be the first in the testimonial daisy-chain, and both Mary Lou and Alan are issuing subpoenas like supermarket coupons.

But there will be an inevitable push-back. Half the power structure of San Diego is going to come charging, and the Baja Cartel as well, and Boone doesn't know which is more lethal.

He looks around at the group of his friends as he takes the fish off the grill. Sliding the pieces into tortillas, he passes the tacos around. They *are* friends again, but it really isn't over, he thinks. I have relationships to mend – with Dave and Hang, Johnny and Tide especially – and that's going to take time.

It's going to require some good surf sessions, some days hanging together on the beach, some nights talking story. Maybe it's going to mean that we take a fresh look at ourselves. Like Sunny had e-mailed him.

Hey B,

Heard about all your craziness lately. Wow. Double wow. Sounds like the Dawn Patrol has gone through the washing machine. But you know how it is – if you make it through to come out the other side, the world looks a little different. Kind of fresh. I remember something Kelly used to say. 'Your view is as much a mirror as a window.' It's a pretty cool view, B, for you and all our friends. Enjoy, yeah? And take care of each other.

Mucho lovo,

Sunny

P.S. How'd the booty call go?

Boone looks out at the ocean.

The surf is beginning to build.

There are waves. They're small, but they're waves.

Not Kansas anymore

Maybe . . .

South Dakota.